Avoiding Commitment

A novel by

K.A. Linde

Copyright © 2012 K.A. Linde

All rights reserved.

ISBN: 1478132744
ISBN-13: 978-1478132745

December 9th

1

PRESENT

Vibrations reverberated throughout the miniscule apartment. The sound dulled and then died, not even registering on the tiny figure wrapped in a heap of hand-me-down quilts. Again, the electronic noise pierced the early morning silence. Lexi groaned, nearly rolling off the twin sized bed. Her hand fumbled clumsily for the alarm clock, slamming on the snooze button several times before realizing that it wasn't even plugged in, let alone set for an early Saturday morning wake-up call.

She peeled her eyes open searching desperately for the obnoxious noise before zeroing in on her crummy old cell phone. It was situated between a box of photographs, last night's cup of coffee, and her laptop, which had turned itself off when she hadn't been kind enough to plug it in for the night. She stared across the room, debating whether the call was worth getting out of her cozy nook so early on a Saturday morning, just as the third ring blared through the apartment. Shoving the covers off of her bare legs, she stumbled out of bed, immediately stubbing her big toe on her nightstand. She swore profusely and barely kept from falling over as pain shot through her toe. Reaching out for the cell phone, she extended her arm and barely saved it before it vibrated over the side of the cluttered desk.

"Mmm hmm?" she mumbled groggily into her phone. She succumbed to the throbbing pressure in her foot and collapsed on the grey area rug she had indefinitely borrowed from her college roommate.

"Lexi." It was a statement not a question. The voice was familiar, but it was so ridiculously early, she wasn't going to blame herself for not immediately recognizing the deep masculine tone.

Lexi pulled the phone from her ear and looked at the time. She groaned when she saw it was only six; four hours before she needed to be awake. The number glaring blindly from the screen wasn't programmed into her phone, but this came as no surprise. She had accidentally dropped her phone into a toilet two months earlier in a nightclub. The phone had miraculously survived, but she had lost all of her numbers.

What perplexed her was that it wasn't an area code local to New York, where she had been residing the last two years for law school. Strangely enough, it was an Atlanta area code, and the only people she still talked to from home were her parents. When she had replaced the numbers in her phone, she hadn't retained any other Atlanta phone numbers. Since moving to New York City, she had tried to let go of her past and move on to her bright future.

"Lexi, are you there?" the unidentified voice repeated into the phone. "I know…"

"Who is speaking?" she asked cutting him off abruptly. "Do you realize it's six o'clock in the morning on *Saturday*?" she questioned him further. "Some people do like to sleep in," she spoke sharply into the cell phone, adjusting her seat so as to assess the extent of her injury.

"Yeah, look, I'm sorry," he implored her. "I would have *never* called if I didn't absolutely have to."

Her brain was trying to signal to her that she knew that voice. It sounded so familiar, but there was no way it could be *that* voice. Lexi rubbed her tired eyes before allowing herself to speak again. "Sorry," she mumbled. "Who did you say this was again?" The person on the other end didn't say a word. Lexi knew that wasn't good.

The silence prolonged as neither person seemed willing to speak up. Finally, he emitted a tiny sigh and said, "Lex, it's Jack."

Chill bumps broke out across her arms and neck as his name registered and she was able to finally place the voice…*that* voice. It was him. Oh God! Why was he calling her?

The sound of her heart palpitating inside her chest could be heard out the door, down the hall and quite possibly outside in the nearby construction zone through the jackhammer slamming against the concrete…not to mention through the phone. Her mouth felt like she had been chewing on chalk all night. Butterflies whacking their tiny wings violently against her insides suddenly assaulted her stomach. All she could do was cough in disbelief. Her mind was whirling with indescribable possibilities for the purpose of his phone call, each new idea seemingly more ridiculous than the last.

She wasn't sure if she was overreacting. So she hadn't heard a word from him since their last encounter over a year and a half ago, that didn't mean that he couldn't randomly drop her a line at six o'clock in the morning. After all, they had been friends, of sorts, for nearly six years now.

"Look, I know I shouldn't have called so early. I didn't mean to intrude," he said quickly.

She was terrified that he might hang up after only a few short minutes of his time. "What? No. Of course you're not intruding. I just wasn't expecting…well you. I wasn't expecting you," she could hear how breathy and uneven her voice had gotten and wanted to kick herself with her hurt toe for being such a girl.

"Yeah, I'm sorry. I know it's been awhile since we last spoke." That was an understatement.

"Yeah, well, I lost all of the numbers in my phone." Not that she would have called him. Anyways, he likely didn't have the same excuse.

He didn't say anything for a second. She figured he just didn't have a response to that. "I guess I'll just cut to the point," he finally stated. "I need you."

Lexi froze, not able to comprehend what she had just heard. Her mind poured over the countless interpretations of that statement. "You what?"

"I mean, I need you here."

Her eyes bulged out. She could feel them drying out, but somehow couldn't bring herself to blink. She couldn't process what he was saying. He needed her? Not just needed her, but needed her there with him. Needed her home. She shook her head realizing she must be misunderstanding him. There was no way, after everything that had happened between them, he would ever call her like this. "I'm sorry…what?"

"I'm not getting this out right. It's kind of hard to explain. Do you have a minute?"

She glanced around her tiny room, as specks of light began to filter in through the window. She visualized her planner, filled to the brim with meetings and appointments weekdays, and then her lame Saturday with only a haircut on the schedule. All she had was time. "It's six in the morning. Go ahead, Jack," she said letting his name roll off her tongue the same way he had…she stopped herself. No point in letting her mind venture there.

"Are you sitting down? This is kind of a strange story."

"Uh…yeah, I am," she said glancing around her tiny apartment. Her bedroom walls were covered in cracking soft green paint that had probably been there since the dawn of time, and a collage of hooks and holes from previous tenants. Her floor was scattered with dirty laundry and destroyed textbooks. The sparse amount of furniture she had been able to haul up the seven daunting flights of stairs still managed to make the space look cluttered, something she had never quite been able to figure out. "So…uh…what is this strange story?"

"Okay, well, just hear me out, because I promise I wouldn't have called and bothered you if it wasn't for a reason I thought was worthwhile." He sucked in a long deep breath before continuing. "So, I've been dating this girl," he began, coughing a little at the introduction to the conversation. "She's really great. Actually, I think ya'll would get along. Anyway, she is really into uh…marriage," he said awkwardly. "And…well…you know me."

She did know him. He despised the idea of marriage, the idea of being tied down to one person, suffocating under the monogamous bonds forced upon you by a legally binding document. Knowing that after that moment, there was no turning back. Except, of course, there was always divorce. She was pretty sure that the only thing he hated more than marriage was the idea of divorce. Breaking up was bad enough without the added effort of divvying up possessions, possibly children, moving out, starting a new life, and not to mention court fees, custody battles, and worst of all, lawyers. She giggled a little on the inside at that last thought. After all, she had spent the last two years of her life studying law. "Yeah, I know. Mr. Anti-Commitment," she said only half-joking.

He breathed out heavily. "Now that you mention it, that's kind of what it boils down to."

"What? The fact that you have the capability of convincing women to hold out for you until you break their hearts?" she asked coldly. Really, she had no idea where this was leading. Why was he talking to her, of all people, about possibly marrying his girlfriend? He hadn't spoken to her in over a year and a half, and she was pretty sure *her* opinion on marriage was irrelevant to his decision. After all, her opinions on relationships, in general, had always been irrelevant.

"Yeah," he replied very softly into the phone. She almost hadn't heard him. "Yeah, that's what this is about." She waited for him to elaborate. After a brief pause, he began to explain the mess he had gotten himself into. "My girlfriend asked me if I wanted to marry her. Not like a proposal or anything," he quickly corrected, "more like a question to see where our relationship was headed. I didn't have an answer for her. I mean what kind of guy has an answer for that? But as you know…I mean because of my parents…the thought of marriage tends to make me run head first in the opposite direction. She pinned me down though, said she would leave me that second if I didn't give her an answer, which really took me off guard."

Lexi felt like she was sitting on the edge of her seat about to witness a train wreck. Any girl who had ever tried to pin Jack down for *anything* experienced rejection like a blow to the face.

"So I told her that was what I wanted."

"What?" she sputtered helplessly into the phone. "You told her you wanted to *marry* her?" Her mouth dropped open forming a little "oh" of disbelief.

He chuckled lightly at her reaction. "I told her I could see myself marrying her, but that I wasn't ready to commit yet. I mean we've only been dating for a year and a half." Jack cleared his throat before continuing. "Luckily, she took that as a positive answer and didn't break up with me. Then comes the part of the story where you come in."

"Me? I don't see how I could possibly come into a story about you marrying someone else."

"Well, she wants to meet you."

She could have never prepared for that answer. "What? I think I must have missed something. The girl that you are dating, that you *want* to marry, wants to meet *me*. Why? I'm so…insignificant," she mumbled disheartened. She couldn't even think about the different times her and Jack had tried to form a relationship. Nothing had ever worked, and the last time… She stopped herself again from entertaining the thought. The hole that Jack left still ached when prodded, and she avoided irritating the wounded feeling that crept through her.

"Don't say that. You know you're not insignificant." She let silence settle between them, not wanting to be the first to speak next. After listening to her breathe heavily for a while, he spoke again. "She got this idea in her head that she wants to meet every girl I've dated to find out why I was unable to commit to them. I guess she think it will help her figure out why I'm not committing to her. And don't try to say this doesn't apply to you because we didn't date. I wouldn't have dragged you into this Lex, but she heard about you from Kate."

Lexi recoiled at the mention of Jack's ex-girlfriend. "So by the way you say that, I'm guessing you actually went through with this insane decision. You are letting this girl pick and pry through your past just so that you don't have to commit to marrying her right now?" This was low…even for him.

"It's not like that," he stated defensively. "I let her talk to them, because I wanted to show her I had nothing to hide. When Kate mentioned you and I didn't, you can guess how she reacted."

Lexi couldn't help nodding even though she knew that he couldn't see her. She wouldn't be happy. Any female would be unhappy with the description Kate had likely bestowed upon her. Knowing the way Kate felt about her, it probably went along the lines of temptress, devious, manipulative, conniving, two-faced whore with a few added expletives just for good measure. "So Kate told her what happened which is how she got my name, but we were never um…together," she said not certain if that was the correct word.

"She doesn't seem to care. She thinks that since I didn't tell her about you, you somehow must hold all the answers as to why I am the way I am. I tried to tell her that the last I had seen or heard from you was before we'd even started dating, but she is almost as persistent as I am. So, I guess what I'm saying is that I need you, Lex," he said affectionately using her pet name. "I need you to meet Bekah and convince her I'm worth keeping around."

Lexi rolled her eyes to the ceiling in exasperation. She didn't even want to consider whether or not Jack *was* worth keeping around. Nonetheless, she mulled the idea over. She was, in fact, overdue for an Atlanta trip to visit her family. She had never intended to see Jack, especially if that included parading around with his fiancé-to-be and explaining their history. Pass on that. "You've failed to explain how any of this is *my* problem," she stated as firmly as possible. "It's not like I can dash away from my busy schedule to take a wonderful jaunt in the park with you and your girlfriend, or fiancé-to-be, or whatever the hell she is. I have other things to do. I'm kind of busy."

She could practically feel him cringe through the phone. "I know you're busy, but I thought that maybe since school wasn't in session, you might be able to take some time to get off work."

"Actually, I'm interning. I've been working my ass off all summer. I don't even know if the firm would give me the time off. No one takes time off, and I don't particularly want to be the only one," she stated telling only a partial truth. The other three interns had taken time off at the beginning of the program, but it had been before the work had drastically increased. Lately, the interns barely had time to breathe, let alone think of taking a weekend rendezvous out of state. She may have had a quiet Saturday planned, but that hardly kept her from being on call.

"I'm sorry. I didn't realize," he said quietly. "I guess I'll just have to tell her you weren't able to get off work. Please let me know if you happen to change your mind. It really would help me out immensely."

Jack had a talent for making her feel bad about the decision she made, especially if it wasn't directly in his best interest. "I'd really like to help," she said, lying through her teeth. "There's just no way that I can get the time off, and anyway I couldn't afford the flight," she said off-handedly.

"I wouldn't make you buy your own ticket," he added hastily. "You would be doing me a huge favor. Of course, I would take care of you…uh…it…the ticket."

"Oh." The last time she had seen him he was just out of college, poor, and practically starving for a job. Of course he would be doing significantly better financially two years later. Unlike her, sitting in a hundred thousand dollars of student loan debt with a year left in school.

"I guess I'll let you get back to your morning. Sorry for waking you up so early. You have my number now," he said as if that solved all the issues. "You can call me if you want."

"Right. Okay. Thanks," she stated dumbfounded. Why would she ever have to call Jack?

"Later."

"Bye."

She hung up the phone closing it with brutal force. Somehow, she restrained herself from flinging the stupid thing across the room. She was so angry and worked up and also terrified he would never call again. Too many emotions were roiling through her body right now so she did the first thing that came to mind. She quickly added Jack's name into her contacts despite the nagging urge to erase his number, all recollection of the phone call and him.

Lexi ground her teeth in frustration. She couldn't believe that after all of this time, *this* was why he was calling her. He called her because he was in love with another woman. Well, he hadn't come right out and said that, but it didn't matter. Jack would never contemplate marriage without due cause. She shook her head hoping she could wake herself from the nightmare of what she had just heard. When that didn't work, she pushed herself off the ground, careful not to put too much weight on her sore toe, and stalked out of her bedroom into what only a resident of New York City would consider a living room.

In all honesty, the living room, dining room, and kitchen were all compacted into one puny space with two doors leading into the bedrooms on either side. Grimy yellow paint crusted the walls with navy smudges appearing more prominently in some places where the top coat was peeling off. The crown molding was cracked and grungy. Her roommate's sofa, which luckily had a maroon cover to hide the seventies-esque pattern, took up the majority of the room. Two large bean bags, one brown and one turquoise, sat to one side, and a black Ikea table donned the other. A brown coffee table, left over from the previous owner, was cluttered with old newspapers, coffee stains, and seemingly endless dents from late night escapades. The only remotely spectacular item in the living room was the flat screen television her parents had given her as a move-in present.

Dusty wood floors creaked as she walked to the kitchen to brew the pot of coffee she so desperately needed. An off-white refrigerator hummed noisily along the far wall closest to Lexi's door. A window was etched into the wall above the aluminum-plated sink revealing a glossy view of the street below. After Lexi prepared the coffee, she leaned back against the cool counter and ran her fingers through her brown matted waves.

Her laid back Saturday had gone from relaxing to a spastic panic attack in the span of a fifteen minute phone call. When the timer went off, she poured herself a mug and guzzled the steaming coffee as quickly as she could muster before moseying back into her room to take a shower. Even though she drank the coffee black, the caffeine barely hit her. She knew by the time she was out of the shower, any signs of consuming it would have all but dissipated. She scrubbed her body vigorously with cranberry body soap. After applying shampoo through her long tresses and rinsing, she cut the shower off, dried her body, and slicked her hair back into a high ponytail. She threw on a pair of red Nike track shorts, a flimsy black tank, and a pair of running shoes. Making her way back into the kitchen, she poured the remaining pot of coffee into a travelers mug and scribbled a quick note for her roommate since this was the one morning she had actually woken up before her.

Forgoing a cab, Lexi trekked on auto-pilot across town, haphazardly knocking into eager tourists staring skyward. She remembered being one of those clueless people when she had first arrived in town. Now, she could navigate the city nearly as well as any homegrown New Yorker, except for her best friend, Chyna.

That was precisely who she was after as she meandered down Park Avenue on the way to the Upper East Side. It always baffled her that her best friend was more wealthy than she would likely be in her lifetime. But they got along and Chyna didn't seem to mind the financial discrepancy.

Lexi and Chyna had met nearly two years ago standing in line at a nightclub. Well, Lexi had been in line. Chyna absolutely refused to be subjected to waiting outside, when there was fun to be had on the inside. Lexi was next in line, wearing a scandalous outfit more fit for her home in Georgia than fall in York. She had been freezing her ass off for the past hour when Chyna arrived at the front entrance of the same locale gliding out of an onyx-colored town car, and directly through the rope.

Having seen one too many of these girls flounce into the club in front of her, Lexi began throwing a fit yelling about another skanky whore taking her place inside, not even caring that the bouncer looked like he was itching to kick her out of line. Surprisingly, Chyna stopped in her tracks, turned towards her, and asked her directly what she had said. Lexi repeated herself, smiling through chattering teeth the whole time. The bouncer's eyes had bulged at her comments and moved to remove her from the line, but Chyna put her hand out stopping him in his tracks. She then demanded he allow Lexi inside. Ever since that night, they had been all but inseparable.

Lexi planted herself on the front steps of Chyna's apartment building, smiling at the doorman. "You're here early, Miss Lexi," Bernard said opening the door for her and signaling for her to enter.

"Yeah, I had a pretty shitty morning to be honest, Mr. B."

"I'm sure it was nothing you can't handle," he said with his ever enthusiastic smile.

"Thanks, but you give me too much credit," she said producing a smile of her own. "Chyna upstairs?" she asked as she stepped through the entranceway.

"Yes, ma'am."

"Alone?" she threw the question over her shoulder.

He smiled that all-knowing smile and winked at her. Lexi laughed wondering if Chyna *ever* slept alone.

Lexi took the elevator to the top floor, listening absentmindedly to the classical ballad playing through the speakers. After exiting, she located the door to Chyna's apartment, slid the gold key into the lock, and twisted it. Swinging the door open, she smiled inwardly at the new renovations Chyna had effectuated into her foyer.

Her taste was constantly changing, and with a trust fund hovering somewhere around the nine digit range, why not adjust your life, home, and wardrobe whichever way the wind blew. At present, a crystal cut vase overflowed with seasonal flora on top of a square, white, sculpted table in the middle of the pristine entranceway. She prayed she hadn't tracked in mud or sidewalk grime on the freshly waxed marble floors as she strode through the foyer and down a small flight of stairs into the sunken living room. Lexi couldn't imagine a space contrasting with her apartment more than Chyna's den. In square feet, the living room along was larger than Lexi's entire residence. The pure white carpet was constantly steam cleaned to maintain its perfection. A sofa, loveseat and recliner – all a matching set of soft black leather – centered on an entertainment center rivaling a movie theatre. Original oil paintings Chyna had collected while traveling throughout Europe decorated several walls and black and white photographs floated in a collage of frames against one another.

Advancing across the room and through the arching hallway, Lexi made her way to Chyna's bedroom. She cracked the door open, and peered into the expansive room to see if Chyna did, in fact, have a companion in her king-sized, four-poster bed. "Chyna," she whispered into the darkness. "Chyna. Wake up, chica."

A deliberate grunt sounded from the other end of the room. "Go away."

"Get your tiny ass out of bed! Is there someone in there with you? I'm not afraid to do jumping jacks on your five million thread count sheets," she taunted with surprisingly more enthusiasm then she thought she was capable of that particular morning.

"You wouldn't," a muffled cry emanated from the darkness.

"Come on. How well do you know me?" Lexi questioned.

The covers flew to the foot of the bed and Chyna sat up grudgingly. "All too well," she grumbled swishing her glossy black hair over one shoulder.

Lexi pursed her lips with envy as Chyna slung her long olive-toned legs over the edge of the bed and hopped down. With the genetics of an Italian supermodel, Chyna was enviable from head to toe. Chyna felt more comfortable sauntering around in skimpy lingerie than probably anyone else in existence. But why not? She was rail thin with large perfectly perky breasts and a petite ass that didn't even look remotely fat in white, ultra skinny jeans. Her flawless complexion had never seen a blemish. Her large emerald eyes were almost always smoky and seductive. She was one hundred percent her mother's daughter in appearance and her father in personality, which explained why she didn't get along with either.

Her parents had made a public mess of their divorce when she was in high school, spreading their personal affairs all over the tabloids. Chyna wasn't sure why they had gotten so angry with each other. She had known since she was ten years old that both of her parents were having affairs. It had been pretty obvious. She couldn't understand why they hadn't realized that as well, but they hadn't. Or at least they had pretended they didn't know, possibly for her sake, but more likely, they looked the other way to hold on to some semblance of why they had gotten married in the first place. Money. Love. Who knew? Now her father couldn't look at her, and her mother couldn't be around her.

"What are you doing here so early? Unbelievable, Alexa," she chided, using Lexi's full name as always. "You know I need a minimum seven hours of beauty sleep or I look like shit all day. Do I look like I went to bed at midnight?"

Lexi smiled at her. Chyna looked like she had never gotten less than seven hours of sleep in her life. "Oh wow, I'm sorry," she said in mock repentance. "You look like an ugly old hag this morning. Perhaps you should sleep for another three hours."

"You're right," she nodded. "I've only been sleeping for four hours."

Lexi sighed dramatically. "The world will end."

Chyna poked Lexi's shoulder playfully. "Shut up, you."

"Bernard mentioned there was someone with you?" Lexi asked cocking an eyebrow at her.

"Oh, phew on him. What do I pay him for anyway? I threw that boy out hours ago," she said smiling mischievously. "Now, what in the world are you doing here so early? Our hair appointment isn't for a few more hours." Lexi brushed the flyaways behind her ear anxiously, a clear indicator of her anxiety. "Oh God, it's a boy," Chyna squealed in excitement. "Tell me everything!"

Chyna always got excited when Lexi mentioned a new guy. Mostly, Lexi figured because it happened so infrequently. Pretty much since she had moved to the city, she had been too preoccupied with school, and relationships had been placed on the backburner. Every now and then, she would go out on dates with guys from class or someone Chyna recommended, but, it never worked out. When it came to her luck with men, Lexi preferred just to avoid the situation entirely.

"Well, it's kind of a strange story," she began, realizing she had exactly mirrored Jack's words. Chyna nodded enthusiastically, bouncing on her toes in anticipation. "So, you remember Jack?" she asked tentatively, forcing herself not to wince when she said his name.

Chyna's faced clouded over and a crease formed between her eyebrows. "Oh no, not him," she said pleadingly. "Please tell me that this has nothing to do with him."

"What's wrong with him?" Lexi asked, strangely enough, finding herself getting defensive.

"Alexa, Alexa," she scolded, "do you not *remember* yourself after that boy left?"

Lexi did remember. She could still feel it every time she thought about him. When she stumbled across a picture of them together or passed a particularly cozy looking coffee shop, she remembered it all like it was yesterday. Only in the past six months had a numbness started to take over that feeling. Sometimes it still hit her fresh nearly two years later. He was capable of eliciting such emotional and physiological responses to this day, even though they had never officially been together. She was amazed she had turned him down over the phone after no contact for that long. If he had called for *anything* else, she was certain she would have crumbled.

"Yeah, I remember," Lexi said softly.

"Well, then, why would you bring him up?" Chyna demanded

"He called me," she said brushing her hair back several more times before meeting Chyna's disapproving eyes.

"And?" Chyna asked with a look of firm protectiveness taking over her features.

Lexi sighed, and then quickly gave Chyna the run down on the mess Jack had gotten himself into, and what he had requested of her. She forced all the words out in quick procession, not allowing Chyna to get in one word edge wise. When she finished, she breathed out heavily and looked up to find Chyna staring at her curiously. Somewhere throughout her story, Chyna's features had changed, softened. Lexi wasn't quite sure what it meant. "So yeah, that was my morning. Sounds great, doesn't it?"

"You turned him down?" she asked clearly surprised. After everything she had been through with Jack, her feelings for him were unrivaled.

"Yeah, I did. Aren't you proud?"

"I think you should do it," she stated simply.

"What?" Lexi asked bursting from her comfortable lying position on the bed. "This morning is just nuts. Jack calls, and then you, of all people, tell me that I should go visit him and meet his fiancé?"

"Fiancé-to-be," Chyna quipped letting a naughty smirk creep onto her face.

"Whatever! Just explain this to me. Why should I go see him? Nothing good ever comes out of me being around him. I know this and you know this. The whole world should know this. Give me one good reason I should go see him." Chyna couldn't be serious! After all, Lexi had been so proud of herself for turning him down for *once* in her life.

"Closure."

"I don't need closure," Lexi stated stubbornly.

"Come on. Honestly, Alexa. I'm not sure you have ever gotten over this guy. I've tried to get you into a relationship, and you've dated a few of the people I've thrown your way, but it was never anything substantial. You need to move on, but how can you do that when you're still hung up on a guy you haven't heard from in two years? Oh wait, you can't!" she exclaimed cocking her head to the side to really examine Lexi. "Now you've been through some rough times, and honestly you've been a bit of a depressive. I get it. I've been there too, and I understand. Maybe not with a guy, but my parents and I have all those issues. You need to go to Atlanta, meet this girl, tell her exactly how much of a scumbag Jack truly is, and then get the hell out of there!"

Lexi hesitated and then nodded seeing her logic. "Maybe you're right."

"No, I know I'm right," Chyna said hopping off the bed and moseying into her walk-in closet as if that ended the discussion.

Lexi stayed seated considering Chyna's argument. The girl had a point. After everything she had gone through with Jack, maybe this was exactly what she needed, even if it wasn't necessarily what she wanted. Still undecided, Lexi joined Chyna in her closet. As Chyna chose something to wear, Lexi remained lost in her thoughts. She knew that Chyna's statements made sense, but how could she ever face Jack? Once Lexi had realized who was on the line, she had nearly hyperventilated. How would she react when she saw him in person? She really didn't know, but she didn't think she could turn down the opportunity to see him either. "Ok, I'll do it."

"I knew you had it in you," Chyna said sliding on a pair of brown strappy sandals and exiting the closet. "Now go make that phone call while I fix my hair and makeup."

Lexi gulped as Chyna walked into her bathroom, likely not to surface for a while. She had agreed to do it; now she just had to calm herself down enough to make the call. Her palms felt slick with sweat as she sat down at the mahogany writing desk and pulled her phone out of her black handbag. She hesitantly flipped it open and scrolled through the address book. Lexi was thankful, at least, that she had added his number to her phone this morning instead of erasing it.

She worked up the courage to press the button, then immediately hung up. Her hands were shaking so furiously, she nearly dropped the phone. Taking a few breaths to try to calm down, she punched the send button again. Listening as the phone rang twice nearly unnerved her, but then the line clicked over.

"Lex," Jack said surprised. "I didn't expect to hear from you."

"You implied," she began her voice cracking slightly with the effort of staying calm, "that I could call you."

"Sure. I said you could call me. I just never thought you actually would."

"Yeah, I'm full of surprises," she said trying to play off her apprehension.

"Always were," he said quietly.

Lexi sighed before venturing forward. "My internship ends in two weeks. I will probably be coming to Atlanta to see my parents after that. So, I guess, what I'm trying to say is…that I'll do it. I'll come see you," she paused before allowing the last part of her sentence to roll off her tongue, "and meet your girlfriend."

2

SEPTEMBER SIX YEARS EARLIER

When Lexi first arrived at her freshman dorm, her resident assistant called a hall meeting for all the freshman students. At the meeting her resident assistant distributed a directory listing local restaurants, clubs, bars, and an array of study nooks for the incoming freshman. Nearly every girl tossed the packet into the garbage as soon as they left the meeting, but Lexi held onto it hoping it would come to good use in locating a perfect locale to study. She investigated a handful of these locations, but found them not to her tastes.

When she finally stumbled upon one particular coffee shop near the end of the list, she instantly fell in love. The coffee shop itself was nothing spectacular. To be honest, it was on the small side, especially for a college town. But the rich aroma of freshly ground coffee beans that enveloped her senses when she set foot in the dimly lit shop sold her. It was perfect! Twenty unmatched tables were tightly pressed together with barely enough room to squeeze between. Green filtered lamps of various shapes and sizes rested atop each table casting a pleasant emerald glow upon the customers. Counter space was nearly impossible to acquire.

As the winter months gradually approached, a roaring fire crackled in a corner fireplace. Cushioned green lounge chairs and dilapidated couches were scattered haphazardly against the walls and surrounding the fireplace. On any given day, the tables were occupied by students and professors alike discussing anything from nuclear physics to Aristotelian philosophy to Freudian psychology.

After Lexi spent a few late nights in this cozy nook, she laid claim to one of the tables facing the counter. She had chosen that particular table specifically for the instances when *he* was working. At first, she hadn't even really noticed him. But the more time she spent there, the more often she crossed paths with him. And she couldn't stop coming by hoping to catch a glimpse of him. Her friends, who preferred to study at the university learning center, kept trying to rouse her from the coffee shop. None of them could understand why she would want to work in such a loud, crowded, poorly lit space with a feeble internet connection. When they asked her why she refused to leave, she gave them the excuse of enjoying the atmosphere, but they finally weaseled it out of her.

Him.

The next day after her secret was revealed, Lexi found herself sitting at her usual table with her friend, Olivia, for company. "Well, what do you think?" Lexi asked as she flipped through her introductory philosophy class notes, skimming through the most recent lecture on Empiricists.

"You're right. He is pretty hot," Olivia confirmed, running her fingers through her bleached blonde pixie cut, letting the tiny strands of hair fall effortlessly back into place.

"I meant about Locke."

"He's dead right?" Olivia asked uninterested.

Lexi rolled her eyes. "No, I mean...what's his idea about knowledge?" she asked trying hard not to glance up at him while Olivia blatantly ogled the eye candy.

"Honestly, I don't care. I hate this stuff. I might just drop the class altogether. I don't get it," Olivia said shrugging her shoulders at her own indecipherable notes. She glanced back up at the guy working the counter. "Him, I can *fully* understand. You should give it a shot."

Lexi brushed her off, feeling the weight of her gaze uncomfortably. "No, what I need to shoot for is an A on this test."

Olivia rolled her eyes dramatically. "Whatever, you know you're going to get an A, but don't you want to at least meet him? Know his name?"

It was Lexi's turn to shrug. "Yeah, I guess," she conceded.

"Have you ever even had a boyfriend?" Olivia asked giggling a little at that inexplicable possibility.

"Of course I've had a boyfriend," Lexi retorted defensively. "I'm just not looking for one now."

"I didn't say you wanted or even needed a relationship. We're freshman. We're just supposed to have fun and make mistakes anyway. So you should at least meet him and hang out with him," she uttered persuasively. Lexi shrugged noncommittally returning to her notes.

After a pause, Olivia changed topics, "So, anyway, are you coming to Nick and Neal's show tonight at The Theatre?"

"Yeah, I should be there," Lexi confirmed.

"Good, I've been helping them plan this for a month. I need as many people there as possible." Lexi just nodded since she had heard this same rant nearly every day since Olivia had decided to become their publicist. "I'm going to get myself a drink from sexy Coffee Guy," she added a wink just for good measure, "and then I'm going to head back to the dorm to get ready for tonight. You comin' with, doll?"

"Nah, I'm going to finish here," she said gesturing to her notebooks sprawled on the table. "But I'll meet you later," Lexi said scribbling a quick note into her study guide. She watched Olivia slink over to the counter to get her coffee. Lexi quickly averted her eyes to avoid watching her shamelessly flirt with the guy she was interested in. She figured it didn't really matter that much anyway. This guy was no one to her. He was just a pretty face in a sea of pretty faces in the crowd or at least that's what she tried to convince herself.

*****

A few hours later, Lexi, Olivia, and fifteen other people they had managed to drag out of the dorms were casually standing in front of the stage at The Theatre waiting for Nick and Neal to begin their set. The Theatre was a large open space with couches positioned around the perimeter and for smaller shows, like tonight, on the main floor.

As the time passed, the room gradually filled with regulars and other locals. Considering this was Nick and Neal's first real performance, the crowd was relatively large. A unanimous bounce began as the throng of people fell into rhythm with the flow of the music that Nick was spinning, Neal's original lyrics filling the room. Lexi sang along with some of the words she remembered from hanging out with them.

"You're not bad. Maybe you should show them how it's done," someone said to her.

Lexi laughed out loud letting her curls bounce lightly. She turned to address whoever had addressed her and was face to face with *him*. She froze mid-laugh.

"You think so?" she asked trying to recover from her shock at seeing him here, standing next to her, talking to her.

"Honestly, no," he said with a sly smile.

"Well, thanks. I'm very offended right now." Lexi placed her hand over her wounded heart. "So...do I know you or do you always just insult people when you first meet them?"

He bent down so he she was better able to hear him. He smelled like a heavenly combination of soap and sexy cologne. "I think you study at the coffee shop where I work."

She turned her head up to face him. His brown hair fell neatly across his eyes as he looked down at her. She had never noticed just how clear blue his eyes really were until they were set intently and solely on her. "I think you might be right," she confirmed giving him a coy smile. She was having a hard time breathing with him looking at her so intently. She could practically feel the energy crackling between their bodies at his nearness. Trying to ease the sexual tension she was feeling, she asked him, "Are you much into college boy rap?"

His laugh was easy and sincere and she loved the musicality of it. "No, not really, but this guy's not bad. Is he a friend of yours?"

"Yeah, he lives in my dorm." She cringed realizing she had just given away her youth. She had no idea how old he was or whether he would consider a freshman to be worth his time.

"Nice. Those guys over there." He gestured with his thumb to three guys clustered behind him. "They lived on my hall last year in the dorms. Which one are you in?"

Lexi let out the breath she hadn't even realized she had been holding. "Um...Russell."

"That's where we were," he said smiling bigger. "Fifth floor east. You?"

"Five north," she told him. If she had only been a year older, she could have lived on the same hall as him for a year. Her head swam with the thought.

"Small world."

"Yeah, it is. How exactly did you hear about the band? I mean, if you don't really listen to the music," she couldn't help but ask.

He reached into his back pocket and pulled out a folded piece of purple paper. He opened it revealing the PR flyer Olivia had been relentlessly handing out for the past two weeks. "I believe a friend of yours gave this to me," he said pointing to Olivia over the crowd of people.

Lexi giggled. That little devil. Olivia hadn't been flirting with him when she had gone to get her coffee earlier that afternoon. In fact, she had been helping her by convincing Coffee Guy to come here. "Well, yeah, that's Olivia for you," she said shrugging, making an attempt at nonchalance. "Oh, I'm Lexi, by the way." She extended her hand out to him.

"Lexi...hmm...I like that," he said taking her outstretched hand firmly in his. "Jack. It's nice to meet you,"

Silence fell between them as the show progressed. The hip-hop beats blaring in the background made it difficult to carry on a conversation. The crowd filed outside for intermission when the set was complete, allowing the main act time to set-up on stage. Several people lit cigarettes as soon as they exited The Theatre, but Lexi steered clear of them. She watched as some of her friends made their way to the back entrance of the black building to meet up with Nick and Neal. Lexi waited awkwardly with Jack at the front of the building waiting for Olivia to surface.

A few second later, Olivia exited through the doors covered with a collage of torn flyers advertising upcoming shows. She bounded up to them humming one of the songs she preferred. "Hey, sweetie," she said kissing Lexi on the cheek. Her eyes were glazed over a little and her low cut blouse smelled strongly of beer and secondhand smoke. Before Lexi had a chance to respond, she stumbled along after the rest of the group.

"I guess she's a bit drunk," Lexi commented shrugging her shoulders as she let her gaze land back on Jack.

"A bit?" he questioned with a smirk. "Hold on one second." He directed his attention on his friends hovering behind him. "Hey guys, I'll meet you at Chamber. I think Chasity said she was working." Nodding, the three guys disappeared down the street leaving Jack and Lexi alone.

Lexi assumed Chasity was a bartender, but refrained from asking. She had no desire whatsoever to know how they knew each other…or how well. "I'm not sure what my friends are doing," she said glancing around the corner. The group she had arrived with were stumbling around outside with Nick and Neal at the center. "But by the look of things, I'm going to have to carry half of them home." At only a couple inches over five feet, that really would be a feat. "I should go catch up with them before they get into any trouble," she said concerned.

"My friends are probably lost without me too," he said jokingly.

"Are you working tomorrow?" she asked not anxious to leave his presence.

"Are you studying tomorrow?" he countered flirtatiously.

"Yeah," she confirmed, thinking about the daunting stack of homework on her desk.

"Then I should be there."

She stood with him another second taking in his near flawless appearance. He wore dark snug-fit jeans, a black button-up rolled to three-quarter length, and worn navy Chuck Taylor's. He was taller than her by more than half a dozen inches with a well-toned muscular physique. She figured she wouldn't be able to reach his lips if she stood on her tip-toes, but he was strong enough to pick her up to them. Quickly pushing the idea out of her mind, she snapped herself back to reality. "Guess I'll see you there."

"Sounds good," he said as she turned and began to walk down the alleyway toward her friends. After a moment's hesitation, he called out to her and jogged down the street after her. She turned on her green high heels to find him standing before her again. "I know you have to study tomorrow, but what are you doing Friday?" he asked hesitantly.

She paused giving enough time to make it seem like she was considering her schedule. "I don't have any plans," she finally responded, fighting the uncontrollable silly grin contorting her features.

"Do you want to hang out?"

She nodded. "I thought you'd never ask."

*****

Friday night Lexi found herself pacing her tiny dorm room twining her dark curls around her fingers. The room was nothing special, but she and Jennifer made it look the best they could with the space provided.

Two beds were lofted on opposite sides of the room. A black futon rested under Lexi's; two mini fridges and a tiny tube television sat under her roommate's. A red and black print rug covered the tile floor and red curtains blocked out the view of the other high-rise dorms surrounding them. Lexi's side of the wrap-around metal desk held her black laptop and a selection of her favorite books and textbooks. The wall adjacent her desk held a collage of photographs neatly arranged. Jennifer's desk was a mess of multi-colored paper clips, geometrically shaped Post-It notes, and furry-topped pens. The walls were lined with sorority initiation paraphernalia that made Lexi roll her eyes every time she glanced over there.

"Jen, do you think I look okay?"

Jennifer gave her a once-over. Lexi wore black, slightly-worn, skinny jeans, a pale green camisole with lace-trim and black thong sandals that strapped around her ankle. Her hair was pulled up into a high ponytail with the dark bouncing curls streaming out of the rubber band. A light coat of black mascara brushed her eyelashes and a hint of shimmer lip gloss adorned her lips. "Mmm," Jennifer murmured tilting her head to the side before turning back to her Latin homework spread out across the futon.

Lexi placed her hands on her hip exasperated. "What does *mmm* mean?"

Jennifer shrugged. "You should probably pull your hair down, run a straightener through it, and put on a cute dress," she said as a matter-of-fact. She hadn't even glanced up from her five-subject notebook. "I have this perfect purple ensemble that will do wonders to detract from your plain brown eyes."

Lexi was starting to get used to this behavior. Jennifer was remarkably honest, to a fault. But she was also incredibly judgmental which made her blatant honesty not as flattering. "I think we're going to be outside though," Lexi told her, turning to face the full-length mirror hanging on the back of their door.

"It's like seventy degrees outside," Jennifer said. Her gum smacked against the roof of her mouth as she spoke. "You can still wear a dress."

Jennifer thought everyone should wear a dress, all the time, for every occasion, even when it was freezing. Lexi was pretty certain that the only time Jennifer went without a dress was when she showered. She was even lounging in a dress while studying Latin!

Both her parents came from old southern money dating back pre-Civil War. The Country Club, where they resided, played host to a number of stars. She had once complained about missing Halloween away from home, because that year a certain male rapper had actually answered the door to pass out candy.

"Well, it could be colder tonight," Lexi grumbled snatching her cell phone off her desk and cramming it into her plum purse. "I'm going to see Olivia. Have fun studying."

Lexi darted down the hall as her phone trilled inside her purse. Opening the cold metal clasp, she retrieved the cell and answered. "Hey, do you want me to come upstairs?" Jack asked from the other line.

"Nah. No point in making you try to get past security. I'll be right down." Lexi scrambled down the four flights of stairs as fast as she could, making it to the landing before the elevator dinged. Racing down the steep hill that led to the street below, Lexi recognized his little silver sports car waiting with the hazard lights blinking. She slipped her hand under the handle to pop the door open and slid smoothly onto the black leather seat. He let off the clutch and slung the car into gear as soon as he heard the latch click. "So, where are we going?" she asked relaxing back into the soft material.

"It's a surprise," he said, shifting gears as they picked up speed.

"Hmm...I like surprises."

"I thought you might." He glanced at her briefly before turning left.

Lexi hadn't been sure whether or not to treat this as if it were a date. He had asked her out, but when they talked on the phone, he had acted as if it was no big deal. She didn't care to agonize over it though. She didn't know him yet, so as far as she was concerned the status of their relationship, if you could even call it that, was hardly relevant. One step at a time.

John Mayer's acoustic cover of *Free Fallin'* filled the silence as Jack drove them away from the center of town. Jack tapped his fingers against the steering wheel in time with the guitar chords. "Do you play," she asked watching how well his fingers moved.

"A little," he said with a sexy smirk.

"Oh yeah? What instruments?"

"*Just* guitar, bass, piano, saxophone, and some drums, but I'm really rusty."

"Jesus! All I can do is sing."

"Oh, and I sing," he smirked as he hit the break at a red light.

"Well don't you seem to be good at everything," Lexi said staring up at him through thick dark lashes.

She could tell that he was watching her out of the corner of his eye. "You just wait and see."

"I look forward to it." She giggled turning back to the road. Something about Jack seemed to just fit. The flirting, the desirous looks, the uncomplicated conversation was all so easy between them.

Lexi's eyes widened as they turned onto a stretch of university property that until now had been empty fields. Instead, a bright twirling Ferris wheel had been erected in the center of the field with an array of carnival rides and booths displayed around the centerpiece. "I didn't know a carnival was coming through town!"

"One night only," he said wiggling his eyebrows up and down. "The university sets up celebrations like this throughout the year. Since you're new, I thought I'd take you to the first one of the year."

A plump older man in an orange vest holding a light stick directed them into a makeshift parking spot on the lawn.

The couple trekked across the muddy terrain towards the vinyl ticket booth. Handing over their student identification cards, the student association representative slid the cards through a reader. The machine dinged each time authorizing their authenticity. "Have a good time and don't forget to grab a complimentary t-shirt on your way out," the woman said handing them back their cards with one hand and gesturing to a display of boxes containing hundreds of bright green tees.

"Thanks," Jack said grabbing Lexi's arm and racing through the entrance.

They made it only a dozen feet before unexpectedly running into Jack's roommates, Seth, Luke, and Michael, who were with two of their other friends, Clark and Hunter. Each looked more excited than the next. Between them they were counting out what looked like several hundred orange paper tickets like little kids in Chuck E. Cheese.

Seth snatched up a handful out of Clark's palm and deposited them in his pocket. "Hey, what the fuck are you doing?" Clark cried launching himself onto Seth.

Seth chuckled as he sidestepped Clark's advances. "You don't need all of those," he said tauntingly.

"You took all of my goddamn tickets, jackass," Clark yelled grabbing at Seth's pocket as the rest of the guys burst out laughing.

Seth threw his hands up. "Geez, Clark, you're very forward. I feel like we've just met. At least take me to dinner first."

"Ha. Ha," Clark said sarcastically, placing his tickets firmly back into his own pocket.

"Hey guys," Jack said laughing along with the rest at their behavior. "Not sure if you've met already, but this is Lexi."

The guys gave their names and nodded hellos. That was all the introduction they afforded her before they were ready to attack the rides. "Let's hit the Bumper Cars before the line wraps around the park," Seth said edging towards the far side of the field.

"Bumper Cars? No way. I'm never riding Bumper Cars with you assholes again. Ya'll gang up on me every time," Luke complained. "Can we just do something like the Scrambler?"

Seth rolled his eyes. "Don't be such a fag, Luke. We would never pick on you. How old do you think we are?" This coming from the guy who just snagged someone else's tickets.

After finally convincing Luke to join them, the group moved over to get into line for the Bumper Cars. Jack sidled up to Lexi. "We actually do gang up on Luke," he whispered in her ear, laughing. "Better make sure you join in on the fun. His reaction will be well worth it."

Of course, he was right. Luke instantly began pummeling anything he could get his hands on, even knocking over a tiny blonde in his angst. His friends' laughter only egged him on further.

Jack slung his arm across Lexi's shoulders as they doubled over in a fit of giggles. "I cannot believe him," she said wiping away tears of laughter.

"He is a riot," Jack confirmed watching Luke try to take a swing at Seth who ducked under his half-hearted blow easily. "Why don't we get you something to rot your teeth," Jack suggested pulling her away from his friends who had begun to brawl outside of the Bumper Cars and directing them towards the cotton candy machine. "So tell me, Lex, what do you normally do on Friday nights?"

She shrugged. "I hang out with my roommate or Olivia, go downtown, see movies, game nights, dinners, fraternity parties," she added at last.

"Cool. I like to do all of those things," he said with an easy-going smile.

"Fraternity parties?" she questioned raising an eyebrow.

"Mike's in a fraternity. So, yes, even fraternity parties. Probably not as often as my freshman year though."

Lexi snatched a piece of the sweet pink cloud and stuck it in her mouth as they walked towards the Ferris wheel. The sticky goodness dissolved almost instantly leaving a trail of sugar across her lips. Jack's eyes had zeroed in on the traces of the candy still on her lips. She licked them experimentally tasting a mixture of her lip gloss and sugar. "You're such a mess," he said indicating where she had missed a spot. His eyes gave away other thoughts.

The Ferris wheel line had already begun to wrap around the edge of the giant machine. The two placed themselves at the back of the line and continued their conversation. "What's your major?" he asked plopping a piece of the cotton candy into his own mouth.

"As of today, I'm undecided," she proclaimed cheerfully.

"An indecisive one, I like it."

"I'm not indecisive. Just open minded."

"Same thing."

"Well, what's your major, Mr. Decisive."

He shook his head. "I'm not decisive, just practical. I'm Pre-Business, likely going to the accounting route. Not so sure though."

Lexi wrinkled her nose. "Eww. I'll forestall practical. Thank you!"

His laugh boomed out of him. "Yeah, it's what I'm good at."

"At least there are a lot of jobs out there for you. Not much a person can do while being undecided and what I really want to do has only a few more jobs than that," she said shrugging her shoulders helplessly.

"And what is that? What do you *really* want to do?" he asked giving her a very serious meaningful look.

Lexi considered not telling him for an instant then gave in. "Gymnastics." Her eyes glazed over at the thought of being able to fly through the air, jumping effortlessly from a spring board, weather-worn calluses coating her hands from the uneven bars.

"That's awesome. Have you talked to the Gymnastics Team here? If you like it so much, you should try out," he said enthusiastically.

She shook herself out of her cloudy visions. "No," she responded solemnly.

"Why not?"

"You don't just try out for the Gymnastics Team here. They're amazing. If they don't recruit you, then you have no chance. No walk-ons. Nothing."

"How do you know that? Were you recruited?"

"No, I wasn't," she said a bit sharper than she had intended, the bitterness sneaking into her voice.

"Oh, well, I know one of the gymnasts. I bet she could talk to the coach. Even if you can't be on the team, you could probably practice with them." The glance she gave to him was as if she were approaching a Martian. "Ok, maybe not," he said raising his eyebrows and taking another bite of the cotton candy to prevent himself from speaking again.

"Even if I could get to talk with the coach, there would be no way she would let me practice with them," she stated matter-of-factly.

"Never know until you try," he said swallowing the remaining bit. "Here we are." Jack handed the man four orange tickets, and ushered Lexi into a big swinging yellow bucket with the number twenty-five plastered against the back.

Lexi felt weightless as the machine cranked them around in an endless circle. They rotated three or four times, Jack shaking their bucket back and forth until he rattled the whole ride. A large girl with too tight jeans and a way too tight shirt rode in front of them threatening him the whole time. "Calm down," she said putting her hand on his knee. "We don't want to get kicked off."

"I know the guy who's running it. No way we'll get kicked off," he said throwing his arm across the back of the bucket seat, but stopping nonetheless.

As they made their final rotation, the ride crawled to a stop leaving Jack and Lexi on the very top of the ride looking out across the open fields. Jack's arm fell from the seat back and landed gingerly across her shoulders. She allowed him to pull her into him, her head falling into place between his shoulder and neck. She sighed contentedly, gazing out across the night sky filled with twinkling white stars burning in the distance.

They spent the next several hours perusing the carnival life. He even won her a huge teddy bear from a darts game. She held it tightly as they made their way towards the exit with the rest of the crowd. A plump associate stuffed two green t-shirts in their hands as they stepped across the threshold. The distance back to the dorm felt like only seconds compared to earlier in the evening. Jack skidded to a halt in front of the hill that led up to the dorm entrance.

"Do you want me to park and walk you up?" he asked turning his warning blinkers on again.

"No, not necessary. Thanks," she said grabbing her purse from the floor and raising it to her shoulder. With shirt and bear in hand, she popped the door open.

"Hey, wait," he said putting the car in park and darting around to the other side.

He reached her, immediately pulling her into him. She slid her arms up around his neck feeling him press up against her. He picked her up letting her legs dangle when he stood up straight. "I hope you don't mind, but I couldn't leave without a hug," he said squeezing her a little tighter.

"Oh no," she breathed, "I don't mind at all."

Jack placed her back on her feet, and she stared dreamily up into his eyes. He bent down planting a light kiss on her cheek before straightening up once again and making his way back to the driver's side. Lexi waved as he barreled down the road leaving her standing there breathless. It had definitely been a date.

*****

The next few weeks went by in a blur. Lexi and Jack were together as much as humanly possible. When he was working at the coffee shop, she could be found studying across from his counter. When her classes let out, he was waiting for her outside the old brick building with a steaming cup of her favorite brew and a moist slice of pound cake or a blueberry muffin. She became a regular in their household staying up late into the night playing video games. His roommates didn't mind her coming over, mostly because they loved the look on Luke's face when she kicked his ass at Mario Kart.

The only time they didn't spend together was football games. Olivia's legacy went back several generations, and Lexi usually followed her to their tailgate spot on North Campus along with the rest of their friends. Jack typically had a space reserved with his buddies on East Campus. Since he was from Savannah, he tended to return there during away games, and Lexi found that she missed him more than she was willing to admit. That's why she had designated Sunday movie night.

On this particular movie night, Lexi accepted his easy hug as she walked through his door. She snuggled up into his sweater inhaling the familiar smell of his cologne as it lingered on his skin and in his clothes. "This weekend seemed to drag on forever," Lexi whispered into his ear.

"I know. I missed you too," he murmured directing her towards the couch. When he looked at her again, he said, "You're beautiful."

A smile stretched across her face. "Thank you. You don't look too bad yourself," she said knocking her hip against his before falling against the brown suede couch. He landed next to her. Throwing her dark chocolate boat shoes onto the carpet, she stretched her legs out crossing them on the coffee table. "So, what are we watching tonight?" she asked scanning his impressive collection of movies.

Before he had a chance to answer her, his phone buzzed on the table. Attempting to be courteous, Lexi reached forward to hand it to him, but he was too quick. He eagerly snatched it up off the table and stood to read the name on the caller id. After a brief pause, he clicked a button to silence it.

His eyes turned back to her, and Lexi met his gaze expectantly. "I'll call them back," he said falling back into his place at her side. He wrapped his arms around her waist and pulled her into his lap, burying his head into her hair. "You smell like Heaven," he said taking a big long whiff.

She giggled, smacking his hand playfully. "I showered before I came over."

"Well…that's a nice change."

She smacked him harder this time, pushing at one of his arms that was holding her tightly in place. "Stop sniffing me like a dog."

"Then stop smelling so *damn* good," he said breathing her in several more times. His face was so close to her body that she could almost feel his lips against her bare neck. She stopped struggling and tuned into how her body was reacting to him being so near. Her breathing had quickened and her body felt warm all over. His nose brushed lightly up against her ear. She shivered as goose bumps broke out across her arms and down her back at his touch. He didn't let her go, and he didn't back off. This was new and she liked it. "God, I want you, Lex," he said running a line of kisses down her exposed jaw line.

Lexi's eyes closed of their own accord. As his kisses intensified moving from her jaw to her ear and then down her neck, she sighed heavily cocking her head back to allow him easier access. He laid her gently back against the couch moving his body so that it was hovering just above her with one leg positioned between hers. Their eyes met briefly before his mouth moved from one cheek to another experimentally. She sighed as he inched closer to her wet, trembling lips. Her hardly contained desire let loose a moan as he pushed himself against her. Lacing her fingers through his hair, she gazed up into his crystal clear blue eyes practically begging him to continue. He leaned forward to meet her lips. She sighed happily waiting for that moment, but it never came. Just before his lips touched hers, his phone buzzed noisily in his pocket. His attention wavered and he pulled back from her body.

"Don't stop," she urged him, leaning forward and planting a kiss of her own on his cheek. "You can call whoever it is back," she reminded him. The limbo he left her in was like torture. She hadn't said so, but her desire for him was overflowing and they had yet to even kiss.

He smiled at her lovingly and kissed her cheek before moving from his position on top of her. Fishing the phone out of his pocket, he took a look at the name, and once again silenced it. "You're right. I can just call them back."

He hopped off the couch and quickly scooped her up into his arms. Lexi laughed unexpectedly as he effortlessly carried her into his room kicking the door open with his foot. She fell back against the navy blue comforter, her shirt sliding up nearly to her chest. She stretched languidly, allowing him a full view of her lean muscled body. He crawled from the foot of the bed up to her abdomen and left one lone kiss next to her bellybutton. His hands raked the bare skin as he traveled upwards from there. Sighing contentedly, she felt his lips make their way back to her neck. He darted his tongue against her tender skin making her writhe.

"Oh, Jack," she breathed. Bringing his head up to look at her, she noticed his breath was coming in short puffs. She teasingly wiggled her hips first from side-to-side and then in small circles, watching as he groaned on top of her.

"You're so mean."

"Really? I thought I was being *really* nice," she replied twirling her hips in a figure eight.

"A little too nice." He sighed closing his eyes as she ran her tongue along his earlobe. "You've found my weakness," he moaned grabbing her arms in his hands and pushing them above her head, forcing her back against the bed.

"Well, if I found your weakness, then you shouldn't push me away." Her eyes were smoldering. One thought and only one thought filled her head; she did not want to be away from him. A cute flirtatious smile crossed her face. She glanced from his baby blues to his pouty lips and back, not sure which she preferred more at that moment.

"I don't want to push you away, but I'm going to take advantage of you if you keep doing that," he said rolling over to the other side of the bed.

Lexi flipped her leg as he rolled, straddling his body. "I haven't even gotten a kiss," she said leaning in close to him, "so I don't feel as if I'm in much danger of being taken advantage of."

"You are the most amazing girl I've ever met," he said brushing his fingers across her cheek.

Her lips landed lightly on his and instantly knew she wanted more. Just as he began to react, his pocked vibrated making Lexi jump backwards in exasperation. He swore under his breath. "I'll be right back," he said yanking out the phone as he casually adjusted his erection. She watched him exit the room and turn towards the back door out of earshot.

Falling back against the bed, she sighed heavily. She couldn't tell if she was being too forward. Even though they had only been hanging out for a couple of weeks, she could tell he was really into her. She was unbelievably ready for his lips to be on her. Normally, when she was in this position, guys were absolutely dying to get in her pants. It's not that Jack hadn't acted like he wanted to kiss her…do more than kiss her. He just hadn't even tried. She respected that he respected her, but enough was enough. She yanked her shirt back into place and sat up straight-backed against the black headboard folding her arms across her knees.

"Sorry about that," he apologized as he came around the corner scratching the back of his head.

"It's alright." Her smile had lost its fire. "How about that movie?"

They retreated back to the living room; both attempting to forget that they had been so close to ravishing each other's bodies only a few short minutes earlier. As time went by, their encounters continued, each with as much or more intensity as the last. Then, they would stop, always just a little bit farther than the last time. He captivated her thoughts, and was even beginning to make his way into her dreams. The previous night, her dream had felt so real. When she had woken up to find herself in her dorm room, rather than wrapped in Jack's arms, she had been so frustrated she had actually woken Jennifer up. It was safe to say neither girl had been pleased.

The next day, Lexi forced herself to survive her three classes before driving over to Jack's house. She knew that he had the day off, and was anxious to see him. After the exceedingly vivid dream, she could hardly concentrate without images of him pressed against her entering her mind. She knocked on the door to announce her presence, and then pushed it open without waiting for a response. Jack was standing in the living room talking on his cell phone. He glanced over at the door as she entered and held up a finger as if to tell her he would just be a minute. He moved into the bedroom and closed the door as she sat down on the couch to wait.

Lexi had gotten dressed with extra special care today, hoping to make an even more vivacious impression than usual. Even Jennifer, whose endorsement was practically nonexistent, had approved when she had chosen a short purple dress that buttoned around the neck with a key hole revealing a portion of her breasts. She slid her grey pea coat off and deposited it on the couch armrest.

Jack wandered into the room and she eagerly hopped up from her seat to greet him. The smile he returned to her was weak and he held up his hand. "Lexi," he said her name as if reprimanding her. She couldn't help it, she radiated with energy. Her curls bounced in her face as she backed away obediently. She looked at him concerned, her eyebrows furrowed in confusion.

"Sorry," she said smiling playfully, trying to play off the seriousness of his appearance. She didn't know why she was sorry just that he off somehow.

"No, Lex, it's fine. I just need to talk to you about some stuff," he said averting his eyes. Lexi paused in her excitement and took a good hard look at him. Large black circles ringed his eyes as if he hadn't slept the night before…for several days even. Obviously, he hadn't been having the same dreams as her. His clothes, which were normally in pristine condition, hung off him wrought with wrinkles. He hadn't even given her a hug when she had walked in. Something serious was going on. "Oh, ok. Well go ahead. I'm all ears," she said pretending to stay upbeat despite the awful feeling forming in the pit of her stomach.

He sighed heavily, finally meeting her eyes. "I have a girlfriend."

"You *what*?" she practically screamed at him, shock evident on her now very pale face.

His head fell to his chest and he wouldn't meet her gaze. "She doesn't live here. That's how you haven't come across her. We've been dating since high school," he added the last part in an almost whisper, his voice breaking.

"You've got to be kidding me," she shrieked, tears unintentionally springing to her eyes. "How can you stand there and tell me that everything we have is a lie?" She pushed past him and into the kitchen running her hands against the sides of the cool countertop in an attempt to calm herself. It didn't work.

"It's not a lie."

She glared at him fiercely, her jaw locked tight. "How?" Lexi asked through her teeth, smacking the countertop with the palms of her hands.

"Lex, I can explain."

"Oh, can you?" she asked turning to face him. "How can you *possibly* explain?"

He paused, achingly watching the tears stream down her cheeks. "Look, I'm sorry."

"Oh, you're sorry?" she retorted, throwing her hands in the air. "What good does that do? How does this solve anything? I don't need your apology, and anyways you still haven't given me an explanation." She stood straight-backed in front of him, nostrils flaring, staring him down. "You said you could explain. Well, try. Please try to explain to me how any of this can *possibly* be okay. How could you lie and deceive me like this? All those things that you said," she cried running her fingers through her tangled curls. "God, did you mean anything you said?"

"Please don't cry. We weren't even really together." She shot him a look of death. "I know we spent a lot of time together," he said throwing his hands up in defense.

"Enough time that the fact that you had a *girlfriend* might have come up, don't you think?"

"Yes. I wanted to tell you so many times."

"Don't give me that bullshit, Jack. If you wanted to tell me, then you would have. Obviously, you didn't want me to know. You wanted to double dip."

"Oh, stop with that," he said taking her shoulders in his hands. "I stopped what we were doing before anything serious happened."

"Before anything *serious* happened. Really? Are you serious?" she asked venom apparent in her tone.

"Lex…I…"

She cut him off, not really wanting to hear his definition of what serious was. "Is that what all those phone calls were? All those weekends at home? You were visiting your…girlfriend." He nodded solemnly. "You let me go through all of this, let me feel like we were working towards something, while the whole time you were parading around with your *girlfriend*?" she asked weakly, her voice cracking. "What kind of person *does* that?"

"Lexi, please."

She couldn't listen to him pleading with her. She just couldn't do it. Suddenly, her voice shifted from despair to anger. "So, tell me, what did your girlfriend say when you told her that you had let some other girl sleep in your bed? What did she say when you told her that you would trail kisses across that same girl's face and down her neck with countless promises for more?

Hmm?" she asked forcefully pushing him away from her. "What did she say when you told her how beautiful you thought I was, and how much you had never met *any* other girl as amazing as me? Was she happy? Wait, let me guess, you didn't tell her," she spoke fiercely, accusing him. "Of course not, because *had* you told her, then she would be the one crying right now. Not me."

Jack brushed his hair back from his eyes and paced away from her. "Please, Lexi, God, I didn't want this to happen."

"You didn't want this to happen?" Lexi asked in disbelief. "God, are you blind? Why did you even ask me out in the first place, if you were so set on not letting *this* happen?" she threw the question at him angrily. "You didn't have to. I was walking away. You could have and *should* have just left it at that. Just answer me that, since you can't seem to answer anything else."

"I hesitated," he started lamely. "I wasn't going to ask you out, but I thought that I could hold you back. That we could just be friends and maybe, you could even meet Danielle. Then we started hanging out, and I was in deep over my head after the first time we hung out. You were…are," he corrected himself, "amazing. I didn't want to stop what we had, and I never wanted to hurt you like this. But, by the time I realized I should tell you about Danielle, it was too late."

"You're right. It is too late. Good-bye, Jack," she said shoving him against the pantry door, snatching her jacket off the couch, and marching towards the exit.

"Lexi," he called rushing after her. He latched on to her elbow and spun her around. "I told you because I want us to still be friends. I didn't want to hurt you."

"Don't feed me that," she quipped, struggling to yank her arm free. He held on tight, not letting her loose. "Let me go," she cried warningly.

He ignored her command. "I'm not feeding you anything. The time isn't right for us, but I don't think that means there won't be a time for us," he said, his blue eyes pleading. "Please, Lex."

"You tell me you have a girlfriend. A serious girlfriend, of what, two or three years?" He nodded. "Then you tell me that the time isn't right for us, but you think you *might* want to be with me in the future? How can you even ask that of me? How much more selfish and pigheaded can you possibly act?"

He winced as she berated him. "I'm not asking for you to wait for me."
"Good, because that's never happening," she said under her breath.
He forged onward. "I just mean, don't give up on this. We haven't even begun, and I don't want us to be over."

"You're right. We haven't begun, and we never will. Thank God, this was over before I let you fool me any longer, before I actually acquired feelings for you." He winced again. She was saying these things just to hurt him now, and it was working. "Now, let. Me. Go," she demanded, indicating with her forehead that he was still tightly holding onto her elbow.

"I really am sorry, Lex," he said finally releasing her.

"Save it," she said cutting off any further retorts. "Just do me one thing, Jack." She yanked open the front door.

"Anything," he volunteered eagerly.

"Don't you dare ever lie to me again," she said as she slammed the door behind her.

3

PRESENT

Open the door.
Don't open the door.
Open the door.

Lexi hovered in front of the plain black door with the silver handle resting in her palm, indecision distorting her features. The lock had already been clicked to an open status with the metal key still sticking out from the hole. Her bright purple luggage lay against the blue and cream patterned carpet. She had made it this far. There was no turning back. Taking a deep breath, Lexi twisted the handle and shoved the door open to Jack's apartment.

Adjusting her black laptop sleeve, Lexi hoisted her carry-on bag to her shoulder and threw her black purse on top of it. Grabbing a hold of the extended arm from her rolling suitcase, she pushed through the open door, down the hallway, and into the living room. She recognized the brown suede furniture he had owned in college. The furniture was facing a mounted flat screen with several video game consoles underneath and surround sound hooked into a killer receiver. Two black bookshelves sat on either side of the TV, each overflowing with movies. An assortment of vinyl records covered one wall with an original copy of the Beatles *White* album proudly showcased at the center. Glass sliding doors opened to a balcony overlooking the Atlanta skyline. To the left was a stainless steel kitchen with black granite countertops and a breakfast bar. Lexi peeped into the adjoining room and found a small dining room with four high-backed chairs tucked into a rectangular wooden table.

Lexi left her bags resting against the loveseat and ventured down the hallway on the right. She chose the first door on the left and entered a large master suite. Each piece of furniture was in pristine condition and appeared as if it had been directly relocated from an Ashley's Furniture store. The deep walnut collection looked exquisite against the caramel coated walls.

Lexi paused in the doorway. She didn't want to overstep her bounds and being in his room made her feel as if she might be invading Jack's privacy.

Quickly closing the door, she turned and faced the one across the hall. She assumed this would be the guest bedroom Jack had mentioned. Her breath caught at the sight as she passed through the frame. She felt as if she had just traveled through time. The room was laid out in exact replication of his college apartment. Memories flooded her vision, and she took a steadying breath. She wasn't sure if she enjoyed having memories rush her mind about that room...that bed.

Recovering her state of composure, she raced back into the living room, snatched up her luggage, and distributed it in the bedroom. She quickly stripped down into a red satin tank top and black sleeping shorts.

Despite the fact that she had taken a late flight into the city and had worked for nearly fifteen straight hours the day before, Lexi couldn't even imagine falling asleep yet. Jack was away on business until the next morning and had offered her his guest bedroom. She had been wary at first; even more wary now that she was actually situated in his apartment with all the familiar sights and smells surrounding her. However, with the alternative of driving forty-five minutes out of town to stay at her parents as her only other option, the convenience of the arrangement had won her over in the end.

Lexi grabbed her cell and dialed Chyna's number. "Hola chica," Lexi uttered into her cell phone. She made her way back to the kitchen to search for something to get her mind off the fact that she was in Jack's apartment. Rummaging through his cabinets, she zeroed in on the box of snack bites. After fishing out a pack, she pulled out a Coca-Cola from the refrigerator and set it on the counter.

"Alexa!" Chyna yelled through the blaring background noise.

"Where are you?"

"What?" Chyna screamed into the phone. A giggle broke through the line.

"Chyna, where *are* you?"

"Hold on. Gimme a second." Lexi pulled the phone from her ear to cancel out the obnoxious techno vibes blasting through the wireless. A short minute later, the noise started to fade. Then, it turned into just a buzz in the background. "Alexa, I'm so sorry," she slurred slightly into the receiver, clearly inebriated.

Lexi laughed. "You're drunk." She should have guessed that Chyna would be in this condition on a Saturday night. She had known her for a long time, and this was pretty much par for the course.

"Psh, I'm just a liiiiiitle tipsy. It's my natural state of being, but you know that. What's up?"

"Just wanted some other human being to know that I landed fine."

"Oh fantastic," she said another giggle filtering through the line.

"You don't sound concerned," Lexi said feigning hurt feelings.

"Why would I be concerned? Flying is way safer than driving," she said nonchalantly. "Stop, stop," she squealed obviously flirting with some random guy.

"Do I know your man of choice for tonight?" Lexi asked popping open the soda and taking a long swig.

"I have no idea what you are talking about," she feigned innocence.

"Sure...right."

"Ohhhh..."

"Are you moaning into the phone? Are you fucking serious, Chyna? Can you chill out for one second to talk to your best friend who just traveled a thousand miles away from home?"

"You're from Atlanta so it's like going to your home away from home. So...no, I'm not concerned." Lexi heard her shoo her boy nonetheless.

"I'm locked up in my sorta-non-ex-boyfriend's apartment, and you're not concerned?"

"Is *that* how you refer to me?" a voice questioned from behind her.

Lexi whipped around in surprise. Her mouth dropped open and the phone slipped from her hand hitting the tile floor, and shattering into several pieces.

"Jack."

He looked exactly as she remembered him. Maybe a bit more handsome. He leaned against the kitchen doorframe, one leg crossed over another, hands resting in his pockets staring at her with his piercing blue eyes. His shaggy brown hair was at her favorite length, just before he needed a haircut. Black slacks with charcoal pinstripes hung loosely on his narrow hips. A black long-sleeve button-up was open at the neck where a charcoal tie had been pulled loose from its proper place; a matching overcoat had been left unbuttoned. A smirk crossed his face as his eyes scanned her scantily clad body. Lexi couldn't really be embarrassed that he saw her in her ridiculously small night clothes. Let's just be honest, he had seen her in less.

She could feel her heart beating like a marathon runner at the sight of him. Yet, she felt frozen in place. She hadn't been prepared for this. She assumed she would have all morning to look presentable, and get herself into the right state of mind. Then, she would have been able to face him. But this was completely unexpected. What was he doing here? He wasn't supposed to be back until tomorrow.

His smirk widened at her apparent shock. "I guess *surprise* doesn't really cover it, does it?" he asked her, bending forward and retrieving the loose pieces of her cell phone that had scattered across the cool tile floor.

"Not...not exactly," she warbled. She watched as he slid the battery back into place, secured the backing, and switched it on. Lexi felt a chill run down her spine when his gaze returned to her. Reaching out, he handed her back the cell phone letting their hands brush briefly. Lexi commended herself for not flinching. "So," she began clearing her throat, "what are you doing here?"

"I live here," he said smiling down on her.

Lexi rolled her eyes. "Jack, come on. What are you doing here? You weren't supposed to get in until tomorrow."

"Wow, Lex," he said using her pet name as if it had been only yesterday when he had been in New York City with her, "no, hello how are you? No, oh my God, I've missed you? Not even a hug? What the hell?"

Lexi couldn't help herself. She giggled. This was the Jack she knew and loved. "Hello. How are you? Oh my God, I've missed you," she said tossing her phone onto the counter. She swung her arms around him in earnest, knocking her body against his. He pulled her into him, gently wrapping his arms around her slight waist. What she had intended to just be a short, almost dismissive hug had instantly changed as she felt him breathe her in.

"I know you were just joking, but it really is good to see you," he whispered into her ear.

When they pulled away, she watched as Jack took an extra step farther from her. His eyes had gone crystal clear blue, and seemed to be looking straight through her. She knew what that look meant, and every muscle in her body willed her to step forward into him. It was with great effort that she broke his determined stare and took another step backwards.

Lexi reached up and brushed her hair behind her ears several times anxiously. It was a habit she had never been able to kick. Even as she did it, she knew she was giving herself away, but she really couldn't help it. As if saved by the bell, her phone began to buzz noisily on the countertop. She glanced down at the screen groaning as she saw the hairline fracture across the surface. "Hey," she said answering the line.

"What the fuck happened, Alexa?" Chyna screamed into the other line. "I've been trying your cell for five minutes. Are you okay? Did something happen? Were you robbed?"

Lexi could hear the concern evident in her voice. Suddenly, Chyna sounded sober, and very serious. Not one ounce of her previous whimsical attitude showed through. Zero thoughts of Chyna or really anything considered to be coherent had filtered through her head after Jack had entered the room. She was ashamed that she hadn't called Chyna back right away. She felt even worse knowing that without her phone call she wouldn't have remembered at all.

"No, no, nothing like that. I was just surprised, and I dropped my phone."

"What could possibly surprise you to the point of not calling me back?" she asked. Lexi contemplated answering that, but didn't get the chance as Chyna gasped on the other line. "You said he wasn't going to be there."

Lexi glanced up at Jack who eyed her humorously. She could practically read his thoughts. *Ha. Ha. You're in some shit now.* A blush crept up her neck and landed a light pink hue on her cheeks. Chyna was practically screaming through the other line, and Lexi wasn't sure if Jack was able to hear her. "I don't know what you're talking about," she said lying through her teeth.

Jack raised an eyebrow and mouthed to her, "I thought we were over that."

He meant the lying, but Lexi just shrugged her shoulders ignoring his penetrating gaze. She had no desire whatsoever to talk to Chyna about Jack's unexpected arrival, especially not while he was standing directly in front of her listening to every word. "Alexa, you know *exactly* what I am talking about! You *cannot* be alone with him under any circumstances. We talked about this. Remember?"

Chyna was speaking so loudly that, Lexi had to pull the phone away from her ear. "Yes, I know we talked about this. But your concerns are completely irrelevant," she stated sharply.

"Don't bullshit me, Alexa Mae Walsh!" Lexi couldn't help laughing. The only time Chyna ever called her by her full name was when she was absolutely livid, which made the whole situation even funnier to Lexi.

"Calm down. Calm down," Lexi shushed her, feeling self-conscious as Jack continued to watch the stand-off intently. She tried to avert her eyes as he effortlessly stripped his jacket off and held it in his arms. He just looked so good it was hard to resist staring.

"I'm not calm, damn it!"

"I realize that. But I have to go," Lexi said abruptly, already wanting out of the conversation.

"No, you need to leave. Go catch a cab. On *me*," she added hastily.

"Love ya, chica," Lexi said closing the phone lightly.

Her phone lit up in her hand again, but she switched it to silent, and turned the screen face down. No more interruptions. The stillness in the room was disconcerting. Last time she had been alone with Jack, she had been in a state of hysterics. Life with Jack in general was a state of hysterics. The rollercoaster her emotions rode when in his presence sent her stomach rolling and every nerve standing at full attention. The strange euphoria that had settled over her at the familiar touch of his hands encircling her had dissipated with Chyna's urgent cautionary reminder.

He was not supposed to be here.

Even more important, Lexi had sworn she would not be entrapped by him again, and that included finding herself alone with him.

"Well, it was nice seeing you." Lexi began edging towards the doorframe. Unfortunately, he didn't move a single inch. She felt her breasts, covered only by a thin piece of flimsy material, brush against his arm as she passed. Holding in a gasp, she walked as quickly as possible towards the guest bedroom.

"Nice seeing you?" he questioned following her down the hallway. "We haven't spoken in two years, I surprise you, and all you have to say is nice seeing you?" Lexi let her nails dig into her palm. The jolt of pain was the only thing holding her back from snapping at him. "Well, it's nice seeing you too," Jack retorted, his tone resolving to calm neutral.

She forced a half smile in his direction. Clicking the tiny button at the rear of her suitcase, Lexi felt the arm release. Her hand extended forward retrieving the rest of her luggage.

"What are you doing?"

The earnest in his voice surprised her, and she looked up into those clear blue eyes in surprise. Something had changed. A flicker of doubt cast across her features; her mouth formed a circle with a question hanging off her delicate lips.

"You can't leave," he stated simply; a command not a request.

Lexi shook her head. This was so typical. "I can and I will."

"Lex, please, I don't want you to leave."

"I know this might come as a surprise to you, but it's not always about you. And contrary to what you may think you know, I don't care what you want," Lexi said fighting to keep her cool.

He repositioned himself in a similar fashion in the doorframe. "You wouldn't be here if you didn't."

"I didn't come here for *you*," she spat.

He nodded his head in mock agreement. "Then why did you come?"

"I came here for your lousy fiancé. I came here," she paused, slowly walking towards him, "to help her not make the same mistake that I did." Anger continued to well up inside her especially since his expression had yet to change at her remarks.

"That's nice, except for the part about my fiancé. I don't have one." A smart-ass smirk made its way onto his face.

"Oh details," she said waving her hand in the air dismissively.

"I'd say that's a fairly important detail."

"Either way. She is your girlfriend. Right? That hasn't changed overnight?" Jack shook his head confirming that nothing had changed. "Well then, I should be going." She grabbed a hold of her rolling suitcase and walked towards the exit.

"Would you stay if she wasn't my girlfriend?" he asked letting her pass by him.

She stopped abruptly and turned. Her lips were tight, jaw set. "You never change."

"Oh come on. I'm teasing you," he said reaching forward and touching her hand, gently extracting the suitcase from her grip. "If you feel that offended that I came back all the way from Nashville just to see you, to make sure you were alright, then fine, leave. I'll hail you a cab or drive you myself."

A flustered sigh came out of her mouth. How could he always do this? Somehow he had turned everything against her. Now, she was the bad guy for trying to storm out of his house. She was the bad guy for wanting to leave when he had made all the effort to get her to stay. She was the bad guy despite his unexpected, unwelcome appearance.

"Maybe you should do that," she managed to get out. She knew it was the right thing to do. She couldn't be here. Their history prevented them from being casual, from being just friends.

His face dropped. He had been expecting her to give in. "You really mean that? You don't even want to hang out for an hour? A half hour?" he pleaded. "For old time's sake?"

"Jack, I can't. You can't ask that of me." Her voice came out just louder than a whisper.

Still grasping the handle of her suitcase, he yanked it around and protectively placed it behind him. "I am asking it of you." He took a step closer. "What do you *really* think is going to happen? Things are different now, Lex."

As she stared up into his gorgeous blue eyes, she couldn't help thinking that things weren't that different for her. He had obviously moved on and rather quickly, but that was not the way it had happened in her world. She had tried to move on...unsuccessfully. Deep down she knew that if he bent down to kiss her just then, she wouldn't have stopped him. As much as that fact irritated her, it was the truth. Even after everything.

"Look, I just want you to feel comfortable. If I can only have ten minutes of your time before tomorrow, then I guess I could settle for that. If you'd rather me leave, and come back in the morning when we were scheduled to meet, I can do that too. Or if you'd rather us hang out all night reminiscing, even if it means we have to sit on separate couches. I would prefer that option."

She hesitated before speaking. "Jack, I..."

"You're going to say you can't, but you can. You just won't," he said taking a step into her personal space. She could feel the heat coming off of his body, and smell the cologne he wore that took her mind to places it shouldn't.

"Stop, just stop," she murmured stumbling backwards. "You know what you're doing, and you can just stop that. If I'm going to stay, it will be because I want to. Not because you are using all your damn seductive magical powers on me."

He looked amused as he gazed down the hallway at her. "I have magical powers now?"

"Don't act like you don't know what I'm talking about." She glared at him.

He held his hands up in defeat. "Fine. Magical powers it is. Now will you please stay?"

"Fine," she stated only partially reluctant, "I'll stay."

His smile was electric, as compelling as ever. He marched down the hall and threw his arms around her lifting her effortlessly off the ground. A giggle escaped her lips as she latched onto him for support. He quickly placed her back on her feet not wanting to press his luck.

After a short break in which Jack changed into a familiar faded green t-shirt and black athletic shorts, the pair arranged themselves on separate couches in the living room as promised. Jack flipped on the TV setting ESPN's college football predictions as background noise. Lexi lounged back against the brown suede. Her eyes took in the space, focusing in on things she hadn't previously noticed. Two copies of Sports Illustrated, a week old Wall Street Journal, and a copy of Maxim were laid out against the walnut coffee table. Heavy black marble coasters sat in a neat stack within a matching enclosure.

What was strange was that there wasn't a single picture frame in the room. As she thought about it, she couldn't remember there being a single picture frame in the whole house. When they had been in college, he had an array of picture frames of his family at his parent's country house when he was younger, ridiculous acts captured with him among his college friends, and some amazing photos he had taken himself when he had been in a photography class for a semester. Now, none of that was here. It was like he had erased his past. Lexi felt suddenly out of place. She was a part of his past that he had so easily gotten rid of. She let her eyes rest back on Jack as she tucked her hair behind her ears several times.

"Why are you so nervous?" he asked, resting his arm across the back of the couch and fixing her with an attentive gaze.

"I'm not nervous," she mumbled.

"You're doing that thing with your hair," he said pointing it out just as a lock was placed behind her ear. She caught herself doing it and quickly snapped her hand down to her side. "It's kind of endearing, but you always do it when you're nervous or anxious."

"Well...I haven't seen you in a long time. I just can't believe I'm actually here."

"I can't believe you're actually here either."

Lexi's eyes made their way back to him. "Hey, that shirt!"

He looked down at what he was wearing. "Yeah?"

"Oh my God, you're wearing the carnival shirt," she said seeing the worn outline of a Ferris wheel.

"Oh, yeah. I guess it is. It's the most comfortable thing I own." She stared longer, her mind whirling. "Do you still have yours?"

She giggled then sprinted to the guest bedroom. When she returned, she had a flimsy green shirt in her hand. The material had several tiny tears. It had been washed and worn so many times it was practically sheer. He nodded his approval with a smile. She tossed the shirt onto the back of the couch and returned to her earlier position.

After a brief pause, Lexi spoke up again. "So, what did Danielle and Kate tell the new girl? I mean I'm guessing that's who she talked to."

"Yeah, she met both of them. It was almost as strange as calling you. Well, maybe not quite that strange." Her eyes narrowed when he winked at her. "Anyway, Danielle agreed immediately. Thankfully, she had no qualms about meeting Bekah. Her and I broke up on good enough terms, you know, for it not to be an issue."

Lexi giggled. "That's not how I remember it."

"Luckily, that's how she remembered it," he said sighing. "I haven't spoken to her much since then, but her sister lives in Atlanta now so she came and stayed with her for the weekend."

"Does she still live in Savannah?" Lexi thought it was humorous that she was able to have this conversation at all. When she had first found out that Danielle even existed, she was so furious that she was certain she would never talk to Jack again, let alone spend time with him.

"Yeah. She's married now to some redneck that dropped out of high school the year I graduated. He's a real winner," he added smugly. "She's raising his two kids from a previous marriage, and she's pregnant with another. You could only just tell when she was here. Anyway, she told Bekah our story; that we dated in high school and my first year or so of college. The distance thing," he stated vaguely, "didn't work out for us, and so we broke up. End of story."

"So, nothing about me then?" Lexi asked just trying to get all the information she could.

"Uh...I never told her about you," Jack said shifting uncomfortably.

"Oh, well that's probably for the better," she said trying not to convey her emotions too strongly. There had been plenty of reasons for Jack and Danielle breaking up. The distance and Lexi were just two of the many. But if Danielle hadn't said anything about the others, Lexi wasn't going to be the one to bring them up. "What about Kate? Obviously she brought me up, so I'm sure her story was interesting," she stated sarcastically.

"Ugh," he groaned. "Do we have to talk about Kate? I know how you feel about her. I know how she feels about you. And now Bekah knows how Kate feels about you. And let's just say, it wasn't a conversation I wanted to be present for."

"Oh," Lexi replied slightly taken aback. She hadn't really thought about what Kate might have said about her beyond the usual. Lexi had been so concerned with what she was going to tell Bekah, that it hadn't even crossed her mind what Kate might have said about her. "Did she claim that I was the reason that you wouldn't commit to her?" she asked finally.

He let out a puff of air. "Not exactly, but you didn't help anything either."

"Me?!? *You* were the one…"

He cut her off. "I *said*, let's not talk about Kate."

She quieted, her chest heaving up and down in a familiar burst of anger. "Fine."

"What are *you* going to tell her?" he asked hesitantly.

She shook her head deep in thought. She still wasn't sure herself. At first, she had been certain that she was going to tell his girlfriend how Jack was an awful terrible person, and that Bekah better get out before things went downhill. After all, that was what she had told Chyna she was going to do. That's what she had screamed at Jack in the hallway. But, after finally being in his presence, Lexi wasn't sure if she could do it. "I'm not sure yet."

"There's just so much you could tell her," he stated vaguely. Lexi could tell he seemed a bit anxious about the whole situation.

"I know." And she did. Their history went back for six years and the fact that they hadn't been together made the whole story juicier.

"Did you mean what you said in the bedroom? That you were going to tell her not to make the same mistake you did."

"I did when I said it," she offered. "But I was angry, and now I'm not so sure."

"I guess that's a good thing," he said, optimistic to the prospects. She could tell he wanted to ask more questions, but he held his tongue. Lexi was grateful for that. She didn't really want to have that conversation.

Lexi pushed her hair behind her ear again before asking the question that had been nagging at her since Jack had called the first time. "Why didn't you tell her about me? You had to know Kate was going to say something."

He ran his hands back through his hair several times thinking the question over. He adjusted his position so that he was lying with his head back against the armrest before addressing her. "I didn't want her to know about you. I..." he paused collecting his thoughts once again. "I met Bekah shortly after you and I...well...you know. I had no interest in dating anyone. But when I told you she was about as persistent as I am, I wasn't lying. After a few unremarkable dates with her, I called the whole thing off."

Lexi looked over at him surprised. She had assumed their relationship was picture perfect. It was refreshing to hear that it wasn't. "Why? What happened?" she asked curiously.

"She wasn't you."

Lexi gulped. She wanted to just scream at him for not calling her afterwards, for not calling a month later, a year later. They could have worked things out if he hadn't run out, if he had just come back to her. But instead he had been with another woman. Now the distance between them was unbearable.

"Bekah doesn't take no for an answer," he continued. "I was pretty messed up after I left New York, and she slowly brought me out of all of that. I stopped trying to see you in her, and I found that things went much better. I found I could like her. Soon we were together all the time. The relationship progressed rather quickly from there."

Lexi sighed heavily. The way his eyes lit up at the mention of their relationship pained Lexi. She could tell Bekah made him happy...happier than she had ever been capable of making him. Their relationship was everything she had hoped for with Jack, but had never been afforded.

"I don't know how much more you want to know, but Bekah wanted to move in with me when her lease ran out. Her parents are pretty well-off and have been helping her financially. They told her they would cut her off if she moved in with her boyfriend before she got married. That's pretty much where we are now."

"So, it's not because she wants to get married so desperately? It's about money and moving in with you?" Lexi asked trying to process this new information. Jack had made Bekah situation seem much more...desperate on the phone.

"No. No. No. It's really about her wanting to get married," he remanded hastily. "She is playing it off like those are the real reasons. Honestly, she doesn't need her parents' money or approval," he finished. Even though Lexi wasn't really looking forward to meeting Bekah, she had obviously captured something with Jack. Lexi was kind of curious about her.

"Can I ask you something?" Lexi asked sitting up to get a better look at him.

"You just did."

"Ha. Ha," she said dryly. A smile appeared on his face as he sat up to meet her gaze.

"Sure, go ahead."

"Where are all your picture frames?" Whatever he had been anticipating, that hadn't been it. "You used to have a ton of them, but I don't see any."

"When you were snooping?" he asked playfully. She nodded. His smile waned slightly when he responded. "The glass broke in a bunch of them when I moved here, and the rest are in my closet."

"Why didn't you put those up? I mean at least the woods shot," she said remembering a particular black and white photograph of a rickety bridge over top of a creek surrounded by age old pine trees at sunrise. It had always been her favorite.

"I don't have it anymore," he said sheepishly, his eyes fixed on the floor.

"Where did it go?" she asked intrigued. He had always loved that picture as much as she had. For the longest time, it had hung in a thick black poster sized frame above his bed.

"I destroyed the frame."

Her mouth hung open as she imagined his prized portrait torn to shreds. "Why would you do that? It was your favorite picture."

He shook his head. "It was your favorite."

Realization dawned on her. He had gotten rid of it because of her. He couldn't look at it anymore because of her.

"Two days after I threw it away, I felt terrible and fished it out of the garbage. The picture was still intact except for a few small tears from where the glass broke. I gave it to my mom."

Lexi forced the conversation to lighter subjects. She didn't want to continue to suffer from long lost memories. She told him about school and her internship. He bored her with accounting information, and how his immediate supervisor was an older woman he couldn't stand. They watched highlight reels from last year's mediocre football performance from their Alma Mater. Luckily, the team was still ranked in the top twenty-five due to good recruiting. She listened when he told her about his Fantasy Football strategy for the upcoming season, and gave him pointers on who she thought was going to play well. He regaled her with stories from Seth's bachelor party in Las Vegas earlier that summer. She told him about Chyna's congratulatory weekend in Atlantic City when Lexi had been accepted into her internship.

"This feels so familiar," she breathed leaning her head back against the arm of the loveseat.

"Yeah, I suppose it does," he agreed amicably.

"You have a girlfriend."

"You don't have a boyfriend," he added.

"I could have a boyfriend," Lexi said popping her head up to look at him eyebrows raised.

He laughed lightly. "You don't have a boyfriend," he said as a matter-of-fact.

"How do *you* know?" Her eyes narrowed.

"Lex, I've known you for a long time…years, in fact. You don't have a boyfriend right now."

"Fine. I don't have a boyfriend," she conceded, "but I could."

"You could, sure. But you don't. Either way, we've been here before."

"We've been everywhere before," Lexi stated running her hands through her long waves and let them fall off the side of the loveseat.

Jack coughed into his hand covering up a laugh that began to break through. "I wouldn't say *everywhere*."

"Oh, Jack, stop it!" she exclaimed catching his double entendre. Hefting the pillow out from behind her, she threw it with full force across the room and into his still amused face. Shocked, he picked the pillow up off the white carpeted floor and tossed it back in her direction catching her in the chest.

She coughed upon impact, the weight of the pillow knocking the air from her lungs. She threw the pillow back in his direction with as much force as she could muster. He was prepared this time, and caught the pillow out of midair. Jumping up, he dove to the loveseat and smacked the pillow down into her shoulder. Lexi curled into a ball protectively covering her face.

"Do you surrender?" he asked holding the pillow high.

Just before he was about to bring it down on her one more time, another pillow materialized her in hand. "Never," she declared swinging the pillow hard, hitting him full on in the chest. He teetered for a moment before regaining his balance and toppled his pillow down on her. When she didn't even seem to register his attack, he bent down over her and began to tickle her between the ribs. She giggled uncontrollably, kicking out wildly with her feet, gasping for air.

"That's cheating. You're cheating," she squealed attempting to pry his hands away from her. "Stop. Stop. Oh God, Jack, stop."

He paused, his body starting to register the position he had found himself in. Lexi had unwound from her fetal position and was sprawled across the couch. Her bare legs were slightly spread with her hands above her head. The silky material of her shirt did very little to hide her hard nipples underneath. His knee touched hers while his arms remained circling her waist in the same position where he had been tickling her. His body rested only a couple inches from her.

As she recovered from his assault, her chest heaved up and down so hard she could almost touch him. Her chocolaty eyes were wide and wild, rimmed with tears of laughter. Flushed, her cheeks showed a splatter of red; her lips bare and showing slight signs of chapping. Even her hair was unruly and untamed, weaving curls and waves all across the sofa. All together, she was the epitome of uninhibited, unbridled beauty.

Lexi's eyes gazed back at him seductively. She could feel how close he was, and despite herself, despite it all, she wanted him closer. She licked her lips watching as his whole body seemed to relax into her. He was only a couple inches from her mouth at that point. So close, in fact, she could just reach her head off the armrest to meet him.

In that moment, she knew. All that stuff about things being different had been bullshit. He wanted to kiss her. He wanted her.

Lexi heard a gentle trill come from the direction of the bedroom. "I think that's your phone."

His eyes roamed her face once more, and then glanced up at the clock. "Fuck, is it really 3:30?"

She arched her body up, feeling herself press up against him as she got a good enough angle to read the red digital numbers. He hadn't pulled away from her, and she could feel him easily through his basketball shorts. "Yep, that's the time," she said sliding back down against the suede couch. His weight eased back against her as she moved. God, she wanted him. This was the reason she had promised Chyna she wouldn't be alone with him. "Perhaps, you should go answer that."

"I can call them back," he said automatically. Lexi felt as if she had traveled back in time six years, and Danielle would be on the other line.

"You know, perhaps this feels a little too familiar," Lexi said sitting up and pulling away from him.

He coughed uneasily and righted himself on the sofa. "You're right. Sorry."

She could tell he wasn't. It didn't matter though. He was doing the right thing. She was doing the right thing. For once.

4

AUGUST FIVE YEARS EARLIER

Flashes of silver light careened around the open dance floor sending blurred, refracting images across the wide-eyed girls shaking their bodies in time with the rap beats blaring from the projection speakers. Saturday night at Chamber showcased incredible DJ spinning talent, and for the sea of wall-to-wall listeners nothing could get better. Several bartenders distributed lethal quantities of whatever one's heart desired in alcohol. The medium-sized rectangular room was divided in two by sliding glass doors keeping the dance space and the more secluded lounge area separated. A raised platform designed in an L-shape was constructed against one wall and had a long bar against the open side.

Beefy security guards in bright yellow Chamber polo's remained stationed in precarious locations as a rather deliberate reminder for the drunkards to keep their cool. One too many customers had found themselves sprawled on their ass on the pavement outside after a fight broke out or the Fire Marshall deemed the building to be over the maximum occupancy.

"I need six lemon drops, three Bud Lights, two Jager bombs, and an Amaretto sour," Trina demanded of the tiny red headed bartender. The girl looked frantic pulling random bottles off the shelf and replacing them almost instantly. She grabbed several shot glasses placing them haphazardly on the bar before glancing up at her customer helplessly.

"How many shots did you want?" the girl asked her voice coming out mousy.

Trina rolled her eyes exaggeratedly. "Honey, why are you working the busiest night of the week if you can't take an order? I said six."

A blush crept up across her cheeks and down her neck. "I...uh..." the girl stammered not anticipating the harassment.

"I mean really, what was Joe thinking hiring someone so incompetent?" Trina questioned her further leaning forward against the bar. Her eyes were locked with the mouse who looked terrified. Several of the surrounding customers glanced anxiously over at Trina. Some just looked angry that she was taking up so much time with the only bartender in the vicinity. A small blond girl standing to her right nudged her lightly in the ribs giving her a *shut the fuck up* look. Trina didn't even register the jab. She was smiling, instead, at the girl behind the bar. "What's your name sweetheart?"

"Mary," she said fumbling with the bottle opener. Mary, getting even more flustered, managed to drop the metal opener. She quickly ducked down to retrieve it.

Trina smirked at the girl maliciously. "Seems like you are better suited for church... Mary," she said dragging her name out. The girl just glanced up meekly, not even able to form words. Her eyes were beginning to well with unshed tears.

"Trina, stop being such a bitch," another girl said materializing next to the redhead. The voluptuous bartender scooted Mary to the side with her hip and began expertly filling the order.

Trina's smile widened at the sight. "Chasity, I thought I would have to break your newbie before you got over here. What took you so long?"

"I'd like to remind you that you are underage darling," Chasity quipped pushing the beers across the counter. "Might I also point out," she said thrusting the bottle opener into the back pocket of her micro-mini jean skirt and leaning into one hip, "that three-fourths of the people in the room know that."

Mary's eyes bulged. "Oh my God, Chasity, I had no idea. I wouldn't have served her if I'd known."

Chasity rolled her eyes at the girl. "We don't ID at the bar silly girl, just at the door." Mary's blush returned in full force. "Anyway, you should recognize Trina here as one of our All-American gymnasts."

"Thanks for the introduction. Why not add a lemon drop to that order for yourself and little Mary too," Trina said fishing out her credit card and passing it to Chasity who stuffed it into her red bra strap. Chasity added two more glasses to the counter and began filling them with clear liquid. Trina held a shot over her head beckoning the couple off the dance floor.

Lexi brushed her side-swept bangs off her glistening forehead as she made her way to Trina and the rest of the group. Trina smiled as she approached, a shot appearing in front of Lexi's face. "For you, my dear," she said passing her the drink.

Lexi reached forward to extract another shot from the bar and passed it to the guy standing behind her before diving back in and retrieving two sugar-coated lemon slices. The eight people in attendance smacked their glasses against one another and downed the contents feeling the familiar burn of vodka. Quickly inserting the lemon slice into her mouth, Lexi felt the dizzying effects of the alcohol, even stumbling a little. "Ugh," she groaned leaning back against the guy's shoulder, "I can't feel my legs. Is that bad?"

He wrapped his arm around her tiny waist securing her in place. "Don't worry. I gotcha."

"I know you do," she said nuzzling her nose into his neck affectionately.

He jumped upon contact. "Damn. Your nose is freezing. How are you that cold?" he asked breaking away from her. She shrugged leaning forward against Trina's chair.

"Who's the new girl?" Lexi asked nodding towards the red headed bartender.

"Mary," Trina said cocking her head sideways as she studied the girl. "Chasity was just introducing her to me."

Lexi's head shot up at the name. Her head swiveled around the bar expecting to catch a glimpse of very familiar dark brown hair and piercing blue eyes. No matter how many times she came to Chamber, she had the same reaction at the mention of Chasity. After all, Jack had been a regular of hers at one point in time.

"Hey, Lex," Chasity said winking at her. Lexi's heart skipped at the casual use of the nickname that she had never really allowed anyone else to call her after. "I was actually just chastising Trina for acting like a bitch to Mary here. You're on the team, right? You should learn to keep her under control." Chasity swirled her hips in time with the music looking all the more sensual for her adoring customers. She flipped a bottle of whiskey three or four times experimentally in her hands before tipping it upside down and emptying it into a glass brimming with cubed ice.

"Oh no, I'm not on the team," Lexi corrected hastily. "I just practice with them."

Last semester, Lexi had received an email from Krista, the captain of the gymnastics team, asking if she was available to attend a meeting with the coach. Lexi had thought it was a cruel joke. She had only told one person about her desire to be on the gymnastics team, and well, she hadn't spoken with him since that fateful night in October. Her response had been dripping with sarcasm and questions in regards to the real sender. Krista had instantly responded that in no way was she joking about the offer, but that if she wasn't interested then to forget it. As fast as she could get a reply out, Lexi apologized and agreed to the meeting.

Krista met her at the entrance to the athletic training facility. She was petite, even compared to Lexi, with stick straight brown hair to her shoulders covered in red and blonde highlights. A distinct hole in her eyebrow, nose, and lip showed where piercings were beginning to close up. An old, destroyed, university, warm up shirt hung loosely on her tiny frame sliding off one shoulder and allowing her bellybutton ring to peek out from underneath. The elastic of her grey sweatpants had been cut off so that they barely hung on her narrow hips. Lexi liked her already.

The meeting with the coach went surprisingly well considering the fact that the lady had been characterized as the epitome of bitchiness. Shortly afterwards, they had set up some time on the mat, and Lexi had wowed them into allowing her to practice with them. It had been like a dream come true. The only thing that could have made it better was if they allowed her to compete. She wasn't going to hold her breath for that though.

Lexi had been fortunate enough to begin training out that same week. The first day at practice she met the guy standing behind her. Spencer was a student athletic trainer for the gymnastics team that season. He frequently attended practices to prepare him for meets.

After successfully completing her first practice, Lexi's entire body felt physically assaulted. Seeing the amount of pain she was already in, Spencer had pulled her to the side and offered to do post-stretch work outs with her to soothe her aching muscles. At first, she had turned him down thinking she didn't need it, but when she found she could hardly make it to the locker room, he had insisted. He nursed her over-used muscles making sure that she hadn't done any serious damage.

Then after proclaiming her fit, he had nervously asked her out that same day. Agreeing to the offer was a no brainer, and they had been dating ever since. Seven months later their relationship was still going strong.

"No one can keep Trina under control especially if she is trying to make up for Krista's absence," Lexi said leaning back from the bar and glancing up into Spencer's warm chocolate-colored orbs staring lovingly down upon her. His dark blonde hair was buzzed so short it was almost military official with just enough in the front to spike up. Cheek bones were prominent against his pale skin; a strong square-set jaw line fit perfectly with the rest of his features.

"And no one can make up for Krista," Chasity said flipping the tops off several beer bottles.

"She's probably glad to have graduated," Trina commented. Lexi narrowed her eyes at her. Trina had been making similar comments since she had been named captain. "What?" she asked defensively. "I just mean that now she doesn't have to take her piercings out every January."

The group laughed along at Trina's joke. Lexi found she could only produce a forced half-smile. She really did miss Krista, and her spontaneous vivacious personality that seemed to light up any room. As soon as she had graduated, Krista had hightailed it out of town. She had ended up in Las Vegas and was now performing nightly at some Cirque de Soleil show. The team wouldn't be the same without her.

Lexi pulled her phone out of her tiny black purse to see if anyone else from the team had responded to her mass text. Sighing, she looked at the blank screen. "Guess everyone else is busy tonight," she mumbled under her breath.

Then, her phone vibrated in her hand. Lexi perked up and wondered who else was coming out. She flipped her phone open and stared numbly at the name that flashed onto the screen: Jack Howard.

Lexi quickly glanced backwards at Spencer. He was occupied by Ashley, a blonde leggy gymnast in her third year. She had never mentioned anything about Jack to him before. Even if he had seen the name, it wouldn't have meant anything to him. Despite that fact, she angled her body to block his view of the screen.

She was unsure whether or not she should click the little green button to view the message. He had contacted her several times shortly after he had confessed to having a girlfriend. However, he had ceased his attempts at contacting her when she didn't answer a single one. It had been difficult, of course. She had wanted to reply. After all, she had fallen head over heels for the boy, but she couldn't share him.

Just enough alcohol coursed through her veins that her finger fell on the button opening the message.

"*3 o'clock.*"

Lexi stared down at the cryptic text message, confusion written across face. Her brow furrowed together as she tried to decipher the meaning behind his words. The time was 1:30 in the morning. Was she supposed to meet him at 3 o'clock? If so, where was she supposed to meet him? No, that couldn't be it. He would have said more if he wanted her to meet him, some explanation at least.

3 o'clock.

She stared off into space feeling the alcohol loosen her muscles and continue to cloud her judgment. Then, as if woken from a dream, she turned slowly. There he was. Sitting at the end of the bar, beer in hand, at her 3 o'clock.

He raised his glass to her as if to say cheers. She couldn't take her eyes off of him. He looked *so* good. She had almost forgotten how his shaggy hair fell messily into his eyes. The natural way he jerked his head to uselessly move it out of the way...only to have it fall back into his amazing blue eyes. The way his smile warmed her inside out.

"Want to go back out on the floor?" Spencer asked breaking her out of her trance. She averted her eyes and snapped her phone shut.

Lexi shook her head. "I'm going to stay here and wait until I can stand straight. You can go ahead," she offered. She had never lied to him before, and she didn't particularly like it. But if Jack was here, she wanted nothing less than for them to cross paths.

"Alright," Spencer said a little reluctantly. "Are you sure?"

"Don't worry about me. I think Ashley needs someone to dance with," she said gesturing towards the tiny blonde gymnast waiting patiently for them to come to a decision.

He shrugged and went to kiss her on her lips. She turned at the last second letting it brush her cheek. He glanced down at her, a glimpse of pain evident in his eyes. A forced smile moved across her face, but she knew he wasn't satisfied with that.

"I'll check on you in a bit," he said finally before making his way back towards the mass of bodies. Lexi leaned back against Trina's chair and rested her head on Trina's shoulder. She didn't want to chance a glance back up for fear that Jack would still be there—or worse—he'd be gone.

"Don't you dare fall asleep on me," Trina said bumping Lexi off her shoulder.

"I'm not. Swear."

"Well, take my chair. I'm going to go dance. You better not be asleep when I get back," Trina said pointing her finger in Lexi's face.

"Have no fear. I'm sure Chasity will take care of everything."

"I sure hope not with your tolerance," Trina called over her shoulder laughing as she walked away.

Lexi watched her friends meander through the crowd of people. As soon as she lost them in the mass, Lexi turned her head, and searched for Jack again. There he was, seated in the exact same spot, waiting for her. Without really realizing what she was doing, she stood and made her way to him. As she approached, she fully assessed him. Stubble had grown in across his chin and jaw line making him appear older. The blue vertical striped button-up he wore brought out the ice blue of his eyes. He seemed even more fit than the last time she had seen him, but she couldn't be sure under all those clothes. Not that she was thinking of taking them off…of course.

She smiled slyly trying to keep from letting her eyes roam his body further. She wasn't sure how she had forgotten how attractive he was. His gaze met hers. She felt as if he was looking straight through her. A blush rushed up her neck and to her cheeks. She couldn't decide if the cause was the alcohol or the way he looked at her like he could just take her right then and there.

"Lex," he said extending an arm out for her to walk into. She did the motion automatically, feeling herself fit against his body like she was the missing puzzle piece. His cologne overpowered her senses, and she hastily backed up a few paces remembering the last time he had been this close to her. Her groin throbbed at the recollection of his knee resting in that same spot. Something about that smell…about him just made her hot all over.

His look of desire hadn't changed despite her speedy retreat. She knew that he shouldn't be looking at her like that. She definitely shouldn't be having this type of reaction in a very crowded, *public* place with her boyfriend only a hundred feet away. Anyone could walk over and see them together. It's not like anyone could mistake the looks that were cast between them.

"Um…how are you?" she asked awkwardly averting her eyes attempting to break his spell.

He shrugged nonchalantly. "Single."

Her body tensed at the statement. That hadn't been her question, but for some reason it was the answer she had wanted, the real question she had been anxious to find out about. "Oh yeah?" she asked trying to remain cool and not let her heart beat speed up any further at the prospect of him being single. "How did that happen?"

"As a birthday present to myself."

She scoffed, her eyes bulging. "Are you serious?"

He smiled brightly. "One hundred percent."

"That's a story I'd like to hear."

"I'd like to tell it to you," he said standing up and closing the distance between them. Her breath caught in her throat. "Come be with me tonight."

He issued it as a command not a request. And God, did she want to be with him that night. Her mind slowly started to catch up with her wanton body, and she began to shake her head wishing his request had come some six or seven months earlier. "No, I can't."

Stepping just a few inches closer, he pressed his hips against her. She sucked in a good deal of air. His fingers found her palms and gently stroked upwards. When he reached her shoulder, he redirected his movement downward slowly but deliberately grabbing her hips and pressing himself against her.

"Jack," she moaned, glancing back up into his baby blues. Involuntarily, her eyes moved to his lips and back up.

"Come be with me," he repeated himself.

She reached her hands up and pushed lightly against his chest, giving herself a few inches of space. He didn't pull his hands away from where they rested on her hips. "I said that I can't," the words came out feebler than before.

"I heard you," he said licking his lips.

"I should um…probably get going actually."

"Mmm hmm." But still she didn't move away from him. She felt his thumb make a small circle on her exposed hipbone. Just as his finger met the hemline of her skirt, she backed up roughly running into a large woman seated at the bar.

"Sorry," she said skirting around the woman and entering open space to the right. Her eyes shifted back to Jack. "I haven't heard from you in a long time."

He shrugged. "I was letting your cold shoulder thaw." Her head jerked to the side and she puffed out angrily. All of a sudden, she felt his cool fingertips graze her neck. They moved to her chin and gently forced her to look back in his face. "I've missed you, Lex."

She seriously thought that her heart stopped in that instance. "Jack, this isn't fair."

"I don't want it to be fair," he said not letting her chin go, but taking another step towards her, invading her personal space.

The words kept filtering through her consciousness. She knew she should probably tell him. She should say it right now. There was no way she wanted to do the same thing that he had done to her. She had a boyfriend for Christ's sake. A real boyfriend. Someone she had been dating for close to seven months. Things were so good. She should really tell him right there. "Well, you've accomplished that," she said, ignoring her conscience.

He snaked his other hand up and threaded his fingers through her hair. "I saw that guy," he said trying to make it easier on her.

She knew she should tell him right there. She gulped. "Yeah?" She was having trouble thinking with his hand running through her hair.

"What's his deal?"

"I thought you didn't want things to be fair," she said smarting off to him.

He smirked arching an eyebrow as if to say *fine play it that way*.

She had no idea what she was doing. There was no way that this would end well. Her friends could return at any moment. If they walked over and saw her close to sexing it up with some apparent stranger, she had no idea what she would do. She had no idea what Spencer would think or do, and she didn't want to find out.

"Then you won't mind if I do this," he said his head dipping down to plant a kiss on her lips.

She froze watching his descent as if in slow motion. Her eyes started to flutter close and she could almost taste him just as her mind finally kicked in. "I don't want to lie to you, Jack," she murmured feeling his breath hot on her mouth.

"Well seeing as you've said next to nothing, doesn't seem like you're lying to me," he said suspended before her waiting for her to continue.

"We both know that *not* saying something can be just as much of a lie," she reminded him.

"Well, what aren't you saying?" he asked backing up just enough to look deeply into her dark brown eyes.

"That guy is my boyfriend."

He didn't back away. In fact, he didn't move at all. His hand had stilled on the back of her head; the other had moved affectionately to the soft spot under her jaw line. He just stared at her with those ice blue eyes. After that brief pause, his hand started working through her hair again almost like he hadn't even heard what she had said.

"Jack...did you..."

"Yes."

"Then why..."

"Because I want to, and I've wanted to for too damn long."

She loved his forcefulness even though she knew she shouldn't. He should have backed away by now, apologized for interfering with her relationship, and then immediately left her if not the premises. But he didn't.

Sighing heavily, she spoke again, "It's not that simple." She reluctantly took a step backwards. Gently, she extracted his hand from her hair, and moved it back to his side. His other hand followed.

"You're the one making it complicated."

"Me?!" she exclaimed. "You're the one doing *that*."

"Doing what?"

"I don't know. Just *that*. That thing you do."

"Oh, how original. Doing that thing you do?" he asked mocking her.

"You know what I mean."

"I have a feeling that I don't."

"Oh Jack," she groaned crossing her arms over her chest. "We can't do this again."

"I'm not sure what *this* is, but it feels very different then whatever *this* was last time."

"It's different, because I know the truth," she said bitterly.

"I promised I'd never lie to you again, and I meant it," he said trying to bridge the distance she had put between them.

As if they were in some synchronized dance, she moved with him. When he stepped forward, she stepped back not giving him any room to touch her again. If he touched her, she would be lost. "You can't just say that. How can I believe you?"

"I hardly expect you to." She narrowed her eyes waiting for the catch. "But I plan to make it up to you."

She liked the sound of that. "How do you plan on doing that?" she asked cocking her head to the side and trying to keep the flirtation out of her voice, but damn that was hard to do.

"I've got a few ideas," he said, a smirk appearing on his face. "I think you'll like them."

"I'm sure I would," she mumbled, images of him kissing her senseless appearing before her eyes.

"I think we're back to square one. Why don't you come and stay with me tonight?" She looked helplessly up at him. He could tell that he was wearing her down. She wanted to say yes.

Just then a hand snaked around her waist from behind and a head nuzzled into her neck. "Hey babe, I've been looking for you all over. I thought you were going to stay at the bar," Spencer said leaving one last kiss on her neck before straightening and turning towards her.

She stared at him dumbstruck. "I…uh," Lexi stammered.

"Did Chasity give you anything else?" he asked with concern evident in his voice. "You're not going to be sick are you?"

"Oh, well…" she began fumbling for words. "I just ran into a friend."

Spencer glanced up and looked around completely ignoring Jack who was standing directly in front of them. "Where did she go?"

Lexi couldn't help laughing out loud. "No, no, this is my friend," she said gesturing to Jack, but being careful not to touch him as she directed Spencer's attention towards him.

He glanced at Jack uncomfortably. She could tell that Spencer wasn't too happy that this was her friend, but regardless he stuck his hand out. "I'm Spencer."

Jack took his hand in his own and gave a quick squeeze. Lexi saw the smirk cross his face. "Jack."

Spencer looked between Jack and Lexi awkwardly. "Sorry if I was looking for a chick, but, well, I don't think I've ever heard her mention you before."

"Not surprising. We haven't seen each other in a really long time," Jack said. "Anyway, I've got to get out of here. My friends were just heading out when I ran into you. I'm gonna go catch up with them."

"Alright. Nice meeting you, man," Spencer said putting a deliberately protective arm across Lexi's shoulders.

"Likewise, I'm sure," Jack responded, that smirk never leaving his face. "I'll see you around, Lex."

She watched his departing back, sad that he didn't even give her a backwards glance. Had that really just happened? She couldn't be sure, but all of a sudden she felt terribly uncomfortable in Spencer's grasp.

"I thought you didn't like being called Lex," Spencer said turning to face her and sliding his other arm around her.

Lexi smiled. "I don't."

5

PRESENT

Navy blue covers crinkled and scrunched around Lexi's lithe form, and a down pillow lay crushed against her chest. One bare leg was revealed while her feet remained tangled in the matching sheets. A sharp knock on the door roused her from her reverie, and she buried her face farther into the pillow. The door creaked open uninvited. "Lex, it's time to get up," Jack whispered into the darkness.

"Nuh uh," she grumbled shaking her head against the pillow.

"I thought you could use a shower," he said flipping the light switch and holding up a white fluffy towel. "I realized that I washed all the towels before I left so there aren't any in the bathroom. But if you don't want it," he said tauntingly, waving the towel back and forth in front of his face.

Her head popped up from the comfort of the pillow, and she looked at him groggily. They had been up way too late and her eyes weren't happy with the early morning wake-up. She flipped over on her back and leaned back against her elbows giving her eyes time to focus. "What are you going to do?" she asked stifling a yawn. "I don't mind walking around naked...and wet." She bit her lip at her own suggestive behavior.

She successfully elicited her desired reaction from Jack. He tried to stay calm, but she had known him long enough to be able to interpret his subtle movements. His eyes bulged as they crawled down her body, his imagination running away with him. He licked his lips as he thought of her wet, naked form sauntering around his apartment...or in his shower...or on his bed...or pretty much anywhere. His chest rose and fell irregularly, and the crotch of his pants jumped just a little bit, just enough for her to notice. He gulped uneasily. "Uh...yeah...well then, I guess you'll need this," he stammered walking into the room, and placing the towel at the foot of the bed, trying not to show his arousal. Then, he quickly turned to leave before he did anything he might regret...or she might tell his girlfriend.

"Jack," she said stopping his exit. She kicked the sheet to the foot of the bed and stretched out arching her back. He just stared at her hungrily. She was so bad.

"Uh...yeah?" he asked his hands clenched in fists at his side.

"Things aren't going to be awkward today after you know...last night, are they?" she questioned him, sitting up and hugging her knees to her chest.

"No, things will be fine...normal." She wasn't sure what normal was for them. Normal could be *so* many different things. "You look concerned."

"It's just...you did tell your girlfriend you were coming back last night, right? She knew I was staying here?" Lexi asked watching his eyes shift uncomfortably.

"Well..."

"You didn't tell her," she said interpreting his behavior once again. "As I thought."

"No. I couldn't tell her. She wouldn't understand why I'd let you do that."

"That's funny. I don't understand either," she said still staring him down waiting for his eyes to meet hers.

When they finally did, she could tell he was just as confused about his actions as she was. "Can we just talk about this later?" he asked.

She nodded. "Yeah, sure. But you'll explain it later, right?"

"I'll always be honest with you, Lex," he said before exiting the room, pulling the door closed behind him.

Lexi threw her head back against the covers and smiled half-heartedly up at the ceiling. Yep, things were going to be *way* awkward.

She quickly showered and diffused her loose curls. She unzipped her suitcase and stared at the different outfits she had planned for the day. A brown sundress she knew would go perfectly with her golden tan. Blue and white striped seersucker shorts coupled with a white tank top would have the same effect, but she was as indecisive as ever. Did she want to be cute and friendly like she *should* be or would she rather dress a bit sexier? After a moment longer, she opted for the shorts combo. No need to dress the part Kate had drawn her to be.

"You can't wear that," Jack said, entering the room without knocking.

"I could have been naked," she cried.

He smirked. "Yep," he said cheerfully, "looks like I waited too long."

She scowled at him. "*Anyway*…why can't I wear this?" she asked gesturing to her outfit. "I think I look good."

"Plans just changed. Unfortunately, we're going to the Country Club."

Lexi crinkled her nose up at him. "Why are we doing that? I thought you said we were going to get brunch, some much needed coffee, and then get this ridiculous conversation over with," she mumbled the last part under her breath.

"I just got off the phone with Bekah, and there was some miscommunication with her parents."

"And?" Lexi asked clearly irritated.

"And we have to postpone our afternoon engagement." Lexi sighed, not a good choice of words. "She thought her parents were having their monthly Club brunch next weekend, but she just found out it's today."

"Okay, well, you have fun with that," Lexi said taking a seat on top of the bed stubbornly.

"Come on. I can't leave you. I already told Bekah that you made it here. She'd find it weird if I didn't bring you along."

"Jack, I'm not going to some snooty country club with your girlfriend and her parents! How would you explain me? How would you explain why I'm here?"

"Lex, please," he whined. She just glared harder. No way was he winning this. She had made the mistake of going home with Jennifer, her college dorm mate, for a weekend at the Club her freshman year of college. She had been completely humiliated when the rude, stuck-up, rich members found out that her parents weren't wealthy. She had utterly refused to go back. A repeat performance was not something she ever wanted to endure.

"No! You can forget it."

"It will be easy. I'll just tell them that you're an old friend of mine who's here from out of town…which you are," he added. "We don't have to give them details. They don't give a shit about anyone else besides themselves anyway."

"Oh, that's *real* comforting," she spat back at him.

He strode across the room and stood directly in front of her. "You know what I mean. They aren't going to care who you are or where you're from as long as you are with the right people."

She tilted her head up to look into his face. "And *you're* the right people?"

He nodded. "Bekah is the right people."

Lexi's stomach rolled at that sound. All she could picture about this girl was some blonde bimbo following daddy's orders and spending daddy's money. And, yes, she was certain Bekah was blonde. Jack *always* dated blondes. Not to mention, her parents were Country Clubbers. She groaned at the thought. No wonder Bekah was so worried about her parents cutting her off from their finances. "I'm not going," she said crossing her arms and legs at the same time and putting on a determined face.

"Okay, alright, I can't make you," he said throwing his hands up. "I'll call her back and tell her you can't make it. It would just be for a couple hours, but...whatever." He turned to walk out of the room.

Lexi shook her head from side to side arguing with herself. Did she really come all this way just to bicker with him? She had come here for him...even if she didn't really want to admit it. She might as well go along with his charade. "Jack," she said standing up and catching his arm before he exited.

"Look, Lex, I get it. You're a different person and blah, blah, blah. But come on, the direction you're going in life, you could be one of these people someday. I mean, what's the worst that could happen? You could make some useful connections if you decide to head back to the South?" he asked speaking roughly to her. "So stop spouting bullshit. I know why you don't want to go. I remember what happened with Jennifer. I thought you were better than letting one bad experience cloud your judgment."

Her jaw clenched as she listened to him rant. She didn't want to hear any of this. "Ok. Ok. Jesus Christ, Jack, just shut up." He paused and looked at her expectantly. For a second, she got lost in his gaze. His baby blues clouded over with grey as he let anger take him over. Something about that stare froze her in place.

"Lex?" he asked. She hadn't even realized he had been speaking. "Were you going to say something or just stare at me?" he asked amused.

"Oh. Oh yeah," Lexi mumbled recovering. "I was just going to say that I'll go with you...you know...before you said all that shit."

"Oh."

"Yeah," she said shifting her weight uncomfortably.

"Well, then, you better change."

Lexi glared at him. "Are we back here?"

"Well, now that you've agreed, you have to change," he snapped, but his anger was gone. He actually looked bemused that she had caved so easily. She tried to not let that shake her.

Lexi changed tactics. "And what would *you* like to see me in?" she asked cocking her head to the side and looking at him from beneath her side-swept bangs. The flirtatiousness in her voice was evident, but this was how she and Jack worked. They argued. They made up. They fucked...oh wait...she meant flirted. Damn it!

"We don't have time for that." She glanced up at him innocently. "Or that. Now, go put on a sundress. You brought heels right?"

Lexi shrugged. "Fine, whatever, but you know you owe me, right?"

"I always repay my debts. Now go," he said pushing her into the room. She could imagine this conversation if they were together. He would kiss her softly on the mouth and smack her ass as she went to change. He would follow her and ravish her body before they departed for their afternoon together. She sighed. Then again if they *were* together, he wouldn't dare drag her to a stupid Country Club. Oh yeah, and that whole girlfriend problem.

Lexi poured over her dress options. The brown sundress was too short for a Country Club especially if she was going as a guest. That left her to decide between a strapless ivory eyelet dress with a salmon-colored satin belt and a bright green spaghetti strap number that billowed out around her knees. Frustration started to take over as her indecision intensified. She didn't really want to go to this brunch, and the fact that she had to put so much effort into her outfit made it even worse. Finally, she threw on the ivory dress with a pair of brown peep-toe mules leaving the green dress for a less judgmental audience.

"Ready?" Jack asked as she entered the living room. He looked as gorgeous as ever. A rather expensive, as she could judge by the quality, baby blue button-up fit him perfectly even cutting in a bit at the waist to make him look leaner. A tri-colored blue, black, and silver tie hung from his neck to his light grey dress pants. The shirt brought out the blue of his eyes, and when they rested on her, they seemed to be a million times more intense than normal. She wasn't sure if that was because of her or not.

"As ready as I'll ever be."

They set off for the twenty minute drive out of town. A vast array of music filtered through the speakers. Lexi hummed along to what was playing as they pulled up to the gate of the Club.

After being cleared by the overweight security guard, they drove past the million dollar homes and around the immaculate eighteen-hole golf course to a mansion of a Club House. Jack parked his car into an available slot between a BMV SUV and a tiny Mercedes convertible. Sauntering past the other meticulously detailed luxury vehicles, they made their way towards the daunting Club House.

Lexi took in the massive arching entranceway and polished marble floors as her heels clicked noisily across the surface. The room was over-air conditioned, and smelled strongly of flowers. When she glanced around, she realized why. Hundreds of flowers of various types and colors were scattered in prearranged vases all around the entranceway. Lexi didn't remember that from the last time she had been there, and didn't much like it either. The whole thing made her want to sneeze.

She followed Jack through the foyer and up to the receptionist seated behind a desk large enough to swallow her whole and covered with similar vases brimming with carnations, lilies, and tulips.

As they approached, the aroma grew stronger and she did sneeze this time. Jack touched her arm briefly, smiling in her direction. After Jack announced their presence, he ushered her down the hall towards the colossal dining hall. Lexi glanced around her at the couples sitting in overstuffed arm chairs sipping on tea and reading the newspaper. She scoffed and several heads swiveled to get a look at the interruption. She skittered down the hall after Jack. Her hand instinctively went to her hair and began threading it behind her ear repeatedly.

Jack looked over at her and stopped moving. She took a few more steps before recognizing that he wasn't alongside her anymore. "What?" she asked turning to face him.

"Don't be nervous," he said taking her hands away from her hair.

"Oh yeah, well, I'll work on that."

"There's no need to be nervous."

Lexi shrugged not wanting to have this conversation in public. "I'm going to go to the restroom," she said seeing the blue sign behind his head.

"Alright, do you want me to wait?" Lexi shook her head, anxious to be alone and calm. "You'll be able to find me?"

"No problem," she said making a beeline towards sanctuary.

After about five minutes staring apprehensively at herself in the mirror, Lexi figured it was about time to get out of there. When she walked out, she was caught off guard by the man standing just outside of the bathroom talking to a woman who couldn't be a day under eighty. Lexi assessed the gorgeous specimen standing in front of her. She was quite certain he had one of the tightest asses she had ever seen. The suit he wore was obviously tailored for his build. An extremely muscular build, if she did say so herself. She figured he had to work out with a personal trainer…daily. His hair was a sandy blonde. Not that ugly highlighted look that so many guys were sporting, but a color that seemed infused with sunlight as if he lived at the beach.

A look of disdain quickly crossed her face as realization hit her. It was pretty obvious that he was just another asshole country clubber like every other person here. Of course he was handsome. They bred them that way. His incredibly amazing physique was likely mandatory. His blonde hair doubtlessly *was* from the beach. No. Now that she thought about it, he probably owned the beach!

She crossed her arms uncomfortably. Whoever this guy was she already didn't like him. There was no way he had a personality. Last time she had been here, Jennifer had been the closest thing to a human being in the establishment, and God *that* was saying something. Just as she began to move away from the attractive man in front of her, he finished his conversation and turned around nearly knocking Lexi over.

"Oh, sorry. Excuse me," he said reaching out to steady her.

"No problem," she said coldly, backing up a step out of his comforting grasp. Her dark brown eyes shifted up to his extremely handsome, apologetic face. He really looked concerned. Strange. She turned away from his strong jaw line and high cheek bones, ignoring his expression. When he didn't seem to get the hint, she returned her gaze to his face. "Yeah?" she asked rudely.

"Uh…sorry…do I know you?" he skeptically asked, his eyes roaming her face.

Lexi rolled her eyes. Was he really playing this game? That had to be the most overused line ever. Why would she know him? "Um…no, I don't think so," she said diverting her attention again. "I have to get to brunch." Lexi attempted to side-step him, but he cut off her path.

"No really, I think I know you from somewhere."

"You're in my way," she pointed out to him. She couldn't help how rude she was being. She wasn't really sure why he was eliciting such a reaction either. It's not like he had been rude to her, but Lexi didn't want to give him the chance.

"Oh yeah, sorry, but really we've met before."

"No, I don't think so."

"Have you ever been here before? I think it was here. Actually, I'm almost certain it was here."

"Just once a long time ago, but really I need to leave, and you've blocked my path." Lexi didn't want to have this conversation. She didn't want to remember anyone she might have met that day when she had come with Jennifer.

"Okay, yeah, I definitely remember you now," he said cheerfully. "You came with one of my sister's friends. But she wasn't here, of course. I mean you wouldn't know that. My sister went to Duke. So she wasn't here. Which I already said. But you were here with her friend, I'm pretty sure. And man, she's really annoying." Lexi looked back up at him skeptically. Had he just called Jennifer annoying? Of course, Lexi thought Jennifer was annoying, but she was pretty sure he wasn't supposed to think that. "Oh no," he said staring down at her apologetically, "I mean she's your friend. I didn't mean that the way it sounded." She stared at him longer unable to believe what she was hearing. This guy was babbling. She was certain there was an unwritten rule somewhere preventing this from happening. "Wow, this isn't coming out right at all."

Lexi looked up at him incredulously. "Right then, I'm going to go," she said attempting to dodge him again.

"Oh right," he said seeming to step out of her way, but only blocking her path further. She sighed heavily, stepping in the opposite direction. He had the same idea and moved in front of her once again. He laughed heartily. Probably a little too loud for the environment. The people she had been attempting to remain invisible from turned in their direction and began staring. She cringed and pushed her hair behind her ears.

"Okay, stop," Lexi commanded, reaching out and grabbing his arm to prevent him from moving farther. "I'm going to go right. Just…don't move."

"Who are you here with?" he asked, ignoring her demand.

"That's none of your business," she snapped, extracting her hand from his suit.

"You're right," he said sheepishly. "It's just I don't know if you remember me, which I guess you don't, but I remember you."

She wasn't sure what that meant and didn't plan on finding out. "That's great," she stated sarcastically.

"Is Jennifer here?" he asked glancing over her shoulder to see if Jennifer was about to appear at her side.

"I don't know, but I'll send her your way if I find her."

"So, you didn't come here with Jennifer then?" he asked. She flinched, realizing that she had unintentionally given away a piece of information.

"No, I didn't. What's it to you anyway?" Lexi demanded getting more flustered the longer she stood in front of him.

"I'm just curious about you is all. You've been here before, and you came back," he said in disbelief. "That never happens."

"Right, well, I see that I'm a fantastic spectacle for you to wonder about, but once again, you are in my way. I'm going to be late for brunch, and frankly, I'm starving." Not to mention she was sure to be humiliated if she arrived a second behind schedule.

"Oh yeah. I keep forgetting about that," he said, bringing his hand up and scratching the back of his head thoughtfully.

"Well, I haven't. So…yeah…nice meeting you," Lexi said offhandedly, finally getting herself around his solid figure.

"But you didn't. I didn't even tell you my name or get yours for that matter."

Lexi turned letting her loose curls trail down her back. "That's alright. I've survived this long without it." He walked forward towards her. "What are you doing?" she asked throwing her hand out to stop him from walking further.

"I can escort you to your seat," he offered, his perfectly straight white teeth appeared as he smiled brightly at her.

"Absolutely not."

"Do you even know where you are going?"

"*You* don't know where I'm going," she reminded him. "And I'm sure I can find my way just fine, thank you." She took another step forward and he followed her. She clenched her fists. "Jesus, why don't you back off?" she exclaimed raising her voice for the first time. She regretted her actions almost instantly. The obnoxious middle aged members, who had only been half-listening to their conversation, now went silent and turned their full attention to her, making her cheeks burn bright red. It didn't help that she had taken the Lord's name in vain in the Bible belt. Goddamn it, New York had changed her! She took three calming breaths before glancing back up at him and smiling through gritted teeth.

His smile had never wavered. Country Club manners through and through. "Well, if you are sure I can't be of any assistance, I'll just let you find your own way," he said politely.

Lexi watched him purposely walk off in the opposite direction. Clenching and unclenching her hands several times calmed her down enough to allow her to search for Jack. To be honest, she had no idea where to begin. She should have let that guy help her. But after he had been so goddamn pushy, all she wanted to do was get away. She searched around unsuccessfully before noticing Jack quickly approaching her.

"Where have you been?" he asked concerned and a little annoyed.

"I ran into someone and they wouldn't stop talking to me," she complained.

"Well, let's hurry up. We should get in there before they start taking orders," he said smiling down on her, his annoyance dissipating the longer he remained in her presence.

Her throat caught as his hand rested gently on her elbow and nudged her in the appropriate direction. She had wanted things to be like this for so long. It hurt to know that the only reason she was here, the only reason he was even talking to her, was because of his girlfriend. His perfect girlfriend whom he intended to marry. His perfect girlfriend that she was about to meet. She sighed, mentally preparing herself, and followed his lead into a side room with a large gold plaque labeled Anderson, Bridges, and C. Brown.

The dining room that Lexi entered opened onto a balcony overlooking the ninth hole fairway. Cream-colored walls and blue patterned carpet decorated the large space. Three elegant oak tables filled the area with matching cushioned chairs placed around them. Nearly all the seats were occupied, and roughly thirty people glanced up from their prearranged silverware to stare at Jack and Lexi as they entered the room. Lexi smiled repentantly and ambled after Jack to their assigned seats.

"Sorry we took so long," Jack said taking his seat across from his girlfriend.

"Uh...hi," Lexi said adding a tiny wave before scooting into her seat and tucking her dress underneath her.

Lexi pulled her eyes from the table and let them rest on Bekah. She knew that she didn't like her as soon as Lexi laid eyes on her. Bekah was definitely beautiful in a cookie-cutter sort of way. The pin-straight blond hair,

Lexi had predicted she would have, was all one length cut to the middle of her back. Chunky bangs covered her forehead. Big blue eyes popped out from Bekah's naturally beautiful face which was hardly tainted by make-up. Lexi felt sick upon realizing that Bekah had as nearly flawless skin as Chyna. Her pale yellow, square-cut sundress was modest yet fashionable all the while accentuating her best features. Eleven millimeter white pearls dangled from her earlobes and matched the thin chain of pearls draped across her neck. What bothered Lexi the most wasn't that she knew that this woman was one hundred percent Jack's type, but rather that she had something that Lexi had never appeared to have.

Innocence.

Okay, to be fair, Bekah probably wasn't all that innocent either. After all, she was dating *Jack*. But she sure as hell gave off the appearance. Lexi, on the other hand, had never given off that appearance. Something about Lexi's dark, tangled, curly hair, the way her eyes looked smoky without make-up, the way her characteristically bold personality tended to intimidate strangers, and the way she almost always felt completely comfortable in her body gave off the impression not that she was easy, but certainly that she was *not* innocent.

"It's so nice to meet you," Bekah said. A row of brilliant, white teeth were revealed as she smiled across the table from her. Something in that smile held a secret. She had no idea what it was. But when she looked upon her full for the first time, Bekah looked at her as if she had seen her before…as if some light bulb of recognition had just gone off in her mind.

"Likewise," Lexi said coughing uncomfortably and glancing away from her doe-eyed gaze. The rest of the table was filled with mostly respectable middle aged men and women in high-quality attire. She was introduced as Jack's friend from out of town, but failed to really take in any names. She didn't plan on remembering any of them anyway. Lexi nudged Jack. "Don't you want to sit next to Bekah?" she asked indicating the empty seat facing her.

Lexi had thought it strange that the seat was unoccupied. He smiled at her. "Well, yeah, I would, but this is where I sit."

Lexi cocked an eyebrow at him condescendingly. This must be some Country Club thing. Not that she wanted him to leave her side. "Alright," Lexi said not pushing the subject. "Are we missing someone?"

"My brother," Bekah answered. "He should be here shortly. He tends to run behind."

"Oh." Lexi didn't know what else to say.

Bekah leaned over the table smiling secretively. "Sorry about that. He's a bit of a troublemaker. He likes to upset my parents by showing up late for brunch, talking a bit too loud in public and the like." Lexi tried not to roll her eyes. This girl was serious. Talking too loud in public? Had she ever left her bubble? "I don't mind it so much though. I think it's humorous."

"I'm sure it is." Lexi tried to smile. She had just used *humorous* in a sentence. Fantastic.

"Yeah, Ramsey's a riot," Jack interjected.

Bekah smiled even bigger, her blue eyes glittering with unspoken revelations. "He is...something else," she said dropping her voice. "But anyway, I am so glad that your flight landed as scheduled. I would have felt terrible changing plans on you if you were still in transit. Jack wasn't sure if you would accompany us for brunch, but I'm very glad he was able to convince you."

Lexi jerked her head to the side and glared at Jack. "What?" he asked defensively, a slow smirk creeping onto his face.

"You forced me to be here," she muttered angrily.

"Well, it convinced you didn't it?"

"Did you not want to come?" Bekah asked crestfallen.

She swore under her breath. Then she remembered where she was and furiously bit her lip. Lexi could not believe this! Why would she want to be here? This was the most awkward situation she had ever been in, and then Jack had dragged her tooth and nail to the one place she absolutely despised. Of course she didn't want to be here! It was just dumb of Bekah to think that *any* outsider would want to be trapped in their dumb old-timey Country Club. But even Lexi couldn't blurt that out in front of complete strangers. So she just smiled and said, "Oh no, it's fine."

Jack chuckled under his breath. The laugh turned into a cough as Bekah turned her blue eyes on him. "Well, I'm glad you made the trip," Bekah said cheerfully.

Before Lexi could embarrass herself further, several stuffy-looking waiters entered the room and began to fill beverage orders. Lexi sighed as she listened to all the requests for sweet tea. She had forgotten how addicted Southerners were to the stuff. If they could have sweet tea poured directly into their veins, they would do it. What was even more disgusting was how the women, all diet-addicted forty year olds pretending to be twenty-five, ordered their drinks with Splenda, as if the alternative sugar option wouldn't give them cancer like everything else. Lexi ordered coffee.

"Sugar and milk?" the man questioned, staring down at her through his thick black-rimmed glasses over the bridge of his large nose.

"Uh, no, thank you. Black is fine."

"Mmm hmm," he said hotly and turned on his heel.

"Sorry I'm late everyone," a familiar voice said pushing past the snotty waiter and over to their table.

Lexi heard the chair in front of her scuff against the carpeted floor before she had a chance to glance up. When she did, a short gasp escaped her tight set lips. Recognition swept over her. *No.* She didn't want to believe it. This couldn't really be happening to her. Really, she should have just expected obnoxious bathroom guy to be Bekah's brother. She had been rude enough that she should have more surprised not to see him. The smile he sent her way was practically unbearable. Life couldn't get any worse.

"Oh, hey you," the guy said when he noticed her.

"Hi," she managed to say through her gritted teeth.

"You know each other?" Bekah asked, the surprise exceedingly evident in her voice. She had perked up even further than Lexi had thought possible. Bekah's eyes glittered as she glanced between the two of them several times catching Ramsey's gaze briefly. A look passed between them.

"I wouldn't say that exactly," Lexi responded. She sat back against the hard-backed chair and began pushing her hair behind her ear forcefully. Jack peered at her reaction curiously.

"Oh, don't be like that. We go way back," he said openly smirking.

"Oh yeah?" Lexi asked leaning forward and crossing her arms on the table. "Then what's my name?" she asked, raising her eyebrows in a challenge.

A voice from the other end of the table cut off his response. "Ramsey, where were you?" a man Lexi recognized as his father asked in an obviously controlled neutral tone. Ramsey just shrugged, his eyes remaining on Lexi's face. "I'm talking to you son," he growled. The room fell silent.

"Yeah, I heard," Ramsey said finally turning his attention to his father. "I got lost."

Lexi could tell his father was boiling over. The only thing holding him back was the fact that he was in the midst of friends and colleagues. "You've lived here since you were a boy," his father pointed out. "It's not possible for you to get lost."

"Sure it is. I got lost in a broom closet," Ramsey said shrugging his shoulders as if this was common place. He also said the words as if it were suggestive of foul behavior. Behavior that should not be spoken of over afternoon brunch at the Country Club...or perhaps anywhere. "Anyway, can I get back to my conversation?"

"Ramsey, may I have a word with you in the hallway?" his father asked menacingly.

"I just got here, remember?" he said smirking. "Wouldn't want to miss brunch."

"That's enough Ramsey," Bekah whispered letting her hand rest gently on his forearm. Bekah glanced down to her father's seat and smiled sweetly. The implication was clear. She was going to handle the situation. No need to embarrass the family over something simple, even if these things pushed her father over the edge. Bekah whispered something in Ramsey's ear that he didn't appear to be too pleased about, but he cooled off nonetheless.

Ramsey's smirk returned as his focus shifted back to the matter at hand. "Your name, right," he said scratching the back of his head thoughtfully.

"You said you know her, but you can't remember her name?" Jack asked dubiously glancing between the two of them.

"You're telling me that's never happened to you before?" Ramsey asked raising his eyebrows.

Jack chortled at Ramsey's implication then turned back to Lexi. "I was pretty sure you didn't know anyone here." He sounded concerned, even a bit jealous. She smiled despite herself.

"He doesn't know me, Jack."

"But you recognized him," Bekah pointed out. She reached forward and took a sip of the ice water that was placed before her. "I mean, right? You did recognize him."

"Well yes," she finally conceded.

"So, you do know him?" Jack asked. Yep, she could definitely detect a hint of jealousy. She reveled in it for a moment.

"I'm not sure why it matters whether or not I know him. He's just messing with you guys," she pointed out. Ramsey snickered. Her eyes turned fiery. "What, may I ask, is so funny?"

"I'm sorry," Ramsey said stifling another laugh. "Did you just say *you guys*?"

"And if I did?" Lexi snapped. She clenched her teeth. Here it goes again. She was being rude. Why was she being rude? Why was she letting this guy – Ramsey – bring out the Yankee asshole in her when she had sworn she was going to stay in Southern hospitality mode?

"Oh nothing," he remarked glancing into Bekah's blue eyes, an all-knowing look passing between them.

"What? What's wrong with that?" Lexi demanded turning her eyes from one to the other.

"Oh, it's nothing," Bekah muttered at the same time as Ramsey began asking, "You... you're just not from around here, are you?" His green eyes glittered with humor.

"She's from New York," Bekah said cheerfully filling in some information for her brother.

"Oh, a Yankee in our midst."

"I'm not *from* New York," she quickly corrected. This girl obviously knew nothing about her. Lexi figured, at least for now, that was probably for the better.

"Yeah, she went to college down here with me," Jack interjected, not enjoying the fact that his girlfriend was providing details about Lexi to Ramsey...or anyone.

"So, where *are* you from then?" Ramsey asked, his interest spiking with her annoyance.

"I'm sorry. The investigation begins later. You'll just have to wait your turn." Lexi announced abruptly. Bekah's face instantly turned a bright pink hue, and Jack, hoping to quiet Lexi, nudged her in the arm. Lexi turned towards Jack and shrugged. It's not like he had told her that her reason for being here and everything surrounding the awkward circumstances was supposed to be a big secret.

Ramsey smiled but his eyes held suspicion. "Okay. Just let me know when you are open for an investigation, and I'll be there."

Lexi rolled her eyes catching his sexual undertone. "Whatever."

"But I have one condition."

"There are no conditions."

"Well, I need to know your name first."

"And I thought you said you knew it."

"I could try and remember, but I have a feeling that would take longer than the time we're allotted."

"Probably," Lexi agreed, averting her eyes.

"Okay, wow," Jack began turning his head between the two. "How did you say you know each other?"

"We don't," Lexi barked.

"No, no, we do know each other. She came here with Jennifer once," he explained turning to his sister. "I guess they went to college together or something."

"You know Jennifer?" Bekah asked Lexi perking up again.

"Wait, you know Jennifer?" Jack asked directing his question towards Bekah.

"Well, yeah, we went to high school together," Bekah admitted. "How do you know Jen, Jack?"

"Jennifer and I dormed together freshman year," Lexi told her at the same time as Jack said, "I know her through Lexi." Jack had never liked Jennifer much, and he knew Lexi thought she was one of the most annoying people on the planet. The fact that his new girlfriend not only knew her, but grew up with her was just plain weird.

"Small world!" Bekah exclaimed.

"So your name is Lexi?" Ramsey asked speaking up for the first time since the beginning of this exchange. "Hmm...I like that."

Lexi groaned inwardly glaring daggers at Jack for revealing her name. "Yep. That's me. Lexi."

After their introduction, conversation shifted to other topics. Brunch was served as the table began to discuss the upcoming golf tournament, specific techniques, and possible favorites in the match. Lexi withdrew from the conversation. She had learned how to play in college, but didn't much care for the game, or at least, not enough to continue talking about it.

Instead, Lexi took this time to assess Ramsey for the first time since she had set eyes on him. She wasn't sure what to make of him. He was pushy and forthright. For someone born and bred in this environment, his personality depicted rebellion despite his impeccably controlled appearance. He was dressed the part head-to-toe, but he looked more like he was in character. He was damn persistent as hell when he wanted to be, but as soon as he found out her name, he had done a complete one-eighty. He spoke to her only when polite conversation demanded it, and though his flattering tone and overwhelmingly charming demeanor never wavered, she could see, perhaps, underneath that there was something more. She wasn't quite sure whether more was good or not.

Jack, at least, seemed to act normal…or at least normal for Jack. For that, she was grateful. If this new girl had changed him, or at least if she thought she was capable of changing him, things were going to get very interesting quick. Jack Howard did not change.

Seeing him speak with Bekah like he had always done with her was disconcerting to say the least. But after all, she had volunteered for this torture so she was might as well endure it with some dignity. Not that she had expected it to quite play out quite like this.

Bekah's father stood and thanked everyone for attending their monthly brunch celebration. Lexi followed everyone's lead and scooted back from the table to leave. Jack moved in front of her and grabbed Bekah's hand entwining it with his. She could feel herself close to gagging. She quickly covered her mouth so as not to draw any unwanted attention to herself.

"You don't mind if I escort you this time, do you?" Ramsey asked holding out his arm. His green eyes were twinkling again as a smile broke out across his face.

After contemplating her options, Lexi rested her hand in the crook of his elbow, and trailed behind the crowd exiting the dining hall. "I might mind, but I'll allow it," she said glancing up at him mischievously. She hadn't realized how tall he was the first time around. Now standing directly next to him, she noticed that the top of her head just barely reached his shoulder. He had to be well over six feet tall.

"So, are you just here visiting Jack?" Ramsey asked.

"Kind of," Lexi said neither confirming nor denying anything.

"Specific. Are you visiting your parents?"

"I plan on it."

"So are you staying with Jack?"

Lexi saw Jack's head swivel in front of her. He had obviously been eavesdropping on their conversation. "Um…no. I don't think so."

Ramsey nodded, but kept his face neutral. "Do your folks live in the city? Are you staying with them?"

"Why do you care?" she asked snootily.

"Why are you so snippy?" he questioned right back at her.

"Sorry, *yankee* thing," Lexi said drawing out the word.

"Right, but you're not from there," he pointed out. "Either way, I was just curious about you is all. I told you that before."

"Okay," Lexi said eyeing him warily, "well my parents live on the south side of Atlanta about an hour maybe an hour fifteen south of here. I'll probably be staying with them."

"That's pretty far away. Why don't you just get a hotel?"

She rolled her eyes. This was typical. "Money. As in I don't have any, because I'm in school," she told him coldly.

"Oh, right. Stupid me," he said smacking his forehead with his available hand. "Well, I think Bekah and Jack are coming over to my place later for drinks with some of my friends. You are welcome to join them, if you are interested," he offered graciously.

"Oh my God, we would just *love* for you to come," Bekah exclaimed interrupting their conversation. "Why didn't you think of that, Jack?" she asked him, hitting him playfully on the arm.

"Must have slipped my mind," Jack commented glancing from Bekah to Lexi and then down to where Lexi's hand was still placed on Ramsey's expensive sleeve.

"Then it's settled," Ramsey confirmed, "I'll see you tonight."

Lexi had come here for one purpose. Country Club brunches and parties were not on that list. She didn't want to get to know Bekah or her family. She didn't want to think about what a better lot Jack could get by marrying into this family…this girl. She didn't want to go back to New York feeling worse about her situation and the way things had ended with Jack then she already did. She couldn't imagine what that would feel like. She just wanted this to be over with.

Why couldn't closure be easier than this?

6

SEPTEMBER FIVE YEARS EARLIER

"Jack, I can't come over," Lexi told him for what felt like the hundredth time. She rested her flip phone between her ear and shoulder while directing her car into an available parking spot in front of the grocery store.

"Sure you can. I don't live that far away from you. What's the drive, like ten minutes?"

"It's not the distance that's the issue," she told him, getting out of the car and walking towards the entrance. She dodged a white SUV that zoomed in front of her. Lexi flipped off the driver as she skidded to a halt in the middle of the crosswalk. "Jackass."

"What? No need for name calling."

"Oh, sorry, I wasn't talking about you," she told him cautiously jogging the rest of the way to safety. "Some crazy driver."

"I really want to see you."

"I know. I want to see you too," she confided in him. She bit her lip at the thought of going over to his house, and then quickly diverted her attention. She couldn't let herself go down that path.

"Well then, come see me. Nothing's stopping you."

"You know there are plenty of things stopping me from coming to see you." She grabbed a buggy and pushed it down an aisle.

"Alright. How about this: I'll come see you. That way you don't feel like those reasons apply."

Lexi shook her head. "You forget my roommates." She threw a few items aimlessly into the cart and continued down the aisle.

"Are they there right now?" Lexi knew they weren't, but there was no way she was telling him that. She didn't know her roommates' schedules by heart, and if she was found with Jack, there would be a lot of explaining to do. And explaining why she was talking to him again was not something she was interested in. "Silence means they're not?" Jack guessed.

"I don't know when they are or are not there," she told him noncommittally.

"I just really want to see you. We've both been so busy. It feels like forever since I ran into you at Chamber."

"Yeah, about that. How did you know I was going to be there? You never told me," she said switching ears to adjust the uncomfortable feeling creeping through her shoulder. She couldn't afford to have aching muscles with gymnastics conditioning beginning soon.

"Don't try to change the subject. When do I get to see you?"

"You can't see me until you answer."

"I won't answer until I see you."

"Well, I guess we're at a stalemate," Lexi said attempting to maneuver the shopping cart one-handed.

"Okay fine. If I tell you, you promise you'll come see me? My roommates are out of town, and we'd have the house to ourselves."

All of a sudden, the invitation seemed very enticing. God, she knew she shouldn't even be talking to him. Spencer had no idea about the conversations they had been having, and she had no real desire to tell him. Sometimes she swore that he knew that something was different about her. Jack made her different. That wonderful month they had shared together, even though he had had a girlfriend, had changed her. Jack just made her glow, which was the exact reason she could *not* tell Spencer about Jack.

Spencer would never understand. Sure he acted goofy and played everything off like it was a joke, but she knew that he would see more into it. And there wasn't more to it. At least, that's what she kept telling herself.

"So, what do you say, Lex? You'll come over?" he asked, persuasion etched in every line.

She weighed her options. Spencer was also out of town for the weekend. His great-aunt something-or-other from some no name city in Vermont was visiting his parents, and he was obligated to entertain her. She hadn't been too keen on the details. No matter how many times he argued with his parents about having previous arrangements, he couldn't' get out of it, and she couldn't accompany him. His family was very old fashioned.

He would be none the wiser if she happened to spend a few hours of her afternoon at an old friend's house. Then again, she felt guilty enough for not telling him about the phone conversations and text messages. How would she feel if she spent time with Jack? A knot formed at the pit of her stomach.

"Just to talk?" she peeped, already knowing his answer.

"Of course, if that's what you want."

"You can keep your hands to yourself?" she practically whispered into the other line. She glanced around the nearly empty aisle checking for people she knew or potential eavesdroppers...anyone at all that looked suspicious. If she found one person, she would turn him down flat. But she didn't notice anyone.

"I can if you can," he deadpanned.

"Well, I don't know," she said prolonging the moment.

"You don't know if you can keep your hands to yourself?" he asked with a chuckle. "You should definitely come over."

"Oh, ha. Ha. I don't know if I should come over."

"Lex, I already told you I just want to spend a little time with you. I know you want to come over, and there's no reason for you not to. If one of your other guy friends asked you to hang out right this instant, what would you tell him?" She remained silent. He already knew what she was thinking. There would be no reservations in going to hang out with another guy. Any other guy wasn't Jack. Plain and simple. "That's what I thought. So, come see me."

"You know what. Fine. Whatever. If you say we're just going to sit around and talk and hang out, then I'll come over. But only if you tell me how you knew I'd be at Chamber," she said giving into him.

"Okay, that's an easy one," Jack said coolly.

Just then, Lexi's phone began to beep in her ear. "Hold that thought," she said, glancing down at the number beeping into the line. She swore as she read the name.

"Hey, can I call you back?" she asked Jack impatiently. "I have to take this call."

"You're still coming over right?"

"Sure. And you will finish your story there."

"Alright. See you soon."

Lexi clicked over to the other line. "Hey baby," she trilled into the phone. "How's hanging out with the fam?"

"It's so dull without you here," Spencer complained. "Maybe I could still convince them to let you come up here and visit."

Lexi giggled. "In what lifetime? Your sister got married last year, and they still have trouble letting her husband come to family events."

"You're right, dear. I wish I could change things."

She waved the comments off. No need for him to be even sweeter than normal. That would just make her feel worse. "Your family is the way it is. There's nothing wrong with that."

"Well, I don't agree with you on that, but I appreciate it. It would make me feel better if you were with me though. There's only so much family backgammon I can take," he said chuckling heartily. "So, what are you doing? Have any big plans for the evening? Weekend get-away while I'm not in town?"

Lexi stopped dead in her tracks in the middle of the frozen food section. Did he know about her plans? She shook her head. Of course, there was no way for him to know. She had just decided herself. How could he know something like that? She steadied herself on the shopping cart and let her breath even out. "Nope. I'm probably just going to be boring while you're gone. Hang out with Olivia. Finish my Spinoza reading. Stuff like that," she said terrified that guilt was creeping into her voice and he would notice.

"Aww…baby… just because I'm gone doesn't mean you can't go out and do something. You know what?"

"No," she croaked.

"I want you to have a good time, a really good time while I'm gone. It's my fault you're all by yourself this weekend. I feel obligated to tell you that you need to do something fun and crazy. I don't want you sitting at home doing homework on a Friday night."

"I…well…"

"Nope. That's final. If you don't have a good time tonight, then I'm the one to take the blame. So go home, put on something cute, and go out tonight, okay?"

"Okay," she mumbled.

"Oh, I'm so sorry I'm not there," he moaned, misinterpreting her guilty conscience.

"It's…it's fine. You have family stuff."

"I just wish I could be there with you. I have to go, but I'll call you tomorrow to find out how your night went. You'll let me know how great it was, right? I love you, baby. Bye."

Spencer hung up so fast he didn't even hear her whispered good-bye or the fact that she completely neglected saying I love you too.

Lexi tucked her phone back into her pocket. She felt worse about going to see Jack now that she had spoken with Spencer. He wanted her to have a good time, and she knew she would if she actually went to Jack's house. It just wouldn't be the kind of fun that would be in her best interest, or her relationship's best interest.

She couldn't go see him. He had promised they would just talk, but she just couldn't do it. What she remembered the most about Jack was the lack of control. Her actions were compelled by him. She was compelled by him. Every time she found herself in his presence, she acted as if she was possessed. It was easy to conjure up how she had felt when she had been so enraptured in him that she could hardly sleep at night. She couldn't let herself go there again.

Her temples began to pulse painfully as she contemplated her options.

She wondered if maybe she was overreacting. She had stopped anything from happening with Jack at Chamber, and she had been drunk! What she had felt with Jack before had stemmed from her understanding that they were moving towards a relationship. Now that she was with Spencer, perhaps they could just work towards a friendship.

Deep down, she knew that what she had felt with Jack nearly a year earlier had been real. That had he been single at the time, they would have worked out. She had wanted *that*—for them to be together—more than anything she wanted now. And that fact scared her.

Lexi tried not to think about it too much as she finished her grocery shopping and drove home. Pulling into a parking spot in front of her four-bedroom flat, she unloaded the groceries.

"Need any help with that, roomie?" Olivia asked, skipping into the living room her pixie-cut bouncing as she went.

"No thanks. I think this is the last of it."

"Okie dokie," she trilled, plopping down cross-legged on the white carpeted floor. She snatched her acoustic guitar from its stand and began absentmindedly strumming one of her new tunes. She alternated to a fast-paced picking for the chorus and her soprano filled the room.

"I like that last part," Lexi told her pushing aside three half-full cartons of milk to make room for some of her groceries.

"Thanks, sweetie," Olivia murmured halting her guitar playing to look back up at Lexi. "What are your plans for tonight?"

"Uh…" Lexi froze. She hadn't come up with an excuse for being out, because she hadn't expected Olivia to be home.

"The guys," Olivia began, referring to their other two roommates, "went on some fraternity bonding retreat." She gagged. "Spence is gone right?"

"Um…yeah he is."

"Cool, girl's night!"

"I'm going to have to pass," Lexi muttered uncomfortably. As soon as the words came out, she regretted it. Olivia looked crushed. She always wore her emotions on her sleeve. "I want to, but I made plans with Jennifer," Lexi improvised quickly. Olivia despised Jennifer which was the only reason she had used her name. That way she had effectively cut off Olivia attempting to join her. God, this was getting too elaborate.

"Oh…eww…why?" Olivia asked crinkling her nose.

"Ex-roommate bonding something or other," Lexi told her vaguely.

"Right…okay. Have fun with that," she said making another gagging noise.

"Will do," Lexi said, retreating to her bedroom to decide on something to wear. At first, she threw on a loose pair of jeans and a red baggy t-shirt. She stared at her reflection in the mirror, and sighed heavily. If she was going to pretend to hang out with Jennifer, she had to play the part. Sliding the jeans and t-shirt back off, she rummaged through her closet until she found a navy, three-quarter length, scoop neck blouse, and a grey skirt. Lexi placed a tiny silver chain with a sideways heart pendant around her neck and black flats. Jennifer would have never been seen in public with Lexi in what she had been wearing previously. Or at least that was her excuse for dressing sexy.

Apprehensively, Lexi slid back into her car to head over to Jack's apartment. Two hours had passed since their phone call, and he probably thought she had bailed. After all, she shouldn't be seeing him at all.

She just hoped nothing would go wrong. As long as they both knew that this wasn't going anywhere. They had gone down that path, and had seen how poorly it had ended.

But this time there was no girlfriend holding him back from showing his true feelings for Lexi. The only thing preventing him was himself. She hoped that was enough.

Lexi skipped up to Jack's doorway and found it open just as she arrived. He had been waiting for her. "Here you are," he said looking her up and down. "Wow, you look great." He was obviously ogling the length of the skirt revealing so much of her tanned thighs.

"Thanks."

"I didn't know if you were going to show," he stated as she skirted past him into the living room.

"Me either."

"Well, I'm glad you did." She nodded not letting herself admit that she already felt better by being around him. "Did you want to watch a movie or something?" he asked.

"Sure thing." She grabbed a movie off of the shelf and went to put it into the DVD player remembering their movie nights all too well.

"Actually, I just got a TV for my room, if you want to watch it in there," he said casually.

She could read him though. He knew if they were in his bedroom that she would be forced to sit next to him. But she couldn't decide whether or not she minded. "Okay. We'll go in there, but don't think you're off the hook about the Chamber story," Lexi said pointing the movie at him.

He raised his hands in defense. "Of course not."

They moved to the bedroom, and Jack put the movie in turning the volume down until it was more background noise than anything. He sat next to her on his bed, but was careful not to touch her. He was being courteous and respectful, which was good, so far.

Lexi poked him in the ribs playfully. "So spill mister! How did you know I was going to be at Chamber? That's been bothering me for awhile now."

"I already told you, that's an easy one."

"Yeah. Yeah, but how?"

"Krista told me."

She stared at him blankly. "Huh?" That didn't add up. Krista, last year's gymnastics captain, was currently residing in Las Vegas. How would she know that Lexi was at a bar on any given night? And why would she tell Jack about it even if she did find out?

"You asked me how I knew, and it was because Krista told me."

"Yeah, but how do you know Krista? And why did she tell you?"

"Well, one – I knew her before you did. She dated one of my friends freshman year. When they broke up, we remained friends." Her eyes narrowed. "Just as friends," he added quickly. "And, two – she received a text or something from you. She told me you were there, because I was the one who told her about you."

"You told her about me?"

"Yeah. After you stopped returning my messages, I just went ahead and told Krista about you. I gave her your email and told her that you were worth her time. I think you know the rest of the story."

"You did that for me?" she asked wistfully, realizing for the first time that Jack had single-handedly secured her position with the gymnastics team.

"Of course, I did it for you."

"I mean, I figured you had something to do with it since I hadn't told anyone else about it."

"You hadn't told anyone else?" he asked in disbelief.

She blushed at the admission. "Uh…no."

"But why? I mean, why did you tell me?"

"Well, first, you asked and second, I don't know…it sounded like you were honestly interested. I thought that gymnastics was part of my past. That since I hadn't been recruited out of high school everything had been a waste. And I hated admitting that to myself. Let alone to anyone else."

"But you told me."

Lexi nodded. "I told you."

"Because you trusted me," he said, his voice lowering.

"That's right."

"And I ruined it," he said looking away from her. She could tell he was in pain about what had happened. He looked just as hurt now admitting that he had hurt her as he had nearly a year earlier. It was almost too much to bear. Why was he so damn sexy and caring? Why couldn't she see past that? Why couldn't she stay angry at him for playing her for a fool?

Finally, he met her gaze. "Let me make it up to you," he said scooting closer so their knees were almost touching.

"Jack," she said in warning, but she didn't move away.

"I *need* to make it up to you. I told you I'd never lie to you again, but that's just the beginning. That's not enough."

Lexi just stared at him. She didn't know what he had in mind, but she knew that she wouldn't…couldn't stop him…whatever it was. The feeling was exhilarating.

"You deserve more than that," Jack said reaching out and caressing her cheek with the back of his hand. It was the first time he had touched her. His hand turned and cupped her cheek affectionately, lifting her face up to his. His hands were warm and she could feel the calluses from working for his dad. Yet, the touch was kind and gentle. There was so much affection in that gesture she thought she might break right then and there. "Will you let me prove that to you?" he asked his piercing blue eyes set solely on her.

She couldn't believe what she was doing. His lips were only inches away from her. She was putty in his hands. The instant he had touched her, she was lost. Her eyes were closing of their own accord, and she could feel her head tilt back to reach him. She was craving his sweet kiss. Her conscience told her to run from him, but she just couldn't. Despite the fact that she had promised herself that all they were going to do was talk, she didn't pull away from him. Everything about the situation was wrong, and she knew it. But it felt so right to be with him, and she couldn't seem to process anything else.

"You made me promise to keep my hands to myself," Jack whispered, his breath hot on her lips. She could feel her body tense in anticipation. "Do you want me to stop?"

Lexi whimpered as his hand moved to the nape of her neck pushing up into her dark brown curls. She needed to tell him to stop. Her mind needed to clear, and not concentrate on the chills she found running down her spine at his touch. But her voice wasn't working. She didn't really want him to stop, and the effort of conjuring up those words seemed to be too much.

"Lex, look at me." Her eyes fluttered open and she stared dreamily up at him. She wet her lips as she waited for him to continue. "I want to make it up to you, but I don't want to cross a line. You'll tell me if I am?"

Lexi thought about it for a second. She was having a hard time thinking when he was so close to her; his crystal clear baby blues seemingly staring straight through her. To be honest, she wasn't sure how he was even controlling himself. Just a slight touch from him had sent her body into overdrive. Her pulse was racing, and her nipples were erect.

But could she let herself do this? Guilt creased her features for a brief second before he kissed her worries away. He had never kissed her like this before. The passion they had both been feeling overflowed as he parted her lips. His tongue licked across her bottom lip before moving in and meeting her tongue. She moaned as the kiss intensified. He pulled her into his lap and pressed their bodies firmly together, letting his hand rest on the inside of her bare thigh.

Almost as soon as the kiss began it ended. Lexi ended up straddled on top of him in her grey mini skirt. She could feel the course material of his jeans against her inner thighs, and felt his erection pressed against her barely-there, red, lace thong. She was panting as she stared at him from her precarious position.

"That didn't cross the line?" Jack asked pressing one more kiss on her lips. She shook her head. Words still wouldn't come. She just wanted more. Her eyes moved from his eyes eagerly back to his lips. She leaned in and gave him another, more demanding kiss. She could feel him smiling against her mouth.

"I'll take that as a no." Picking her up, he effortlessly flipped her over on her back so that he was situated on top of her. She adjusted her position so that her head rested comfortably on a pillow. This did nothing for her skirt which rode up to the very tops of thighs as she moved.

He seemed to ignore this fact as his hands crawled up her shirt and cupped her breasts through the red lace bra she had put on before coming over. His head moved towards her skin as he pulled down the bra, and grasped her nipple between his lips. She gasped at his forwardness, but didn't disapprove. Actually, whatever he was doing with his mouth was working. Groaning, she wiggled her hips in appreciation. While his tongue began working on her other breast, his hand snaked underneath and unclasped the bra.

"And this," he said flicking his tongue across her hard nipple, "isn't crossing the line?" Her eyes snapped shut, back arching at the delicious feel of him. All thoughts of stopping had completely left her. She had come this far. She wasn't sure if she could stop him even if she wanted to. And she didn't want to.

"I don't think you'll need this," he said pulling her shirt over her head, and tossing it along with her bra to the floor.

She couldn't believe herself. Here she was, all but nude, on Jack's bed. Her practically see-through thong hardly covered anything, and her skirt seemed to be on just for show. It wasn't really preventing anything.

"You know I think you look more beautiful now than I've ever seen you," Jack said moving to kiss her on the lips. She breathed him in. Everything about him turned her on. The way he had so easily riled her up; the way his lips and tongue had turned her to jell-o. She couldn't imagine what it would be like if he went farther. Her body liked that thought, and she could feel her thong begin to soak through. Really was there a point for her having it on? She couldn't remember.

She hadn't even realized that her hands were digging into his back until he pulled back to strip off his shirt. Her gaze fell on the perfectly toned abdomen muscles. Instinct made her reach out and trail her fingers down his six-pack enjoying the feel of each solid muscle. He groaned as her hand reached his waistline. She ran her thumb underneath the hem of his jeans across the sensitive portion of skin.

Jack reached out and laced his hands in hers, then forced her back against the bed roughly pushing her hands above her head. "We'll get there later," he said, teasingly pushing his erection against her as he bent forward and kissed her ear. An even louder gasp escaped her lips. "This is about you. Me making things up to you."

She closed her eyes again and lost herself in the feel of his hands running down her arms, across her breasts, along the line of her stomach, catching the curve of her buttocks, and then teasing her thighs with his fingertips. She let loose a moan as he unexpectedly nipped at the inside of her right leg, spreading it open wide.

"Jack," she moaned as his mouth moved up her left thigh successfully spread-eagling her legs in front of his face.

"Yes, dear?" he asked his finger trailing the line of her thong.

"Oh, Jack," she gasped feeling his finger get replaced by his tongue.

"Mmm hmm?" he asked his breath hot against her lace thong only increasing the wetness across the flimsy material. "Do you want me to keep going?"

She wasn't sure if she could handle this any longer. God, she wanted him so bad. She had wanted him to do this for a year. The sexual build-up was killing her. She knew her body was already so close to release that if he so much as laid one finger in her she would be gone.

"Lex," he moaned pressing his thumb gently against her clit.

"Yeah...yes...um...yes?" she asked, her body tightening at the feel of the pressure on such a sensitive area, even through her thong.

"You didn't answer," he said relieving the pressure briefly. "Do you want me to keep going?"

She wanted to say no, to push him away and run out of the house. Or at least, she knew that's what she should want, but she didn't. She wanted him to keep going and not to stop until she was spent. Lexi found herself nodding. Then realizing he couldn't see her with his face buried in her crotch, she finally uttered, "Yes."

"Yes?"

"Yes, I want you to keep going."

"You're sure?"

"God, please, touch me."

Ever so slowly, he hooked his finger under the thong and began to massage her clit in a circular fashion. When she began to buck her hips against the immense amount of pressure, he removed her skirt and thong, and threw them to the floor. As soon as they left his hand, he dove down and began flicking his tongue against her clit in short, quick, back-and-forth motions. Her legs began to shake from the exertion of holding them open, and allowing him to have his way with her. Her body began to overflow with pleasure as she got closer to climax. He rotated between licking and sucking motions enjoying the taste of her all over his mouth. His fingers appeared and slid between her lips opening her up fully to him. She pushed her hips up eager to meet his fingers that were positioned over her moist opening.

Instead of fingering her like she so desired, he ran his fingers across the wet sides of her lips hitting each sensitive nerve perfectly. Her back arched and she let loose a low moan, feeling her body reaching all new heights. He was drawing out her pleasure, knowing that each touch was sending her farther and farther over the edge. He was increasing her bliss by prolonging the time until her climax, waiting until he allowed her to orgasm. When he knew she couldn't take it any longer, he inserted two of his fingers directly into her. He felt her instantly clench around him, causing his erection to harden even further in his jeans.

Lexi began laboriously panting as she felt her climax take over her body. Jack's fingers were working in a come-hither motion on the inside of her sending her over the edge. She moaned even louder, only just resisting the urge to scream in delight.

Her legs were shaking convulsively by now as he removed his fingers and swiped at his mouth. "I've wanted to do that for so long," he said leaning forward and kissing her. "And damn, do you taste good."

She blushed at his words. Even after what had just happened, sexual references still made her blush. This made her giggle. She felt euphoric.

"Damn, Lex, you look cute like that." He assessed her naked form. "You should always be naked around me."

She blushed even deeper. "Come here," she commanded snaking her arms around his neck and pulling him in for another kiss. "I want you," she moaned against his lips.

"You want me?"

"Inside of me. Now."

She didn't have to say it twice. He quickly undid his belt and tugged his jeans to the ground. Lexi smiled sweetly at his blue boxers covered with tiny yellow fish. He tore those off as well and repositioned himself over her. It was his turn to pant while his erection hovered only inches above her soaking wet opening.

His crystal clear blue eyes bored into her as he got ready to meet her. "Are you sure, Lex?" She could tell it was taking every ounce of self-control he had not to just shove himself right inside of her, taking her for his own. Every inch – yes, *every* inch – was hard-pressed and ready to go.

But was she sure? She hadn't been sure the whole time. In fact, the only thing she had been sure of was having the most amazing orgasm she could ever imagine. She wanted him inside of her, but something was nagging at her. If she went ahead and slept with him right then and there, like her body was begging her to do, there would be no going back. Maybe if they stopped where they were, she would be able to recover from what happened, but not after sex. Sex was final.

"Lex, you're killing me here. I want you. I just need to know if you are sure this is what you want."

She sighed heavily, her hands coming to cover her face. "Oh Jack, it's what I want." He sighed happily, and moved himself so that the tip just barely touched her. He then shifted his hips to rub it up against her gently. She moaned at the feel of him, and then pushed herself away. "But I can't," she whispered sitting up against the headboard.

She watched his face fall as he realized that she wasn't going to go through with it. But he wasn't going to pressure her. If she said no, then he was going to be okay with that.

He rolled over to the other side of the bed and lay back against the sheets. "I just want to make everything up to you. If you don't want to go further, that's okay," he finally said after his breath began to even out.

Lexi hopped off the bed and quickly began throwing on clothes. "Actually, I don't think you should make it up to me."

"What?" he asked, concern written on his face.

"Jack, I have a boyfriend. I can't believe I just did that." Guilt washed over her.

"But you said it was okay."

"I know I did. You didn't do anything wrong. You asked me if it was okay. I was wrong for not stopping you."

"No, Lex, you weren't wrong," he said joining her on the carpet and grabbing her hands in his.

"I was wrong. I can't be around you, Jack."

"This is something you want though."

"Not while I'm with someone else," she said, lifting her face to meet his. Tears were welling in her eyes and she quickly wiped them away. She was so ashamed of herself. "I just have to go."

"Lexi, please, don't run out like this," he said tugging on his boxers and jeans.

"I can't be around you," she yelled, hating herself for raising her voice when he had done nothing wrong. She just wanted to crawl into a hole. She felt like such a creep. How could she go on? How could she live with herself? She had been so lost in the moment – in him – that she couldn't even think straight. She couldn't process that she was ruining her life by being there with him, by letting him touch and kiss her like that. No matter how wonderful it had been, the guilt she was feeling was so much worse.

"Don't beat yourself up about this," he whispered to her as she threw her purse onto her shoulder and moved towards the bedroom door. "I don't want you walking out the door and never talking to me again."

"Jack, what I feel for you…I can't feel like this when I have someone else. I'm not supposed to be this person. I'm not supposed to do these things. You have to understand. You're too much for me."

"I can't understand that. We're right for each other."

"But not right now," she said, hollowly repeating his own words. Her brown eyes glanced up and met his. "Isn't that right?"

"No," he said reaching out for her. "Right now is right." She backed away not wanting to be touched by anyone, especially not him. All she needed was a scalding shower and a few nights of repentance. Thank God, Spencer wouldn't be back for a couple days. Maybe by then he wouldn't notice.

"No, Jack," she murmured shaking her head. "I'm sorry. I can't be around you."

"Lex, come on."

"No," she stated firmly. "I'll miss you." Her words came out weak.

"I don't want to miss you again. I want to see you more. I want us to hang out. God, I want us to finish our movie."

She shook her head adamantly. "I shouldn't have come over. I knew this was going to happen. I'm such an idiot. I can't resist you. Good-bye," she said reaching out and giving him a fleeting kiss before yanking the door and rushing out of the room.

When she reached her car, she let the tears flow. She pulled out of his driveway nearly blinded by tears.

>How had she thought that this could be some innocent night?
>How could she lie to herself about what she was doing?

7

PRESENT

The coffee shop Bekah chose for them to finally have their conversation in was delightful. In some ways, it reminded her so much of the place where she and Jack had first met. It wasn't well-lit, and there were so many people milling around that it seemed damn near impossible that they were going to find a table. On the other hand, the establishment was huge. Unlike chain and small town coffee shops, this place had three stories and took up an entire corner of a building. Lexi never bought coffee at places like this. For her, it lost the cozy atmosphere with the size.

Meandering through the densely populated shop, they went on a search for an unoccupied table. Lexi veered away from Bekah hoping to spot an available table in the opposite direction.

Jack had dropped her off outside the coffee shop after brunch. He had complained the whole way back about having to wear a tie, and had ditched her as soon as they arrived. He claimed he would be gone only as long as it took for him to change. She was pretty pissed that he had left. After all, he was the whole reason for this stupid conversation.

She didn't know if it made it easier or harder knowing that Jack wouldn't be hearing everything she said. On the one hand, she would be able to speak more freely about their relationship, because she wouldn't feel constrained by his memories. But at the same time, she might be more convincing if Jack was there to back her up.

"Lexi?" a voice called out to her.

She turned in a half-circle hoping to find Bekah finally seated at a booth. She just wanted to get this over with. But Bekah was nowhere to be found. She heard her name called again, and this time she recognized the direction of the voice. Turning slowly, she stopped and gawked at the person who had called out to her.

"Oh my God! Krista is that you?" Lexi asked rushing to hug the petite girl who had once been her gymnastics captain in college. "I hardly recognized you."

"Yeah, I get that a lot," she peeped standing to accept the embrace.

"Your hair…it's all one color…brown," Lexi exclaimed in awe. "And who would have guessed anyone would ever find you in a business suit!"

"Not in a million years," she said adjusting her silky v-neck blouse to reveal a bit more cleavage.

"I thought you were in Vegas. When did you move back to Atlanta?" Lexi asked enthusiastically. Krista giggled. The girl actually giggled holding out her left hand to reveal a huge diamond surrounded by four others on a white gold band. "Oh wow, that's beautiful." Lexi stared transfixed at her ring. The rock was enormous. Lexi didn't believe anyone actually wore diamonds that large out and about, but Krista always liked to catch people by surprise.

"I got married last winter. My husband's company has an Atlanta branch. He knew how much I loved it out here so he relocated. I'm working with an interior design company. It's kind of dull but the hours are flexible. If they weren't, I'd quit that shit and go fulltime at the gym. We've got some amazingly talented girls. Last year, we had one make it almost all the way through the Olympic trials," she explained.

"That's amazing!" Lexi exclaimed truly happy for her friend.

"So, what are you doing here, missy? I'd heard through the grapevine that you were in fucking New York City," Krista said her green eyes glimmering.

"Yeah, I am. I'm just here visiting a friend." Lexi paused remembering that Krista and Jack knew each other. "Actually, I'm visiting Jack. Uh…Jack Howard."

"Holy shit! Jack fucking Howard. Now that's a name I haven't heard in awhile. I thought you two would be married by now. Run off together or something," Krista noted.

Lexi blushed. "Um…no."

"Damn. You always seemed like a perfect pair to me," Krista told her. She watched as Lexi's complexion colored even further. "So where is he?" she asked her head swiveling hoping to catch a glimpse of him. "He's so delicious. I'd love to see him again."

Lexi laughed remembering why she had always liked Krista. She was so straight-forward and vulgar. It was refreshing. "He actually just dropped me off. I'm here with his…" Lexi trailed off realizing that she had been standing here for awhile and had completely lost Bekah.

"With his what?" Krista asked curiously.

"Uh…hold on." Lexi pivoted trying to look through the crowd, but she was too short. She couldn't see anyone.

"Who are we looking for?" Krista asked scanning the throng of people.

"There you are. I've been looking everywhere for you," Bekah stated calmly as she walked towards them from the opposite direction of where they had been searching.

"Yeah. Sorry," Lexi stated awkwardly turning to face her. "I just ran into a friend."

"What a coincidence," Bekah said turning to face Krista. "Bekah Bridges." She extended her hand formally.

Krista took it, but glanced at Lexi conspiratorially. "Krista Hammond."

"Pleased to meet you," Bekah replied properly. "Wait. Hammond?" she asked eyeing her appearance. Krista nodded, one eyebrow arched perfectly. "Any connection to Hammond, Stern, & Birch?"

Krista's eyes narrowed. "That depends," she muttered. Krista, always blunt, asked her, "Who the hell are you?"

"Beg your pardon?"

Lexi stepped in. "Krista, this is Jack's girlfriend. That's what I was going to tell you. I'm here with his girlfriend."

Krista stared blankly from Lexi to Bekah and back. "*You're* dating Jack?" she asked Bekah. "Jack Howard?"

"That's right."

"Not Lexi?" Krista demanded.

Lexi wanted to cover her face with her hands. This was not going to help anything.

"Well, no," Bekah said confusion crossing her face.

"I already told you Jack and I aren't together," she reminded Krista.

"I'm sorry. How do you know a Hammond?" Bekah snootily asked Lexi before turning to Krista, "And how do you know Jack?"

"I used to fuck one of Jack's friends," Krista said nonchalantly at the same time as Lexi announced, "We were on the gymnastics team together."

The look Bekah shot Krista was a mixture of disdain and confusion. Lexi figured she wasn't used to being around such crudeness especially not from someone who had a *name* she recognized. This just reminded Lexi why she couldn't stand being around Country Club types.

Bekah shook her head letting her golden blonde hair swish around her face. A bright smile appeared out of nowhere. "Well, it is so nice to meet another one of Jack's friends," Bekah said adapting to the situation. "Perhaps we could get together sometime," she offered. "You know coffee or lunch. Whatever works best for you."

Krista glanced at Lexi. "Yeah, maybe." Lexi could read her expression clear as day. *No chance in hell.*

"So, just out of curiosity, are you in any way related to Matt Hammond?" Bekah nosily asked.

"Yeah, we got married last winter," Krista told her showing off her massive ring.

"Ahh," she said admiring the crystal clear cut. "Well, this is a small world, isn't it? I've known Matt since childhood. He actually used to be a pretty good friend of my brother's even though he spent the majority of his time in Las Vegas. I'd heard he had just gotten married and was in town running his daddy's company. My apologies that I couldn't attend the wedding." Bekah smiled sweetly. "Will you tell him that I said hello and that he needs to visit."

Krista had one eyebrow arched. "Sure thing," Krista said diplomatically. "Hey, Lexi, I've really got to be going. It was great seeing you. If you can, you should stop by the gym," Krista said wrapping her in a hug. Just as she got close, she whispered in her ear, "How is Jack with her?" Lexi giggled finding it hard to believe herself. Krista slipped her a business card, grabbed her brown paper cup, and made her way towards the door.

"Well, that was interesting," Bekah said rubbing her finger around her pearl earring.

"Yeah, I guess," Lexi said standing awkwardly now that the comfort of Krista's presence had dissipated.

Bekah turned to face her. "I heard what she said you know."

Lexi stared at her uncomfortably. She wasn't sure which part Bekah was referring to, but with her luck it had to be the part about her and Jack. "Uh...what?"

"That she figured you and Jack would be married," she stated simply.

"Uh huh." Lexi wasn't sure what Bekah wanted her to say. She hadn't seen Krista in years, and after all, Jack was the reason that she knew Krista in the first place.

"I just want you to know that I don't think any less of you."

Lexi gawked at her. "Um, what?"

"I mean, that girl was so vulgar. I have no idea how Matt... you know what? Just never mind. Let's not go down that road," she said running her French manicured finger nails through her pin-straight hair. "I just want us to be open and honest with each other. I heard what she said about you and Jack and it made me a little uncomfortable."

Lexi could tell Bekah was waiting for her to say something, but she didn't know what she was supposed to say. So Bekah had eavesdropped on their conversation? Lexi didn't give a shit. She had told Krista that they weren't together. She and Jack had never been together *together*, in fact.

"Well, now that that's out of the way," Bekah chirped. "I found us a table."

Lexi had no idea what to think of this girl. She was all over the charts. She wanted to be completely honest one minute, and then her best friend the next. Lexi wasn't sure if she could handle this anymore.

Lexi plopped down in the booth. She twirled her hair around her finger several times before shoving it carelessly behind her ear.

Bekah faced Lexi. "I think we got off on the wrong foot."

Lexi forced a smile. "Why do you say that?" Lexi could have given a million reasons why she could never...would never like this girl. She still wanted to hear what Bekah thought on the subject.

"It's just...we were supposed to get this over with in the morning, and then I half-dragged you to meet my family. I just don't want those things to cloud your view of me," Bekah said twirling her earring again.

"Oh...um, ok," Lexi said noncommittally. Sure the Country Club experience made being around her more difficult. However much that bothered her, nothing bothered her more than just the plain fact that she was dating Jack. This girl, who seemingly had nothing in common with Jack, this girl, who he hadn't even wanted to date to begin with, this girl, who was practically forcing him to propose to her so she wouldn't be cut off from daddy's money, was who he had picked over her. *Somehow*, she just didn't think their friendship could recover from that.

"Well, either way, I suspect you know why Jack asked you here," Bekah said smiling sweetly.

Lexi fixed her with a blank stare. Was this girl serious?

"But I just...I really don't want this to be awkward, you know?"

Lexi didn't know. She already thought this was awkward enough.

"So, I thought we could just get to know each other a little bit. I mean, I know I wouldn't confess...or tell a perfect stranger about my past, especially not my love life."

"I have a hard time talking to anyone about my love life," Bekah said easily blushing at the statement.

"Uh huh," Lexi finally added in.

"It's just that I make a good judge of character. Jack obviously liked you at some point." Lexi couldn't even form words for *that* statement. "Ramsey seems to know and like you. Though, he isn't exactly the best judge of character...or the best character, but regardless. I mean not to mention, you put up with Jennifer for at least a year, and nothing short of a miracle can make a person go through that."

Lexi's mouth dropped. "You don't like Jennifer?"

Bekah's crinkled her little nose. "She's a little much for my tastes."

"But I thought Ramsey said you were friends."

"Friends is such a loose term. Our parents are friends so she was always…around," Bekah said shrugging her shoulders. "What I'm saying is that I know nothing about you."

Lexi hated how sincere Bekah was being. She was supposed to hate the girl. She was supposed to think she was an annoying Country Clubber like everyone else, and go home with a semblance of closure. "Yeah, I don't really know anything about you either," Lexi admitted.

"Right. Well then, tell me about yourself, Lexi," she said immediately returning to her diplomatic demeanor. Lexi hadn't exactly been prepared for the shift. "You don't mind me calling you Lexi, do you?" Bekah asked politely, her smile strained at the edges.

Lexi returned her fake smile. "That's my name."

"Oh, of course. I didn't know. I thought, perhaps, it was a nickname of some sort. I've never met a Lexi before."

"Well, it's sort of a nickname. Birth certificate says Alexa. I never much felt like an Alexa though, if you know what I mean," Lexi said trying to fall back into Bekah's more personable character.

Something about her statement must have worked, because this time Bekah's smile was sincere. "Yes, I think I do. I've never felt much like a Rebekah. Now, please, tell me about yourself. Jack has not said a word about you besides that you went to college together and as soon as you graduated you zipped right off to New York City. Of course, I know some other things," she said her eyes shining mischievously. "But as a whole, he has left you a complete mystery to me. And I do love solving mysteries," she commented folding her arms across one another at the table.

Lexi didn't even know where to begin. She knew that Jack hadn't told Bekah about her in the beginning, but he hadn't told her that Bekah knew *nothing* about her. How awkward! He hadn't even bothered to prep Bekah with the basics about their um…relationship even after Kate had run her mouth. So, thus far, Bekah had only heard terrible things about her. Great!

"Um…well, what do you want to know?"

"Just, whatever you want. It's up to you. I can tell you a little about myself if you like." Lexi just stared at her. Bekah, taking that as an affirmative, said, "I graduated *summa* from Duke with degrees in business and psychology. Let's see. What else? I currently work for my father as a Senior Vice President of Bridges Enterprise. He wanted Ramsey to run the business, but well…Ramsey always has his own ideas about things. I'm sure there's more, but I'd really like to know about you."

"Oh, well, I'm at NYU Law, about to start my third year. I worked all summer at a criminal law firm in the city. Anyway, that's really about it," she said.

"I'll be the one to judge that," Bekah stated. Lexi smiled weakly. "Did you want to go into criminal law or did you have something else in mind?"

"Oh, I'm really not sure," she told her honestly. "I've been doing a good deal of alternative dispute resolution cases in class. You know mediation, arbitration, and negotiations." Bekah nodded along even though Lexi wasn't sure she knew what she was talking about. Though if she had been raised in a Bridges household, then maybe she did. "But a part of me wants to go into a big corporate firm working seventy hours a week making a ridiculous amount of money. I don't know why. It sounds awful, but once I do that, I really think I could do anything."

"Hmm…interesting. I would have pinned you more as environmental law or public interest work."

Lexi laughed heartily. "Um…no. It's not that I don't care about those things. I just couldn't see me concentrating in anything like that."

"Well, if that's what you're into," Bekah said with a shrug. "Oh…hold on. There he is." Bekah waved at a tall, lanky, disheveled looking man who immediately veered towards them.

"Rebekah," he said as she hopped out of her chair. He gathered her up in a hug. "You look fantastic. You're not in here enough. You need more coffee for that stressful job of yours."

"You know perfectly well that it's not stressful. And anyway, I don't really drink coffee, Connor," she reminded him.

Connor was over six-feet tall with wiry brown hair and dull brown eyes. He'd obviously had acne problems when he had been younger. His nose was a bit too large, but it kind of fit him in a strange sort of way. He wore brown corduroy pants with a faded green coffee-stained, deeply wrinkled button-up, and tweed vest. This was not someone that Lexi would have ever in a million years pictured Bekah knowing let alone hanging out with.

"Oh, I'm so rude," Bekah said tearing her eyes from Connor. "This is Jack's uh…friend, Lexi. Lexi, this is Connor. He owns the coffee shop."

Lexi was able to put the pieces together. Bekah seemed to only know people who were important enough for her. If this guy owned the shop, then he must be rolling in money, even if his appearance didn't give that away. "Nice to meet you."

Connor took their orders and let them know that the drinks were on the house. As soon as he left, Bekah got right back to business. "So, I don't really know where to begin with you, to be honest." Lexi didn't know what that meant. "I had a plan when I talked to Danielle and Kate."

Lexi rolled her eyes and then let them wander around the shop. She had completely tuned out what Bekah was saying. It's not like she really wanted to talk about this. She just wanted to get things out of the way.

"Did you hear me?" Bekah asked, touching Lexi's arm lightly.

"Oh, I'm sorry. I spaced out."

"I just asked how many serious boyfriends have you had?"

"Well, two since high school." Hearing the words out loud really made Lexi want to crawl into a hole. She hadn't thought about the fact that she hadn't had a serious boyfriend in so long. Sure, she had dated, and she had been in strictly uh…sexual relationships, but she didn't count those. So her number still stood at two. Two guys in six years. Pathetic.

"So one other than Jack?" Bekah asked lacing her fingers together.

Lexi swiftly glanced up trying to read Bekah's expression. Was this girl clueless? "Um…no. Jack and I were never together."

Bekah narrowed her eyes. "What are you talking about?"

"You already met Jack's two serious girlfriends: Danielle and Kate."

"Right," she said leaning forward in her chair. "But ya'll *were* together. I mean I talked to Kate."

Lexi blushed at the accusations that were clear in her tone. "I wouldn't believe *everything* Kate told you."

Bekah twirled her earring contemplating what Lexi had just told her. "I realize Kate is probably biased to a degree. But she said that ya'll were together so I just took her word for that. I'm sorry."

"I'm not sure why you're sorry. You claim to know nothing about me. And anyway, it's an easy thing to misconstrue. You heard the conversation I had with Krista. I haven't seen her in years, and she thought Jack and I were together. But it simply isn't the case."

Connor reappeared with their drinks. "Okay. So you and Jack weren't together."

"Nope."

"I guess that clears up why he didn't tell me about you," she said under her breath. Lexi decided to just pretend like she was deaf. "So, how did ya'll meet?"

Lexi desperately shoved her hair behind her ears. She hadn't thought that a simple question could seem so difficult…so terrifying. So much of what she and Jack had gone through had been covered up and hidden for so long. The thought of peeling back the layers and revealing it to someone else constricted her. She reached out for her coffee, realizing for the umpteenth time that morning that she was desperate for the stuff…maybe even something stronger.

"Sorry," Lexi said smiling weakly. "I haven't really talked about Jack to anyone in a long time. Our uh…situation wasn't exactly healthy, to put it nicely."

"What do you mean by that?" Bekah asked sipping on her chai tea.

"The reason we were never together was because every time we tried, things or uh…people," she said averting her eyes, "just kept getting in our way. For the longest time, I thought that Jack and I really were going to end up together." She could feel her skin warming with embarrassment at the statement. "But some shit went down between us, and we just stopped talking. Pretty much end of story. I'm not sure what else you want to know," Lexi stated bitterly.

Lexi could feel Bekah's piercing gaze evaluating her. It wasn't a comfortable look, and the silence that followed was even worse. "I get that ya'll aren't together and haven't been for quite some time. I mean, I'd at least surmised that much," she said giggling. "Jack and I have been together for a year and a half, and he's never mentioned you before."

"Not that he would," Lexi said under her breath.

If Lexi had thought the last look she had received from Bekah was uncomfortable, it had nothing on the look she was giving her after that comment. "Excuse me?"

Should she tell her? Yes. She had come down to Atlanta to talk to this girl, she might as well start from the beginning and with the truth for once. Slowly, pulling back the first layer of their relationship, Lexi began, "You asked how we first met. We met at a coffee shop, similar to this one actually, where he worked for some time in college. We were together constantly for more than a month before I found out he had a girlfriend. And Danielle *never* found out about me," Lexi said bluntly. Bekah's jaw dropped slightly. Whatever she had been expecting, that wasn't it. Not even close. "So when you say that you had never heard about me, I wouldn't take it for granted that was because we hadn't spoken."

Lexi hated admitting all of that stuff, but the girl had asked for the truth. She might as well be frank with her. Jack had always been best at lying. Some people were good at sports. Some people were good at school. Some people were good at working. While some people were good at commitment, Jack was good at *avoiding* commitment.

"So, you're saying that ya'll have spoken or...done more than speak since we've been together?" Bekah asked, getting choked up at the thought.

"Uh...no," Lexi said awkwardly. She hadn't meant to imply that. "I haven't spoken with Jack since he left New York almost two years ago. Well, up until he called me about you."

"What kind of point *were* you making?" Bekah asked getting riled up.

Lexi pushed her hair behind her ears before continuing. "I wasn't making a point about *your* relationship. You wanted to know about the type of relationship I had with Jack. So, I was telling you. It was one full of lies."

"Lies?" Bekah's blue eyes were glimmering with wonder. Lexi was pretty certain that her interviews with Danielle and Kate had been exceedingly dull compared to the dirt Lexi was sending her way. Then again, Danielle and Kate had had perfectly normal...ish...relationships with Jack. They had flirted, dated, and broken up like normal couples. They had had normal emotional responses to situations, and had gone through relatively normal cycles of development. Nothing about Jack and Lexi had ever been *normal*.

"He lied to me about Danielle. Then, swore he would never lie to me again. And to this day, I don't think he has," Lexi said wistfully.

"But I thought you said your relationship was full of lies."

This time Lexi did look Bekah directly into her naively, innocent eyes to answer her, "It was. We just lied to everyone else."

Lexi was pretty sure that after that last statement, she would never meet the personable Bekah again. The two stared stonily at each other for a few moments before breaking eye contact and uneasily sipping on their beverages.

Finally, Bekah broke the silence. "So, what happened next?"

"Uh…when?" Lexi asked surprised that the girl was even still talking to her. She certainly wouldn't be happy with someone if she had just heard that.

"After he lied to you about Danielle."

"I refused to talk to him again for awhile…almost a year. But after he broke up with Danielle, he came looking for me, hoping that I would forgive him. And I didn't at first."

Bekah nodded. "He'd lied to you. That must have been hard. He's never done that to me."

Lexi blushed not really wanting to correct her. She had been in town less than a day and already Jack had lied to Bekah because of her. Wow, things weren't that different. "It's just this time around I had a boyfriend. When I told Jack about him, he didn't care. He pretty much persuaded me to come to his house and seduced me." Lexi heard the faint gasp that escaped Bekah's mouth, but she continued on. "I broke up with my boyfriend shortly after that. Mostly out of guilt."

"But you said you and Jack weren't together?" Bekah asked her stony gaze still not wavering. Lexi could tell she was getting more and more reserved and withdrawn. She wasn't sure how much she should actually reveal, and Bekah looked to be having the same idea.

"No. We weren't. I just couldn't talk to him after that. I had really strong feelings for Jack, and they scared me. Made me do things that I normally wouldn't. Made me act in ways that I…I couldn't control." Lexi glanced up at Bekah to see her nodding along.

"I know what you mean," Bekah whispered.

Lexi hardly believed her. Bekah was another Danielle…another Kate. Everything they had was normal and expected. There was no way that she could have even a semblance of understanding as to what she had gone through. "The lying really got to me. I was terrible at it. Jack wasn't." Lexi knew she was reminding her about the lying just to be cruel. She wanted Bekah to ask Jack questions about it. She wanted to make her uncomfortable. She just couldn't stand the idea of sharing a feeling with this girl. It felt wrong. "He didn't understand why I wasn't okay with lying to my boyfriend, when he thought we were so perfect for each other. When he thought that there would never be another girl as amazing as me," Lexi added spitefully.

Bekah's blue eyes met Lexi's, and the understanding that had been there only seconds before was replaced by the deep loathing Lexi had seen the last time lying had been brought up.

"Well, if it isn't my two favorite girls," Jack said coming up to them seemingly out of nowhere. It was obvious in his absence that things hadn't gone well. The tension in the atmosphere could be cut with a dull butter knife. Bekah looked pissed and Lexi would rather be anywhere else right then. She always had a strange effect on people, but Jack hadn't considered what kind of toll that would take on Bekah.

Bekah glared up at him as the last words left his tongue. Lexi just smiled weakly, not entirely sure how to take that statement.

"Uh…I brought your suitcase," he told Lexi offhandedly, attempting to make conversation. "I thought we could just go to Bekah's before the party tonight, and you could change there. Her place is right around the corner."

Lexi arched one eyebrow in disbelief. He actually believed that she was going to go to this party? After the disastrous conversation with Bekah and the embarrassing confrontation with Ramsey, there was no way she ever wanted to hang out with these two again. "Oh, well I'm not going."

Jack opened his mouth to protest, but Bekah got there first. "What do you mean you're not going? You already said that you would go."

"No, I never actually said that. Everything was just kind of decided for me," she reminded them. The events of that afternoon had transpired so quickly that Lexi hadn't even had time to decline the party invitation.

"But Ramsey assumes you'll be there," Bekah told her.

Lexi wasn't sure why Bekah was trying to get her to go to this thing. She obviously didn't like her, and that was just fine with Lexi. All Lexi really wanted right then was an extra-large New York-style pizza, sweatpants, and endless hours of super sappy chick flicks. "Well, he'll just have to get over it. I can't make it."

"What do you have to do?" Jack asked.

"Family stuff."

"Aren't you spending the rest of the week with them?" he continued to probe her.

"Well…yeah."

"Then you can come out for one night with us," Bekah told her, standing and possessively entwining her fingers with Jack's.

Lexi thought she might vomit at the sight. Her stomach was rolling and she didn't like it. She just needed to get away. She needed to get away right now.

Something was up with Bekah, and Lexi knew it. This girl couldn't be everything she acted like she was. Her emotions were all over the charts. She took every statement as if it were a personal blow against her. And Lexi was just trying to be honest! Well, so maybe she was telling the truth a little too blunt, because this girl got under her skin. But who cares?

As soon as she had met Bekah, Lexi knew that this *couldn't* be the girl that Jack was going to marry. He could not be with her. The sweet and innocent act only went skin deep, and Jack could do better. He had dated *her* after all…well, kind of.

With all these thoughts rolling around in her head, Lexi knew that the best thing for her would be to get away as soon as possible. She didn't want to do anything to sabotage their relationship if this was what he really wanted. If Jack had wanted Lexi, then he would have tried to make things work between them. But he hadn't. And Lexi had to deal with that fact. She had to deal with knowing that he hadn't chosen her. He didn't want her.

It hurt. Damn, did it hurt! But she couldn't do anything to change it.

But the other side – the less logical side – kept wondering why, if Jack did want Bekah, did he almost kiss Lexi last night? Why did he come home a day early from his trip to see her, and not tell Bekah about it?

That was the side that agreed to go to Ramsey's party. The side that wanted to know if Jack still cared about her the way that she cared about him. If perhaps, Bekah was just the next best alternative.

8

MAY THREE YEARS EARLIER

Lexi stared wistfully out the backseat window across the changing terrain. The rolling hills eased into a flat expanse anticipating the coming ocean front. She could almost smell the distinct scent of salt mingled in the air. Decrepit signs, interspersed amongst the neon bulbs flashing from the street side, caught her eyes briefly before they locked onto the next tethered old business vying to compete with the beach community only twenty minutes away. Palm trees had started springing up about forty-five minutes back, and Lexi's desire to be beach-side, sprawled out with the sand between her toes, had grown exponentially since then.

"Babe, chill out. You're doing that thing with your hair again," Clark said snatching her hand from her face and clutching it in his.

Startled out of her daydreams, she glanced into Clark's soothing green eyes. He had on a green intramural soccer shirt which only intensified the gorgeous shade.

"Sorry," Lexi said biting her bottom lip and suggestively raising her eyebrows at him, feeling the all too familiar desire to kiss him creep through her.

He traced the palm of her hand with his thumb and gave it an affectionate squeeze. "We'll be there soon. I know you're anxious."

Lexi giggled looking at him coyly across her shoulder. "Oh yes, I'm very…anxious."

He smiled warmly back at her, but was interrupted from responding by Seth. "None of that lovey-dovey shit back there. We're not even putting you two in the same room. The walls are too thin for all that," Seth said laughing as both their faces turned to pouts.

"Whatever, Seth," Lexi said leaning forward across the center of the seat. She ignored Luke seated in the passenger seat ogling the cleavage bulging out of her low-cut halter top, and ruffled Seth's hair. "You can't honestly expect us to stay off of each other."

"I'm not expecting it. No. But you can do that shit during the day. There isn't enough space at night for you two to be in the same room." Lexi leaned forward farther giving Seth a decidedly better view of her rack. "And," he responded taking in the full view of her, "if you think that," he pointed at her breasts, "is going to change anything, you're wrong." Despite his comment, she could tell his breathing was getting shallow. Men!

Clark grabbed her waist in his hands and pulled her back towards him. He snaked an arm around her shoulders, drawing her into him, and kissed her passionately. "I think we'll make up for it. Don't you?" he asked nibbling on her bottom lip.

A small moan escaped her mouth, but she pulled back shortly afterwards. She didn't mind being flirtatious around their friends, however, she had to draw the line somewhere. Clark rarely liked where the line was drawn when it came to PDA. She let her gaze shift back out the window as they reached Seth's parents' beach house.

Seth's parents were celebrating their twenty-fifth wedding anniversary by cruising for seven blissful days in the Mediterranean. He had taken the liberty of securing…uh stealing a key to their new house from his younger sister, and invited as many of his friends to join him for the conveniently planned week before graduation. Many had turned down the invitation since it did fall so close to graduation, but eight had eventually agreed and were now in two cars driving towards their vacation destination.

Lexi had initially been concerned about the arrangement. Several people in attendance had lived with Jack at one point in time, and all of the people going knew him. But when Clark had excitedly invited her for his pre-graduation vacation, she hadn't been able to tell him why she felt unsure about going on a free week-long trip to the beach when her summer job hadn't started yet.

Clark. She smiled just thinking about him. They had met through Jack originally back in her freshman year. He hadn't known all the details of what had gone on between them at the time, but he had learned enough to put the pieces together. When Clark had stumbled across Lexi walking around the mall, he hadn't been able to stop himself from asking her out even knowing something had gone on with her and Jack. He unintentionally confessed that he had always thought she was way too good for Jack, and not even close to

Jack's type. Lexi hadn't been sure if she wanted to say yes to the offer. Clark was a friend of Jack's. Awkward. And even worse, he knew at least some of what they had gone through. Even more awkward.

Clark hadn't been offended by her lack of exuberance, but he had continued to pursue her promising her a casual evening out. Lexi had never thought about Clark in a romantic sense. She had always been clouded by her blind desire for Jack. Even as she accepted his invitation, she hadn't realized quite how handsome he was.

Their first date was nothing out of the ordinary. He had taken her to a dinner, not too expensive, but still nice. Afterwards, he took her to a local ice cream shop for dessert. She couldn't remember the last time she had had that much fun. Clark was easy going, yet attentive to her. He seemed to genuinely care what she was talking about, and what she was interested in. Something about him that night remained permanently etched into her memory. Clark just got her. They just clicked. It was strange, even then, for Lexi to feel like Clark understood something about her that, perhaps, even she didn't.

But she couldn't help seeing Jack in him that night. When she looked at Clark, she could remember another time when things had been this easy. Feeling uncomfortable at the prospect of being physical with Clark after having those improper thoughts, she left him with only a simple good night kiss. But after that night, Lexi couldn't deny that there was something about Clark she liked.

He kept calling and eventually, without even realizing it, they were a couple.

A few rather uncomfortable situations had occurred, in which, she was forced into civil environments with Jack. She usually extracted herself as quickly as possible, making whatever excuse came to mind. Recently, it had happened less frequently, and it thankfully made things easier between her and Clark.

Lexi's mind had returned to Jack when Clark had invited her on this trip. She hadn't even meant to ask about him. But somehow it had slipped out, and she had asked Clark the one pressing question she needed to base her decision on: Is Jack going to be there? She could handle hanging out with a bunch of people who knew that her and Jack had had…something at one point in time. But actually having him at the beach house for a whole week looking damn sexy would just kill her. She couldn't do it.

She had been able to hear the disappointment in Clark's voice over the phone. They had been dating for nearly nine months, and she still had to ask about Jack. Sighing uncomfortably, he had told her that he wasn't positive, but last he had heard from Seth, Jack would be out of town for his cousin's graduation ceremony in Savannah. That was all the confirmation she needed, and she had happily agreed to accompany them to the beach. Her tan was waning anyway.

Lexi popped open the door to the Lexus SUV as soon as Seth placed it in park and gingerly stretched out her aching muscles. She breathed in the cool beach air with a smile. Her head swiveled up to the massive beach house Seth's parents called home. The entire place looked modern and chic from the outside. She couldn't wait to see how the interior matched, but all she really cared about at that moment was the beach. She just wanted to sink her feet into the pure white sand and stare out across the Gulf of Mexico.

Clark came around from the other side of the car and kissed her cheek. Taking one last look at her, he said, "Go on." He nudged her towards a pathway leading directly to the beach. "I'll grab your bag."

Without a backwards glance, she rushed the gate blocking her way. Yanking it open, she dashed down the stone stairs, and around the corner. Her breath caught at the sight of the ocean looming ahead of her. Chucking her flip-flops to the side as she reached the threshold, she edged into the sand feeling the heated temperatures against her skin. Then she took off with a burst of energy, loving the overpowering feeling of release at the thought of being here, in this beautiful place, for an entire week.

Just before she reached the sand soaked through from the salty ocean water, she stopped dead in her tracks and stared dumbfounded in front of her. Maybe she was dreaming. Had she fallen asleep while she was in the car? Would she remember that she had been in the car if she was dreaming? Would *he* be here if she was dreaming? She didn't really have to answer that question. He had always been in her dreams, but the real question was whether or not she was dreaming about him right now. Suddenly terrified, she wondered if Clark would hear her say his name. Then realizing she couldn't be dreaming or else she wouldn't be thinking about this, she would be doing…other things. Her mouth opened as he turned towards her.

Had she said his name out loud? She didn't remember.

"Lex?" he asked obviously just as startled as she was. "What…? How…? I…uh…"

"Are you real?" she blurted without thinking.

A characteristic smirk appeared on his face, and she knew. He was real. Even her dreams didn't make him look this gorgeous. Every feature was vividly defined in the afternoon rays pouring over his body, and into his intensely blue orbs.

He took a step forward clearing the gap she had left between them. It had been a safe distance. Now, he was so close their bodies were nearly touching. Her breath caught as she raised her head to meet his intense stare. God, he looked amazing. Her foggy image of his perfect features faded so quickly when he was out of sight. Everything felt right as she stood in his presence, only inches separating them. He reached out placing one hand on her cheek, checking to see if she was, in fact, real. Lexi's heart raced at the gentle touch, her mind returning to a brilliant clarity.

Jack was here.

They both seemed to be in a trance as their looks never wavered. She felt his thumb stroke her cheek lovingly, but she couldn't break away from him. She couldn't remember the last time he had touched her…on purpose. Then, the image of her lying naked on his bed filled her mind, and she blushed deeply. He seemed amused by this and stepped closer to her. They both sank an inch or so into the sand as he shifted causing her to reach out and grab his chest to steady herself. His smirk returned when she didn't pull her hand away from his incredible build.

This couldn't be happening to her. There was no way that Jack would be here. Everyone had confirmed that he was supposed to be in Savannah…far, far away from the beach house. So she let her thoughts return to the possibility that she was dreaming. He was only a few inches from her succulent lips. It would be so easy to close the space. Though she had never envisioned being with Jack intimately on a beach before, she didn't put it past her imagination. And her imagination could be very ingenious when it wanted to be.

Something was off about her dream though. At this point in the dream, Lexi was sure Jack would have practically read her thoughts, and would now be bending down to kiss her. That's how it normally happened. She blushed deeper hoping that her Dream Jack would kiss her already, then colored even further as the time progressed and he didn't.

No, she had been right the first time.

He was not a dream.

"Jaaaaaack," Lexi heard someone yell impatiently from the direction of the house.

Broken out of the spell, he quickly dropped his hand to his side and took a fraction of a step away from Lexi. Her heart thudded in her chest at the absence of his touch…his warmth. She suddenly felt very alone.

"Jack! What are you doing? Who is that?" another whiny cry broke through the serene expanse.

Jack glanced up to the house and did a slight almost dismissive wave, not even bothering to respond in turn. Lexi did *not* want to turn around. She knew that Jack had a new girlfriend, her stomach twisted uncomfortably at the prospect, but she had avoided her at all costs.

"I guess I better get up there. Everyone's starting to stare," Jack said returning to her confused brown eyes.

That broke her out of her dream-like state, and she twisted to find a beautiful blonde leaning over an enormous wooden deck. Slowly, taking in the entire sight, she picked out Clark openly glaring at the spectacle before him. She didn't think her cheeks could redden any deeper than at that moment. After everything Clark knew about her and Jack, this had to appear to be a very compromising situation.

She turned back to Jack, anger flaring up inside. "Why are you here?" she demanded. He sighed contentedly. He had always found her sexy when she got riled up. "Aren't you supposed to be at your cousin's graduation ceremony? Why aren't you in Savannah?"

"It was a cousin on my dad's side. They are too crazy redneck for me. And anyway, I really did not want to deal with the boo-hoo-your-parents-are-divorced speeches for an entire week like they've been doing for the past couple years," he stated calmly, fixing her with a pointed look. "And anyway, Seth and I grew up together. His parents moved here when his sister went to college last year, and they're practically family. Actually," he considered for a second, "they are more like family now."

Lexi knew the details of his parents' divorce and cringed at the harsh words. He had spoken about his parents' divorce before, but generally steered clear of the subject. He hated the fact that they were separated, and just got pissed off when it was brought it up.

"So, why are you here?" he asked angrily.

"What do you mean why am I here?"

"You're fucking Clark. Right. I forgot," he said his voice ice cold.

"Fuck you," she spat angrily.

He nodded his head. "Right. Sorry, I like threesomes with two chicks, but if you're interested?" he asked raising his eyebrows evocatively.

"Jaaaaaack," the girl yelled again, "are you coming back up?"

"Well, that's me. You should consider my offer," he added playfully. "Gotta go. It's good to see you, Lex." He purposefully brushed her hand as he passed by.

She was seething with anger. Clark had said he wouldn't be here. She couldn't even think straight. Why did he have to go shatter the image she had of him in her head? Why did he have to bring is girlfriend? She just wanted to scream with the pain of unanswered questions.

"Oh, hey, Lex," Jack called when he was about ten feet away from her. She counted to five letting her breathing calm, and turned around to meet him. She huffed out her breath trying not to let her eyes veer from his face to his beautiful body. "Nice shirt." He let his eyes travel to her chest, and then winked at her.

She blushed again. What had she gotten herself into?

As Jack plodded through the thick sand ahead of her, she felt eyes boring into her. She didn't want to look up and see the disappointment certain to be evident in Clark's face. No wonder she had demanded that Jack not be present if she planned on attending. She saw him for all of ten seconds, and completely lost control of herself. He sent a rollercoaster of emotions rocketing through her veins. One second she had been elated, ready to jump into his awaiting arms. The next they had been bickering like an old married couple.

God, she hated so much that he got to her. She really would have just given herself over to him right there on the beach as if she was dreaming about him. She groaned feeling stupid for her thoughtless actions.

She ran her hands through her brown curls, and let them fall haphazardly around her face. Nothing near perfection, but it would do in her frenzied state.

When she finally worked up the courage, she tilted her chin up to the hardwood deck, and found Clark all alone still staring at her intently. He motioned for her to come inside, and then without a word, turned and walked inside.

Time seemed to drag as she waited for an opportunity to speak to Clark about what had happened. Seth hadn't been joking about the room arrangements. As soon as she had returned from the beach, she had been stuffed in a room with one of Seth's bimbos. Lexi had completely tuned her out, and instead, let her mind flood with concerns as she dutifully unpacked.

When Lexi was finally alone with Clark, she hissed, "What is he doing here?"

"I don't know," Clark said staring icily back at her. "What does it even matter?"

Lexi had no idea how to answer that question. How could she tell him that she couldn't control herself around him? That she purposefully avoided him, because of the things he unconsciously did to her body. Those weren't things you could tell your boyfriend. "It just…does. You said he wouldn't be here."

"I said that Seth didn't think he'd be here. I guess he just changed his mind. That's typical Jack." His green eyes seemed to see straight through her words. Clark had always been intuitive when it came to her. "Are you going to explain your actions on the beach?"

Why did he have to ask such a difficult question? She had never been able to explain her actions to herself. How did he expect her to explain her compulsion to him?

"I don't know what you mean," she finally mumbled.

His eyes narrowed. He didn't believe her. She could tell. "You're not going to tell me why it looked like you two were about to kiss?"

Lexi's mouth popped open. "We were not! I can't believe you would even think that," she huffed, hating that he had hit so close to home. Why did he understand her so well? Nine months wasn't *that* long.

"I thought you said things were over between you two."

"They are," she grumbled miserably.

"Then why can't you be around each other? Why did it look so much like you were…in love?" he asked struggling on the last words.

She gulped heavily. "We just have history. You know that," she said avoiding his last question completely.

She could tell he was thinking over how to address his concerns. He could see she was lying. After all, he had been watching them together out there. Finally, he blew out his breath and pulled her into his arms. "Okay, baby, if you say so. Can we still have a good time, and just forget that he's here?" She didn't even need to say that that was easier said than done. "I trust you."

Talk about feeling guilty.

"If you say you two are done, then you're done. I've just known Jack for longer than you, and in a much different way than you've ever known him. We were pretty close at one point in time. I know how he treats women, and I know that it doesn't matter to him whether he has a girlfriend or not. So, if there's anything between ya'll still, I'd just like the truth," he said pulling back to look into her guilty face.

"There…there's nothing between us," she said hesitantly.

He let loose another heavy sigh, and then nodded. "Come on. Everyone's getting ready to head out for dinner."

Lexi really wished they hadn't had that conversation. All she wanted was for Jack to leave. The week was going to be *very* long with him here. Lexi bit her lip as she followed her boyfriend into the living room to meet the rest of the group for dinner already lost in thought about the upcoming week.

After assembling into their vehicles, the group drove to a local Mexican restaurant that Seth insisted had the best margaritas. Just as importantly, they didn't check for identification. Since apparently all the girls Seth brought along were under twenty-one, that was a pretty important factor for him.

The dilapidated construction was recognizable solely by the faded green and red paint coating the walls and a rickety sign hanging half-off its hinges that read 'Desperados.' It didn't look promising.

Under different circumstances, Lexi never would have entered the place. The hole-in-the-wall establishment's only perquisite thus far rested in the gorgeous waitress who greeted them at the entrance. She was tall and buxom with wavy brown hair to her waist and cherry red lipstick coating her full lips. A long skirt hung off her voluptuous hips and a white off the shoulder top revealed her other very *full* assets. Every guy in the place stopped to gawk at her as she greeted them with her thick foreign accent.

Seth smirked and made a crude gesture to Hunter before charging forward and introducing himself. The waitress giggled at his obviously rude sexual remark and directed them into a large corner booth. Lexi watched the woman roll her eyes as she turned seated them and left. Lexi suppressed a giggle as she was shoved into the inside corner of the booth next to Jack's girlfriend. She cursed herself for not paying more attention to the seating arrangements.

"So you're Lexi?" the girl asked giving Lexi her full attention.

"Uh...yeah," Lexi said leaning her elbow on the table and resting her head on her hand.

"That's a pretty name. I'm Kate. I don't think we had a chance to meet," she said cheerfully.

Lexi heard a distinct chuckle emanating from the other side of Kate. She couldn't help but openly glare at Jack sitting on the opposite side of Kate. Obviously, Kate wasn't quite as perceptive as Clark otherwise she probably wouldn't be acting as nice as she was right now.

The waitress came back with menus and took drink orders, which mainly consisted of several pitchers of margaritas. Lexi didn't intend to drink much though. Her tolerance was beyond low, and she needed to be fully aware now that Jack was sticking around. Great...what a fun trip...

"Jack, thanks for giving me a heads up about your arrival," Seth said acting perturbed.

Jack shrugged effortlessly. Lexi tried not to stare at the light stubble on his chin and up his jaw line that made him look older and more handsome. "I couldn't stay away. You know that," he said cocking his head to the side and smiling suggestively at his friend.

"Oh baby, baby, take me now," Seth cried passionately. He cracked up laughing and smacked the table with his hand hard enough for the water glasses to shake. "Man, I've been meaning to tell you about this chick..." He wasn't afforded the luxury of finishing his sentence as Luke forcefully smacked the back of his head. "Ugh..." he croaked. "What the fuck was that for?"

"There are five women at the table, are you sure you want to finish that line of conversation?" Clark asked raising his eyebrows in warning.

"Yeah man, I don't care who hears." He shifted his attention back to Jack. "So I was fucking this..." Another vicious slap came, but from his other side this time. "What. The. Fuck. Sandy!" he cried glaring at the leggy brunette seated next to him.

"I can't believe you were going to..." she trailed off as she realized everyone was staring at her.

"I wasn't going to tell them whether or not it was you." A blush crept onto her cheeks, but she remained resolute. The other two girls at the table seemed to find this highly amusing. They were facing into each other and giggling, then began whispering something that they obviously didn't care to share with the rest of the table. "Anyway," he began again massaging the back of his head, "like I was saying, I was banging this girl from behind, and she did this amazing..."

Lexi blanched at his next comment. She knew Seth was crude, but this was over the top even for him. She heard Kate whimper. When Lexi flashed her eyes towards the girl, she realized she was tugging on Jack's sleeve, begging him to make Seth stop.

"Alright man," he said grabbing Kate by the upper thigh and pulling her into him. She giggled a little. Lexi felt like gagging. "How about you tell me what she did when we're not about to eat?"

"Your loss man," Seth said running his hand down Sandy's back.

The night proceeded smoothly after that point. Lexi managed to carry on an entire conversation with Jack's girlfriend who, as much as Lexi hated to admit it, seemed like a genuinely nice person. Jack remained civil, but they both purposefully avoided all means of communication. Sometimes when Lexi would say something referencing something from their past, he would catch her eye and grin devilishly. At those moments, she tried to keep the desirous glint out of her own eyes, and reminded herself repeatedly that she was sitting at the table with her boyfriend. Her very lovable, amazingly intuitive boyfriend…who would notice if she kept up the flirting signals Jack was conspicuously sending her way.

At the end of the night, Seth boasted about getting the waitress's number, all the while having each arm slung around another girl. Lexi wasn't all too sure how he did it. But she was pretty sure that the waitress, at least, had given him a wrong number.

Since they had arrived so late in the afternoon, and the majority of them wanted to be awake as soon as possible to hit the beach, they all separated into their rooms to sleep. Lexi simply couldn't get comfortable in her room. The queen-size bed she was sharing with Sandy, felt lumpy despite how expensive she knew it was. She turned onto her back and felt a sharp elbow dig into her side. Lexi shot up in bed wondering if this girl was feigning sleep with how cruel her jabs were. After experimentally pushing her body, she decided Sandy was actually asleep. Apparently, she was just a brutal sleeper. Not that Lexi could really sleep anyway. All she could think about was Jack.

Besides his occasional chuckle and rather suggestive eye contact, he hadn't really done much else to entice her…whether good or bad. The sane part of her told her that that was a good thing. She should definitely consider that to be a good thing. But being this close to him and having him nearly completely ignore her…well, it damn well irritated her.

So what if he had an adorably, perky girlfriend? He had flirted with her when he had been with Danielle, and they had been together much longer than that. Hating herself for her thoughts, she kicked her feet over the bed and silently edged out of the room.

The beach house was designed in such a way that when you entered from the front door a large set of stairs off to the right led to the enormous, lofted, master bedroom suite. It took up the entire top floor, and Seth had happily claimed his parents' king-size bed as his own for the week. The front doorway opened to the living room with standard beach decorating, hardwood floors, and a host of stylish wood furniture. Down a hallway to the left, the guys were staying in two standard offices, one with a pullout couch and the other with a black futon. A set of stairs off of the living room led to the bottom floor where Seth's sister's bedroom, where Lexi was staying, and a separate guest bedroom were connected by an adjoining bathroom. A homey-looking den opened to the massive deck Lexi had looked up at earlier that day.

Sneaking out of her bedroom trying not to disturb Sandy, Lexi exited the house through the den and out into the cool night air. The wind caught her hair and whipped it around her face. She breathed in the salt enjoying every second. After grabbing a pink and yellow striped towel, she flew down the flight of stairs that opened to the sandy beach below.

Falling back against the towel, Lexi stared up at the giant luminescent moon overhead. This was much more pleasant than getting elbowed to death in her sleep. She just wished that she could somehow get Jack out of her mind. It's not like her and Clark were currently in a rough patch. Things were going as well as they ever had. He had been a little moody as of late, but she just chocked that up to graduation and the looming prospect of finding a job. Other than that, it was just Jack that was bothering her. Things tended to go very, *very* wrong when she was around him. She had kept her distance since that time she had allowed herself to slip up. She couldn't take that back, but she could try to prevent a repeat performance.

But he was so gorgeous in person! Those baby blue eyes had turned crystal clear with desire at her approach on the beach, and she hadn't been able to stop herself.

The cool environment coupled with the slow rolling of the ocean eventually lulled her to sleep, even as she was thinking these thoughts about Jack.

A hand gently shook her awake and she jumped up from her slumber. She was terrified that she had slept through the entire night out here on the beach. But after opening her eyes, she noticed it was still pitch black outside, and breathed a sigh of relief. She turned to see who had caught her out on the beach alone.

"Hey," Jack said removing his hand from her shoulder. He smiled down on her brightly.

Of course, it was him. If she ran back up to the house right now, would he be offended? Deciding against that course of action, she mumbled groggily, "Hi. What are you doing down here?" A long yawn followed.

"I could ask you the same thing. Scoot over," he directed her, bending down and plopping on the small beach towel. He leaned his elbows back into the sand and stretched his legs out facing the ocean.

She tried to fix her gaze forward and avoid looking at him, but she couldn't. Before he had woken her up, she had been having another…rather inappropriate dream about him. Apparently being within his presence had allowed him full access to her dreams once again. "Couldn't sleep?" she asked to make conversation, even though the silence wasn't that bad.

"I saw you come down here," he told her.

"I thought you were sleeping upstairs." She couldn't help but stare at his well-defined profile in the ambient light.

He shook his head. "Nah, sleeping next to guys…not my style. I took the couch in the den."

She raised her eyebrows realizing that he must have been in the den all along when she had passed through the door. "Oh. How long have I been out?"

"About thirty minutes I guess, before I decided to join you."

"How did you know I didn't go for a walk or something?" she asked curiously.

He turned his head towards her, and by the light of the moon, she got a full look at the beautiful face she had been dreaming about. His eyes traveled over her flimsy sleeping clothes, and then rose back to her intrigued face. Finally, he shrugged and answered, "I just knew."

"You didn't come down and check on me before this?"

"No. I waited to see if you were going to come right back in, but then I realized you weren't. So I came to find you. I just knew you'd be here, Lex. I just know you," he said reaching out and cupping her cheek as he had done earlier that afternoon.

At his touch, her breath quickened, and her lips parted. How did he do that? "I've missed you so much," he said his voice lowering intimately.

"Jack," she whimpered as he trailed his hand down her neck, "you…you can't touch me like that."

He pulled her by her neck towards his waiting lips. Just as they were only an inch apart, he broke her steady gaze and began to kiss down her supple neck. She moaned deep in her throat, and then ripped herself out of his enticing grasp.

"I said no," she cried standing in a fit of anger. He remained seated and rested back on his elbows again, not even looking up at her. "Why are you here? What do you think you are doing? I don't want things to be like that again. My boyfriend…your girlfriend…our friends…everyone is up there right now and could see you doing this," she said pointing up at the beach house. "Don't you care about anyone but yourself?"

Ignoring her other questions, he coolly said, "Lexi, just sit down."

"No! I'm not going to *just* sit down. Why do you have to be so demanding all the damn time?" she cried, her hands resting on her hips. She was glaring daggers at him.

"If you don't stop using that voice with me, I'm going to take you right here on the beach," he told her evenly. "You're so much sexier when you're angry."

Lexi immediately stopped her argument and openly gaped at him. Was he serious? Was he really going to try to calm her down by claiming she was in any way *sexy* by yelling at him? The whole concept just infuriated her further. "I told you to stop telling me what to do. I will do whatever the fuck I want. And I want to know why the hell you're here. You grab me in public and then completely ignore me. Then, just when I'm accepting that, you start kissing me?" she squealed. "What kind of game are you playing? What kind of…"

She was cut off by him standing so swiftly it hardly registered on her radar. He snatched her up in his arms and tossed her gently back onto the towel. From his standing position, he immediately moved over her, pushing his body flush against her. She gasped at feeling every inch of his hard body just as his mouth crushed against her own.

All thoughts left her at that point. She hadn't been aware how much she wanted him…how turned on she already was from being close to him. Her body was aching all over with his mouth against her, moving suggestively from her lips to neck to ear and demandingly back to her hungry lips. He was hardly giving her enough time to breathe as he let his tongue roam her mouth. She let her free hand, that wasn't grasping at the nape of his neck, run down to his hips to pull him closer.

Groaning, he continued his assault on her lips. "I want you right now," he said, fumbling to reach down her cotton shorts.

"Jack, no. No, I can't," she whispered pushing him away.

"Lex, goddamn it, you're killing me," he growled sitting up and straddling her.

"Well, if you'd listened the first time, we wouldn't be in this situation," she said in between pants

"If *I'd* listened?" he asked in disbelief. "I told you I'd take you right here if you didn't stop being so damn sexy. You are the one who didn't listen."

She sat up and shoved him into the sand away from her. "Fine whatever, it's all *my* fault. It's always my fault! It has nothing to do with you being here when you're not supposed to be or you coming down to the beach to find me. It has absolutely nothing to do with you kissing me, for Christ's sake! Taking advantage of me, when you know I can't control myself around you," she spat.

"You can't control yourself?" he whispered into the gusty night, his words almost lost in the wind.

"Don't play with me, Jack," her dark brown eyes were nearly black in fury at this point.

"I'm...I'm not playing with you. What do you mean you can't control yourself? We've been in social situations for the past two or three years, and you've never given me more than one glimpse of your so called lack of control. I think you have *perfect* control. You hardly look at me. You definitely don't *speak* to me. God forbid, we have a normal conversation. So, yes Lexi, what the fuck are you talking about?"

She had never thought about it that way. She figured by avoiding him as much as possible that she would in some way be able to regain the control she lost when suckered into his enticing thrall. But it didn't work. All her efforts were futile, and even worse was she had avoided his wonderful presence and wasted a friendship...relationship for years.

"I did those things because of my lack of control. When you touch me Jack, I completely succumb to you. I give into your every whim."

"But you don't. Can't you see that? If you did, we would have had sex two years ago," he vehemently told her. She let out the breath she hadn't even realized she'd been holding. He was right. He scooted closer to her in the sand, and grasped her hands in his own. "Because I've wanted to be with you every day since then."

Words were lost on her. She had wanted him too, but things were different. She was with Clark now. Spencer had been a short lived thing, but Clark...he was solid. He had everything she had ever wanted in a relationship. He was caring, attentive, understanding, loving...the list was endless.

The only thing he wasn't...was Jack.

Jack. With all of his fiery passion and hopeless desire. Jack. Who had secured her a position on the gymnastics team even though she hadn't spoken to him in months. Jack. Who had always wanted her...since they had first met.

"Lex, I know how you feel about me. I feel that way too. Just...just let me show you what I can be to you," he said playing with her fingers embedded in the sand.

She sighed and gazed into his crystal clear blue eyes. He wanted her. He had always wanted her. "What does that mean?"

"We'll do whatever feels natural."

"You're talking about having an affair," she spoke softly.

"No. It can be platonic. We can be friends," he said taking her hand and interlacing it with his own, "if that's what you want."

What he was allowing her was a way in. A way to be with him...without being with him. The dream sounded amazing. It wasn't everything she wanted, but she couldn't deny it did have its perks. She could be with him again. She could talk to him and be friends with him. They could be around each other without the automatic hot and cold that came from their forced separation.

"Okay, Jack," she breathed. "I'm giving you a chance."

"I'll show you everything I can be for you," he said hesitantly reaching forward and in a companionable manner kissed her cheek.

Her breath caught despite the friendly nature of the kiss. Pushing any negative thoughts away, she scooted closer to Jack and together they sat and watched the ebb and flow of the waves before them.

9

PRESENT

Huffing louder than was necessary, Lexi glanced around Bekah's guest bedroom in disdain. She had been directed in here to change for Ramsey's party, but she was currently having second thoughts about whether or not that was smart. She was going to this party because of Jack. Strike one. She wanted to prove that Bekah was a phony. Strike two. And possibly humiliate her brother miserably. Strike three.

Wow. She was in a low place.

She tried to clear her mind of her dark thoughts and really assess the room with an unbiased eye. It was painted powder blue….Carolina blue. Ironic since she attended Duke. The wicker collection had all white bedding, and navy blue curtains hung across the window. Lexi conceded that it was kind of homey. Though the bed could easily be replaced by a wicker crib, and have the same effect. This couldn't have been an accident. Lexi shuddered.

She realized she simply couldn't be unbiased about Bekah. She had made up her mind that she would never like her…anything about her. Not that the girl was helping out anything by being kind of crazy and having a pastel, Easter egg colored house.

She popped open her suitcase and rummaged around for something to wear to this damn party. Why had she agreed to go through with this? She was such an idiot. If Chyna could see her now. She just shook her head at how awful that conversation would be. Not caring much how she looked, Lexi pulled on a dark pair of jeans, and unable to resist herself, her favorite, blue-green, lace halter.

"Alright. Let's get this over with," she said to herself as she walked into the now empty living room. She wondered where they went, then heard a giggle slice through the silence. Too curious for her own good, Lexi traipsed back down the hallway to the source of the noise.

She stopped suddenly when she heard a loud moan coming from the open door at the end of the hallway. She froze in place, unable to pull away, as she heard Jack and Bekah talking. She knew that she shouldn't eavesdrop on their conversation, but she couldn't help herself.

"Jack, come on, stop. She's right down the hall," Bekah breathed.

"I don't want to stop."

Lexi could hear some more whispers and a few smacking noises that she recognized as kissing. She gulped wishing she had just stayed in the room.

"She's going to hear us, Jack," Bekah squealing smacking his hand.

"I don't care if she hears."

Lexi blanched at his words. He couldn't honestly be saying those kinds of things after last night. This made her want to tell Bekah everything. Not just about their past either. She wanted to tell Bekah about Jack coming home early to see her, the pillow fight, staying up all night with her, and almost kissing her. Her hands were shaking at her side.

"Jack," Bekah mumbled.

"Okay, okay. You're right. She shouldn't have to hear this. I hope she didn't," he said wistfully.

"I wouldn't go that far."

Jack chuckled lightly. "Come on. Let's get out of here."

Lexi darted out of the hallway and back into the living room not wanting to be caught. She wasn't sure what to think of Jack's comments. Of course, she was pissed, because she wasn't certain which part he had meant. He had sounded more like himself when he had claimed that he didn't want her to hear, but she reminded herself that she was biased. Just another thing she would have to figure out before she went back to New York.

When Bekah came out into the living room, Lexi couldn't help but let her mouth drop open at her ridiculously skimpy outfit. She had on a coral high-waist skirt that barely hit the tops of her alabaster thighs, and a see-through, cream, scoop-neck top that did nothing to hide her skinny figure. Four inch brown heels made her already long legs look even better. Lexi felt plain next to her.

"Oh, you can't wear that," Bekah said reviewing Lexi's outfit choice.

"I seem to be hearing that a lot lately," she said giving Jack an icy glare.

"Oh well, Ramsey's parties are a little different than you'd probably expect," Bekah said choosing each word carefully.

"Fine. Whatever. Let's just get this over with. What should I wear?" Lexi asked easily giving in.

Twenty minutes later, the three found themselves climbing the stairs to Ramsey's townhouse in what Lexi recognized to be the ritzy side of Buckhead. The clothing look that Bekah had insisted on was a cross between trampy, smutty, and just a smidge of whore. It had been worth the effort when she had walked back out of the guest bedroom and had Jack, open-mouthed, gaping at her. His eyes traveled from the white lace skirt that accentuated her bronzed skin. Then, he slowly undressed her with his eyes as he traveled upwards to the cleavage bulging out of her blood red tank. Her make-up was smoky and seductive. And though Lexi knew that she looked good without all the added effort, the way that Jack's eyes turned crystal clear with desire at her approach certainly made up for the extra time it took.

Entering the townhouse was like slipping into a new world. The bottom floor was swarming with people vying to occupy as much space as possible. Blaring music emanated from surround sound speakers hiding around the house, and bodies were grinding to the beat. Lights were dimmed low and flashing strobe lights projected chaotically across the space. The people were crowded in so close together that Lexi couldn't even see past the living room. She wasn't sure if there *was* anything past the living room by the look of the place. She couldn't help but ogle the scene in front of her. She felt like she had just entered a nightclub, not a house party.

Bekah took her reaction as a good thing, and smiled at her. "I told you it was going to be a little different than expected," she yelled over the music.

Lexi nodded, her earlier anticipation about coming here dissolving. To be honest, she felt very much at home in this environment. She and Chyna went out nearly every weekend. She just didn't know that house parties were this crazy in Atlanta…let alone by someone like Ramsey. She figured she had a lot to learn about this Ramsey character.

Lexi felt her hips sway unintentionally to the music. "This will be fun," Lexi said to Bekah who appeared hesitant at Lexi's own enthusiasm.

"Yeah, it will," Bekah said reaching up on the tips of her toes and kissing Jack on the cheek. He smiled down at her lovingly. Lexi averted her eyes before either of them could see the horror on her face, but she hadn't done it in time. Jack glanced at her almost involuntarily and saw the haunted look cross her face. He looked like he wanted to say something, but he couldn't in front of Bekah. "Let's go find my brother."

Getting through the crowded living room was a feat in and of itself. Several couples were already interlocked for the evening and disentangling them to create a footpath proved to be rather tricky. Lexi elbowed a girl in the side to get her to move into the mass just an inch further. She squeezed her tiny body against the girl, getting suggestive hip movements pressed against her as she passed. Finally, wedging between two menacing guys, Lexi reached the other side which was surprisingly empty compared to the living room. She trotted into the kitchen and breathed a sigh of relief to be out of that crowd. Jack and Bekah appeared right behind her.

"Ugh...Ramsey's really out done himself this time," Bekah said brushing her fingers through her still perfect hair.

"Yeah, I'd say so," Ramsey agreed appearing in the kitchen. He looked just as good as her memory afforded her. When she had first seen him, she had only gotten a critical look at his back side. And while that was impressive, his whole body was even better for the eyes. It helped that he wasn't in a suit. That way she was able to really see the definition in his chest and arms. He was dressed simply in fitted dark jeans and a black polo. Apparently, the dress code for these things didn't apply to the host.

"Hey big brother," Bekah said giving him a hug. "You remember your old friend Lexi."

Lexi tried not to roll her eyes at Bekah's statement. She was going to be really tired of this party if she had to deal with this type of bullshit much longer. She hadn't been able to keep her cool around Ramsey at the Country Club where your behavior was monitored by a hundred wrinkly socialites. Lexi was sure she wouldn't be able to do it here. "Can I just repeat that I do not know your brother?"

Ramsey turned to face Lexi. His eyes crawled her body and an enticing smile touched his lips as he took in her outfit. It was much the same reaction she had received from Jack, but there was something different. She couldn't quite put her finger on it. Maybe it had something to do with the fact that her clothing option left little to the imagination. No, it was more likely that it had something to do with the fact that Jack had firsthand experience with what was under her skintight clothing.

"You can repeat it all you want, but I'm holding to the fact that we are old friends. And old friends hug when they greet each other," he said swiftly spanning the space between them and lifting her off her feet. She clutched onto his broad shoulders for support. He twirled her around once letting her long hair fly out behind her.

When Lexi felt ground under her weight again, she breathed out in relief. Compulsively she smacked Ramsey's arm as hard as she could muster. "Don't do that. We're not friends."

"You're right. I'm overstepping boundaries...at my own party," Ramsey said sending a full-watted smile her way.

"Oh, shut up," she said giving him a mirthless frown. "I didn't mean it like that."

"How did you mean it then?" he asked stepping into her personal space again.

Why was he always doing that? She cringed and took a step backwards. He followed her as if they were in a synchronized dance. "I didn't mean that you were overstepping boundaries or whatever. Just we're not friends. I don't know you. I've only met you once."

"Well, technically twice. Three times if you count when you were with Jennifer. Four times if you...oh never mind," he said plastering on a smile he as looked at her.

"Four times if what?" she asked curiously.

His smile continued as he entered her personal space again. This time she stood her ground and looked up into his face. He was so tall she had to tilt her head all the way back just to look into his face. "Nothing."

Deciding he was telling the truth, Lexi nodded and said, "Right, well, cut it out."

"You really don't remember meeting me?" he asked ignoring the stares he was receiving from all angles.

"I think I'd remember someone who has no concept of personal space," she muttered. He titled his head to the side really looking at her face from her smoky make-up to her large brown irises to her button nose landing last on her plump lips. Then he took one step back and then another.

"My apologies. Is that better?" he questioned his eyes roaming her tiny clothing once more. Lexi just grumbled an affirmative.

Bekah giggled and clung to Jack's arm breaking them from their argument, and bringing them back into reality. Lexi took a sly glance at Jack. He looked tense and out of place as he slung his arm around Bekah's shoulders. Lexi hadn't even been paying attention to Jack throughout that entire encounter. But as she looked closer, she realized he looked ready to pounce. God, she did not understand him sometimes. Only a few minutes earlier, he had been making out with his girlfriend not caring who heard him, and now he was openly glaring because she was talking with Ramsey! She hadn't even been flirting with him. She had *actually* been annoyed with him. Oh, wait, dammit! He thought she was sexy when she was angry.

Bekah broke the awkward silence that had settled in the air. "Ramsey, you should introduce Lexi to your roommates. I have a feeling they would just *love* her."

Lexi wasn't sure what that meant, but as soon as Ramsey called over his roommates she understood her implication. These two guys, though they had the same appearance of class that Ramsey wore, didn't pull it off quite as well. Lexi could see straight through to the frat boy beneath, and cringed as they collided with her body. She hadn't even gotten the introduction before they were hugging and fondling her. They smelled strongly of booze as if they had been drinking all day...all week.

Ramsey grabbed both of his roommates by the back of their collar and yanked them off of her. "Hands off. She's never been to one of our parties," he said roughly pushing them to the side.

"All the more reason," the one dressed in navy said.

"Agreed," the other, in a yellow Georgia Tech polo, approved.

"Uh...I don't think so," Lexi said pushing her hands out in front of her. Then she caught a glimpse of Jack's face. He wasn't doing a very good job at hiding his displeasure. If she had thought that he had been jealous earlier today, it was nothing compared to the waves of jealousy he was sending her way now. Somewhere deep inside, she knew that she shouldn't enjoy the fact that he felt that way, but she was pretty much ignoring all the things that she was supposed to be doing and feeling. She was in Atlanta for Jack which was bad enough. If Jack was getting some backlash for his bad choices, well then so be it.

"I don't even know your names," she said buying herself some time.

"You don't need our names," Georgia Tech guy informed her sidestepping Ramsey and snaking an arm around her waist. So maybe his roommates weren't as handsome as Jack or even Ramsey, but they were still cute. At least cute enough that she would have flirted with them on any other night.

She thought she heard his friend whisper something derogatory into the other's ear, but she didn't catch all of what was said. The end was something along the lines of 'after we're through with her.' But understanding the looks that were cast between the two of them, she probably didn't want to know the rest. She needed to say something to get their minds off of sleeping with her, because that would never happen.

"So explain this party to me. It's pretty early to drink on a Sunday," Lexi asked glancing between Ramsey and his two roommates.

"It's never too early here," navy guy said.

"Plus, Ramsey comes pretty stocked," Georgia Tech guy answered eye-fucking her clothing choice. It was a good thing she didn't do self-conscious.

"Oh does he?" she asked eyeing Ramsey suggestively. Jack coughed uncomfortably in the corner. Bekah had snaked an arm up to his hair and was gently twirling the longer strands in the back between her fingers.

"I thought we weren't friends," Ramsey reminded her pushing aside his roommates who looked all too ready to devour her.

"We're not," she said smiling coyly at him from under her long lashes. "I'm not this nice to my friends." This was better. She could avoid being rude to him for a few minutes while Jack watched. Though, she wasn't all too sure how long she could hold out the routine.

"Alright," he began, looking at her peculiarly as if wondering when she had become so nice, "I have a good deal of friends who work in late night establishments during the weekend. So, I host parties Sunday nights for them."

That was simple enough. "That's uh...nice of you."

Bekah giggled. "Nice is one word for it."

"Bekah," Ramsey said turning his attention to her. Though the tone wasn't sharp and the look he sent her was the same perfect Country Club smile that gave away nothing, she knew he wasn't pleased. She wasn't sure what it was about him that made her realize it. There was just a slight line of tension forming around his mouth, and his hands were curled into loose fists. Something about the way his eyes clouded over as he stared at Bekah. Lexi seemed to have accidentally stepped into a family dispute, and was feeling all the more uncomfortable as Bekah returned his resolute smile.

Slowly, he shifted his gaze back to Lexi. "Anyway, what they meant is that I have a fully stocked bar," Ramsey said sweeping his arm out to reveal a black bar along the majority of the back wall. The only wall space not obscured by the construction was a back door with a large window opening up to a balcony.

"Ya know, I kind of figured that," Lexi said.

A few people were already ordering drinks from a tiny blonde bombshell whipping up concoctions as fast as they were requested. Jack and Bekah sidled up to the girl hand-in-hand, and began knocking back their drinks.

"What would you like?" Ramsey asked her. "Valentine can make you anything."

Lexi giggled a little at her name. *Valentine* really? God, that was awful. Sounded like a stripper's name or something. She quickly composed herself as Ramsey looked down on her fondly. She hadn't meant to giggle. "A Grateful Dead would be nice," she told the bartender picking a drink at random. Within seconds the drink was before her complete with a cherry and everything. She was impressed. "This is kind of awesome," she admitted. The smile she received from Ramsey was nearly blinding. He genuinely looked ecstatic that she approved.

Another uncomfortable cough emanated from behind them, and Lexi hastily turned around to find Jack looking between her and Ramsey. She wasn't sure why he was acting like this. Honestly, it was ridiculous. He was here with his girlfriend. She was the one who was supposed to be jealous. Not him. But it was kind of nice to have the upper hand in this silly game they were playing.

"We're going to dance," Jack said pointedly grabbing Bekah's free hand and pulling her into the crowded living room. Lexi watched them become enveloped in the mass. She hated how they were acting. Wasn't she supposed to be getting over Jack? She couldn't see how hanging out with him like this was helping anything.

Quite the contrary. She felt as compelled to him as she had when she had first glimpsed his brown hair at the coffee shop or those enticing blue eyes at the club. She had been right to say that things weren't different. And Chyna had been right to say that she needed some semblance of closure. She needed to be over him. She couldn't keep living her life hoping they would one day find the right moment to be together.

Turning back to face Ramsey's perfect smile, she downed her drink as fast as she could automatically reaching out for him to steady her weak legs. "Wow, that's the good stuff," she said returning his smile.

"Want another?"

"Mmm...sure. Wait," she cried stopping him before ordering, "let's do lemon drops! Those were my favorite."

"Were?" he asked raising his eyebrows.

"Yeah, in college. I drank them every weekend. It feels like one of those nights."

The peculiar look he had given her earlier returned. She liked it. He was very cute indeed. He turned back to Valentine. Seconds later, two lemon drops were in front of them. The dizzying effects of vodka coursing through her body were helping her successfully escape Jack's hold. She needed another. After two more rounds of shots her mind was good and cloudy, and she was ready to dance. Ready to forget.

Lexi grabbed Ramsey's hand and pushed her way through to the center of the crowd. He seemed surprised that she wanted to be around him all of a sudden, but got over that as she began to shamelessly grind her ass against him.

There was hardly enough space for her to breathe let alone move around much. That left her the option of being plastered against Ramsey's strong chest, and really she didn't mind. He was a solid rock of muscles. She had to be right in her assessment that he worked out constantly. There was no other option for how strong he was.

The best part was that he was also a great dancer. Each time she would change up her motions, he would follow along perfectly somehow making the movements even sexier. Lexi reached up, and wound her hands around his neck as she stood on the balls of her feet. He took advantage of the opportunity to move his hands along her exposed body feeling the hot skin through her clothing. Leaning back against him, she let her head fall onto his chest, and she stared up into his amazingly well-structured face.

Just as that happened, a buxom blonde shimmied up to them and began grinding on Lexi. The girl was doing things with her body that Lexi had never dreamed people were capable of. She was contorting and twisting all the while touching herself. The girl's eyes were blood shot and unfocused, occasionally rolling back into her head. Lexi had no idea what was wrong with her.

Ramsey grasped the girl's arm forcefully and squeezed. Her eyes snapped open. Lexi stared between the two and stopped moving. "Not tonight Coco." The girl glared at him.

"You sure, baby?" she purred despite the fact that she looked murderous.

"Go get that shit out of your system," he said lowering his voice in warning.

"Whatever," she said yanking her arm away from him and exiting the living room.

Lexi's head jerked back to Ramsey's face. "Sorry about that," he said his voice returning to normal.

"What was that about?" she asked curiosity getting the best of her.

"Just don't worry about it. She comes here like that all the time. She's supposed to be clean," he said grasping her hips that were now facing him and pulling her close.

The hypnotic feel of intoxication was hitting her hard and she giggled compulsively. "Is her name really Coco?"

"Just a nickname," he said swaying his hips in time with her. All of his friends seemed to have nicknames.

She stopped thinking as the next song came on, and focused on dancing in Ramsey's muscular arms. The music and dancing took her back to hanging out with Chyna in New York when she was just able to be young and carefree, dancing all nights in clubs, and drinking an exorbitant amount of alcohol. No matter how often she drank, she was still the cheapest date of anyone she had ever met. Her tolerance never wavered. She was sloshed after the second drink, and would likely be throwing up if she exceeded five.

As she let her body roll against Ramsey, she focused in on a couple in front of her seductively dancing against the wall. Lexi's heart rate picked up as she watched. Bekah pushed Jack back against the wall and began to kiss him feverishly. Lexi couldn't pull her eyes away. She hadn't even thought of Jack since she had gotten out on the floor with Ramsey. It had been a comfort to forget him, but now here he was…on display. Bekah gripped his hips and slid alluringly down his front. She took no care of her tiny skirt as she perched with her head in front of his crotch. Lexi felt as if she were intruding on a very private moment. Their intimacy was so seductively erotic that had they been alone Bekah could have easily been going down on him. She watched as Bekah forced herself up and back against him. He moved easily with her as if this were a common motion…just a transfer of sexual emotion from the bedroom to the dance floor.

Lexi hated to admit it, but they looked good together. It sickened her watching them move together so perfectly…to fit together so perfectly. She could feel alcohol-induced tears welling in her eyes. She turned around so fast she knocked into Ramsey, and nearly fell back from impact. He snatched her before she could fall into another person, and looked down upon her mortified face. The tears were threatening to seep out, and that was the last thing she wanted.

He seemed to comprehend that as he bent down to speak into her ear. "Do you want to get some fresh air? I'm kind of suffocating," he admitted, though she knew it was more for her sake.

The crowd parted as he passed through, and he staved off his roommates. Opening the back door, he ushered her out into the humid August air where they found themselves blessedly alone. She checked her cheeks and found them dry, which was her sole comfort from the entire episode.

"Are you okay?" he asked purposefully giving her enough room to breathe.

Lexi remained silent but nodded. After a few minutes of strained silence, she felt more composed, and a little extra tipsy from the emotional whirlwind she had just undergone. She breathed out heavily, and leaned her elbows back against the wooden banister. Ramsey walked forward and stood in front of her. She couldn't help but notice how attractive he looked in the moon light. She smiled at him endearingly.

"It's good to see that you look better." She shrugged again. The earlier incident, though not out of her mind, was at least momentarily forgotten.

"Thanks. I think I dress up well too," she said biting her lip and staring at him flirtatiously.

"I think both clothing options work for you," he said taking another step closer to her.

"Thank you very much. I have to say…" She eyed him up and down. "Both options work for you too." She hiccupped and leaned forward against him as she giggled. "Though, these muscles are much better in your polo." She placed her hand on his bicep and squeezed.

He smiled his perfect smile, and reached out to help support her. "I'm glad you like them. I spend a decent amount of time in the gym to keep them."

"I didn't say I liked them," she said blushing.

"Fine. I'm glad they look better in my polo," he corrected boldly circling her waist. She let him. It was a nice feeling. He wasn't exactly holding her, but having his big strong arms this close was nice indeed. "You really don't remember me then?"

"Nope!"

"You know I wasn't being completely honest with you," Ramsey said sliding her back another step and leaning her against the balustrade.

"It doesn't matter," she slurred staring at his lips. By now, she wasn't all too sure what he was talking about. She couldn't remember if it was important.

"No, I guess it doesn't, but I could still tell you."

Her head felt heavy and it lolled backwards twice before she looked back up at him. God, his lips looked damn near edible from this close up. They were a soft pink color and perfectly proportioned. He licked his lips as she watched, and couldn't help but let loose a soft breath as her heart rate picked up.

He chuckled quietly when he noticed she wasn't really paying attention to what he was saying. "Lexi, don't you want to know what I'm talking about?"

"Yep," she said letting her focus shift back to his emerald green eyes. "I want to…"

"You want me to…" he began letting the words hang in the silence. Her eyes widened and pupils dilated with longing at the words. "…tell you what I'm talking about?"

"Oh," she said, sucking in her bottom lip in confusion. "That's not what I thought you were going to say."

He snickered again. "What I have to say can wait. What did you want me to say?" he asked leaning into her.

She blushed furiously as her thoughts turned sexual. She tilted her head back to look up at him. Suddenly, she wanted to be sitting on the banister so she could get a better look at him. She wanted to be eye level with him. "Put me up," she demanded slapping her hand playfully on the banister.

"Alright, but be careful," he said hoisting her up and sitting her on the top of the railing. He held a firm grip on her so that she wouldn't fall. A ten foot drop while she was drunk probably wouldn't do her any serious damage, but he didn't want to take the chance.

She liked her seat. Now she was even with him. This was much easier. His hand came up and swept her hair out of her face. "You know, Lexi, you're very beautiful."

She smiled at him through her lustful eyes. "Thank you." Her breathing quickened as she noticed how close they had gotten. She hadn't noticed it before, but he had scooted in between her legs to block the view from the window. She felt her bare thighs press against his sides, and realized her skirt was barely covering her lower half. One hand was wrapped around her holding her securely in place. The other was on the back of her neck gently kneading the muscles. His breath was hot on her face. Their mouths were so close together.

There was no reason for her not to kiss him. She was single. She was completely one hundred percent available. Jack was nothing to her. She couldn't have him. Not the way she wanted him. She might as well go for what was right in front of her. She pushed herself a little closer to Ramsey. She was so close she could almost feel his lips against her. His breathing was wretched with anticipation. As he moved closer to her, something caught her eye in the window. She let her gaze shift fleetingly, and saw the most brilliant blue eyes lock onto her own. Then Ramsey was kissing her, and all thoughts were lost.

10

MAY THREE YEARS EARLIER

Lexi crept back into the beach house just before sunrise. She and Jack had sat together all night peacefully enjoying each other's company. Their attempt at friendship had been mildly successful. Lexi was glad that they had resisted kissing again. She was pretty sure they had gone over the line that was normally reserved for friends, but it was so incredibly mild and tame compared to their normal impulsive demeanor, neither of them had complained.

They had ended the night with a long hug at the base of the stairs. Both were staying on the cautious side, and didn't want to be caught together like that in the house. She checked to see that the coast was clear, and then slunk across the den and into the bedroom. Being extra careful not to wake Sandy up, Lexi gently twisted the handle and secured it into place. When she turned around, she realized all efforts were futile. Sandy wasn't there.

Lexi's heart beat in a panic. She could feel herself beginning to hyperventilate. If Sandy wasn't there, then that meant that she knew Lexi hadn't been in bed. Sandy would tell everyone. Lexi had no idea what to do. She couldn't risk everyone finding out.

Changing clothes, she lay down on the empty bed, and contemplated her options. She could rush out of bed now and start making breakfast or something. However, she wasn't sure at what point Sandy had left last night and it might make her look even more conspicuous. She figured she could go find Clark, and snuggle with him. That would cover her tracks if Sandy came back, but would hardly explain anything if Sandy had snuck out earlier in the evening. And anyway, after staying up all night with Jack, she hardly wanted to see her boyfriend. They hadn't done anything wrong…well after they had talked it out they hadn't. But either way, she wasn't quite ready to wash the familiar scent off of her skin or erase the memories of their night together.

She was fresh out of options. When she was about ready to give up, the door burst open and Sandy sauntered in looking all too pleased with herself. Noticing that the room wasn't empty, she gasped dramatically and swung the door closed behind her.

"When did you get back?" she asked hesitantly, fear evident in her face.

Lexi wasn't sure why she looked so terrified. Lexi was the one who had been out at all hours of the night doing things that she didn't want anyone to know about. Why would Sandy be so scared? "What time is it?" Lexi asked stalling.

"Please don't tell anyone I was out," Sandy squealed rushing to the bed and sitting heavily on the quilt comforter. "Oh God, please don't tell anyone." She looked to be about to go into hysterics. "I didn't expect you to be back this morning."

Now Lexi was *really* confused. Where had she been? Why was she so frantic about people finding out? Luckily, this saved Lexi from being confronted about why she had been out all night. "Where were you?" she questioned Sandy trying to compose her features.

"Okay, I'll tell you, but promise you won't say anything," she demanded grabbing for Lexi's hands as tears began to well in her eyes.

"Sure. I promise." Lexi was just damn curious now.

"Okay. Okay," Sandy said taking her hands back and brushing at her eyes. Obviously, she took some comfort in the fact that Lexi wouldn't say anything. Her hysterics abated, she began speaking. "I woke up when you left. I knew immediately where you were going."

Lexi tried to keep her face neutral, but couldn't help her look of surprise. "Where was that?"

"Obviously you were going to Clark's room," Sandy said making the most girly giggle Lexi had ever heard.

"Oh." Lexi breathed out a sigh of relief. Of course that was where Sandy would think she had been. Most sane women *would* have gone to see their boyfriend in the middle of the night while they were on vacation. That would have been the logical thing to do. She scolded herself.

"Don't worry," Sandy said conspiratorially, "I won't let anyone know that ya'll were up all night."

Oh God, Lexi didn't know it was possible to feel this bad. Lexi bit her lip to the point of pain and then began to push her hair behind her ear. She did not want to cry right now, but Clark was so damn smart. He would know. He would see Jack all over her. He would be able to piece everything together and realize what had really gone on last night.

"But when I saw you were gone, I snuck upstairs to the master bedroom." Lexi nodded along. Really, she should have figured as much. The two had been all over each other since they had arrived. "Seth was very persuasive, and I...well...I stayed most of the night. I didn't sleep much though," Sandy said as if she were confiding in a friend. "I know you and Clark are together, but have you and Seth ever?"

Lexi quickly shook her head no. There was no way in hell. Seth was such a pig. "No. No. No. No. No."

"You should maybe give it a try. He's...wow...amazing."

"Yeah, I don't think so."

"More for me then," she said contentedly. "He made me swear not to tell anyone. It's our little secret. So, if you could just keep it between us that would be great."

Obviously Seth wouldn't want Sandy to tell everyone that they were sleeping together. That way he could sleep with the other two girls he had brought with him without any of them knowing about it. How did Sandy not see that? Lexi didn't really care to find out. As long as they were both under the impression that they were keeping each other's secrets that would work out just fine for her.

She was exhausted, but still she was unable to sleep for very long. Tumbling noises from upstairs informed her that the guys had woken up. From that point on, she would never get any shut eye. Lexi grabbed her toiletry bag and hobbled into the empty bathroom. She stared at her reflection in the mirror in surprise. No wonder Sandy had thought she had been up all night doing the nasty. She was a wreck.

Her hair was tangled and windblown from a night on the beach. Her cheeks were plump and rosy. Her lips cracked and chapping. Two large circles had formed under her bloodshot eyes from the lack of sleep. Luckily, Sandy hadn't noticed the sand covering her body or else she might have asked more questions. Despite her exhaustion and renewed fear that Clark would notice a difference in her, she was ready to start the day. She was ready to see Jack again.

After a shower, Lexi figured she at least looked presentable, and was ready for some breakfast. As she exited the room and began to climb the stairs to search for something to eat, the smell hit her. Pancakes.

She turned the corner and found Clark already in the middle of whipping up a fresh batch. Smiling brightly as she entered the room, she walked up to him and grasped him around the middle.

"Good morning to you too," he said leaning down and giving her a kiss. "You look fresh this morning."

She blushed. "Thank you, dear."

"Go have a seat, and I'll get you some pancakes. Orange juice, yes?"

"Uh…yeah. Sounds great," she said turning away from him. Her gaze rested on the breakfast bar where a certain someone was seated looking smug.

"Mornin'," Jack said tilting his head at her as a welcome. She watched as he poured an exorbitant amount of maple syrup on his pancakes.

"Good morning to you," she said cheerfully, taking the seat next to him and glancing back up at Clark. After pouring several pancakes onto the griddle, he turned around and was staring at her intently.

"Sleep well?" Jack asked between mouthfuls of the oozing goodness.

Lexi leaned back in the chair and prayed she didn't blush. "Sure," she said unable to keep a mischievous smile from creeping onto her face. "You?"

"Nah. Slept like shit. That couch is full of lumps. Feels more like sand," he told her forcing down another bite, but still not looking up at her.

Clark looked between the two, and seemed genuinely pleased that they were having normal conversation. Every other time they were in a room together, Lexi was fleeing the premises or they were locked in a tight, spitfire conversation for several minutes then Jack would storm off. It wasn't pretty.

"Man, that's because it probably is full of sand. Think about how many times people sit on that couch after coming in from the beach," Clark said shaking his head.

A brief, knowing look passed between Jack and Lexi. She tried to hide her delight at Jack's playful comments. It felt nice being able to discuss their night together without anyone…even Clark knowing what they were talking about. To anyone else, all the comments Jack made would seem completely neutral. It was exhilarating.

"You're probably right," Jack agreed scraping the last remnants of his breakfast from his plate. "I probably should have thought about that before I let it keep me up all night."

Lexi accepted the plate of pancakes and orange juice from Clark, and tried not to look anymore impish than usual. As she began to dig into her plate, Kate walked in.

While they had been up all night, they had confided in each other about their relationships—the ups and downs about being with their significant others. At first, Lexi had found it strange to discuss these things with someone who had been feverishly kissing her only minutes before, but after they started talking neither could seem to stop. It was refreshing to be able to speak with someone so openly about her relationship, knowing that they didn't mind…actually reveled in the bad qualities mentioned.

Lexi had found out that Jack and Kate met through a mutual friend of theirs. She was pretty much everything you expected out of a cheerleader prom queen type: average height with stick straight, naturally blonde hair to her shoulders, large baby blue eyes, and a toned build with a killer tan. She wore her emotions on her sleeve, and her bubbly personality only intensified that aspect of her character. The silver spoon she had been fed on since birth made her have a predisposition for expensive name brand clothing, acrylic French manicures, fake and bake tanning, and ultra bright highlights. The only things keeping her from being a snotty brat was the fact that her parents were extremely religious. At least in that respect, she had been humbled from her high horse. The faith had remained with her all through college. No matter what had gone on Saturday night, Kate could be found every Sunday morning sitting in a pew…confessing her sins.

Despite the fact that Jack wasn't on a sports team for the school like her three previous boyfriends, his natural charm won her over. She liked his music and adventurous nature even though she wasn't a big fan of the big wide open outdoors herself. She had been hooked after the first date. He had taken to her to the nicest restaurant in town for a candle lit dinner with wine pairings, roses, and everything. The whole shebang. Afterwards, they traversed a moonlit path around the campus gardens. When he had described it to Lexi, she couldn't help thinking that it was far removed from a simple carnival ride.

They had started talking after Lexi stopped returning his calls, and had been dating for over a year and a half now. Apparently Jack lived by the rules: the best way to forget the last is to move onto the next.

Kate sidled up to Jack in her bright yellow bikini and broad-rimmed floppy sun hat. Lexi watched as she kissed him, and then hooked her leg up onto his lap and swung herself up on top of him.

"Are you ready to go to the beach yet?" she asked wide-eyed.

"Just about," he said circling his arms around her waist and leaning his head against her shoulder. "I could use about five more hours of sleep. You interested?"

"You didn't sleep?" she asked.

"He slept on sand all night," Lexi said taking a long sip of orange juice.

Kate jumped as if just realizing that they weren't alone. "You were on the beach?"

Jack flicked his gaze over towards Lexi in warning. Lexi just continued eating. She knew that she wasn't that great of a liar. She couldn't word things like Jack could. He could manipulate his language so that no one would be able to tell anything was different.

"No, I was telling Lex and Clark that the den couch feels like it's full of sand."

"Oh, gross. You know that I'd come and share with you to make it more enjoyable, but I just cannot sleep on a couch," she said flicking her hair over shoulder. Every time she moved it just bounced back in front. "You need to go change so we can get our asses on the beach," she said sliding off of his lap and tugging him out of the kitchen.

Lexi skimmed her eyes across the departing couple. Her stomach twisted at the sight of Jack's arm hanging loosely around Kate's waist…well a little lower than her waist. She wanted things to work out so that she would be able to be around Jack more often, but so far she wasn't all that certain they could stay like this. She couldn't change the way she felt about him.

"You two seemed to be getting along better," Clark said flipping a pancake over.

Lexi shrugged. "I guess," she said nonchalantly. "I'm going to go change for the beach. Thanks for breakfast." She hopped off her chair, kissed him on the cheek, and then rushed out of the room before she could give herself away.

*****

The next few days passed in a similar fashion. The group would spend a fun filled day at the beach hanging out in the ocean, playing volleyball and Frisbee, and a whole hell of a lot of sun bathing. Each night after everyone passed out from physical exhaustion, Lexi would crawl out of bed and into the den. She would shake Jack from his slumber if need be, and they would slink down to the beach to spend the remaining hours until daybreak together. The next morning, they would wake up at the crack of dawn eager to be in each other's presence. She had resorted to afternoon naps on the beach to keep herself going during the day. Clark couldn't figure out why she was so tired all the time, but she continually blamed it on the sheer amount of alcohol she had consumed coupled with the sun's heated rays.

Lexi was lying back enjoying one of those afternoon cat naps when she was jostled awake. She grumbled as her ear buds fell out of place and drifting ocean noises took over for the tunes that had been playing from her iPod.

"Wake up, sleepy head," Clark murmured as he sat down on the towel next to her.

She swiped at her eyes and pushed herself up against her elbows. "How long have I been out?" she asked sheepishly.

"A couple hours."

"Where did everyone go?" she asked noticing that at least a few rather pertinent individuals were missing from the group.

"Probably doing to each other what I want to do to you right now," he muttered huskily, his voice dipping low.

Lexi gulped. She tried clear her mind of all thoughts of Jack. She did not want to think about him right now when her boyfriend was suggesting rather appealing options. However, she couldn't help herself. All she could think about was whether or not Jack was with Kate, and what they could be doing up at the beach house almost completely alone.

"You want to go join them up there? I'm sure we can find an empty room in that mansion of a place," he said winking slyly at her.

She giggled half-heartedly, her smile not fully reaching her eyes. "Maybe."

Clark moved closer and rested his head in her lap. She wound her fingers through his thick, curly, black hair. He had let it grow longer for the beach, and she enjoyed the feel of it, knowing it would all be gone before graduation. "I bet I can convince Hunter to take the couch tonight if you want to sleep with me," he offered. "You're not getting enough sleep."

In that moment, she was glad he couldn't see her face. Guilt creased her features. The last thing she wanted to do was give up one of her last precious nights with Jack. She didn't care how tired she was. They would never have an opportunity like this again, and she was planning on savoring every platonic second of it. "No, it's fine. Don't worry about me. I think I'm just adjusting to the bed finally," she volunteered the information off hand.

"I was thinking I could give you some more incentive," he said sitting up and pulling her face into his hands. His mouth covered hers quickly and deliberately. Only earlier that week she had reveled in every kiss. Now that she had tasted Jack again, if only briefly, the movement felt robotic and dispassionate. She felt no express desire for him in that moment and that knowledge worried her.

She smiled against his lips and pulled back. "I think I'm going to pass. You heard Seth. Thin walls and all. I'd rather not have everyone hearing us, and then talking about it."

His eyes shifted focus. "Since when are you concerned with other people hearing and being self-conscious?"

"I'm not self-conscious," she muttered tripping over her own lies. "I just...don't want everyone to hear."

"You don't want Jack to hear?" he asked pointedly.

"I don't see how that has anything to do with it," she stated her voicing coming out faulty.

"Look, Lexi, I know you said you took my words to heart, and that ya'll are going to be better. But I just have a really bad feeling about all of this," he told her honestly.

She immediately went on the defensive. "What are you saying, Clark? Do you think that I'd do something?"

"No, I didn't say that."

"Then what are you saying?"

"Baby, I trust you." He took her hands in his and looked into her big brown eyes. "I just don't trust him. I don't think, if he were given the chance, that he'd be able to stay away from you."

"And what, I'm just going to sit by and let this happen?" she asked letting her guilt-ridden anger get the best of her. She had done just that so many times before.

"I'm not saying that either. Stop putting words in my mouth. I'm not trying to start a fight with you," Clark said calmly. "I just have a bad feeling. I was hoping you would reassure me that my feelings are just misguided judgments of a jealous demented boyfriend," he said looking up at her pleadingly.

"I agree with you, at least, about Jack. I'm not sure if he's ever been faithful with anyone he's been with. But that's the reason that you shouldn't be concerned," she said feeling the lie start to form on her tongue. "Why would I let him get to me knowing that?" She really wanted the answer to that question.

He just shook his head. "I dunno, Lexi, but I hope you're right."

"You know me better than that," she said snuggling closer to him.

"You're right. I do. I love you, Lexi."

She gulped. "I love you too."

All throughout dinner Lexi remained withdrawn from the group. Her conversation with Clark echoed in her ears. She couldn't help wondering if she should tell Clark that Jack had kissed her. But if she did that, then she would have to tell him about going out on the beach with Jack. She would have to explain why she had continued to meet him on the beach after that first night, and she wasn't sure if she would be able to do that.

Sure, they had said they were going to just be friends, but she wasn't an idiot. They wouldn't be sneaking off together every night if they were just friends. After everything that had happened between them, Lexi was pretty certain that they could never just be friends.

"You *sure* you don't want to join me? I'm sure you would sleep better in my arms," Clark persuaded hugging her tightly around the middle outside of her bedroom.

"Rain check. I'm really beat," she said nuzzling into his arm. She was really tired. That was the true part of the statement. The only problem was she wouldn't be sleeping again for several hours.

"Alright. If you change your mind, you know where I am," he said clearly disappointed.

He kissed her once more and then trotted up the stairs. Lexi breathed a sigh of relief that he hadn't pushed her further on the subject. She quickly ambled into her room. This was the worst part about the night. Waiting. For Sandy to either sneak out of the room to visit Seth or pass out. Waiting. For the sounds of Clark and the guys quieting down and subsiding to slumber. Waiting. For the coast to clear.

After what felt like an eternity, Lexi extracted herself from Sandy's grip and slinked out of the room. She rubbed her tired eyes as she moved into the den. Her smile lit up when she found Jack waiting for her. He could have been asleep. She was the one who waited for the coast to clear before coming to find him. There was no need for him to wait up for her. Those few hours rest were like gold right now, and he had chose to stay up and wait for her instead.

"Miss me?" she asked sitting down next to him on the lumpy blue sofa.

He yawned in the midst of answering her, "Ohhhhhh...yeaaaaah."

"We should probably get out of here," she said feeling his arm come around her middle and hold her in place. He tilted them backwards so that they were spooning comfortably on the couch. She sighed and nestled closer to him. Thoughts of leaving left her as she felt slumber draw close. The soothing feel of Jack's breath hot on her neck caused her eyes to flutter shut, and she could feel herself begin to drift off. Then she felt his lips pressed to that same spot on her neck, and all of a sudden she was wide awake.

It was only one kiss, but it left her heart speeding ahead of her. She rolled to face him, and met his smoldering gaze. Everything about their embrace in that moment showed that they weren't friends. That they could never be friends. That they were stupid for even trying. All she wanted to do was kiss him. Every nerve in her body was pushing her closer towards him. She had never stopped wanting him, as much as she tried to deny the obvious facts. When they were together, she lost all cognitive thought.

Jack moved closer, as if there was any room between them, and she could almost feel his sweet lips on her...almost taste him. A rumbling from upstairs stilled their movement. They waited a second for the noise to die away, but after a few seconds, it returned and stronger.

Lexi swore under her breath. The universe was really *trying* to keep them apart. Jack smiled at her reaction, but his face was strained.

"What's going on up there?" she whispered to him in the darkness.

"No idea, but you should probably go back to your room," he whispered back. His meaning was clear. They could not be in a more compromising situation. If she didn't get back now, everything would blow up in their face.

"No."

"Lex, you have to get back."

"No."

"You can come back once everyone goes back to sleep."

"No."

"No, you won't come back?"

"No, I'm not leaving."

"You're so stubborn. We're going to get caught. Go back to your room."

"No, let's go to the beach instead."

"Do you not hear that upstairs?" he asked pausing to allow her to listen to the continued noise.

"Jack, I hear it, but they're just going to go back to sleep, and then we've missed all our time together."

He stared intensely at her before finally speaking, "Fine. Let's get out of here before they come downstairs." He scooted them off the couch, and after snatching up her hand, dove out of the house and down the stairs.

"How do you know they are coming downstairs?" she asked enjoying the feel of his hand entwined with her own.

"Were you not listening at dinner?" Jack asked lightly swinging their hands as they neared the water line. "I forgot about the conversation when we were…together."

"Oh…no, not really. I was pretty spaced out I guess."

"Yeah, I think I noticed that."

"So, what's going on?"

"Seth dared Hunter to go skinny dipping tomorrow in the middle of the day. Hunter agreed, but only if everyone else did it too. The girls were pretty grossed out by that concept. So Seth said they would do it later tonight when no one else was on the beach."

Lexi giggled. "Yeah, I guess I was really out of it. Somehow I managed to miss that entire conversation."

Without uttering another word, the couple began to take a slow paced stroll along the beach. If they stayed in front of the house, then they would be caught together by the potential skinny dippers.

The feel of Jack's hand in her own almost burned her. All she could think about was how close to kissing they had been earlier on the couch. She would have succumbed to him. The familiar feeling of losing control had taken her over. Instead of steering away from the feeling, she had gotten lost in it once again. And now she was out on the beach with him when any of their friends could find them missing at any moment.

Surprise washed over her when they stopped in front of the pier. The pier was over a mile away from their beach house. Yet, time with Jack had just flown by. She hadn't even realized that they had been walking so long.

He nudged her forward to keep her moving, and they slunk along the wooden planks. Lexi skirted the edge where an old fishing pole rested. They reached the edge and sat down on a green bench set up for tourists.

"I don't know if I can do this anymore," Jack's husky voice muttered sounding defeated. It was such a strange sound coming out of him that Lexi had to stare into his face to even believe that he could feel that way.

Lexi knew what he meant. Her heart was racing knowing that they were so close together, but they couldn't be together. Only a mile up the coast, their significant others were blissfully unaware of what was happening out on the pier. She felt terrible about the deception. Not only was the sleep deprivation killing her, but the lying too. She couldn't keep up this act for much longer. Not when Jack wanted her. The way he had kissed the nape of her neck had proved what she already assumed. He had been trying to hold back how he felt from her all week, but moments like that kept creeping in to their time together. But they weren't supposed to be together. Hadn't she only thought earlier that the universe was just *trying* to keep them apart?

"I know what you mean," she whispered sadly, her chin dropping to meet her chest.

"I'm not sure I want to break up with Kate though," he said miserably.

That snapped her right out of her own pity party. *Break up* with Kate! Holy shit! Where had that come from? Maybe they were talking about two different things. "Uh, Jack?"

He tilted his head to look at her under his thick dark lashes. "Yes, my dear?"

"You've been thinking of breaking up with Kate?" She couldn't keep the disbelief out of her voice.

He nodded choking on his own words. "Ever since I saw you like a vision on the beach the first day you got here."

"Wh…Why would you do that?" She knew the answer. But she wanted to hear him say it.

"I thought that was quite obvious…for you."

She sighed loving the way that sounded coming out of his mouth. She had wanted to hear that for so long. But would he break up with Kate? Could she think about breaking up with Clark? Her heart ached at the mere thought of letting him go. She didn't want things to change with Clark. She loved Clark.

She just didn't know exactly how she felt about Jack, and that scared her. Could she love Clark so much, and still want to spend so much time…have so many inappropriate thoughts about Jack at the same time? God, she wasn't sure, and her head was pounding with the waves of confusion overtaking her.

"For me?" she finally got out.

"How could you not know?"

"I knew, but I thought it was like last time. I didn't think you would want to end things with her. I didn't think you want to…be with me," she whispered into the cool ocean breeze.

Her hair whipped around her head and a long strand landed across her face. Jack reached up and tucked the lock behind her ear for her. He pulled her face closer to his and his voice spoke gruffly into her ear, "*You* have always been what I want. I just made mistakes along the way. I told you that

I would make it up to you, that I would show you what I could be for you, if you would only let me."

Lexi's mind was racing along ahead of his words. He wanted her. Just like she had always dreamed. How could she turn away from him so long as he wanted her? Consequences be damned, Lexi pushed her face forward and moved her lips against his. Taken by surprise, he remained stiff. She was relentless though, and began to tease his bottom lip with her tongue. He moaned and she used the opportunity to insert her tongue in his mouth. She straddled his body and pressed herself firmly against him. His hands came up and wove their way into her thick brown hair. Yanking ever so lightly, he pulled her head back giving him access to her bare neck. She purred as he roughly kissed her neck hard enough to send waves of pleasure through her body, but not hard enough to leave a mark.

She grabbed the base of his shirt and began to pull it off over his head. He seemed to like the idea and did the same to her. He ogled her breasts for a moment before taking them both in his hands and massaging them. She arched her back, and he moved to flick his tongue against her rigid nipples. She was practically feverish for him. Despite the fact that she could feel every inch of him, she felt that there was too much clothing in between them. She wanted to feel his skin against her. She wanted to feel his rock hard abs against her stomach, and his hands rake her naked form. God, she wanted to feel every inch of him deep inside of her.

The way he was touching her made it pretty obvious that he was having similar thoughts. He couldn't get enough of her. The succulent taste of her, her supple breasts in his hands, the way she was reacting to his every touch was sending him over the edge. He wasn't one to resist temptation, and she felt so good. Not to mention she was practically throwing herself at him.

Lexi fumbled for his khaki shorts tugging at the difficult button. Her fingers missed the mark twice, and she was getting frustrated. She kissed him hard on the lips, and then stood up commanding him to do the same. He undid the button for her, and watched as she slid to her knees taking his pants with her. His eyes widened when she didn't stand back up, and instead took all of him in her right hand, and began a gentle stroke. He couldn't stop looking at her. The fluid motion of her hand as it hit the base and then pulled back up to the head. Then as his eyes began to close from an overdrive of emotions, he felt her hot wet mouth close around him. Brushing her tongue around the tip a few times experimentally, she took the rest of him in her mouth and sucked making sure his entire dick was wet. His breathing turned ragged and heavy as she continued her work on him. He groaned as she hit every nerve perfectly.

He felt himself reaching climax, but he didn't want to get there just yet. He wanted her to feel everything he was feeling in that moment. He wanted them to feel that amazing moment of bliss together. With all the energy he could muster, he pulled back from her astounding movements. Her brown eyes looked even bigger than normal as they looked up at him in confusion. Forcing her to stop was even more difficult for him since she looked like all she wanted to do was finish him off. He hadn't thought he could be any more turned on, but after that look, his erection was almost painful.

Grabbing her by her shoulders, he pulled her up and kissed her lips passionately. All confusion was wiped from her face as his kiss clouded her thoughts. Never breaking from their kiss, he scooped her up into his arms and rested her back against the bench. He left a trail down her front as he reached her tiny black shorts, yanked them to her ankles, and then tossed them to the cement ground. He worked his way back up pulling her legs up around his waist as he lay over her.

Lexi stared mesmerized into his gorgeous cerulean eyes. She had dreamed of this moment for so long. Now that it was finally here, she was even more turned on than she had ever imagined. His skin covered her body, and she could feel him pressed into her inner thigh. She whimpered with desire for him. "Oh, Jack," she muttered kissing his bottom lip. He moaned deep in his throat and adjusted his position over her.

"You want me, Lex?" he asked speaking for the first time since his declaration.

"Oh, yes…yes, Jack, I want you," she said swishing her hips so that she brushed her wetness against him.

He nuzzled down into her neck, and then pushed into her. She instantly cried out in pleasure at the feel of him. He buried himself deep into her and enjoyed the feel of her clenching and unclenching her inner muscles around him. She waited patiently as he held that position. She couldn't believe that after all that time, it was finally happening. He was with her. He was inside of her.

She moaned loudly as he shoved harder into her. Then he began to set a slow languid pace. He was already close to the brink after the way she worked her mouth around him, and he was afraid with his overpowering desire for her that he would get there before her. She felt her body begin to flush as he continually pushed himself into her. They fit together perfectly. The feelings he sent throughout her body were unlike anything she had ever experienced.

As the waves of bliss continued coursing through her, she let her hips move with his adjusting her angle so that he hit all new places. Through pants, she managed to get out, "Jack…oh, Jack…"

"Mmm…yes?" he asked kissing her forehead.

"Harder," she pleaded.

He groaned as she begged him. God, she was so fucking hot. She felt him give into her desires, and push into her harder and rougher. With the last few strokes they smacked their hips together, and then came at the same moment. Jack pushed deep into her and hugged her tight to his chest as she cried out into the night air and arched her back. The orgasm that rocketed through their bodies left them breathless and exhausted. A sheen of sweat stuck to their skin

After a minute, Jack lifted himself onto his wobbly elbows, and began to stroke her hair back from her forehead. "That was amazing," she muttered weakly, her eyes still closed.

"I should probably move, but you feel so damn good," he murmured kissing her on her swollen lips.

"Ugh," she grumbled as he rolled off of her and began fumbling around for their clothes. She could *not* believe that had just happened.

They quickly put their clothes back on, and began to walk hand-in-hand towards the beach house. There was no need for words after what had happened. Anything they needed to say to each other could be left for another day…another time. Everything was too blissful and almost surreal to break the mood with thoughts of tomorrow.

As they drew nearer, sounds and jeers emanated down the beach. They both knew what that meant: the guys had actually gone through with their skinny dipping plans. Trekking up through the sand away from the waterline, they attempted a stealthy entrance as they closed in on the beach house. It was clear that there were a few bobbing heads in the water, but the last thing they wanted after what had just happened was to get caught red handed. Jack held his hand out to stop her steps as they heard something crash against one of the surrounding bushes. A light barely illuminated the entwined couple revealing Seth with one of the other bimbos he had brought along. Lexi breathed out in relief knowing that this meant Sandy was still likely fast asleep upstairs. Edging around the oblivious couple, Jack and Lexi sprinted up the stairs taking them two at a time and into the vacated den.

After standing silently in the den and verifying that there weren't any lingering individuals awake, Jack kissed Lexi briefly on the mouth and then pushed her towards the bedroom. She surreptitiously entered the room to find Sandy snoring into the pink comforter. After she changed clothes, she crawled into bed and let her mind wander to the amazing night she had just had, and how close they had been to letting the cat out of the bag.

Before slumber took her, she couldn't help wondering what *was* going to happen in the morning. She had no idea what their relationships would be like after what they had done tonight.

She knew one thing though: nothing would ever be the same.

11

PRESENT

The balcony was spinning.
Lexi was almost certain that the balcony was spinning. She could feel it throughout her entire body. She was being swept up and away as if she was trapped in the *Wizard of Oz*. Her feet were lifting off the ground. Or wait, were her feet on the ground at all?

No, something was off. She couldn't actually be lifting off the ground. Her conscious told her that things like that didn't actually happen to people. Then why did she feel like she was spinning?

Then she remembered where she was. Ramsey's sweet lips were covering her mouth. He was kissing her. She felt her mouth moving against his automatically. He tasted good. Surprisingly he didn't taste like liquor at all. He tasted of peppermints. God, she could keep kissing him all night with how good he tasted. The caress of his tongue on her bottom lip sent a shiver through her body. A low moan escaped her, and he reacted with more enthusiasm holding her tight against his body. She could feel the rippling muscles in his chest pressed to her. Her mind was whirling a million miles a minute. Yet, there was something she was missing.

Party. Shots. Dancing. Balcony. Ramsey. Kissing. She couldn't put her finger on it. There was something else she should remember.

Ramsey pulled back from her mouth to catch his breath. She gulped in two healing breaths in an attempt to clear her foggy head. He smiled at her sweetly and rubbed his thumb back and forth against her jaw line. It was a pleasant sensation, and Lexi's thought process ceased again. They kissed some more, and Lexi was enjoying the emotions he was drawing out of her with every touch. When they pulled apart this time, the fog slowly began to clear and she knew what she was forgetting.

Blue eyes.

Bright blue eyes staring at her from the balcony window. She could pick out those eyes anywhere. She shivered unintentionally as the spinning stopped. Everything came to a standstill as the realization hit her inebriated mind. Jack had seen her kissing Ramsey.

Oh God! Suddenly, a wave of nausea hit her harder than before, and she thought at any moment she might vomit. The last thing she had wanted was for Jack to see her with Ramsey. She hadn't even *meant* to kiss Ramsey! She certainly didn't like Ramsey.

In fact, he annoyed her. Sure, he had been there for her moment of weakness, but that didn't mean she liked him. And that certainly didn't mean she wanted Jack to think she was whoring herself out when she was visiting him.

She quickly covered her mouth as the dizziness returned. She would *not* throw up. How humiliating would that be?

"Are you alright?" Ramsey asked with concerned. He had just seen her near to tears. There was no way she was going to throw up in front of him. Vulnerability wasn't exactly high on her list of things she liked to show in front of complete strangers, especially not ones she had just been making out with.

"Fine, thank you," she said hopping down off of the railing and avoiding his gaze. That was quite enough of the affectionate stuff for her today. She would much rather close herself back off. It seemed to work better. It also usually kept her from making out with random guys while her sorta-non-ex-boyfriend was watching. Ugh!

As she turned to walk back into his apartment, she found herself wobbling and weaving. She didn't remember drinking enough to make her feel this out of control, but perhaps that sexy kiss had something to do with that. No, she wasn't supposed to think about Ramsey's delicious peppermint kisses. That would just get her drunk ass in trouble. And really how much worse could she make her situation?

Just then, her favorite pair of black alligator skin stilettos caught on a nook in one of the wooden planks and sent her toppling to the ground. Ramsey was instantly at her side. Before she met disaster, he scooped her up into his arms, and cradled her body in a gesture that strongly resembled a tango dip. Her cheeks were burning from a combination of embarrassment, relief, and the fact that he was holding her in such an intimate position. She sucked in a few calming breaths, her eyes remaining locked into his emerald orbs. They were beautiful with flecks of gold spiraling away from the onyx pupils. And how had she missed that he kind of smelled like peppermints too? Peppermints mixed with something uniquely his own. Whatever it was, it was damn addictive. And maybe that was just her damsel-in-distress intoxicated view of the world, but he really was unbelievably good looking. Oh and look, his lips were so close once again.

She smiled coyly almost challenging him. He seemed to take that as confirmation that he could close off lines of communication again, and bent his head down to meet her waiting lips. Lexi was overwhelmed with his touch this time. Apparently, her challenging look had changed his mood, because now he was kissing her with reckless abandon. It was invigorating.

As their tongues moved against each other, the back door swung wide open nearly knocking Lexi in the head. Ramsey popped his head up, and came close to losing his balance with Lexi in his arms at the unexpected interruption. Lexi let her head loll backwards to get a look at the intruder. Striking blue eyes filled with venom met her own eyes, and she shivered at the sheer amount of malice he was sending off in waves. Ramsey quickly righted her placing a steadying arm across her shoulders. She gulped.

Jack.

Oh Jack.

She never understood his infatuation with her when she got angry until that moment. He looked smoking hot. Shit! Her beer goggles were fogging up with how gorgeous he was.

"What's going on out here?" Jack spat through gritted teeth.

"I...uh..." she began.

"Lexi wasn't feeling well. I think she drank too much," Ramsey interjected smoothly. "I thought she could use some fresh air." Ramsey glanced from Jack's furious face to Lexi's sheepish grin. She looked like she had just been caught with her hand in the cookie jar.

"Hey baby, ready to go?" Bekah asked announcing her presence in the lit doorway. Her bright smile began to fade as the tension in the air hit her. Something was up. She couldn't figure out why this Lexi girl caused commotion everywhere she went. Was it completely necessary to put everyone's emotions on end all the time?

"Um...did I miss something?" Bekah asked.

Ramsey's eyes remained locked on Jack's face. He was really curious to know what was going on between them. Why would he invite Lexi to Atlanta when he quite obviously had feelings for her? Were they having an affair? That just didn't make sense to him. There would be no point in introducing her to Bekah, and keeping up pretenses if that were the case. Bekah was smart enough that she would see straight through them. At least, he hoped that she was capable of being an unbiased judge about the whole situation.

No, there must be something more to the situation. Something that Bekah quite possibly knew about. He wanted to know what was going on.

While he was stuck under Jack's lethal gaze probably wasn't the best time to start asking questions.

Or maybe he just liked Lexi. There was something so real…so raw about her personality. She didn't hold back. She wasn't afraid to be blunt, to say things that you weren't expecting, to completely ignore someone with wealth and influence. These were not things that people did, especially not the people he hung out with. Everyone was so desperate to please him all the time. And much of the time they were only interested in him for his money. Up until their kiss, which he attributed to the compulsive personality he was beginning to become fond of, he hadn't even really thought that Lexi liked him.

"I don't think so," Ramsey finally answered breaking the silence.

"Why you are all so tense?" she trilled.

"Yeah, Jack, why are we all so tense?" Ramsey couldn't keep himself from asking.

Jack's face immediately lightened. "I don't know what you're talking about. I'm not tense," he said shrugging his lifted shoulders.

"Can we just get out of here. I'm tired," Bekah pleaded her blue eyes opening wide as she looked up at Jack. He didn't even glance at her as his eyes remained locked onto Ramsey and Lexi still huddled together on the balcony.

"Yeah, we were just leaving," Jack growled. "You ready?" he asked nodding his head towards Lexi.

"No. We just got here," Lexi said with a shrug. Actually, she had no idea what time it was, and didn't particularly care.

"It's past eleven. Bekah and I have to work early in the morning so we're heading out. It's time to head out," he demanded.

How had she missed that they had been at Ramsey's for over three hours? Time had just flown by. Lexi's eyes shifted from Jack to Bekah and then up at Ramsey. She knew there was some reason she hadn't wanted to come to this party. Where was she going to sleep now that she was hammered? She couldn't stay at Jack's. They would definitely end up sleeping together. She was already turned on, and with all his bubbling anger she was sure he wouldn't be able to control himself. There was no way she was staying in Bekah's ridiculous Easter egg house. Honestly, she didn't have the money for a hotel, but there was no other option.

"Oh, I see," Lexi said wobbling even in Ramsey's grasp.

"Let's go then," Jack said reaching for Lexi's arm.

Ramsey could see the reluctance on Lexi's face. He remembered her telling him that she was supposed to be staying with her parents tonight, nearly an hour away from his apartment. There was no way she was going to make it there in her condition. For some reason, he felt protective of her.

He didn't want her to stay at Jack's house. Something deep inside him told him that it would be bad news if they were stuck in the same house together.

"She said she didn't want to leave," Ramsey said his voice turning business-like. He had moved just a fraction of a step forward, but it was enough to make Jack drop his hand. "She can stay here and party more if she wants. It's not like anyone else is going to be leaving at eleven." He hadn't intended for his words to come out condescending, but he had managed to get his point across. Jack and Bekah both were looking at him curiously. Almost as if it were the first time they had ever looked at him.

"Ramsey, can I talk to you for a minute in private?" Bekah asked, her voice oozing with sisterly affection.

He glanced from Jack to Lexi and back. He didn't want to leave them alone. Something was gnawing at him, and he didn't know what it was. But it's not like he could always deny them alone time if Lexi was here visiting Jack, and he had never been able to deny his sister anything. Reluctantly, he nodded and Ramsey and Bekah retreated back into the kitchen closing the door behind them.

Lexi and Jack were alone. They both seemed to realize at the same time they had been completely alone since this morning at his apartment. Anyone could walk outside and find them together, but that didn't matter. The electricity between them was intense.

She couldn't remember the last time she had allowed herself to drink this much around Jack. Before, if she knew there was even a possibility that they might end up alone together, she wouldn't touch the stuff. But she hadn't anticipated this moment. She knew she wasn't thinking clearly even as she walked towards him.

"What were you doing?" Jack asked, his earlier anger resurfacing. He had drank a few too many beers himself, but not enough to get him past the tipsy stage.

"What are you talking about?" she asked taking another step closer.

"You were *kissing* Bekah's brother!" he exclaimed unable to control his fury.

"If you already *knew* what I was doing, then why did you have to ask?" she questioned him, her voice laced with sugar-coated inflections.

"How could you do that?"

She stopped her progression. Why was he being like this? God, she was so fed up with him being so goddamn demanding all the time. He didn't *own* her by any means. He couldn't decide who she could see, and who she could kiss. He had no rights, no claim on her...not anymore. "You want to know?" she asked returning his fury.

"Yes, I want to know how you could go and kiss him knowing that I'm here. Knowing what you...mean to me."

"What I mean to you?" she asked in disbelief. He nodded. "I don't care if she hears," she spoke the words softly.

"What?"

"I heard you at Bekah's house. You told her that you didn't care if I heard you with her."

"Lex, I didn't mean it," he said once he realized his mistake.

"I don't believe you."

"I told her that I didn't mean it. Did you hear that?"

"Yes, I heard it."

"And you still don't believe me."

"No, I don't believe you, Jack."

"But why? I'd never want to hurt you again, Lex."

She shook her head furiously. "Don't say those things to me. It's just wrong. You can't *ever* say those things to me again, Jack Howard!"

"Lex, please, listen to me. I swear to you that I didn't mean it. I shouldn't have said it, but I did not mean it."

"It doesn't matter. You don't care about me, Jack. I'm not sure if you ever did." Once the words were out she couldn't get them back. She wasn't really sure if she wanted them back though. She wondered sometimes if he really did ever care about her. Her intoxicated mind told her she was being ridiculous, but she couldn't stop herself. "If you had cared, you wouldn't have left New York," she cried spitefully.

"Lex…"

"Don't tell me what I can do like you always have. Don't tell me that I can't kiss whoever I want. Don't tell me that I can't do what I want."

But he didn't say any of those things.

"How much have you had to drink?" he asked, his eyes hardening again at her accusations.

"Don't you dare try and blame this on the alcohol."

"How can I not? Look at yourself," he commanded her, openly surveying her flustered appearance. "You look like a two cent hooker flushed after securing a sugar daddy for the night," he stated cruelly. She had struck a nerve too close to home, and he couldn't control his retaliation. If she thought he didn't care, well then he would show her what that was really like.

Lexi's mouth dropped open. He couldn't mean that. After all, it was his stupid girlfriend that made her wear this outfit. And sure she was flushed, but it certainly wasn't from Ramsey! August in Atlanta wasn't exactly breezy. The environment was blazing hot and downright sticky from the off the charts humidity ratings.

But Jack wasn't finished. "Are you so easy, Lexi, that you'd rather stay here with someone you don't even know? Someone who is already taking advantage of your drunken state?"

Her mind couldn't even begin to process the nasty remarks Jack was sending her way. Had he really just called her easy? Just accused her of *using* Ramsey for his money? Was he on crack?

"Why are you being such an ass?" she muttered between clenched teeth.

"I'm just being honest. Anyone else who would have stepped through that doorway would have seen the same thing. I just want you to know that."

Despite the falsity behind Jack's statements, her emotions were beginning to get the best of her again. Jack kissing Bekah. Jack dancing intimately with Bekah. Jack fondling Bekah. And now he was accusing *her* of doing things…while he claimed that he cared for her. It's not like he had exactly made that clear. Why was he playing these games? Tears began to well in her eyes, and she rushed to brush them away. Why was she even crying over him? He was only saying these things to get a reaction out of her. She knew that. But she just couldn't stop it.

"Why don't you…just…leave?" she asked between hiccups.

"Why don't you come with me?" he countered making it sound like another demand. He took the last step towards her and placed her elbow in his hand.

She shook her head trying to get out of his grip. "Why would I want…to be…with you?"

"Can't you see that I'm looking out for you? You know nothing about Ramsey," he said trying to reason with her even though he was grasping for excuses to get her away. "He's not exactly a nice guy."

"Neither are you!"

"You know me, Lex. You don't know him. You don't know what he can be like. I know how he is with women, and I know the type of women he associates with. You're better than all of them combined, but if you keep throwing yourself around like them, he's going to treat you the same way. Stop being so stubborn, and let's get the fuck out of here."

"No! God, you're blaming me for drinking too much? I can't believe what just came out of your mouth."

"I wasn't kissing some random guy."

"Now that would be a sight."

"You know what I mean. You were the one making out with a guy you just met, someone you know absolutely nothing about. What's gotten into you, Lex?"

"What's gotten into *me*? You're the one practically getting a blow job in the living room. So don't come here on your high horse and try to bring me down for kissing someone. Last I checked, I could kiss whoever the fuck I want, because unlike some people I'm not attached. Not that it seems to stop you," she snarled crossing her arms over her chest.

"Oh, we're back here again," he huffed. "Haven't we covered the topic about things being different?"

"Right…things are sooo different now. Just…leave me alone, Jack."

"Okay," he began stepping into her personal space and forced her to look up at him. "So maybe things aren't completely different, but they have changed. Let's just get out of here. I don't want to see you get hurt."

He had moved his hand up so that it was cupping her cheek. Her watery brown eyes were looking up at him. How many times had she been in this similar position before? She couldn't even think about that right now. She was fighting off the alcohol induced hormones running rampant throughout her body. He shouldn't have talked about kissing her and then touched her the way he was doing. That just wasn't fair.

"It's too late for that," she whispered stepping away from his comforting touch. "You've done more damage than anyone else."

"Lex, come on. Stop talking like that. Let's just go."

The door swung back open revealing Bekah and Ramsey. Lexi quickly turned around to face away from the door and forcefully brushed away the tears that had seeped out of her eyes. She didn't need them seeing her this way. It was bad enough that Ramsey had almost seen her cry. She could do without Bekah having that advantage over her as well. Not to mention she had no idea what she looked like. Jack completely threw her emotions around. One minute she was on fire. The next she was near tears. Back and forth. She knew one thing though. She couldn't be around him right now. It would surely end in disaster.

"Jack, let's get out of here," Bekah said pulling him backwards away from Lexi.

She didn't exactly look pleased. Bekah shot Ramsey a disdainful look as she yanked on Jack's arm. Ramsey just smiled that perfect Country Club smile. Apparently, he had won out in the end.

"Lex, are you sure you're not coming?" Jack pleaded one last time.

"No, Ramsey's going to get her a hotel," Bekah told him practically dragging him away.

"Oh." He quickly composed himself. "I'll see you. Later," he said tilting his head at Ramsey, giving Lexi one last look, and exiting with Bekah.

Lexi breathed out not having even realized she had been holding her breath. How had she let herself deal with his behavior for so long? She had such strong feelings for him and yet all they could seem to do was argue. God, it was so typical of him. She didn't know what to do. Her head was killing her already. She didn't even want to imagine her hangover tomorrow.

Luckily, Ramsey didn't seem to try to push his advantage. And when he glanced at her, he didn't ask all of the nagging questions he was dying to get answers for.

Lexi wasn't sure if she was going to be able to keep up pretenses if Ramsey wanted to talk about what had happened. She certainly wasn't ready to spill her beans as she had proven when she had spoken with Bekah. There was no way she would be able to talk to Ramsey. She was grateful when he smoothly requested her presence on the dance floor. As emotionally drained as she felt, that definitely sounded like a better option than thinking about Jack anymore.

*****

The next morning Lexi could feel her head splitting open. She couldn't even open her eyes. If she opened her eyes, she was certain the pain would be unbearable. She couldn't even think of anything besides the pain. What could she last remember about the previous night?

She had kissed Ramsey. Yeah, that was pretty clear. The nasty things that Jack had spat at her were still relatively clear in her mind. Though they didn't sting quite as much now that she was sober and had other painful things to deal with.

Then her and Ramsey had danced and danced and danced. She didn't even know how long they had danced. From there things just sort of went fuzzy. Had she blacked out? She was pretty sure she hadn't blacked out since her twenty-first birthday, and the next morning twenty-one slash marks in black permanent marker were on her wrist letting her know she had drank way too much. No way had she had that much last night.

She blearily opened her eyes and found herself in a strangely meticulous bedroom. A very foreign bedroom. Definitely not a hotel room. Shit! This was not good. Hadn't Bekah said that Ramsey was going to check her into a hotel room? Not that it would have looked very good for him to check her into a hotel room in her condition. Don't hotels frown upon that? God, she had no idea. She had never gotten herself into this situation before.

She didn't want to face the truth. Maybe Jack had been right. She knew nothing about Ramsey other than that he came from money and was related to Bekah. If Jack couldn't even vouch for him, maybe he *wasn't* such a good guy after all.

She peered under the huge white down comforter and silky blue sheets to find that she was clothed in a pair of red plaid boxers and a white undershirt that was at least three times too big. Yeah, not even close to what she had been wearing last night. She rubbed her eyes vigorously hoping that maybe something else would come to her. Anything else. But she simply didn't remember what had happened or how she had ended up here in this strange place in some guy's oversized clothes.

Even before she lifted her head off of the enormous feather pillow, she knew it was a mistake. Spasms of pain shot throughout her entire body sending her sprawling back against the bed. The pain was all-consuming and instantly made her feel nauseous. If she had thought she had wanted to throw up last night, it was nothing compared to the desire she was having right now. But realizing she was in a strange person's bedroom with no clue as to where a bathroom was, she lay back down and took several calming breaths before attempting to stand up again.

Steadying herself on the dark wood footboard, she took a swift analysis of her surroundings. The room was plain, but she could tell that the furniture was high quality. A Macbook Pro sat unopened on the desk, but there were no cluttered stacks of papers or half full glasses like at her apartment. The walls were blank giving off a guest bedroom vibe, but something about the space convinced her otherwise. She couldn't put her finger on it. Then she glanced back at the bed. There weren't any throw pillows on the bed. She had noticed over the years that guest bedrooms always had useless throw pillows that most people neglected to place on beds they frequently slept on.

She reached for the nearest door which opened to a rather large walk-in closet. The clothes were organized by style and color. It was almost terrifying how neat the closet was in comparison to her own mishmash of clothing stuffed into the tiny space at home. She shut the door behind her and walked achingly across the room to another door. This revealed a short blank hallway with several other doors and a staircase. She shuffled down the hallway, down the staircase, and around the corner into a familiar kitchen area.

Sighing heavily, she realized she had spent the night at Ramsey's apartment. Panic hit her. Had she slept with him? Had anything happened? She put her hand to her head and trudged over to the sink. Fumbling with a glass she produced from a cabinet, she poured herself some water, refilled the glass and downed another. That helped, but not enough to ease the gnawing ache at the pit of her stomach.

The front door crashed open and she swiveled a little too fast for the headache that had taken residence in her temples. Ramsey, flanked by his two roommates, paraded into the room not taking any notice of Lexi. She became increasingly aware that she was wearing men's sleeping clothes with no bra and she had not seen a mirror. This all added up her looking terrible and wishing she had tried to locate a bathroom. Knowing they were all about to look at her in her condition made her already angry stomach lash out at her.

Ramsey didn't even miss a beat when he looked at her. She looked like she had been through hell and back last night. Her long brown hair was tousled and tangled, and she looked a green tinge to her skin. But it did nothing to detract from her beauty. It was quite apparent that she needed nothing to make herself look good.

"Oh good, you're awake. I was afraid you were going to die up there." His roommates gaped at her before smirking at each other and venturing upstairs, leaving her and Ramsey alone.

Lexi had no idea what time it was. Apparently, this was starting to become a trend around Ramsey. "What time is it?" she croaked hating that her voice sounded all throaty in the morning.

He could have listened to her speak all day with how sexy her voice was in the morning. "Nearly two."

"Oh my God!" she yelled too loud for her own ears. She pushed her palms to her temples and cringed. "Two in the afternoon?" she moaned.

"Yeah, we would have brought you back lunch, but we weren't sure what you wanted. I just got you coffee," he said holding up a brown Starbucks cup. She stared at it like it was her lifeline.

"Uh…thanks," she said awkwardly reaching for the paper cup. "How did I end up in your guest bedroom last night and not at a hotel?" she asked meekly.

"You were in my room," he corrected her taking a step into her personal space.

It was as she had dreaded. She had slept with him. God, she just wanted to bury her face in her hands. She didn't even remember sleeping with him. Had he been good? Had they been careful? Ugh…she felt like such a slut.

"I dragged you up there after you passed out on my couch last night. I got you awake enough for you to change," he gestured to her clothing. "Then tucked you into my bed, where you proceeded to pass out again. And now here you are," he muttered quickly.

"Wait, we didn't sleep together?" she asked blushing furiously as the question tumbled out of her mouth.

"I didn't know you wanted to," he chirped smiling down brightly at her. How did he look so good in the morning…oh wait, afternoon?

"Oh, I didn't say that I did. I just assumed…" she trailed off.

"No, I did exactly what I said I was going to do except the part where you slept in a hotel. I thought you would like better accommodations than that."

"Where did you sleep?"

"Couch."

"Oh, well, thank you." So she had been wrong. She liked knowing that her judgment was still intact. Jack had been misguided…just jealous ramblings of an ex-lover. Fantastic.

"Anytime," he said still not leaving her personal space.

"I know that you did a great thing by letting me stay at your place, but we really need to work on your manners, Country Club boy," she quipped.

"*My* manners?" he inquired.

"Yeah. Personal space," she reminded him sticking her hand out and pushing him back a step.

"Right. I forgot."

"Oh, black coffee. How did you know?" she asked after guzzling a good quantity into her system.

"I paid attention at brunch yesterday."

"Oh God, was that yesterday?"

"Yeah, hey, do you want to go get some lunch?" he couldn't help asking.

Lexi stared at him amazed. Was he asking her out? No way was that happening. Sure they had kissed and he had let her stay at his place, but that probably happened all the time. He was just being kind. And besides, she looked and felt terrible. He had to see that on her. Was he just humoring her?

"Uh...I don't have any clothes. They were in Jack's car."

"He left them," he said evading her first excuse.

"I still feel kind of shitty," she admitted.

"Alright. How about dinner?" he asked prepared for this.

"Oh," she began chewing on her bottom lip and pushing her hair behind her ears. What was she supposed to say? He had been very generous and all she had been was rude to him. She figured she at least owed him that much. "I guess we could do that."

"I mean, you don't have to go," he said misinterpreting her hesitation.

"No, no, we should go. I appreciate what you did for me last night."

"Hey, it's no problem," he said scratching the back of his head thoughtfully as he looked at her.

She smiled for the first time that morning. He had decided that he liked her smile much more than the frown she normally sent his way. He wasn't sure how he elicited such anger from her, but he would work much harder from now on so long as she continued smiling like that.

"Alright. Sounds like a plan."

"Like a date," he corrected sending her the most charming smile he could muster.

12

NOVEMBER TWO AND HALF YEARS EARLIER

"*You busy?*"

Lexi read the text message she received from Jack and smiled. She relaxed back against Clark's passenger seat. They were on their way back to his place from eating at a quaint downtown deli before finals.

"*Not sure. I'm w/ Clark. What's up?*"

"Who's that?" Clark asked his eyebrows furrowing as he watched her fingers slide against her beat up phone.

"Oh," she said her head snapping up as she pressed the send button, "Jack's just seeing what we're doing tonight."

"*I want to see your sexy little body.*"

Lexi's grin widened at the message. "*You miss me?*"

"What did you tell him?" Clark questioned her, taking the turn a little faster than she had anticipated. Lexi's shoulder slammed into the doorframe, and she readjusted in her seat glancing nervously at her boyfriend.

"That it was up to you," she told him returning to her text message.

"*It's been five fucking long days!*"

"*Well, in that case, maybe I can get away.*"

"Did you want to do something?" Clark asked attempting to read the message over her shoulder.

"Doesn't matter to me. We can if you want," she said her head still buried in her phone. "Did you want to?"

"*Do that. I can't wait another minute without you.*"

"I mean, I was planning on going home," he said checking her reaction.

She snapped her phone shut and turned to face him in her seat. "You want to leave?" she gasped. "I thought we were going to do something together this weekend. You were gone all last weekend with MBA stuff. Don't go." Clark had been accepted into their school's prestigious Business graduate program at the end of last year. It had been extremely beneficial that he had received the offer since that meant that he wasn't leaving for Atlanta to find a job. Instead, he would be able to stay in town for her senior year.

"I'll try. No promises."

"Lex, I'll make it worth it."

"I haven't seen my parents in a long time though. You know that."

"I know, but Thanksgiving isn't even until Thursday. Do you have to leave so early?" she asked. They had originally planned on going to their parents separately on Wednesday and staying through until the next weekend.

"You could come with me," he offered.

Lexi crinkled her nose. Lexi loved Clark's parents. They were caring and loving and always wanted to take them out, but she had thought they were going to spend some much needed alone time together. Guess he had a different agenda. "You know I have that big paper due."

"Oh I know you will make it worth it."

"Then what's stopping you?" Jack asked.

"It'd only be for the weekend. You'd still have the rest of the break to work on your paper."

"Yeah, maybe. I just feel really behind. With applications, LSAT, and everything, I've just had no time to work on this paper, and it's due as soon as we get back."

"Maybe I'll just go tonight and be back to be with you tomorrow. Would that give you more time to work on it?"

"Clark."

"..."

"I shouldn't. I can't."

"You won't. It's different."

Lexi stuck out her bottom lip. "I'll miss you."

"I'm sure you will."

"What if he's in town? I can't get away."

"You'll figure it out."

"So, what's Jack doing tonight?" Clark asked eyeing her suspiciously. "I didn't think ya'll were still talking that much."

"We're not really. I guess he's just bored. He's talking about going out downtown."

"What about Kate?"

"What about her?"

"Is he trying to get a group together?" Clark asked curiously.

"I guess so."

Clark pulled his phone out of his pocket and lit up the screen. "Hmm…I'm surprised he didn't message me too."

"We come as a match set. There'd be no reason to send messages to both of us," she informed him.

"How are you going to get away from her?"

"I don't know. I'll just tell her I don't want to hang out tonight."

"That simple?"

"Yes."

"I suppose you're right. Maybe after you're finished with your studying you could go out tonight. Hang out with the crew and all. You've been too stressed lately."

"Maybe," she stated uncertainly.

"Clark thinks we're all going out tonight."

"Why did you tell him that?"

"He was asking a lot of questions…"

"You should text Seth and see if he's going. That way you're guaranteed a good time, and plenty of girls to diffuse his advances," he said chuckling to himself. "Want me to text him?"

"Oh, no," she said quickly. She was pretty sure Jack hadn't messaged anyone else about it. "I have his number."

"You'll leave early with me if we go out?"

"Of course. Don't invite Clark."

"Like I'd want to."

*****

Hours later, after kissing Clark good-bye and getting all dolled up, Lexi waited rather impatiently in her apartment. She had refused Jack's offer to pick her up for proprieties sake. If they were going to be out in public, she would rather not make it look like a date. She had planned on driving herself. However, Olivia had decided she wanted a night out and had insisted on driving. That was fine with Lexi, but Olivia was pretty much the slowest person on the planet. It took her at least thirty minutes longer than anyone else she knew when it came down to getting ready to go out.

"Geez, Olivia could you take any longer?" Lexi asked pacing in front of Olivia's bathroom.

"It could," she muttered.

"You don't even have that much hair," Lexi pointed out.

"Which is why I have to make sure every tiny strand is perfect," Olivia said pulling her flat iron through her bleached blonde pixie cut again.

"No one is even going to be in town," she whined.

"Lexi, darling, that is the reason I *should* take so long. I'll spend more time with each person individually. This inevitably means I should spend more time on my hair," Olivia said taking pleasure in Lexi's growing discomfort.

Lexi groaned loudly. "I don't see why you have to take so long."

"I don't see why you have to be so impatient. Your boy isn't even going to be out," Olivia said letting her brown eyes flutter to Lexi's face.

A small blush crept onto Lexi's face. "So…"

"So chill out," she cried.

"Let's just get out of here."

"You can't rush perfection," Olivia explained placing the straightener on the off-white counter top. Her hand reflexively reached out for the tall hairspray bottle.

Lexi groaned again. "Honestly, how much of that stuff do you put in your hair?"

After spraying on another layer, Olivia snuck a glance at Lexi. "Alright, fine. Are you going to tell me *why* you are being so impatient?" she asked raising one eyebrow inquisitively.

"I'm always impatient."

"Not like this."

"I just…uh…miss Clark. I want to get out of here so I can get my mind off of him being gone," Lexi said anxiously pushing her hair behind her ear. She really was a terrible liar and did not want to have to deal with Olivia being any nosier than normal.

Olivia raised an eyebrow further. "You sure that's all it is? You look like you're anxious to see someone?"

"I don't know what you're talking about."

"Oh come on. I know that you've liked Jack since the beginning of time. It's not like you have to hide that fact from me," she said coolly leaning against the sink.

"Jack and I are just friends."

"Yeah, and pigs can fly."

"Livy, cut it out. You've been on me about Jack since you managed to get him to that concert. I just don't want to hear it anymore. You know what happened between us after that catastrophe. Leave it be for once," Lexi cried vehemently.

"I'm just looking out for your own good."

"Sure," Lexi said rolling her eyes.

"You know you can tell me anything, Lexi," Olivia said, her tone turning serious. "I wouldn't tell Clark if something happened with you and Jack. You're my best friend. I hope you'd trust me with anything. Or at least all the raunchy details," she said giggling.

Talk about a guilt trip. Lexi wanted to trust Olivia with the details of what had happened with Jack all those months ago, and what was continuing to happen to this day. Something deep inside told her that the only person she could trust with what she was doing was herself…and Jack, of course. Sure the gravity of the situation was eating away at her, but even that wouldn't open her mouth. How could she tell anyone how she felt when she was having issues discerning that on her own? She just could not imagine her life without Jack in it anymore, yet she was still with Clark. He was still with Kate. Neither of them had talked about breaking up. Yet, they still spent time together whenever possible. She didn't know what to think about that.

"I know I can trust you with anything, but there's nothing to tell," Lexi lied smoothly. "Can we get going?"

Olivia clicked the off switch on her straightener, glanced at her perfect appearance, and then nodded. Ten minutes later they were pulling into a rather fortunate parking spot down the street from Chamber. Lexi twirled her own stick straight hair around her finger as she approached the door.

"Stop fiddling with it," Olivia said swiping at her hand.

"My hair doesn't look good straight like yours," Lexi whined. "I can't believe I let you talk me into this."

"Whatever, shut up. Everyone is going to love it."

Lexi strutted to the door and smiled playfully at the bouncer. "Hey, Max," she said kissing him lightly on the cheek as she breezed through the door without him even bothering to ask for her identification.

To say that Chamber was dead this Saturday night would have been an understatement. They had gone out a little earlier than usual, but it still seemed that everyone in the city had gone home for Thanksgiving break. Lexi passed the empty dance floor marveling at how hollow the room appeared without bodies swarming the inside. Music filtered through the speakers at a surprisingly reasonable volume for a Saturday night. The only constant in the place was the voluptuous woman behind the bar.

"What do you want, girl?" Chasity asked sidling around the corner to give Lexi a hug.

"Whatever you want to make me," she responded easily.

"Dragonberry, Red Bull, Sprite, cranberry…the works," she mumbled to herself. "Liv, you want one too?"

"I'm driving," Olivia pouted.

"You volunteered," Lexi said pushing her lightly.

Chasity shrugged her shoulders. "I guess that means you'll stick to beer tonight then?" she questioned thrusting an open Bud Light at her.

"You know me so well," Olivia said cheerfully.

"Oh dear, look at who just walked into my bar," Chasity said fanning herself.

Lexi's head swiveled to find out who she was making a fuss about, but she really shouldn't have bothered. Jack was a damn good sight for anyone's eyes, but with Seth and Luke flanking him they were a sexy set. Jack was gorgeously built with his shaggy black brown hair and steely blue eyes. Seth towered over the other two and had a very boy-next-door look about him that made him appear to be safe. Well, at least until he opened his mouth. Luke had tousled blonde hair and light brown eyes, and was extremely clean cut. Though Lexi knew that Chasity was whistling at the trio, her eyes were solely focused on one boy. His easy smile upon seeing her sitting at the bar sent unexpected butterflies in her stomach. She couldn't tear her eyes away. She didn't even have the excuse of not seeing him often. She just wanted to drink in his every feature. The way he looked right then and there in his worn jeans, tight fit t-shirt, and navy jacket.

"Hey," he said nodding his head at the bunch. "Whoa, your hair." He immediately went to Lexi's side and fiddled with a straightened strand.

She smiled up at him, goose bumps kissing her skin at his gentle touch. "Do you like it?" she asked hesitantly.

"You look great," he said before he could filter his enthusiastic response.

"See, I told you!" Olivia cried. Lexi's smile widened.

"So, let's start the night off right. Shots all around and give me a hug," he demanded of no one in particular.

Olivia giggled and nudged Lexi forward as if he had been talking to her all along. She didn't need much coaxing as she nestled into his arms. He squeezed her tightly around the middle before releasing her.

"Good to see you," he murmured huskily. "Chasity, shots? Hug? What are you good for?"

Jack scooted around the bar as Chasity poured the clear liquid into six shot glasses. He wrapped himself around her from behind and whispered something in her ear that Lexi couldn't discern. Chasity laughed boisterously and shoved him away. "Whore," she murmured at his turned back.

"I'm not the only one," he quipped eyeing her black crop top and tiny black and white plaid skirt.

"I'm workin' here. Cut me a break."

"I would if you could count," he said sitting in the chair next to Lexi and leaning across the bar.

"What are you talking about?" Chasity questioned glaring at him.

"Seven," he said gesturing to the group.

Chasity's eyes scanned the set in attendance, and then frowned. She quickly shrugged her shoulders and poured another shot. "Not my fault you were hiding the little brunette mouse. Who is she anyway?"

Lexi jerked around to find out what they were talking about. "Sandy," she squealed enthusiastically. Despite the girl having zero common sense, she was beginning to grow on her. Apparently, she was extremely intelligent when it came to book smarts. She just wasn't capable of showing that to anyone. Once you finally got her to open up, she was a real riot.

"Lexi! I didn't know that you were going to be out."

"I didn't even know you were still hanging out with Seth," Lexi said raising her eyebrows up and down suggestively.

"Oh, you know," Sandy said blushing furiously, "here and there. Whenever he's not with some other girl, I'll give him a chance."

"I don't know how you do it. I would die if I had to share." A chuckle emanated from behind her. She glanced warily at Jack, and the smirk on his face grew.

"It's not the sharing that I mind, because I like to sleep with whoever I want. It's just you know how Seth is and how he treats girls. Sometimes he forgets that we're whatever…not trying to be exclusive. Then the lying starts and ugh," she told her shuddering, "I just can't even get into it."

"Bottoms up ladies," Chasity said pushing shots, several limes, and a salt shaker towards them.

"Tequila?" Lexi asked anxiously turning from her conversation with Sandy. "Are you trying to kill me?"

"Nah. Just loosen you up a little. You've been way too uptight lately," Chasity declared licking the crease between her thumb and first finger and pouring a generous amount of salt onto the space.

"Yeah, let's loosen you up," Jack said nudging her playfully.

Lexi glanced up at him and licked her lips provocatively. "I thought you didn't mind me being a little tight," she whispered loud enough for him to hear her.

His eyebrows shot up and he groaned a little at the mental image she was leaving him with. "Don't tease me, Lex."

"Who's teasing?" she asked raising her glass to meet the rest of the group.

"To gettin' fucked up," Chasity yelled as they clinked their glasses together.

Much to Lexi's surprise, Chamber did end up filling up considerably compared to the amount of people who arrived early enough to get personal attention from their sexy bartender. The townies were coming out of the woodworks knowing that much of the college population would be away for the holiday break.

As much as Lexi wanted to relax into their evening, something continued to nag at her. She couldn't figure out what it was. Ever since that fateful night back in May, Lexi had been very careful in situations around Jack. She tried to keep her distance so that Clark wouldn't see straight through her. And though he had never specifically stated that he thought something was up between them, he still commented on her behavior. He complained of her being distant and closed off, among other things...of a more sexual nature. Yet, that wasn't what was bothering her. Every time she would begin to stop thinking about Clark, it was like she could feel eyes on her. The idea was ludicrous. Chamber wasn't full by any means, but there were enough people in the place that no one specifically would be staring at her. She was recognizable from gymnastics meets, but she wasn't the star. There was no real reason for anyone to be watching her.

Olivia left early complaining that she wasn't feeling well. She asked Jack to take Lexi home smirking devilishly. Jack obliged her appeal. Seth and Sandy had not so discreetly located a corner to make out in, leaving Luke as a third wheel. Not too long afterwards, Luke was closely dancing with a large-chested blonde. Even with all of their friends occupied, Lexi still couldn't get over the feeling that someone was watching her.

"Jack," she began taking a strand of her straight hair and pushing it behind her ear.

"How can you be nervous right now?" he asked taking her hands away from her and placing them around his neck pulling her in close to him.

"What?"

"You're messing with your hair. It's a dead give-away," he said letting his bright blue eyes bore into her.

"Right, sorry. I just...I dunno...I feel like someone is watching me."

"Who would be watching us, Lex?" he asked incredulously.

"I said I don't know, but I just feel like eyes are being drilled into the back of my head," she informed him. Even as she said the words out loud she realized how paranoid and slightly delusional she must sound, but still she couldn't shake the feeling.

Jack pulled his gaze away from her and let his eyes slowly roam the dark, crowded room. He paused briefly as if examining the individuals in a particular location then shifted to circle the entire room. "If someone is looking at you, then they aren't right now. I can barely make out anyone ten feet away from me. I don't see how anyone could be secretive about looking at you even if they were watching. Seeing as no one is blatantly staring from where I can see, I really don't think you have anything to worry about."

"You're probably right," she said wrapping her arms around his neck tighter. His lips gently touched the soft spot behind her earlobe.

"If you really feel like that, we can get you out of here," he muttered huskily in her ear. "Actually, I think I should get you home. It's late." He didn't even check his watch.

"I'm glad you are so concerned for my well-being," she stated mockingly.

"Oh, I'm very concerned for your well-being. I want to make sure that you get home at a reasonable hour, tuck you in, and all that."

"Tuck me in?" she asked raising an eyebrow.

"Something like that," he muttered, his lips only inches from her mouth at this point.

She giggled and pushed him backwards. "Chill out. None of that," she said half-heartedly.

"Fine," he said sticking out his bottom lip. "I'm going to close my tab, and then we'll leave."

*****

A short while later, Lexi found herself in a very familiar bedroom wrapped in navy blue sheets. She stretched languidly on the bed and then perched on the edge waiting for Jack to join her. He exited the bathroom flipping the light off as he appeared before her. She couldn't keep her mouth from dropping open at the sight of him. He entered the room in only a flimsy pair of green boxers. He had been doing some serious workouts lately since he was out of school, and the effort was really paying off. His already well-defined six-pack was toned to perfection. His arms and chest had grown in direct proportion making the full package look positively delectable. His tousled brown hair hung just above his crystal clear blue eyes looking at Lexi as if he were about to devour her.

She smiled coyly and patted the bed. He snuck under the covers and pulled her towards him. "You're so little," he said against her collarbone as he kissed a line across it.

"Um...thank you," she said squirming under his light kisses.

"And you should always wear my t-shirts," he said pulling back to examine the grey band shirt she had picked out from one of his drawers.

"You don't like my clothes?" she asked pouting.

"Oh, I definitely love your skimpy little things, but you're so...raw," he said pushing her bangs off her forehead and really looking at her deeply. "So utterly beautiful, my dear."

A slow sweet smile played across her mouth as he stared at her lovingly. "Thank you."

"No," he said letting his fingertips trail across her jaw line. "Thank you." He covered her body with his and pressed his lips firmly against her own. The tenderness and affection he portrayed in that one kiss Lexi thought could last a lifetime. Tears welled up in her eyes as their tongues briefly touched then broke apart. "You're crying," he said concerned.

"I'm sorry. It's dumb," she said swiping at her eyes.

"Is something wrong?"

"It's just…I don't know, Jack. That was *amazing*. I know you can say it was just a kiss, but…"

He cut her off. "No, I felt it too," he said knowing that she didn't have to explain what had just happened between them.

"You…you did?" she asked in disbelief.

He leaned in once more and placed a chaste kiss on her lips. "Yeah. I did. Maybe we should just get some sleep," he suggested.

Lexi nodded as she lay down on his shoulder and snuggled into his muscular chest. She had no idea where to pinpoint that feeling. It was something she had never experienced. It was wonderful, painful, euphoric, and disarming all at the same time. She felt like her heart was ripping out of her chest, and like she had just had the most amazing adrenaline boost of a lifetime. The scariest part was that she had no idea how such a small thing like a simple kiss could make her feel like this. Those were her last thoughts before she drifted to sleep securely placed in Jack's arms.

*****

"Lex…Lex, wake up." She heard her name called, but all she wanted to do was snuggle up further in the covers. "Come on, Lexi. You need to wake up."

Lexi rolled over onto her back and stared up into her favorite pair of baby blues. "G'morning," she mumbled.

"Your phone has been ringing off the hook all morning. You should probably go figure out what's going on," Jack told her.

She felt a jolt of adrenaline hit her body, and she bolted out of bed terrified to find out why her phone was blowing up. She had three missed calls from Clark and four from Olivia. Lexi thumbed through the texts, most of which were from Olivia checking to see if she had gotten in alright last night. Then as Lexi progressed through the messages, she noticed they began to get more frantic.

"Where are you?"
"What are you doing?"
"You didn't come home. I'm freaking out."
"Have you spoken with Clark, because he keeps calling me."
"LEXI, what do I tell him?"
"What if he shows up at the apartment? Can't you just get back here?"

Lexi sighed heavily when she reached the end of the messages, a hard knot forming in her stomach. This couldn't be good. Clark would never call Olivia unless it was important. Maybe something had happened while he was home. She wasn't sure, but she figured she should get home sooner rather than later.

"I've got to get going. Something's going on with Clark. I'm not sure what, but I have to head out," Lexi told Jack as she changed out of his t-shirt.

"Alright, let me know what you find out," he said kissing her briefly on the forehead before she darted out of the house.

Olivia was pacing the living room absently strumming her guitar when Lexi walked through the door. She looked like she hadn't gotten much sleep the night before.

"Where the fuck have you been?" Olivia squealed before Lexi could say a word. She placed her guitar in its stand and stared at Lexi angrily. "Clark kept calling and texting saying that you weren't answering your phone, and that you weren't responding to any of his messages. What did you expect me to tell him?"

"I'm sorry. I didn't expect this to happen. I had a few too many drinks last night and ended up sleeping at Jack's place," she told her. Most of what she had said was true.

"I figured as much, but I wasn't about to tell him that. He would have come back and barged into Jack's apartment without notice."

"He could have. It's not like we were doing anything," Lexi lied biting her lip at Olivia's frustration.

Olivia snorted. "Suuuure. In either case, I finally picked up and told him that you were fine and just passed out in your room from drinking last night. I'm surprised he isn't over here yet. You should definitely call him."

"I'm not sure why you are so frantic," Lexi commented.

"Because I'm lying for you. I don't mind, but you can at least confide in me," Olivia cried. "I'm your best friend, and you can't even tell me the truth. You're a different person than you were when we first knew each other. I think this has to do with Jack, and I'd really like to be clued in."

"For the last time, there is nothing going on between me and Jack," Lexi said storming into her room and leaving Olivia hovering at her door.

"If that's the case, then why didn't he just bring you home last night? Huh?"

"Because he'd been drinking too and he lives closer to downtown," she said, the lie coming out easier this time. She couldn't even count how many she had made by now. They all seemed to be running together.

Olivia seemed to just let it go from there. There was no point in trying to argue with Lexi when she was in this state.

She pulled out her phone again and texted a message to Clark, *"Sorry. I passed out last night from drinking. Hope you're not worried."*

Then she typed out one to Jack. *"Made it safe. No need to worry."*

After several hours of silence from Clark, Lexi was beginning to get worried. If he had been so frantic earlier, why wasn't he returning her message now? It was very strange. When she was about to send him another message, a knock on the door sounded from the living room. As she went to check the front door Olivia was already standing there with it open talking to Clark.

"Hey, I was just wondering about you," Lexi said smiling brightly.

"We need to talk," Clark said walking into her bedroom without another word.

Olivia looked at her anxiously as Lexi followed him into her room, her smile dropping from her face. "I got all your messages."

"Then you know what this is about?" he asked in a very serious tone.

Lexi's stomach knotted together, and she could hear her blood pounding away in her ears. This wasn't about something that had happened when he had been home. No. Judging by the way he was looking at her, she could tell. He knew. She had no idea how he knew, but he did. He hadn't touched her. He had barely looked at her. And those lone looks had been ones of disgust. Not the loving tender looks she normally received from her boyfriend.

"I'm not sure," she answered tentatively.

"Don't do that, Lexi."

"Do what?"

"Lie to me anymore. Just don't lie. Okay? Can we just go through this one goddamn conversation without you lying to me?" he asked running his hand through his shaggy black hair a couple times before resting his green eyes back on her.

"Uh, yeah, sure."

"Tell me what happened with you and Jack."

She stared at him, anxiously holding her hands in place so she wouldn't be tempted to mess with her hair. Everyone kept pointing out that little habit to her, and this would be the worst time for it. "What about me and Jack?" she asked gulping hard.

"Lexi, please!" he cried his breath quickening. "Just *don't* lie to me."

"I'm not sure what you want me to say."

"Just the truth."

"There's nothing going on between me and Jack." She had said the words so often that even she sometimes believed them when they rolled off her tongue.

"Goddamnit, Lexi!" he yelled turning around in place and visibly tensing at her words. He looked as if he were about to throw something across the room. "I already talked to Jack!"

Lexi froze in place. He had talked to Jack? She couldn't believe it. Had he gone to Jack's place after she left this morning which is why it had taken him longer to get here? Jack must have told him everything to save his own skin. Lexi meant nothing to him. She just wanted to cry. Why wouldn't he have at least warned her that he had spoken to Clark. Unless of course she really did mean nothing to him. Everything he claimed to feel for her had just fallen away when he had been confronted by her angry boyfriend…his angry friend.

"You talked to Jack?" she whispered.

"Yes, he told me everything."

"Everything?" she asked in disbelief.

"Yes."

"But nothing happened," she said attempting to stick to her story.

"Lexi," he began shaking his head. "I already talked to Jack. Don't give me that. Now I don't want to believe him, but I need to hear the truth from you," he said facing her cowering figure. "Tell me what happened between you and Jack."

Lexi gulped even harder this time fear glistening in her eyes. She realized that she was compulsively threading hair behind her ears from anxiety. She had never wanted things to turn out this way, but somewhere along the way everything had been flipped upside down. How could she tell Clark what had happened between her and Jack? If she just blurted out the facts, it would make her look bad. Worse than she actually was, but if she left something out that Jack had divulged he would know she was lying and hiding things from him. It was the prisoner's dilemma she had learned about in school. Except there was no winning side to giving away any information. "We slept together."

"You slept with him?" Clark asked hardly containing his disbelief. She nodded. "When?"

"May."

He did the math in his head. "Almost eight months ago?" he cried. "When did you have time? We were together all month."

She choked back tears before answering him honestly. "It was at the beach house."

"Are you fucking joking? While I was asleep in the same house? Has it happened since then?" Lexi sighed heavily and shook her head no. "I don't believe you. You mean to tell me that you fucked eight months ago, and it hasn't happened once since then."

"No, it hasn't. We decided not to."

"Oh, for your own fucking sake," he paced rapidly around the room doing anything to keep from looking at her.

"It hasn't happened again."

"How do you expect me to believe that?"

"Because it's the truth."

"I don't think you fucking know what that is." Lexi remained silent not wanting to egg on his anger. "Have you done anything else since then?"

"Yes. We kissed some, and I would spend the night at his place."

"Oh, you just kissed a little. You want me to believe that you spent the night and didn't fuck? I told you not to lie to me."

"We didn't do anything more."

"What about last night?" he asked cornering her.

"What about last night? Nothing happened."

"I wouldn't say *nothing*! I saw you at Chamber with him all over you."

Lexi's mouth dropped open. She hadn't been manic and delusional. Someone actually had been watching her all along. She couldn't believe it. "You were watching me?"

"Yes and I'm not ashamed of it either. You would have never told me the truth, and I needed to see ya'll together for real."

"I can't believe you would do that."

"I know, because I'm not the scheming scumbag who goes behind people's backs. That would be you and your little fuck buddy. I can't fucking believe you, Lexi. Were you even careful? Did he get checked for diseases? How could you sleep with me after you slept with him? How could you even look at me with those big beautiful brown eyes of yours and tell me you love me? When you obviously don't."

"I do love you," she said quietly.

"I don't want to hear that from your deceitful, manipulative, lying mouth."

"I am so sorry, Clark," Lexi gasped sucking in deep breaths between tears.

"I still can't believe you actually slept with him" He crashed back against the bed burying his face into his hands. "You little whore."

Lexi's glazed eyes stared down at him. Her humiliation was evident. "It wasn't like that."

"You slept with him while you were with me," he said through clenched teeth. Finally, looking up at her, he said, "That makes you a whore." She brushed her palm against her cheeks forcefully. It did no good, the tears kept coming faster. "After all that bullshit you fed me about ya'll just being friends. After all the warnings I gave you about him." She couldn't tear her eyes away from him as his anger intensified. "Fuck, Lexi, you told me yourself that you didn't think he had been faithful with one person he'd ever been with. Why would you let this happen? *How* could you let this happen? Do you think you are special? Do you think he's just going to leave Kate for you? He just wanted to fuck you. And, now he's done that. Try to explain to me how that doesn't make you a whore?" he spat at her.

She had no answer for him. She had never felt so belittled before in her life, and she knew that she deserved every word. She had made a terrible mistake, and then on top of that she had attempted to hide her dirty actions. No wonder everyone had told her that she was acting uptight lately. She had been carrying around such a weight on her shoulders since that night in May. It was almost a relief that Clark knew.

"I just…I need to get out of here and think about this," Clark said standing resolutely. He brushed past her and entered the living room.

"Clark…" she cried as he pulled the door open. "What does this mean for…for us?"

"I really don't know, Lexi. I just can't look at you right now. I'll just…call you tomorrow after I've had time to think about all of this," he said turning away from her and shutting the door.

Lexi crumpled to the floor shuddering from the tears raking her body. She could not believe that had just happened. How had she been so stupid to let this happen? She had just let the best guy she had ever had in her life slip through her fingers.

After a minute, Olivia came out of her room and sat on the floor next to Lexi. She scooped her up in her arms and held her as she bawled.

"Did…did you…h…hear all…of that?" Lexi asked her through her tears.

"Yeah, honey, I heard it. Why didn't you just tell me? You know I would have been there for you. You know I would have kept everything a secret. I can't believe you went through all of this alone," Olivia said brushing aside her bangs. The movement reminded her so much of Jack that it only intensified her tears.

"I…I don't either. I just…thought…that I could…handle this," she muttered.

"Alright, darling. You have to get up. Take a shower, and then things will look a little brighter."

Lexi nodded as Olivia ushered her out of the living room. "No!" she cried suddenly.

"What?"

"I have to go talk to Jack," Lexi decided.

"I don't think that's the best thing for you right now."

"Jack told him everything. How could he do that?"

"I'm almost certain Clark threatened him into it, but that doesn't matter. Seeing that boy while you're in this state is a really, really bad idea."

"No, Livy, let me go. I need to go find out why the hell he would tell him everything and not warn me," she said pulling away from Olivia and running for her keys.

She was in the car before Olivia could utter another comment about staying home. She drove much too fast to Jack's house, swerving to get around rather slow drivers. She skidded to a halt in his parking lot, and dashed out of the front seat. Bursting through the still unlocked door, Lexi darted into Jack's room. She could tell just by looking at him that he had showered. Her heart melted at the sight. She was furious about what he had done, but her heart still longed for him. She wanted things to go back to the way they were only this morning. She wished with all her being that she didn't have to be angry at him.

"Lexi, what are you doing back already?" Jack asked surprise written on his face. "Are you okay? Have you been crying?" He rushed forward to meet her. She backed away not wanting to feel his hands on her.

"How could you tell him?" she asked breaking down into tears for the second time that morning.

13

PRESENT

"Where are you taking me?" Lexi asked Ramsey for what felt like the hundredth time since they had been driving. She hadn't thought much of it at first, but then as her mind registered the direction the car was taking them she began to get more suspicious.

For some reason, she had expected them to stay in Buckhead and have dinner at a fancy five star restaurant over candlelight, perhaps serenade her with live classical music, red wine, and caviar. Show off his wealth to reel her in. She wasn't sure what had triggered that idea beyond just the fact that she had assumed all people in Country Clubs went on ridiculously impressive dates.

Jennifer, her college dorm mate, had told her many times about extravagant opulence displayed before her by men her parents had set her up on dates with. Lexi had always been wary of those types of stories and wondered if women actually succumbed to such antics. One too many towels on Lexi's dorm door confirmed that they did actually work. As Jennifer proved this time and time again, Lexi slowly became adjusted to the fact that lavishness was more like a prerequisite.

She was relieved that she didn't have to go through another awkward situation such as what occurred at the Country Club. She hadn't exactly wanted to go on this…outing with Ramsey, but after how he had treated her she had given in. He had called it a date and she certainly couldn't forget his words. He had smiled so brilliantly at her acceptance that she had almost been duped into believing she had made the right decision. But how could she really feel like that? He had so many strikes against him already. Setting aside the kindness he had showed at his party, he was a member of a Country Club, he was *related* to Bekah, and clearly had no concern for others' personal boundaries.

All in all, she figured this was a huge mistake.

Her brain was working in overdrive attempting to discern where he was taking her. His forced silence on the subject only made her more curious. She had really only known this guy for one day, and the only good quality she had recognized besides his charming good looks was that he hadn't slept with her.

Maybe that was pretty big for guys, but she had blacked out and was entrusted into his care by his sister. Obviously that meant something to him.

"Really, Ramsey, where are we going? We're getting pretty close to my parents' house, which I should remind you, is very far away from your place," she told him.

"We're close to your parents' place?" he asked glancing over at her.

Lexi twisted her fingers back and forth in her lap, uncomfortable with revealing more information. Not that she was ashamed of her family by any means. In fact, she really got along with her parents and two younger sisters. But after being reminded of the Country Club, expensive Buckhead condominiums, and insane parties that resulted from such wealth, Lexi didn't really feel comfortable explaining middle class to someone who had never had a bank account with less than seven digits. She had never even taken Chyna home, and she loved the girl to death.

"Uh, I guess. I mean I don't really know where we are," she explained trying to maneuver the conversation back to their destination and farther away from her.

"We're close," he said adding a wink at the end.

"*We're* close?" she asked arching an eyebrow.

"Are you not close? I mean, you are sitting right next to me," he commented trying to keep the devilish smirk off of his face.

She smiled brightly, happy that she was still capable of flirtatious banter with someone other than Jack. "Oh yes…in the sense," she said looking at him from under her eyelashes.

He burst out laughing in a loud, boisterous, uninhibited manner that she had witnessed at the Country Club before brunch. It had annoyed her the day before even confused her a little, but maybe that was just part of his personality. Perhaps, there was more to him than what met the eye, but she wasn't going to keep her hopes up. She would be polite and let him take her out to dinner this one night.

"So how close are we?"

He jerked his head to the side at her husky tone. He had liked her when they had first met, because she had been completely forthright with him. She cared very little for his status, and showed it. He liked her the night before when she had been drunk, unrestrained, and outgoing. Her endearing personality only intensified with the alcohol. But this woman he was with tonight, he seemed to think he liked the best of all. He saw her possess the same strong-willed determination and unblemished character she revealed in the morning and the natural engaging playfulness that resulted from a combination of liquors. He could certainly get used to her surprising personality.

His eyes roamed her face resting where her bottom lip was caught between her teeth in a thoughtful expression. God, she had tasted so good the night before. He wasn't sure how he had been able to restrain himself. He hadn't told her that she had propositioned him in her drunken stupor. He was almost certain that a woman of her caliber would be mortified that she had been so willing to give herself away. Possibly even more mortified that he had turned her down flat. That he had had to peel her arms off of him and practically wrestle her under the covers, he had also left out of the story. Still, when she had managed to weasel her arms back around him pressing her tiny form against him, he had still found the strength to extract her eager body from him. He remembered how readily his body had reacted to her. He gulped and attempted to force those thoughts out of his head.

"Probably only about ten, maybe fifteen, minutes," he answered her.

She rested back into his comfortable champagne colored seat and felt her phone buzz in her purse. She extracted the old thing and checked the text message.

"You busy?"

Lexi sighed as she stared at the words on her screen. She hadn't exactly been expecting a text message from Jack, and she didn't want to dampen her mood with thoughts of him. She closed the phone and placed it back in its position.

"What's up?" Ramsey asked curiosity getting the better of him.

"Um…oh…nothing," she answered not wanting to address the situation with him. So far it seemed that he knew little of what had happened with her and Jack, and why she was in Atlanta in the first place. If at all possible, she would really like to keep it that way. Jack had a funny way of ruining every relationship she had ever been in. Even though she had no thoughts of that for Ramsey, she wasn't going to risk anything just yet.

Lexi heard her phone buzz again. Annoyed, she stared down at the message. *"Lex?"*

She really did not want to deal with him right now. She quickly shoved the phone deeper in her purse. Hopefully, she wouldn't be able to know if he messaged her again.

As they neared their destination, they listened to whatever was playing on the radio. Neither of them minding what was coming through the top 40 station at that moment. Realization began to dawn on her as stared out at the horizon, but she shook her head in disbelief.

No, he couldn't be taking her there. She hadn't been there since she was a kid. Beyond that fact, it wasn't exactly a place to take your date. She had always gone there with family or church groups. More a place for group entertainment than dating. Not that she was looking for a normal sort of date from Ramsey. She had only been thinking a while ago that she was relieved he hadn't taken her to some special five star dinner, but this was really about as far from that as a person could get.

Ramsey reached the gate and handed over a wad of cash to the eighty-something year old attendant and breezed his Mercedes into the establishment. They took the winding road past rows and rows of pine trees until they reached a valet parking lot at the front entrance.

Lexi glanced around in awe and wonder at Stone Mountain. Her eyes focused in on the giant mural that had been hand-carved into the rock during the Civil War as a testament to their faith in the Confederacy. She felt like a speck next to the giant mountain that tourists from all over came to climb and enjoy the surrounding park which consisted of camping grounds, a water park, train station, and over the summer an amazing laser show. This was the last place she had expected Ramsey to take her. For some reason, that made it all the better. Surprisingly enough, he didn't think that he needed all of his wealth to impress her, and he was right. At this moment, she was impressed.

She flattened out her green spaghetti strap dress she had worn for the occasion and silently thanked God that she had decided on brown thong sandals instead of her heels. Ramsey jogged around the car and directed her towards the stone pathway leading to the lawn reserved for the laser show. She let her eyes leave her surroundings long enough to glance at her date for the evening. He wore a nicely cut polo that matched the green shade of his eyes and fitted khaki pants paired with brown flipflops. She liked his casual attire, and wished she had paid more attention before. She might have realized that they wouldn't be going to some extravagant place had she recognized his flip-flops before this moment.

"I hope you're hungry," he said as they walked around the corner and down another path that opened up to the main lawn.

"Starving, actually," she admitted cringing at how that sounded.

He smiled at her bluntness. Yet another feature that he was starting to like about her. "Good. We have a banquet."

When they reached the grass, they trekked forward through a line of people. Apparently, everyone was setting up for the laser show. It was the last week before school officially started for the public schools in the area, which generally brought out more spectators than any week except Memorial Day Weekend and Fourth of July. Lexi had no idea how they were going to find a quiet place to sit and eat after arriving so late for the show.

She should have suspected something was up when a large opening in the crowd appeared before her. Her mouth dropped open at the display before her. Ramsey had called ahead and had the area cleared specifically for them. A large quilted blanket, much like the ones she slept with back in Manhattan, covered a ten by ten space on the lawn. A giant wicker picnic basket sat at the center of the roped off expanse and a cooler directly next to it. It was the most ideal location for watching the show. He must have done all this hours earlier. A grin broke out across her face.

"Is this the kind of treatment you reserve for all your dates?" she asked sitting down on the massive blanket.

Ramsey smiled brightly at her, still standing. "Not exactly," he admitted.

Lexi had been joking, not expecting an answer in the first place. Though, she wasn't sure if he was telling the truth anyway. It could just be a line. She couldn't picture the type of women she had seen at his party the night before being happy with an outdoor picnic and laser show as their first date. She shook her head realizing that she was overanalyzing. Who cares if he didn't normally take girls on dates here?

Luckily, he had learned his lesson and sat on the opposite side of the blanket from her giving her a wide berth. He was always so up in her face and it really just brought out the worst in her.

"I didn't know what you wanted," Ramsey began digging into the basket, "so I just got a bunch of things. You can decide what you like."

"When did you have time for this?" she asked. She had stayed at his house all afternoon. Granted, she had felt like shit much of that time and took nearly an hour long shower.

"I just made a list and had some people take care of it," he said sheepishly.

"Oh." She should have figured. It could have been worse. He could have not gone to the trouble. She shook her head again in frustration. Why did she care whether or not he went and picked out dinner for them? She had to keep reminding herself she didn't *really* want to be here. Right?

Lexi watched him extract a bag of green grapes from the bag and immediately snatched them out of his grasp. He jolted in surprise. She sent a smile his way and popped one into her mouth.

Ramsey couldn't help himself from staring at her. Lexi's cheeks were flushed from the Georgia summer heat and lips wet from licking off the grape juice that had squirted onto her bottom lip. He gulped heavily fishing around in the basket for something to distract him. He uncovered the remaining food and removed two cans of Coke for them.

She caught him watching her, and in her eagerness scooted closer towards him so they were nearly touching. "Want one?" Lexi asked holding a grape between her fingers. He nodded and before he could reach out to take the fruit, she pressed it in between his lips.

He crunched down on the fruit trying to act as if that hadn't affected him. "Thanks."

Lexi batted her eyelashes before sitting back on her side of the blanket. Her hand brushed her bag and felt the vibrations through the material. She retrieved the device and flipped it open. *"Are you okay? Where are you? Why aren't you returning my texts? Lexi?!?"*

Lexi sighed heavily and bit her lip as she read through Jack's text message. She had completely forgotten about messaging him back. She quickly typed out a reply and closed her phone. *"Sorry. Alive."*

"You got to your parents safe then?"

Turning her head to look at Ramsey's perfect bone structure, she giggled a little to herself. Man, if Jack knew where she was at this moment, he would have a fit. She wasn't sure if she wanted to tell him though. At least, not over text message. Not when she couldn't use the information as leverage. *"Safe."*

"Anyone important?" Ramsey asked casually taking a bite of the sandwich in his hand.

Lexi rolled her eyes. "Just Jack again." God, she hated how familiar this all felt.

"Ahh..." he said unsure if he was prepared to broach that subject.

"Do you want to come over tomorrow or something?"

Lexi sighed again. Did she want to go see him? Yes. No. There wasn't really a good answer. If she was honest with herself, the answer would be yes. The answer would always be yes. She always wanted to see him. She hadn't spent any time with him in two years, and she missed him. A part of her always missed him. They had gone through so much, it was hard to not want to be around him. Even though things always ended so fucked up, her brain wouldn't let her forget the in between times when things were oh so good.

"Yeah. I'll let you know."

"Great."

"So what's up with you and Jack?" Ramsey asked against his better judgment. Lexi's eyes immediately darkened.

"Oh, just...you know," she stated vaguely unsure how much she wanted to reveal. He didn't know anything now which was probably for the better.

"Not really. You two seemed pretty heated last night. Was he just drunk? I'd never seen him that way before," Ramsey admitted hoping to push the right buttons. He could see her begin to visibly relax as the attention fell away from her.

"I've just known Jack for a long time, and he's pretty protective. Kind of like an older brother," she said dryly. She couldn't help thinking that Jack would make *the* worst older brother in the world.

Ramsey smirked noticing the ever-so-slight twitch in her muscles that indicated she was lying. He had always considered himself a great judge of character even when his parents hadn't. Lexi's phone began to buzz next to her again.

"Hello?" Lexi asked not recognizing the Atlanta phone number. Last time that had happened, she had been led here. That thought almost made her want to drop the call, but the sound of a chirpy voice cut off her line of reasoning.

"Hello, dear," Bekah said from the other line.

Cringing at the uppity sound of her voice, Lexi pulled the phone away from her ear. "What's up?"

"Where are you?"

No way had Jack put her up to this. Then again she had to have gotten the number from somewhere, and Jack was the prime suspect. "I'm busy. Was there something you needed?" Lexi asked avoiding the question.

She let her eyes fall back on Ramsey who looked at her inquisitively. She shrugged and mouth *Bekah* to him. His eyebrows shot up in surprise.

"Yes," Bekah stated rather deliberately. "I don't believe we've finished our conversation yet. Do you have plans tomorrow? I'd really like to take you shopping for Jack's big day, and we can talk then."

Jack's big day? She hadn't heard anything about his big day. What was his big day? What were they celebrating? She had no idea, but she didn't particularly want to give Bekah the satisfaction of knowing that piece of information.

"Fine. How about I call you tomorrow?"

"Sounds great, sweetie," Bekah said happily. "Jack, stop," Lexi heard her mutter playfully in the phone. She didn't even know if Jack was actually there or if Bekah was just being a bitch. She supposed it didn't really matter since it had worked. Lexi could feel her heart constricting and pain crease her temples. Her throat was closing up and she felt her body seizing at the thought of Jack being alone with Bekah. Lexi coughed uncomfortably and said a rushed goodbye before slamming the phone shut.

"What was that about?" Ramsey asked, concern evident in his voice.

"Your sister wants to take me shopping," Lexi informed him pushing several strands of hair behind her ear forcefully.

"That's nice of her," Ramsey said. Though for some reason, he didn't really think it was.

Lexi snorted. "Nice. Right."

"You don't have to hang out with her," he stated absentmindedly. He passed a sandwich to her, and she reached into the basket to investigate the contents further.

"Yeah, I know, but Jack wants me to," she said shrugging.

"Why is that?" he asked honestly curious.

Lexi shrugged again. "Beats me. We've known each other for a long time, and I guess since I'm here he wants me to get to know his girlfriend too."

Ramsey took a deep breath to keep from asking too many more questions. "How long are you here for exactly?"

"School starts on Monday. I guess until Sunday then. A week total." Lexi smiled at the grimace that crossed his face. She wasn't entirely sure if that was because she was staying too long or too short, but she was going to go with the latter. She had found herself in quite an interesting scenario.

"I guess you'll be here long enough for Jack's birthday then," Ramsey said leaning back on his elbows and examining her reaction.

Lexi's mouth popped open in surprise. Oh my God. How had she forgotten his birthday? Of course, it was his birthday this weekend. And, if she recalled, this was a big one indeed. Twenty-five years old. Wow. A quarter of his lifetime gone by, and she had known him since he was just nineteen. She couldn't believe she had forgotten. "Oh, yeah. What is he doing exactly?"

She couldn't believe she was asking Ramsey for information about this. Why hadn't Jack mentioned it? Had he assumed she wouldn't come? Did he not want her to be there? There were so many questions that she needed answered. At least now she understood why Bekah wanted to go shopping for *Jack's big day*.

"You don't know?" he asked skeptically.

"I wasn't really filled in," she admitted awkwardly.

He sure thought it was strange that she had come to visit Jack, but he hadn't even invited her to his birthday celebration. "It'll be a surprise for you too. Want to go with me?"

Lexi was interrupted from answering as her phone went off in her hand. "Goddamn it. Who wants to talk to me now?" Lexi popped open the phone. "Hello."

"Alexa!" Chyna squealed on the other line. "Oh my goodness, chica, I have missed you. How have things been going with, you know, everything? Are you planning to come home to me sooner rather than later?"

Lexi's laughed as soon as she heard her best friend's voice. "Chyna, it's so good to hear from you." Lexi glanced over at Ramsey who's expression had lightened in accord with her own enthusiasm. "Sorry to disappoint, but it doesn't look like I'll be joining you back home anytime soon. Though I do miss New York terribly."

"I knew you would," Chyna trilled. "How could you not? I know the summer is scathingly hot, but to get away to go somewhere not only hot, but humid? Disgusting."

"You convinced me to come down here in the first place," she reminded her, getting lost in their conversation and not realizing that she was giving away information in front of Ramsey.

"Yes, well, how does closure suit you?"

"Actually," Lexi said pushing her hair behind her ear as she glanced at Ramsey's all too curious face, "I can't really talk about that right now."

"And why not? You're supposed to be with your family tonight, right?"

"Err..."

"Oh my God, Alexa, you are *not* with him right now are you?"

Lexi's brows furrowed together hoping to God that Ramsey couldn't hear Chyna's end of the conversation. "No, no, no, no, no," she muttered quickly. "I'm just...um."

"Do not lie to your best friend."

"I'm not lying," she quickly corrected. "I'm just...on a date." Ramsey's bright smile at the recognition of their date was totally worth it. This guy seriously had everything going for him. Which begged the question, what was he doing with her? But she couldn't think about that right now.

"What?" Chyna squealed. Then thinking the better of it, she asked, "With whom? Jack? It better not be Jack. Your vague texts over the past two days haven't been enough. Fill me in. What's going on?"

"Chyna, I'm kind of in the middle of something here," Lexi reminded her.

"Oh geez, Alexa, I'm sorry. I'll let you go, but I better get some details. You know how long I've been waiting for this to happen. If you don't call me by tomorrow..."

Lexi cut her off. "Good night, Chyna." Lexi closed the phone and turned the damn thing off not wanting another such distraction. "I'm so sorry. I'm usually not this popular," she admitted smiling at Ramsey who just shrugged off the statements.

"No problem at all. Was that someone from home?"

"Yeah, my best friend," she told him.

Luckily, there were no interruptions for the remainder of the evening. The two managed idle chit chat with little interrogation or their normal rude behavior towards one another. The sun set as they finished their meal and an announcement went out signifying the beginning of the laser show. Lexi got lost in the twirling lights and loud popular music blasting from the speakers. She couldn't believe that they were capable of displaying scenes to go along with the music that were large enough to cover the entire side of the mountain. The couple involuntarily snuggled closer together as the show continued. Ramsey had even ventured to lace his fingers with hers.

When the show ended, the surrounding families and groups began to pack up. Lexi sighed finding it strange that she was actually sad that the evening was coming to an end. She began to pull away from him, but he pulled her back down.

"It's not over yet," he muttered into her ear.

"But everyone's..." she began gesturing to the crowd.

"Wait a second," he said smiling down at her.

Lexi glanced around hoping to find out what he was talking about. Half of the people were already exiting the lawn, and they hadn't even moved yet. She knew it would take awhile to get out of the park and was ready to start the long ride back to his place. If there was more to come, then no one else had been informed. She was about to tell him that he had been misinformed, when a loud pop sounded from the mountain.

Lexi's eyes darted up to the sky as a red firework exploded, covering the night sky. There were never fireworks this time of the year. They only ever had fireworks for the week of the Fourth of July. The surrounding crowd had halted their urgent packing to look up at the shimmering colors falling towards the earth. Several more fireworks erupted from their perspective locations producing earsplitting booms and crackling popcorn. Lexi stared on in wonder as more and more fireworks colored the sky.

"I can't believe they did this," she whispered into the night. "I didn't think they had fireworks this late in the season."

"They don't."

Lexi shifted her gaze momentarily to stare into Ramsey's shining green eyes. "They don't? What do you mean?"

He smiled at her, reaching up and cupping her chin. "I thought you'd like the surprise."

"You mean...you did this?" she asked putting the pieces together.

"For you."

She couldn't do much more than nod before his lips touched hers gently. She knew they had kissed the night before, but she had been drunk at that point and acting without inhibitions. This kiss occurred because she wanted it to. It was gentle and brief, but he sure did taste wonderful. She had no idea how he still tasted of peppermints. She hadn't seen him eat one or anything. When he pulled away, she couldn't help but whimper at the loss of his warmth. He chuckled and placed one more kiss on her lips as the fireworks display came to a close.

He took her hand and pulled her to her feet. "Come on. Now we can go."

"Shouldn't we pack up?" she asked looking at their feet.

"Nah. I'll have someone take care of it. Let's get you back. I'm sure you're exhausted."

Lexi filtered in and out of consciousness on the ride back to Ramsey's apartment. After last night, all she felt like doing was sleeping. Her evening with Ramsey had been magical. She was pleasantly surprised that he was capable of being well...human. She had such a terrible stigma against anyone from a Country Club that she had immediately thought he would be just like everyone else. And though at times, he did play that part, and obviously he had a good deal of wealth, she didn't feel like that was the main part of his character. He was able to be a fun-loving guy, who just happened to have money, rather than the other way around, as she expected.

"I appreciate you taking me out and letting me stay here the night before," Lexi told him truthfully, pushing a piece of hair behind her ear. She followed him up the stairs to the front door. "I guess I should probably get a hotel or something tonight."

He stopped and turned to look at her. "You could come inside if you like."

Lexi gulped not feeling comfortable with the direction of that statement. She wasn't really prepared to take this to another level. "Uh...I don't think so."

He scratched his head thoughtfully. "Sorry. No. I didn't mean it to sound like that. I have a guest bedroom. If you'd like to stay here another night, you are more than welcome."

"Oh, well..." She didn't know whether or not to accept the invitation. She was dead tired, and couldn't exactly afford a hotel. "I guess that's alright."

Ramsey veered her towards the guest bedroom on the top floor and left her to get dressed for the evening. She changed into her own sleeping clothes and brushed her teeth. A soft knock sounded on the door and she pulled it open. Ramsey stood before her clad in nothing but a pair of black athletic shorts. Her eyes traveled to his six pack and then back up. She gulped unsure if she would be able to control herself if he came into the room.

"I wanted to give you a proper good night," he informed her bending his head and crushing their lips together. She breathed him in enjoying every bit of pressure he was exerting onto her lips. She could tell he was trying desperately to keep himself from going further just like she was. She wasn't exactly known for her ability to resist temptation. Her body was still flush against him when he pulled back, his breathing ragged, and his pupils dilated.

"I...uh," he muttered pulling back a fraction of an inch.

"Yeah," she agreed her own breathing coming out in short puffs.

"You know you never did answer me earlier this evening," he said resting their foreheads together.

"About?"

"Will you accompany me to the birthday festivities?"

"Sure," she said just as he captured her lips again. She moaned as his tongue slid against her own. Satisfied with her answer, he pulled back again.

He cleared his throat and stepped back into the hallway. "Well, good night."

"Good night," she whispered closing the door and leaning back against it.

"Shit," she muttered to the empty space. "What have I done now?"

14

DECEMBER TWO AND A HALF YEARS EARLIER

"How could you tell him?" she asked breaking down into tears for the second time that morning.

"What are you talking about?" Jack asked glancing helplessly into Lexi's bloodshot eyes.

"You told Clark about what happened. You told him everything."

"Lexi."

"How could you do that?"

"Lexi…"

"I've been lying to him for months, he confronts you about it one time, and you tell him everything. And for what, Jack?"

"Lexi, please let me…"

"No! For what? What could you possibly gain from telling him? Do you think he'll spare Kate the knowledge of what we did? Because I don't."

"Geez, Lex, can you give me a minute?"

"A minute? Oh yes, so you can try to explain? No, I don't want your explanations. I already know what happened. You told him, and he's going to tell Kate. All because you told him. I can't believe this is happening," she said her breath coming out uneven. She could feel the characteristic tingling feeling in her fingers and lips that let her know she was hyperventilating.

"Lexi," he said stepping towards her, mouth hanging agape.

"Don't touch me!" she shrieked pulling away from him. "I can't believe you."

"Could you listen to me for one goddamn minute?" he asked finally raising his voice.

She stopped her rampage. "Fine, say what you wanna say."

"I didn't talk to him. I didn't say anything."

Lexi's eyes shot up to his face, her heart full of hope. Then she shook her head. "How did he know? He said you told him everything. You must have told him, Jack."

"I told you I'd never lie to you again. Look at me," he commanded. "Lexi, look at me. Look in my eyes and tell me I'm lying."

Her eyes lifted to him once again. She searched those beautiful blue eyes for some sign that he wasn't telling the truth. For anything that made him seem like he would tell her boyfriend to spare himself. Anything at all that said he didn't care about her. But she found nothing there. He looked as sincere as he could get.

But how could she believe him? He could lie his way out of a lie detector test if need be.

"I...I don't know what to think. Why would Clark say that if it wasn't true?"

Jack's face had gone pale at the realization of what she had said. In his earnest desire to let Lexi know he hadn't breathed a word to Clark, he had completely skipped by the fact that Clark knew.

"He trapped you, and you told him everything," he finally said soaking in the information that Clark knew...and Kate would soon follow. "Fuck."

"Oh God, this is so fucked up," she cried falling to the couch. "He actually didn't talk to you. The conniving little..." she trailed off. It was useless to be angry at Clark. She should have told him in the first place, and it was her fault that he was finding out this way. How could she have let this happen? How could she have let this thing with Jack spiral so far out of control?

She was acting just like Jack had while he dated Danielle. Only three years ago, she had screamed at him for doing less with her behind his girlfriends back. Now look at where she was. How had she changed this much over the past couple years? She would never have let herself get into his kind of position with anyone else.

Damn it! Why did Jack do this to her? It was so exhilarating being in his presence that sometimes she felt like she never wanted to leave. After the amazing night they had shared, she couldn't believe they were sitting here like this. Less than twelve hours since that amazing kiss, lying wrapped up in his arms, and here they were arguing and freaking out about the people they were *actually* dating finding out. God, they were pathetic.

Beyond that, she had no idea what to do. She had come here ready to be angry at Jack for the rest of eternity, and now what? He hadn't done anything wrong. In fact, she had been the one to spill the beans. If anything, Jack should hate her, but the way he was looking at her said a different story.

"What are we going to do?" she whispered through her fingers. Her head rested in her hands and tears trickled down her face collecting in a pool in her palms. She felt the sofa adjust next to her as Jack's weight shifted the cushions. He slowly brushed her hair back several times pushing a few loose strands behind her ear just like she habitually did.

"We'll figure it out," he said soothingly.

Lexi sobbed into her hands as he continued to stroke her hair. There was nothing he could do or say that would make her feel better at that moment. She was lost in her own misery.

"Are you going to tell Kate?" Lexi asked finally looking up at him.

His hand stilled at the nape of her neck as their eyes met. "I…uh…I dunno."

"Jack, you know he's going to tell her about it. He was so angry. If you had seen him, you'd understand what I'm talking about."

"Did he say he was going to tell her?" Jack asked her.

"Uh…well, no," Lexi admitted. She assumed Clark would tell Kate everything. If she was in his position, that's what she would do. Jack had ruined Clark's life. It seemed only fitting for Clark to return the favor.

"Maybe he won't tell her," he said wistfully.

Lexi stood swiftly. "So, what? You're just going to go on with your life?" she asked through her tears. "You're just going to go back to Kate? I don't understand you at all. Even if he doesn't tell her, she's sure to find out. She's not all that bright, but she's not an idiot. She had to know something was up. Clark did."

"I doubt she would find out," he said looking down.

"What? How could you say that?"

"You said it yourself. She's not as bright as Clark, who obviously figured this all out on his own. If he didn't say anything about telling Kate, then maybe he's not going to tell her."

"And you're not going to tell her?"

He met her fierce gaze. "I don't see why I would."

"Oh…you don't see why you would."

"God, Lex, you wouldn't tell Clark if the positions were reversed." She didn't really want to think about that. She had no idea what she would do if the roles were reversed. "And anyway, I would never let Kate have any idea what we were up to."

Lexi gasped. "Are you implying that I set this up for him to find out?"

"I'm not implying anything. Stop putting words in my mouth. All I'm saying is that there's no way you would tell Clark. You'd have no reason to tell him."

Lexi's mouth just hung open. Was he serious? He could find no reason to tell his girlfriend that he had been cheating on her? She sighed heavily. "I don't know what I would do, because circumstances aren't reversed, but I'd at least be smart about it."

"Fine. Tell me how to be smart about all this. You think telling Kate is a *smart* decision? Well, you're wrong. Kate and I have been together for years, and if I told her it would crush her."

"Maybe you should have thought about that," Lexi said.

"You think I didn't think about that? I fucking think about it all the time. But you…I don't even know. Once I remembered what it was like to be with you, I didn't want to let it all go again." Lexi allowed herself a small smile at his admission. "But I wasn't ready to get rid of Kate either. And I'm still not ready to get rid of her."

"But you're ready to get rid of me?"

"No, that's not what I'm saying. God, I don't even know what I'm saying. All I know is that I can't tell Kate just yet. I couldn't imagine being the one to crush her. She would never be the same."

Lexi shook her head in disbelief at everything he was saying. It was like last time except now she knew about what was happening. She had allowed herself to get into this position for the second time with the same guy.

Not that she had been prepared to let go of Clark, but that seemed to be the obvious course of action. This was something that wouldn't go unpunished. Clark was the kind of guy who could find a million different girls to be with, and he had chosen her. At the flip of a switch, he could have any other girl.

A part of her knew that was coming. It was inevitable that Clark was going to leave her. That inevitability wasn't in place for Jack. But even so, she couldn't even count the number of times she had thought about actually being with Jack in a relationship. She had imagined them together for so long, it was strange to see that for the third time they had screwed up beyond repair. Jack wasn't leaving Kate. Lexi knew it, but she couldn't come to grips with that reality. She had always assumed that if things broke apart in their relationships, that they would be together. Not that they would be apart. She had never believed they would be apart.

"Jack, be realistic. She's going to find out one way or another. If you don't tell her, then Clark will. Then where will you stand?"

"What do you expect me to do, Lexi?" he asked standing forcefully. "Think about it. What would *you* do in my place? You have this great life with an amazing girlfriend who would do anything for you, and you would throw all that away?"

"If your life was so great, then what the fuck is this? What have we been doing since May?" she screamed gesturing between the two of them.

"I don't know, Lexi. God, I don't know. Give me some time to think about all this."

Lexi's mouth dropped open. "You need some time to think? I didn't have any time to think when Clark confronted me."

"That's not my fault! Alright!"

"I thought we were in this together," she said weakly. Her mind was whirling. Clark was right. It's not like this actually mattered to Jack. He may not have told Clark about what had happened, but it wasn't like he was going to leave Kate for her either. He had set her up in his mind to be the *other* woman, and that's where she resided. That's where she had always resided. She had never come first with him. Even when his relationship was threatened, he couldn't see past his "amazing" girlfriend to what was really in front of him.

"This is all so sudden, and I just need time to get things straight. I can't rush over there right now and tell her what happened. Even if I did that, it's not like we could be together. You still have to straighten things out with Clark. So let's put this whole conversation on the brakes. You're already upset. I don't want to continue to cause you pain."

Too late.

Lexi felt completely drained as she left Jack's house. Somehow she managed to get back to her apartment in one piece. She collapsed onto the couch. Glad, at least for the moment, that she had no more tears to shed. Her eyes were bloodshot and puffy from crying. Her complexion had drained of color. Her lips were only a soft pink. The messy ponytail she had forced her hair into that morning had all but fallen out. She realized for the first time that she didn't even match. She wore purple sweatpants coupled with a ratty orange t-shirt and blue zip-up hoodie. She kicked off her red, black, and white sneakers to reveal one orange and one neon yellow sock. She couldn't even remember changing.

Lexi stared upwards pathetically counting the number of dots on the ceiling. She reached a number somewhere in the triple digits, forgot which ones she had already counted, and then started over again. Then she started losing count of how many times she had numbered the same area. She closed her eyes hoping to block out the pain she was feeling. All she wanted to do was forget that all of this had happened. Close her eyes and wake up to find that everything was back to normal or at least skip to the part where she felt like a human being again.

She wasn't sure how long she had been lying there when her phone started buzzing. She didn't even realize she had stuffed it into her pocket. A feeling of dread took over her body as she stared at the screen flashing Clark's name. Her stomach curled in around itself wondering whether or not she should answer. Of course, she knew she *should* answer, but she really didn't want to hear him say the words that she knew was coming. How could she let this all be over?

She felt the phone buzz once more, and then with a loud sigh answered the phone. "Clark," she mumbled into the phone.

"Hey, baby," he said from the other line. Lexi's heart fluttered at the pet name. Well that was a good sign. She shook her head. No, it was more likely a habit. She wasn't sure if she was supposed to respond to him or if he was going to do all the talking. Her throat felt like it had a handful of cotton balls shoved down it, and even if she had wanted to initiate conversation, she would probably need a full glass of water before she could even attempt to manage it.

"We need to talk." Lexi gulped. That didn't sound good. How could he sound so calm after blowing up this morning? How was he so controlled? She was all over the charts. She had cried for hours, and then stared at the ceiling for God knows how long. Clark sounded more like he had just taken a brisk morning jog, gotten out of the shower, had breakfast, and was ready to start the day.

"Alright," she began, clearing her throat. "Let's talk."

"Come meet me for coffee."

Lexi's head swam as a vision of Jack standing behind a counter handing her a paper cup brimming with coffee filled her. She snapped her eyes closed hoping to clear her head. The last thing she needed to think about right now was Jack. "Can I...just come over?"

"I'd rather not be at one of our houses."

Why did she always have to associate coffee with Jack? She just wanted to hit herself. Everything seemed to remind her of Jack. She needed to focus on what he was going to say to her. She needed to remain calm as he broke up with her.

"Coffee it is then," she said weakly. "See you soon."

"Yeah."

Lexi decided that it really didn't matter that she was going out in public in something resembling a clown outfit. If all she was going there for was to be broken up with, then what did it matter? It didn't really add to the humiliation. She couldn't humiliate herself any more than she already had.

*****

Her eyes traveled the familiar building, her heart aching with memories. She entered through the side entrance to avoid getting a glimpse of the counter area and her all too familiar study space. She breathed in the rich aroma of freshly brewed coffee and appreciated the dull green glow that emanated from the lamps resting on every table. At least this light didn't hurt her already damaged eyes. She saw Clark nestled in an overstuffed couch next to the fireplace with two cups sitting before him. They both appeared to be untouched.

Their eyes met across the room. She felt frozen in time in that second as she stared across into his hazel orbs. Clark had always been so intuitive, so knowledgeable. Even from her spot rooted to the floor in front of the entrance, she could tell something had changed in him. In the short time they had been apart, he had come to a decision. A decision that Lexi knew would change everything.

Lexi meandered through the crowded room, and plopped down next to Clark on the sofa. He handed her one of the cups. "Black, like you like it," he said taking a sip of his own cup.

That was strange enough in itself, because Clark didn't drink coffee. He was one of those self-motivated people who could survive the morning without that extra buzz. She eyed his cup like it might explode any minute. He followed her gaze to his cup, and revealed a half smile that quickly dissipated. "It's hot chocolate," he confessed.

"Oh."

"You're probably wondering why I asked you here," he said.

Lexi didn't really wonder. She knew why she was here. He needed time before to think about things, and then after thinking things through he was ready to break up with her. He might love her, but Clark wouldn't be second best. He wouldn't let this slide. However, all she said was, "I guess."

"I just…can I ask you something?" he questioned putting his cup back down on the table and turning to look at her.

"You just did," she said meekly, "but sure, go ahead." She wasn't sure why he was prolonging this. It would just be better to get this over with. Cut the strings and all that.

He gave her another half smile before it fell off of his face again. A curl fell into his eyes and he pushed the hair back into place. Lexi hadn't even realized he had let his hair get so long. He normally cut it all off before it was long enough for her to play with. How had she missed the fact that she was able to run her fingers through his thick mess of curly hair? Had she been so lost in her other world that she hadn't really been present in this one? Her heart contracted at the knowledge that she would never again have the privilege of playing with his beautiful hair.

Had Jack been right? If the roles had been reversed, would she have given everything up? Would she have willingly given up Clark? Her eyes followed the curly hair down to the five o'clock shadow across his chin, up to the plump lips, and then finally resting on his hazel eyes. Now with him right in front of her, she couldn't be sure.

"Do you want to be with me?" Clark asked breaking her out of her thoughts.

"Of course I do," she said without another thought.

"Why…" he began taking a deep breath. "I want to ask why you would do this to me if you claim you want to be with me, but I know that is a useless path to take. You did it because of Jack. I should have known all along. I should have seen the warning signs. I *did* see the warning signs. I just didn't want to believe that anything had happened. I wanted us to stay exactly where we were. We were happy, right?" he asked his eyes pleading with her.

"Yeah. We were happy."

"I knew from the get go what Jack meant to you. I could see it every time his name was mentioned. I could see it every time he was near you. I knew it every time you had to run away from him. You did that to save us. I can see that now," he said. "Then, I forced ya'll to be around each other. What did I expect by doing that? I should have known that ya'll wouldn't change. Ya'll would only continue to harbor the same affection you felt previously. Right?"

Lexi gulped and then nodded.

"That's what I thought. Now, I didn't think ya'll would sleep together. I thought that perhaps you would be smart enough to realize that this would be done if that happened."

Lexi gulped again even harder. There. He had said it. They would be over if that happened, and it had.

"I guess I didn't expect it to continue. I tried to turn a blind eye. I tried to be with my girlfriend, but you weren't the same girlfriend. I guess you haven't been for a long time," he said, his eyes momentarily darkening. "That's when I couldn't deal with it any longer. I couldn't be with a shadow of the woman I love. And that's what you've become." He reached out and took her hand. She was so shocked by his grasp that she nearly dropped her drink. "So please, Lexi, baby, my dear, my sweet, my love, answer me honestly. Do you want to be with me?"

Her heart fluttered at his words. After everything they had been through and all the good times they had shared, did she really want to give that up? Jack didn't want her. She had to know that by now. He wanted Kate. He had all but come right out and said that earlier today. They couldn't be together. A part of her felt like she was dying with that thought. Jack had been such a large part of her heart for so long, she wasn't sure if she would ever be the same person without him. As cheesy as it sounded, she felt complete with him. A completeness she had never felt with anyone else, not even Clark. Yet, Jack didn't want her and she needed to move on from that.

"I do want to be with you," she answered.

He searched her face for a lie or some sign of falsehood, but couldn't locate any. Lexi was a terrible liar, and he could almost always pick out when she wasn't being honest with him. But as he stared into her big chocolate eyes, he realized she was telling the truth.

"I want to be with you too," he said pulling her into a hug.

Lexi couldn't stop the tears from streaming down her face again. How had this happened? How had she come out of this scenario unscathed? Well, almost unscathed. After all, she had lost Jack. She pushed that thought away. No need to think about him. He was gone.

Clark still wanted them to be a couple. She was having a difficult time processing that information. For the third time today, everything had turned out completely opposite of what she had been expecting. She had been mentally preparing herself for a break up, and he hadn't wanted a break up at all.

When he pulled away from her, there was something different in his eyes that she didn't recognize. "I just need one thing from you, if we're going to stay together."

She should have expected this. No way was he going to let her walk away so easy. "What is it?" she asked warily.

"Lexi, you really want to be with me, right?" She nodded, the anticipation rising. "Alright, if you really do want to be with me, then you have to tell Kate."

Lexi's mouth popped open. "What?" she squealed.

He wanted her to tell Kate what they had done. God, what a terrible thing for him to ask her to do. She couldn't imagine what Jack would think of her if she did tell Kate. No, actually, she did know what he would think of her. He would never speak with her again. He would never want to see her again. He had flat out told her that he didn't want Kate to know. He didn't think Clark would tell her, and he wanted to get on with his perfect, amazing life with his perfect, amazing girlfriend.

"If you want to be with me, then it won't matter that you tell her," he stated simply.

She couldn't close her mouth. She was in such a state of shock. She had never realized how vindictive Clark could be. He was asking her to ruin another person's relationship, another person's life like she had been so easy to do to her own.

So, it came down to whether or not she was willing to give up Jack. Because after this, there was no turning back. Jack would never forgive her for this. Earlier he had seemed slightly unsure, but she knew what that meant. He had already made his choice in Kate, and now she was going to go and ruin that for him. No, he wouldn't forgive her, because Kate would surely leave him. Lexi knew the news would crush Kate. Jack had been right in that at least.

"But, Clark…it would…it would, I don't know," she mumbled incoherently.

"She has a right to know the truth about him," he said darkly.

"Of course. Of course she does," Lexi said nodding. "But to have me tell her."

"I don't see a problem with it."

"It would be the ultimate insult."

Clark smiled the first true smile since she had arrived. "Not to her."

Lexi bit down on her lip...hard. Of course Clark would want to get back at Jack, and having her tell Kate would do just that. "Clark, I...I don't know about this."

"Lexi, it's really simple. You said you wanted to be with me, and you do want to be with me. I can see that. I'm just asking you to do one simple thing. Tell Kate what happened."

What he wasn't saying was that he was actually asking her to do two things. She would have to give up Jack and not just his friendship and the relationship that they had grown into. She would have to give him up forever. No contact with him at all. Telling Kate would ensure success in that aspect. Could she do it? Could she actually go without Jack?

"Fine. I'll tell her."

Lexi pulled out her cell phone and found the number that she had never used waiting for her. She clicked send without thinking about it. If she thought about it, she would never actually go through with what she was about to do.

"Hello?" Lexi heard her answer.

"Kate. Hey, this is Lexi."

"Lexi! Oh my God, I haven't heard from you in so long. What have you been up to?"

"Um...yeah, not that much. Can we meet somewhere to talk?"

Kate was silent on the other line for a minute, and then she answered, "Sure. Jack and I were going to hang out tonight because he was busy last night. But he won't be here for another hour or so. Where did you want to meet?"

Lexi tried not to show her guilt at her words. Jack had been busy last night because of her. He had told Kate he couldn't hang out, because he was with Lexi. "Um...wherever you want. I can come over if you want."

"Sure, sounds good."

After getting directions, Lexi left Clark at the coffee shop and made her way over to Kate's house. She had never been to her place, and she was dreading making this her first visit. The house was situated in a small subdivision outside of downtown. Each house was a bright color ranging from yellow to pink to baby blue. Most were single stories, but the one Kate resided in looked to be a two-story townhouse with a small yard and white picket fence. The area was trying to bring the suburbs to the city, and Lexi had always found them adorable. Well, until now.

Kate let her inside on the first knock and ushered her into the living room. Lexi had a faint idea based on Kate's appearance that Kate's family was relatively wealthy. As she looked around the townhouse, she realized this was definitely the case. An olive green couch sat on one side and two brown chairs occupied the other side. The television that was mounted on the wall fit the size of the room to perfection. Picture frames hung tastefully on the walls and the oak side tables were filled with pictures of her friends. The most common face Lexi noticed other than Kate's was Jack. He was all over her house. Scattered in nearly every picture frame. A brown jacket she recognized as his hung on a hook at the front entrance. A Wall Street Journal, Jack's favorite newspaper, sat on the coffee table.

Lexi gulped and looked up into Kate's enormous blue eyes. "Have a seat, sweetie. What did you want to talk to me about?" Kate asked gesturing to the seat next to her on the sofa.

Taking a precautionary seat in the adjacent chair, Lexi shoved her hair behind her ears several times. She had no idea where to begin. She opened and closed her mouth several times before looking down at her fingers resting in her lap. She glanced back up at the oblivious girl, her heart going out to her for what she was about to do.

"Have you noticed anything different about Jack lately?" Lexi began.

"Different? Different how?"

"Uh...just anything."

Kate chewed on her bottom lip gloss covered lip seriously contemplating the question. "No, I don't believe I have."

This was going to be harder than she thought. "You haven't noticed that he's been missing a lot more than usual?"

"Well...I guess he has been missing, but not really more than usual. We've always had an understanding that we don't have to be together all the time for our relationship to work. He can have time away from me if he wants, and I have the same privilege. It's just how we work. Not many people would be okay with that, but we are. Why?"

"Okay, I don't really know how to say this so I'm just going to dive right in. Jack and I slept together."

The silence that followed was unlike anything Lexi had ever sat through. She wasn't sure if Kate was going to lunge at her or break down in tears. She looked shell shocked for sure. That had to have been the last thing she had been expecting. The tension could have been cut with a spoon. Lexi wasn't sure if she should run now. Her heart was hammering in her chest with the anticipation of Kate's response.

"Why would you tell me something like that?" Kate finally asked barely above a whisper.

"I had to let you know and Jack wasn't going to tell you."

"Why would you think I'd want to know something like that?"

"I just…thought you'd want the truth."

"I didn't," she said shaking her head forcefully from side to side. "I didn't want to know that."

Lexi just stared at her. She didn't want to know. She had crushed her for no reason. "I'm sorry."

"Sorry?" Kate asked her eyes glaring at her. "For what? Fucking my boyfriend or for telling me that you fucked my boyfriend."

"Uh…"

"Just…just don't answer that. I don't want to know. I don't want to hear any of it. I just want to forget you. Forget you ever existed. Please leave my house."

"Kate."

"No, I don't need any other information from you. Thank you. Get the fuck out of my house," she said standing and pointing towards the door.

Lexi stood in complete shock at Kate's reaction. "Are you going to tell Jack that I told you?"

"No. I'm not telling him anything. Now leave."

"Why are you so calm about all this?" Lexi couldn't help asking.

That question seemed to change everything about Kate. Lexi had never seen the girl anything but way too perky, but she looked damn well furious. "You think I didn't know that he fucked you? God, I am not stupid, you fucking whore." It was Lexi's turn to look shell shocked. Kate had known all along, and she hadn't said anything. "I knew the first day that it happened."

"You did?" Lexi couldn't believe it. No one else had been out on the pier that day. No one else had known they were there. Kate certainly hadn't even been awake that night. "How did you find out?"

"I was there. I walked into his house, because I have a key that he gave me. He had his bedroom door open, and there you two were on his bed." Lexi's mouth popped open. "I just loved Jack enough to see past that one incident."

"That wasn't the first time," Lexi admitted to Kate the information she had withheld from Clark.

"What?"

"That was about a month ago, right?"

"That's what you were talking about, isn't it? You were feeling guilty, and you had to let me know about it. Well, fuck you, I already knew that it happened. I knew and could get over the fact that he was unfaithful that one time."

"No. You have it all wrong. The first time was at the beach house."

Kate turned and stared at her. "That was in May."

Lexi nodded watching the news dawn on Kate. "That's what I came here to tell you."

"No." Kate murmured falling back down onto the couch. "Ya'll have been sleeping together since May? Why is he with me then?" Lexi shrugged. Lexi, of all people, did not have an answer for that. "If you've been sleeping together since then, why are you just telling me now? Why are you telling me at all?"

"Clark found out, and Jack wasn't going to tell you. I thought it was right to let you know."

"I never thought he would do this."

Lexi rolled her eyes and then felt bad for doing it. Of course, he would do this. Then again, he probably didn't reveal this side of himself to too many people. Lexi just happened to be on the wrong end of this scenario twice already.

"I mean, I'm a virgin."

"What?" Lexi squeaked. She steadied herself on the molding to the front entrance. "You're a what?"

"I just thought that if it was one time, he would get it out of his system since we don't sleep together. We do everything else, but we don't have sex. I didn't think it was that big of deal, but this...this is different."

Lexi couldn't do anything more than stare at her. She's a virgin. Jack had never mentioned that. Not once. The look of despair that passed over Kate seeped into Lexi. How had she done this? It was a question she couldn't help repeating to herself. She had slept with Jack and Kate hadn't. Jack and Kate had been together for years and never slept together. Lexi couldn't process that information. Jack had no self-restraint. He was completely incapable of it around her. Just like she had no control around him. How was he able to go years without sleeping with Kate?

"Get out," Kate said. "I can't stand looking at you. You took something that wasn't yours, and you don't even seem remorseful. If I ever set eyes on you again, it will be too soon."

With that Lexi pulled the front door open and rushed out of the house to her car. She was so lost in what had happened that she hadn't even noticed the very familiar Mazda 3 pulling into the driveway. She tried to dart into her car before he would notice her, but she wasn't quick enough. Jack hopped out of his car and sprinted to her side.

"What are you doing here?" he asked venomously.

"She is a virgin," was the only thing Lexi could get out at the sight of him.

"Oh God," he said running his hands through his hair. "What did you do?"

"She is a virgin."

"Lexi," he yelled grabbing her by the shoulders. "What did you do?"

Tears began to form in her eyes again as she looked up at the handsome face. "Why?"

"I came here to tell her."

"Why?"

"So we could be together."

"You didn't want to be with me," she said feeling her weight sinking in his grasp.

"Lex, I've wanted to tell you for so long…that I love you."

Lexi's head snapped up. "You what?"

"You've known for a long time. You say it to me all the time with your eyes. I came here to straighten things out with Kate. To make things right for us."

"Did you say you love me?"

"Lex, you know I do."

"No, no I don't," she said pulling herself away from him and slamming into her car door.

"You're just lying to me."

"I'll never lie to you again. I've told you that so many times. Just let me straighten things out so we can work this out."

"I don't want to work it out," she said numbly staring at him. She was still shell shocked and saying the first thing that came to her mind. How could he say those things to her? After everything he said, how did he expect her to react? Did he think she was going to roll over for him? She had made a decision in that coffee shop with Clark and she was going to stick by it. He couldn't just come in here with his sweet talk and think everything would just go back to normal. He wanted her now, maybe, but that wasn't good enough. He had to want her all the time. He had to need her. He had to put her first. If he loved her, that's what he would have done from the beginning. But Jack had never put anyone first in his life. "I want to be with Clark. He wants to take me back."

The look on Jack's face hurt more than Lexi ever thought would be possible. "Fine. Go be miserable with your little lap dog. Forget what I said. Just forget it," he said turning away from her, and pushing aside the lone tear that had managed to seep out of his eye. "Forget it all."

But she would never forget.

15

PRESENT

The next morning a town car pulled up in front of Ramsey's place and waited on Lexi with breakfast and coffee. It wasn't the type of hospitality Lexi had been expecting to receive from Bekah. When they had last parted, it hadn't exactly been on good terms. So far, everything had officially gone completely opposite of how she had planned. All she had wanted to do was tell Bekah her story and leave Jack behind. By now she was supposed to be sitting on the back porch of her parents' house sipping on a margarita and enjoying the remaining week at home. Instead, she found herself being whisked off to some boutique to go shopping for Jack's birthday party.

She sighed and took a long sip of the black coffee hoping the caffeine buzz would kick her brain back to its proper mode of functioning. If she could get out of this situation sooner rather than later that would be better for her rattled nerves. The only problem was that she wasn't sure what to tell Bekah.

Things with Jack had never been simple enough to put a label on.

For some reason, everything had to be complicated when it came to Jack. If they had just dated and got bored with each other like normal couples, then maybe she could just go to Bekah and tell her a very simple story. But under the circumstances, Lexi thought it did their relationship a disservice to reduce it to such simplicity.

How she felt about Jack crossed lines that she wasn't sure many other people ever experienced. The way he looked at her, touched her, and seemed to understand her made the whole scenario much more difficult to explain.

And it's not like she could tell Bekah the entire story. No one had ever heard the entire story. She was all but certain that Jack hadn't confessed anything. No way was he going to tell anyone else about New York, and Lexi never had the heart to reveal all the details to anyone else.

So that left her back at square one. What should she tell Bekah?

Lexi had expected to pull up in front of some swank boutique. To her surprise Phipp's Plaza appeared before her eyes. The mall parking lot was already swarming with expensive cars bustling to feed their owner's shopping desires. Lexi hadn't been inside since high school and the only reason she hadn't returned was because she hadn't been able to spend a dime in the place. It wasn't a Manhattan boutique, but it wasn't like Lexi could afford this either.

She pushed her bangs off her forehead as she entered into the overly air conditioned shopping centre. She felt out of place in her loose fitting purple tank and khaki shorts compared to all the fake princesses clicking along the marble in their four inch Manolos and swishing their tiny butts in professional garb.

When Lexi had received the message from Bekah, she had just been about to go out on a morning run. She hadn't had much time to do anything but change shorts and throw her hair into a slicked back ponytail. Bekah probably wasn't going to approve of her choice, but there wasn't anything she could do about it. She hadn't let Chyna persuade her into a five hundred dollar t-shirt, and that was her best friend. No way was she going to let this be any different. Lexi dealt with high end, wealthy people every day of her life. She was almost certain that there was nothing Bekah could send her way that would throw her off track.

Bekah's nose turned up ever so slightly as Lexi approached the entrance to Jimmy Choo. She placed a fantastic pair of brown leather boots back on the stand and sauntered up to the tiny girl. Bekah had never been one to put much effort into her appearance. She had always been the beautiful Southern Belle with long flowing blonde hair, baby blue eyes, and a clear complexion. She always stood out from the crowd and the wealth her parents bestowed her only helped with her wonderful wardrobe.

Under differing circumstances, she could see why Jack had thought she would get along with Lexi. She had the same no theatrics beauty, and carried herself as if she owned the world. She looked just as beautiful, if not more so, than any of the other women who spent millions every year trying to achieve the flawlessness that came to these two women naturally.

This girl obviously had charm.

"Lexi, how wonderful to see you," Bekah trilled giving her a quick hug.

Lexi was momentarily caught off guard by Bekah's continued hospitality. This girl really was an enigma. One moment she was a snotty nosed bitch out for her life, and the next she was all happy-go-lucky girl next door. What was scarier was that Lexi didn't know how to predict her actions. Was it something that Jack had said that forced this woman to play nice with her today? Did Jack even know that they were out together again? Lexi hadn't bothered to call him. She knew she would have to speak with him eventually. She just didn't know how much of him she could handle yet. He acted as if everything was fine and there was nothing between them, but then there were moments…shining moments where he was *her* Jack all over again. And she knew in those moments, she was lost. He would somehow work his magic and make her remember what it was like to be with him. That was when she needed to be on guard the most. She had to get closure. Wasn't that what all this was about?

Her thoughts seemed to press in at her temples, and she forced a smile onto her face as the pain continued to crush in on her. She didn't want to think about that right now. She had been able to forget for the briefest of moments about Jack while she had been with Ramsey. That had been her break. Now, she needed to get back to reality and fight out this battle so she could move on with her life.

"Good to see you too," she said pulling away from the embrace. "What are we up to?"

"You'll never believe it," Bekah began ushering her away from Jimmy Choo. A slight glint in her eye remained as she passed the high heeled boots she had been holding.

"What?" Lexi asked feigning interest.

"I had this gorgeous one-of-a-kind handmade Vera shipped to me last week for Jack's big day. Well, my seamstress got a hold of it to do some last minute repairs and destroyed it." The look on Bekah's face was pure devastation. "I've never fired anyone so fast, and she's been working for my family for years. You can't go and ruin a brand new dress. I've no idea what she was thinking, but there was no way to salvage it and still have the desired effect."

"So, you need a new dress."

"As do you," Bekah told her angling her body to direct them into Barney's.

"Oh, no I don't think so. I can't afford…"

"Money isn't an option," Bekah said the twinkle in her eye replaced by something else…a bit more mischievous.

"I'd never be able to repay you. I simply cannot accept anything, but I'd be happy to help you find something," Lexi said not wanting to ever be in debt to this woman or anyone else other than the Federal government for her student loans.

"I'll take answers to my questions as payment. How does that sound?" Bekah asked.

"I don't think so," she said uncertainly.

"Let's just talk and if we find something for you, then that was payment, and if not, then you're just fine. Is that better?"

Lexi chewed on her bottom lip not wanting to give in to her. She tucked a lock behind her right ear and fidgeted outside of the store. "Fine, but I doubt I'll find anything."

"Great!" Bekah exclaimed linking her arm through Lexi's and pulling her into the store.

They were immediately greeted by a tall, leggy associate with maroon hair and heavy makeup. She couldn't have been over thirty years old, but somehow with all the caked on layers she appeared older. "Miss Bridges, what a great surprise to see you in the store today," the woman said standing demurely before the perfume counter.

"Thank you, Katherine. My friend and I need something spectacular for Jack's big event tomorrow. Can you try to keep us away from the racks?" she asked smiling sweetly.

"Oh, I think I know exactly what you mean," she said nodding and rushing towards the women's department. Lexi could tell she was excited that they had come in that day since she was pretty sure everyone in this store worked on commission. Selling them two dresses for an obscene amount of money, not to mention anything else Bekah set her heart's desire on, could keep her afloat for several months.

As Katherine bustled around the back of the store, Lexi and Bekah got comfortable in the fitting area. Lexi didn't really know where to go next. Bekah had tried to make the conversation light and civil last time, and that hadn't worked. They both kept getting jealous and unintentionally saying things that made the other belligerent.

Lexi hoped that if she answered the questions truthfully, Bekah could then make up her own mind about Jack's past discretions. Lexi didn't necessarily feel the need to lead Bekah one way or another about Jack. His actions should speak for themselves. If Bekah still felt that Jack was worth her time after the conversation, then that was her decision.

"So…uh…where to begin?" Lexi asked fiddling with her thumbs.

"Can you calm down please?" Bekah asked sipping on some hot tea that appeared before them by another associate. Lexi smiled trying to sweep away her worries. She really did need to calm down.

"Yeah, alright." She didn't sound all that convincing though.

"So, can I start it off then?" Bekah asked setting her tea down on a saucer and leaning back into the green cushion. Before waiting for an answer, she began, "Do you love him?"

Lexi just stared at Bekah. That question hadn't been asked in the past tense. She gulped hard and fully contemplated her answer. On one side, yes of course she loved him. She loved him so much it hurt to breathe. It hurt to think. It hurt to get up every morning without him. But on the other hand, she didn't know if what they had, had ever truly been love. When he said that he loved her, did he mean it? How could she actually know, when they had never been afforded the opportunity to fully appreciate what they had?

"I believe a part of me has always and will always love Jack. Yes," she finally stated in a strangled whisper. She hated so much admitting that, especially to his beautiful, perfect girlfriend. Yes, she was in love with Jack. No matter that they hadn't been together. No matter that he had left her without a backwards glance, without a single act of desperation on his part. She did love him. But something about the feeling had changed and evolved over time. It wasn't really the same question or the same answer Lexi could give had she been asked the same thing two years ago.

"I'm glad that's out of the way," Bekah said blowing out the breath she had been holding. "I was afraid we wouldn't have anything in common."

What a strange thing for her to say.

"Now that that's all out in the open, can we just try and talk about your relationship with Jack. I just want the facts. I want to know why ya'll didn't work out if you actually do love him, and I truly want to find out if I'm actually what he's looking for." Her eyes had enlarged at the last statement and Lexi could tell inadequacy wasn't something she was used to dealing with.

"Can I ask you something?" Lexi questioned Bekah.

"Sure, I guess it's only fair."

"Why would you want to talk to me? I mean, why would you want to talk to any of us? Danielle and Kate and I have all had intimate relationships with Jack. Relationships with him that you will never really understand, because every relationship is in some way different than what you are experiencing. And while you could probably pick up on a pattern of some sort, and coming from an insider's perspective, I really don't think there is one. I've known Jack for a long time, and he's pretty much been the same guy since I've known him. He's had his ups and downs like everyone, but he's pretty much the same. I...well, I don't know why you would want to open up that can of worms," Lexi said spewing out everything in rapid succession.

"I disagree," Bekah said folding her hands one over another, "I think there is a pattern."

"And what's that?"

"I'm not certain yet, but there's really only ever been one constant throughout his relationships. I didn't see it when I first started asking questions or even when I talked to Jack about it."

"But you see it now?"

"Well, I think *you* are the pattern."

"*Me?*" she asked incredulously.

"That's why I wanted to talk to you. I feel that Jack has always had rather strong affections for you. I noticed it when ya'll look at each other, when he spoke to you, when you kissed my brother," she said. "But I also could tell when I talked to ya'll separately. He would get this look on his face. You would get very defensive. It was little things that were out of the ordinary for him," she explained. "Now, if something is still going on, then I'd like to know about it. If not, then honestly I want ya'll to tell me that it's over so that he can move on."

Closure. It always came back to closure. If she was the missing link that explained why Jack couldn't seem to commit to anyone, then how could they ever come to closure?

Before Lexi had a chance to respond, Katherine returned from the back room with two full racks of clothes specifically catered to each individual. They wasted away the afternoon fluttering from one designer to another and discussing the tragic outcome of Lexi's relationship with Jack. She hadn't been able to reveal all of the details as she originally had anticipated, but Lexi was pretty certain that Bekah had gotten enough information out of her that it would sate her desire for the time being. What she did with the information was an entirely different story. Lexi hadn't gotten a single clue as to whether or not what she was providing Bekah with was helping or hurting Bekah's understanding of Jack.

Inevitably, she did end up leaving the mall with a single dress from Barney's. Katherine had been exceedingly accurate with Lexi's size, and without even realizing it, Lexi had found the perfect dress. And as luck turned out, it was also the most expensive dress she had ever had the luxury of trying on her tiny frame. She had gulped at the infinite number of zeros attached to the piece of paper and wondered faintly why God hated her. However, true to her word, Bekah had retrieved a black credit card from her designer bag and handed it to Katherine, paying in full for everything surrounding them. Apparently, she had answered enough questions correctly to deliver payment for her time.

As she made her way towards the entrance, where Bekah informed her that the same town car was awaiting her, she felt strangely at ease. One of reasons she had come to Atlanta again had been successfully fulfilled. No longer would she have to agonize about Bekah, and her potentially deviant plots to get her to confess. Lexi hadn't told her everything, but she had disclosed enough to keep her appetite hampered.

Lexi was almost to the exit, when Bekah stopped her. "Let's just have a peek," she exclaimed, her eyes shifting to her right.

Lexi's stomach dropped at the store front before her. Tiffany's. Bekah had directed her straight to the entrance of Tiffany's. Now, suffice it to say that jewelry stores made Lexi nervous. She had never been able to put her finger on it, but something about the inside of them made her skin crawl. Her body would break out into a cold sweat, and she couldn't help but chew on her bottom lip. She couldn't go in there.

"I really can't..." she stammered.

"Oh, come on. We don't have to get anything. Just a quick look," Bekah said, her smile bright and vibrant at the prospect. She grabbed a hold of Lexi's elbow and hauled her through the well lit storefront. Bekah's eyes barely focused on the stunning collections before her. She ignored the eager looks from the sales associates as she dragged Lexi to the counter. Lexi felt as if she had hit the top of a rollercoaster ride, and her stomach was on auto-pilot down the metallic runway.

Engagement rings clouded her vision. Perfectly cut, perfectly designed, flawless engagement rings on display shining brilliantly in the light. Lexi's hands were shaking as she reached out to touch the glass for support. This was not good. She could not be here with Bekah. It was all fine and dandy when they were shopping for dresses, but this...this was entirely different. She couldn't imagine one of these beautiful stones on Bekah's finger securing her to the man she loved...to the man Lexi loved. She swiped a thin layer of sweat from her brow.

"Aren't they gorgeous?" Bekah cooed, her extra thick blond hair framing her face as her eyes ballooned at the prospect of owning such a rock.

"They're...they're something," Lexi mumbled coughing into her wrist.

"I'd love this one," she said pointing to a large princess cut diamond set on a gold band.

"Would you like to try it on?" the sales associate asked materializing out of thin air with a set of keys. He undid the lock and procured the ring from its home before she even had an option of declining.

"Oh dear," Bekah exclaimed taking the ring and sliding it onto her ring finger. To Lexi's pleasant surprise it was much too large. It would have to be downsized considerably to even look remotely good on her finger. Regardless, the diamond still shone true and her French manicured hands only increased the beauty and perfection that was now placed on her hand. "Well, that won't do quite yet," Bekah conceded handing the ring back to the associate. "Next time perhaps," she added.

"I think...I should go," Lexi said retreating.

"Yes," Bekah said glancing up at her, "we should go. Are you alright? You don't look well."

"I'll be fine," Lexi said hurrying out of Tiffany's and back into the open air. She let out a long breath and felt color return to her cheeks.

"Well, I'll see you Friday, if not beforehand," Bekah said nodding her head at Lexi as she exited. Lexi fell into the cool comforting town car and forced her mind to wander in other directions. The last thing she needed to consider was engagement rings and proposals.

*****

Ramsey had vaguely hinted that he would be out when she returned from her shopping excursion. Something related to work though he hadn't given any details and had evaded any further questioning on the subject. He had slipped a key into her purse before letting her out of the house, and told her that she was welcome back whenever she had completed her errands. After depositing the hanger in the upstairs guest bedroom and letting any remaining thoughts of engagements flutter from her mind, Lexi found that she was surprisingly relaxed. She had a new fabulous dress. She never had to speak to Jack's snotty girlfriend again. And soon enough, she would be spending some much needed time with her family. Not much else could get her this excited. The only issue that she had left to deal with was talking to Jack.

She needed to figure out what was going on between them before she left for New York this weekend. She only had a couple days left, and every time they had been together had held sexual tension or outright anger. If she was ever going to let him go, then she needed to get everything out of the way…out in the air.

That is how she found herself hailing a taxi to take her back to his place. It had only been three days since she had last stepped foot into his apartment, but it felt like a lifetime.

The late night attendant, she had passed while entering the building only a couple days earlier, seemed to remember her and buzzed her through to Jack's floor. She knocked once before twisting the knob, finding it open. The lights were dim as she entered and a flickering of light was coming from down the hall. No sounds could be heard from the apartment, and as she walked past the kitchen, candlelight seemed to take over. A hundred or more candles of varying shapes and sizes filled the living room and more lit the dining room where two plates were set and a bottle of wine sat chilled.

Lexi's mind was whirling. This couldn't be for her. Why would he do something like this for her? Did he just want to confuse her? Granted, it was beautiful. She could feel tears welling to her eyes as they drifted from one romantic scene to the next. Is this what it felt like to have Jack be only yours?

Except he wasn't.

He belonged to Bekah. So, what was he doing making her feel like this now? After she had confessed nearly everything to his girlfriend. After he had flown her down here to convince the new girl that she was what he wanted. Was this a thank you? Did he actually think he had to thank her for what she had done? Because this wasn't helping her ability to get closure.

"Do you like it?" Jack asked from behind her. Lexi turned slowly and took in the beautiful man in front of her. Thankfully, he wasn't over dressed. He wore a pair of dark loose fit jeans and a white linen button up rolled up to his elbows. His blue eyes were momentarily hidden under his midnight hair. His complexion was dark from the summer sun which only added to the exotic effect he was exuding.

"I...well...yes, but why?" she asked her eyes leaving his sexy body and falling on things that she was more capable of discerning accurately with her heart racing like it was.

"Because I needed to apologize," he said stepping towards her.

"Is this how you apologize to everyone?" she asked attempting to keep her eyes averted. He was standing so close she could almost feel the heat rising off of him.

She knew he was smirking without glancing at him. "This is how I wanted to apologize to you."

"You shouldn't have," she said weakly.

"I was out of line when I said all those terrible things to you."

"Jack, you shouldn't apologize. You should let it be," she said turning away from him completely.

"I can't apologize enough for what I've done to you over the years, for what I did to you this week, for having you come here and endure what I put you through. I can't apologize enough for overreacting when I saw you with Ramsey. I can't apologize enough for everything, but I thought I could start with dinner," he whispered sweetly into the ear she had left exposed to him. His arms came up to encircle her miniscule waist and draw her in to him. She tried not to breathe in his delicious smell as old feelings threatened to overpower her senses. He placed a tiny kiss on her shoulder before reaching down, tugging on her hand, and pulling her into the dining room.

"Jack, you really shouldn't have done all of this," she said as he tucked her into the dining room chair.

"I think that I should have, and who are you to turn down a man begging for forgiveness?" he asked with another smirk directed her way.

Lexi sighed and waited for him to be seated before continuing, "We really need to talk."

"I agree," he said, "how is the chicken?"

Lexi glanced down at her food realizing for the first time that there was, in fact, chicken on her plate. She dug her fork into the meat and tasted the morsel. "Good. Did you cook this?" she asked in surprise.

"For you."

She nodded wondering when he had ever learned how to cook. Last she had checked, macaroni and cheese had been too difficult for him. Now he was creating delicious entrees? "Okay, well, thank you, but we really do need to talk."

"You're right. I need to apologize. Would you like me to begin?"

"Uh…"

"I should have never called you." Lexi glanced up from her plate to stare at him in surprise.

"I'm not sure what Bekah told you or what ya'll have spoken about, but I shouldn't have dragged you into this. What we…were shouldn't have been put on display like I've been making you do with Bekah. Does that make sense? What I'm trying to say is that I know why I didn't tell Bekah about you in the first place."

"You do?" Lexi asked finishing off her first glass of wine as quickly as possible. The alcohol was working its way through her system and leaving her with a buzz, which helped.

"I couldn't bear her knowing what I'd done to you, how I'd broken you. And I see it now. I see that I broke you into a million pieces and then left you there. I didn't want her to know I was capable of that. Did you tell her I was capable of that?" he asked directing his question towards her for the first time, expecting an answer.

"I…I didn't tell her that," she whispered watching his face morph from despair to intrigue.

"But why didn't you? You could have told her. You could have told her everything."

"I know, Jack," Lexi admitted placing her fork back down on the plate. The tiny appetite she had entered with had now gone.

"Then why didn't you tell her. She calls me telling me she loves me, telling me that I'm everything to her. She says that you've opened her eyes to who I really am, but does she know who I really am, Lexi? Does anyone other than you know who I am?" he asked standing and approaching her chair. Yanking the chair from the table he rested his hands on either side of the arm rest and bore down upon her.

She tilted her face up to his. "I don't know, Jack. Have you showed anyone else?" she asked staring up into his giant baby blues.

He shook his head letting his eyes close and his head drop forward. She couldn't help but be amazed at his beauty even in that moment. "I've never known how to talk to anyone like I can with you, Lex. I'm not even sure if the woman I've been with the past year and a half has a clue who I am," he announced licking his lips before continuing. "And when I'm with you, I just know. You know?"

She did, but could she tell him that? Should she tell him that? After everything she had told Bekah today and what she had gone through for him every day since they had met, of course she knew what he was talking about. She had been his constant all along. What Bekah had been saying suddenly clicked in Lexi's mind.

She was the reason for all of this.

And that realization in itself pushed Lexi to nod her head in agreement. "I know exactly what you mean."

His head came up. Somewhere in the deep recesses of his mind something had clicked inside of him as well. He scooped her up out of the chair and crushed his lips to hers. He kicked the chair out of his way and pushed her body back against the wall. Tilting his head sideways, he kissed her deeper, feeling around with his tongue for every vantage point. She moaned as his hands grabbed at her waist and hips. His mouth moved away from her lips to kiss her earlobe, neck, and collarbone, taking in as much of her as he could. He returned to her mouth when she clawed at his back begging to taste him again. It had been nearly two years since they had last kissed, but the way they moved together made it seem that like only yesterday. He could still remember every delicate curve of her body from memory, and she continued to revel in the feel of his skin against hers once again.

She wanted him so bad in that moment, but not like this. She wanted him as hers. She wanted him to be her own. No longer could she play the game of sharing him with another. If he was to have her and all of her, she needed the same. She needed him to only belong to her.

"I'm sorry," he said pulling back softly as he noticed her desire wane. "I'm sorry again and again. I couldn't control myself." His hand came up softly to her face and cupped her cheek. "You're so beautiful."

"I'm sorry, too. We shouldn't be in this position again. I want us to be…us," she finally admitted to him. "I want you to be mine."

He nodded. "I know. I know what you mean."

"And I'm okay holding off until you are mine, Jack." He nodded again. "I need to know if that is a reality for us one day or if I'm wasting my time on you."

His thumb caressed her cheek affectionately as the time stretched between them. "I don't think you're wasting your time. When I'm with you, I know I'm not wasting my time."

Lexi nodded letting a smile touch the edges of her mouth. "Oh, Jack," she sighed happily planting another kiss on his mouth. She hadn't felt this euphoric in nearly two years. Something about him always brought out the best feelings in her. And now it looked like things were actually going to work out for them, and they were going to do it the right way.

They let the night recede into morning as they stayed up together sharing stories and remembering what it was like to be in love. The easy flirtatiousness that they had always shared was dampened by the impending emotions that were sure to come forth once they got everything worked out. Instead, they enjoyed each other's company along with the rest of the bottle of wine until the candles died out, and they both fell asleep.

16

NOVEMBER ONE AND A HALF YEARS EARLIER

"Are you sure we have to have this sleepover at your place?" Chyna asked eyeing the dorm hallway reproachfully. "You do know I own a penthouse overlooking Central Park, right?"

Lexi rolled her eyes dramatically. "Yes, I've been there before. It's beautiful, but you can't get the college experience in a penthouse."

"I take it back," she said looking at a particularly large brown stain on one wall, "I don't want to know what it's like to be in college. That's why I didn't go. I've been dating college guys since I was fifteen. If I've managed to avoid a dorm room for five years, then I'm not meant to be in one. Really, I'm peachy keen, chica."

"You're not getting out of this that easy," Lexi growled snatching a hold of one of Chyna's delicate wrists and yanking her further down the hallway. "And anyway, how did you get away with that?"

"With what?" she asked innocently.

"Dating college guys."

"My penthouse was my sweet sixteen present. Happy Birthday princess! We're getting divorced. Move out," she said giggling sardonically. "It really was the best thing they could do for me since I didn't have access to my trust and couldn't purchase it myself."

Lexi had gotten used to this loathing hateful attitude Chyna displayed towards her parents. It was pretty common place. Lexi tried not to broach the subject too often since she had no experience in what Chyna was going through. Her parents, after all, were still happily married after nearly thirty years together. It truly saddened Lexi that Chyna's perception of relationships was so warped. The fact that her parents hadn't completely jaded her towards all human interaction was a miracle in and of itself. "Now that you have access, why don't you get rid of it?" she asked. Though, she couldn't blame her for holding onto the beautiful apartment.

"I've replaced nearly everything inside from knocking out walls and replacing the floorboards. It's not like it's the same place anymore. Did I mention it overlooks Central Park?"

Lexi resisted the urge to mention that the penthouse was also the last gift Chyna had ever received jointly from her parents. She highly suspected that was the real reason for never selling the place.

Lexi could easily admit that an NYU dorm room was nothing compared to Chyna's apartment, but she was far from ashamed of the place.

She shared a common area with three other girls, all who had been admitted into the law school that fall. The space was cluttered with knick-knacks from each other's previous residences. A mismatching couch and loveseat were crushed together in front of the TV. The kitchen didn't even have a stove because it was a safety hazard. This explained why their tiny freezer was always overstocked with microwavable dinners. Lexi had one of the rooms, if you could call them that. She hadn't lived in a lofted bed since her freshman year of college. But if she hadn't put her bed nearly touching the ceiling, nothing else would have fit in the space. A tiny desk, rolling chair, and miniature refrigerator were crammed under the bed. The rest of the furniture was built into the room. Somehow she wasn't embarrassed to bring her rich friend back to her place even if her room was as big as the girl's closet. She was in New York City at a top five law school. This was how people were supposed to live or at least that's what she kept telling herself.

"Here we are," Lexi said hearing the lock click and pushing the door open. Chyna inspected the shared living space while Lexi produced another key and unlocked her bedroom.

"It's so…quaint," Chyna announced cocking her head to the side thoughtfully. Her eyes scanned the room, purposely avoiding the ugly carpeted floors, before landing back on Lexi.

"You haven't seen anything yet." Chyna turned towards Lexi following her into the bedroom.

"Wow. You didn't prepare me for this," Chyna mumbled.

"I didn't think it would be possible to prepare you."

"You're probably right," she agreed in awe. Swiveling in place, Chyna observed the size of the room before saying, "You do realize my closet is bigger than this room."

"Maybe next year I'll move into your closet," Lexi quipped only half-joking.

"Then where would my clothes go?" Chyna asked, her hands placed lightly on her hips.

"I'll work around it."

"Fine. Just don't touch the cashmere," she said giggling.

Chyna placed her hobo handbag in the empty desk chair and sauntered towards the bay windows, which Lexi repeatedly claimed were the only redeeming feature about her bedroom. Lexi watched her for a few minutes recognizing the wheels turning in her mind. Something was going on up there, and Lexi had a feeling it wasn't going to be good.

Whirling on her kitten heels, Chyna faced Lexi with a beautiful smile tacked onto her face. "Can I redo your room? I know this amazing designer. I'm pretty sure he would be able to fix this um…problem."

Lexi rolled her eyes dramatically. "My room is fine the way it is."

"Of course, dear," she said linking their arms and nuzzling close to her friend, "but I could make it gorgeous. You would absolutely love Frederick too. He's a mastermind. He did the renovations in my guest bedroom recently and they're stunning…"

"Chyna…"

"He could really do a number on this place," she continued oblivious to Lexi calling her name.

"Chyna, chill out," she said shaking her out of her reverie. "How about we just have a good time?" Lexi suggested.

"Oh, but Alexa, I'm telling you. The man is a decorating genius."

"I'm sure he is, sweetie, but this is a college dorm room. It's supposed to look like this."

"I'll get to you eventually," she warned poking her playfully in the ribs.

"Yeah, yeah," she said waving her off.

"So…" Chyna drawled, "what do girls do at slumber parties?"

"Haven't you ever been to one?"

"Well yeah I have, but those were different. Usually we took over the house of whoever's parents were out of town that weekend. We'd throw a huge party and get hammered. You know how I like my alcohol," Chyna said with a wink.

"I'll admit alcohol is involved," Lexi told her diving into the freezer of her mini fridge. She pulled out a tray of what looked like frozen gummi bears. "For those of us who had to sneak alcohol past our parents, we made these."

"You made gummi bears?" she asked incredulously.

"No, they're vodka gummi bears. You soak them in vodka for close to three days, then they are as potent as the real stuff, but it looks like you're just eating gummi bears. Not to mention they're delicious," Lexi informed her popping two red gummis into her mouth and letting them slide down her throat.

"Oh, exciting," Chyna said grabbing a handful. "You're right," she said between bites, "these are delicious. I can't taste the alcohol at all."

"It'll hit you later," Lexi told her giggling as she swallowed a white gummi.

"So what do we do after we're drunk from these things?"

"Usually manicures, facials, late night chick flicks, junk food, the works…"

Chyna sucked her bottom lip in between her teeth as she looked at her perfectly done fingernails and imagined the killer work out she would have to endure to process said junk food. "You know…I don't think I was missing anything."

Lexi smacked her arm. "Hey, don't diss on my childhood alchy!"

"I can't help it if your childhood activities don't appeal to a twenty year old," she said playfully. "Let's finish off these gummis and then go party."

Lexi had actually planned for this. Chyna partied nearly every night, and though Lexi couldn't join her most nights since she was in school, they did end up out together at least one night every weekend. "Fine, but we're still staying here tonight without bringing a guy home," she added hastily.

Chyna stuck out her bottom lip adjusting her features into a perfect little pout. "Alexaaa," she whined.

"No buts about it, missy."

"But, but, but, but…"

"No!" she cried tossing a gummi at her.

"Don't waste them!" she squealed ducking the assault and reaching for another gummi.

The girls changed as quickly as Chyna would allow, all the time complaining about the ramifications of four girls sharing one bathroom. Lexi laughed along as she pulled a straightener through her hair which she had let grow near to her waist. She knew it was a poor choice. Even though the evening air was close to freezing compared to the Georgia atmosphere she was accustomed to, the club was sure to be suffocating, and she would be in need of a ponytail upon entrance.

As they exited the building, Lexi recognized an onyx town car which immediately drove up to meet them. Lexi slid against the black leather interior with Chyna following behind her. Apparently, the driver already knew where they were headed, because instead of offering a destination, Chyna popped open a chilled bottle of Cristal resting in a bucket.

"I know it's not vodka gummis," she said filling two flutes full of champagne, "but I suppose it will have to do."

"I suppose," Lexi stated sarcastically.

Lexi took one glass out of Chyna's hand and raised it in the air for a toast. "I toast you, my dear. To being young, fun, and free."

"Not to mention beautiful," Chyna added clinking their glasses together and lifting it to her lips.

The bottle was nearly empty by the time they reached their destination. The driver exited the car and moved to the other side to open the door for them. Chyna floated out of the town car and leaned against the side to steady her already uneasy balance. Lexi stumbled from the car door and nearly collided with the driver. Her alcohol tolerance was practically nonexistent, and the combination of vodka gummis and champagne were really making her head spin. Chyna laced her fingers with Lexi's and plopped a kiss on her cheek. Lexi giggled uncontrollably as she allowed Chyna to pull her towards the bouncer who was openly ogling their display. The rope disappeared as Chyna moved to step across the threshold. Lexi glanced at the long line of waiting customers who, she knew first-hand, were cursing her tiny ass as she walked into the nightclub.

Lexi blinked as her eyes adjusted to the flashes of lights ricocheting off of the mirrored walls. The night was young, and Chyna and Lexi's hotspot was crammed with couples grinding on the dance floor.

Still holding tight to Chyna's hand, Lexi followed her up a winding set of stairs marked for VIP clientele only. Without even batting an eye, the bouncer pulled back the rope and allowed them into the exclusive upstairs bar. Lexi felt that she would never be able to get used to this life with Chyna. Only a month earlier she had been waiting in endless lines hoping for just a peek inside the most illustrious clubs, and now she was drinking for free in the VIP areas with an array of hot celebrities. She couldn't believe this had happened to her. A young NYU Law student didn't get to live this life.

Chyna shimmied to an available couch and gingerly sat down on the red leather pulling Lexi down next to her. "This was such a good idea," she cooed into Lexi's ear.

"It was your idea."

"Alright. This was a perfect idea!"

Lexi smacked her playfully. "My idea would have been perfect if you weren't such a snob."

"Me? A snob?" she asked sticking her nose up in the air, her voice thick with sarcasm. "If I'm such a snob, you can pay for your own drinks today, skank."

"Did you just call me a skank?" Lexi asked placing her hand over her heart as if wounded.

"I call 'em like I see 'em, honey."

Lexi gasped. "How dare you!"

"You're so silly," Chyna said through giggles. "Like you'd pay for a drink yourself looking so smoking hot."

"It's only due to your brilliance," Lexi commended her.

"Yes. I know. It's amazing what designer jeans can do to your ass. You should really let me take you shopping so I don't have to keep forcing you into my clothes when we go out."

Lexi just shook her head. "I'm not getting myself into any more debt."

"You wouldn't have to pay for anything. Te amo mi amor. That's all the payment I request," she replied, affectionately sweeping Lexi's hair behind her ear.

"Oh, please," Lexi said brushing aside her hand.

"Fine. You'll come around. But for tonight, let's find a gorgeous someone who wants to pamper us senseless," she said allowing her eyes to crawl across the room.

Lexi sighed happily and turned to play her friend's favorite game. Under normal circumstances, the game went as follows. Whoever found a hot guy that met Chyna's standards and got offered a dance and a drink first would be able to choose who the other person had hook up with.

"Oh, what about him?" Chyna suggested pointing out a tall blonde in a sleek business suit.

Lexi assessed his features from behind enjoying the view. "We need a look at his face before a final decision can be made." Just then Blonde turned around and brought his beer to his mouth. Lexi nearly gagged as she got a look at his face. "I've never seen a nose like that before. It looks like it's been broken in three places."

"That's because he's a professional hockey player," Chyna said quickly, but Lexi could see the disgust written on her face.

"I don't care what he does for a living. That nose is atrocious."

"Okay, so Hockey Guy isn't for me. Moving on."

They pointed out a few other good looking men, neither of them really satisfied with the selection. Chyna spoke up again, "Oh, him!"

Lexi looked to where her finger pointed out a man wearing dark jeans and a bright blue button-up. Her heart froze as her eyes traveled farther upwards to the shaggy dark brown hair. She couldn't see his face, but her body couldn't resist allowing the butterflies loose in her stomach at the possibility. She could feel the blood draining from her face, and her jaw going slack with fear and anticipation that he might be here. Short puffs escaped her mouth, her chest expanding and contracting with each movement. She tilted her head in hopes of catching a glimpse of Mr. Blue Shirt's face.

"Alexa, sweetie, are you okay?" Chyna asked placing her hand on Lexi's forehead which was already clammy to the touch. "You look really sick all of a sudden. Do we need to get out of here?"

"No, s…s…sorry. He just looks like this guy I used to have a thing with," she mumbled recovering.

"That Jack guy you were telling me about?" Chyna asked bluntly.

"Yeah. Jack. He strongly resembles him."

"If he looks anything like this guy, then he's probably sexy," Chyna couldn't keep herself from mentioning as she took another glance at the Jack look-a-like.

Lexi managed a half-smile. "Yeah, he is sexy, but I just…I don't know. I haven't really seen him in awhile, and I haven't been thinking about him much either. It caught me off guard."

She was lying of course. She thought about him every time she walked around in New York. There were so many dark haired men in blue shirts. It was disconcerting. Not to mention the enormous amount of coffee shops. She was expecting to walk into the store one day, and there he would be standing behind the counter, handing her black coffee, while she studied for her tests. But college was over, and Jack wasn't in New York. Jack wasn't in her life. She didn't have time to talk with anyone, especially Jack. She could lose herself in conversations with Jack for hours if she let herself. Law school didn't exactly permit that kind of freedom. No, Jack was part of her past, and she needed to accept that. She couldn't keep letting herself get so worked up over some guy in a club who resembled him.

"Well, don't think about him. There's no need to when you have so many other men to choose from," Chyna said, speaking like a person who would never have a real relationship. Not that Lexi was one to talk. Her and Jack had never really been functional.

"You're right. Of course, you're right."

"I know it, chica, but you can keep telling me. If you don't want him, I'm going to go see if I can get my obligatory drink and dance out of him. I'll find you someone to kiss when I get back," she said prancing off after Mr. Blue Shirt.

Lexi slumped back against the sofa and massaged her aching temples. She hated that she kept having these ridiculous reactions all the time. She had always been such a strong and independent woman that this gut reaction in regards to Jack was driving her mad. Flashes of him touching and kissing her kept cascading through her vision. Memories of long lost afternoons tucked away in his sheets, wrapped up in his arms as they talked the day away, enjoying each other's company…forgetting that there was a whole other reality that they were supposed to be living in. Those days haunted her day in and day out for the terrible things she had done to the people that cared for them. But even through her despair, she still missed him. She still craved him. He was still on her mind.

Even as she risked massive intoxication, she thought of him. But at least then it didn't matter, because she wouldn't remember it in the morning.

That's the state she was hoping to obtain, when she suddenly stood to patrol for a willing donor to her cause. Her eyes traveled the length of the bar as if she were checking out merchandise on a clothing rack. Her head tilted slightly as one attractive man replaced another in a stool before deciding to proceed.

He was tall…really tall and blonde. Two things she rarely went for, but then again she wasn't searching for a date. She was searching for someone to get her hammered, and this guy fit the bill. She knew an Armani suit when she saw one, thanks to Chyna's scale of men's approved clothing, and this guy was wearing one. That was a step in the right direction.

Lexi sauntered purposely towards his side of the bar. "Oh," she squealed, her heel conveniently faltering right as she passed him. He reached out to steady her, making sure she wouldn't fall. She placed her hand on his chest resting it there long enough to feel the definition under the soft material. His hands were firmly planted on her hips as she righted herself in the four inch Manolos Chyna had forced on her feet. "I am so sorry. I just can't seem to keep my balance in these things," she purred.

"It's no problem," he said still holding onto her hips. "Did you twist you ankle or anything? Did you need to sit down?"

Lexi paused sucking her bottom lip in between her teeth and giving him a doe-eyed expression as if she were contemplating the question. "I'm not sure," she conceded.

"Here. Take my seat. Do you need ice or something?" he asked not taking his eyes off of her as she slid past him and occupied his stool.

"Oh no, I think if I just sit a minute, I should be fine."

"At least let me get you a drink," he said flashing her an award-winning smile.

Lexi giggled checking that off her list. "That'd be great."

"What's your guilty pleasure?" he asked, his voice laced with seduction. "You seem like a Sex on the Beach kind of girl." Lexi blanched at the words. *Sex on the beach.* No, she wasn't supposed to be thinking about Jack. "Or are you more of a whiskey girl. I hear a Southern accent in there. Did you want a SoCo or a Jack and Coke?"

Lexi gulped hard. This guy was supposed to be helping her forget Jack. Not continuing to bring him up even if it was an accident, even if he had no idea who Jack was. She sighed and pushed the thoughts out of her head. He was flirting with her, and if she had been in a different mood, then the comments might not have bothered her. She needed to just relax and know that he wasn't attempting to make her stomach knot.

From the way his green eyes were boring into her brown ones, she could tell that was certainly not on his mind. He had the look of a guy who always got what he wanted. His head tilted in a way that was almost a poker tell on him. He was thinking that this was going to be easy, and soon enough he would be heading out of here with her drunken ass on his arm. Even as drunk as she was feeling, she wasn't prepared to lose herself in some guy. She couldn't do that while her mind was clouded with Jack Howard.

"Shots," she yelled over the music that escalated in the room.

"Do you care what of?"

"Anything *but* Jack," she stated firmly.

He smirked at her answer, and then nodded his head. A minute later two shots were placed before them. More replaced that round and then another round after that. Lexi melted into Armani Guy as all thoughts seeped out of her mind. The alcohol was taking a toll on her tiny body, and she was very pleased with herself for accomplishing her mission so quickly.

"So," she slurred, "what do you do?"

Armani Guy looked at her glazed eyes and leaned in closer to answer her. "Live off a trust right now."

"Oh?" Lexi asked dryly, immediately unimpressed. She never understood why people didn't work themselves. Who cares if your parents left you a fortune? She one hundred percent believed in making your own way in life.

"Yeah. Not really my thing, but it helped me when I was in a pinch," he answered shrugging nonchalantly.

"Well, what are you doing here, Mr. Trust?" she asked giggling at her alcohol infused humor.

"Daddy's work," he said coldly. "Just trying to get a feel on a guy they're thinking of interviewing for a job, and he's in New York. I happened to already be in New York. It was a win-win for them."

"Oh," she said nodding along as if she cared. "Where are you supposed to be meeting this guy?"

"Here, actually. I tend to feel more comfortable in clubs, but he hasn't showed yet," he said his eyes leaving her for the first time to scan the VIP area one more time. "Guess he got caught up."

Lexi pulled his blue and white striped tie between her fingers and tugged lightly. "Well, then it's your lucky day, isn't it?"

He smiled wide, obviously enjoying her advances. "I suppose it is. How's your ankle? Can you dance on it?"

"It's just fine." Lexi nodded checking off number two in her head and wondering if Chyna had beat her to it.

Armani Guy pulled her onto the dance floor. Typically with all the years of formal dance and gymnastics training she had, it made it rather difficult to find a good partner. It seemed that she had lucked out with this one. He moved with her perfectly in time with the music. He anticipated her change in direction and would even guide her hips to his own rhythm when the music took him. She was starting to get disappointed that she had set the rule that they wouldn't be taking anyone home. This guy, whoever he was, was actually helping her forget about Jack, and that was a feat in and of itself.

Lexi didn't know anything about him except that he was obviously wealthy. And though he seemed like a genuinely nice guy, he helped her when he thought she was injured, she simply couldn't let herself get swept up into an imaginary attraction to someone she just met. That never ended well for her.

She needed to take this as far as her drunken brain would allow her. This guy was just like most other men. He wanted one thing and one thing only. When he realized that she wasn't willing to give him what he was looking for, and she kept telling herself that she wasn't, then he would find someone who was.

"Do you want to get out of here?" he questioned into her ear.

She leaned her head back against his chest and swayed to the music. She wanted to leave with him, but she had promised Chyna. She hadn't even thought about Chyna for ages which could mean that she had already ditched her for someone else except Chyna was usually good for her word. If she agreed no guys for the night, then she would find Lexi by the end of the night and they would both go home alone. Lexi sighed…*both* go home alone. She needed to find Chyna. "I'm here with a friend. I can't leave without her."

He located her much more quickly than Lexi would have been capable of alone. His height gave him a distinct advantage. "Chyna, time to go," Lexi commanded peeling her off of some guy she had locked lips with. Whoever he was didn't look too pleased, but after seeing Armani Guy he quickly backed off and vacated the premises.

"Alexa," she shrieked, "the love of my life!"

Lexi giggled as Chyna tackled her, forcing them both back into Armani Guy's hard chest. "Oh, excuse us," Chyna trilled batting her long lustrous eyelashes.

"It's not a problem. I was just helping, Alexa, find you," he said smiling politely at Chyna.

"Ohhhh," she said her eyes moving from Lexi back to Armani Guy. "Well, thank you for that. She's hardly ever able to find me on her own."

"So she told me."

"It is time for me to go," Chyna said faking a yawn. "I guess I should check out. I'm sure you can find your own way home, right chica?"

Lexi knew this act. It meant that Chyna approved of her choice. "Can you excuse us for a minute?" she asked Armani Guy. As he nodded, she yanked Chyna out of earshot from him. "No guys, remember?"

"Yeah, but did you see that Armani suit?" she asked, her eyes leaving Lexi's and glancing back at his build.

"Yes, I did," she said snapping at her to get her attention back on her.

"Did you see those muscles?"

"Yes, I did," Lexi growled.

"Did you see the way his green eyes blazed at the sight of you?" she purred.

"Chyna, cut it out. I saw, but it's a girl's night. I can hook up with him another night."

"You are insane, but I love you!" she exclaimed planting a drunken kiss on Lexi's lips.

Lexi rolled her eyes. "Yes, I know, dear."

"Just for the record, I think you should go for it."

"Well, I'm not going to. Some other time," she said as she turned towards Armani Guy. "Sorry, we have to get out of here."

"We?" he asked incredulously. She pointed between her and Chyna and his face transformed at the realization that she was going to leave without him. He had put in all that work for nothing. She could tell he wasn't pleased. They had hit it off, but she wasn't ready to go home with him yet. Not tonight at least.

"Sorry. I know you have that meeting," she quickly improvised. "Maybe we can meet up some other time."

"I'm leaving the city tomorrow, but maybe I could get your number and the next time I'm in town we can meet up."

Chyna grumbled something in her ear, but she swatted her away not wanting to hear her voice of reason. Of course she should go home with this guy, but that really wasn't going to help her tonight. She was too drunk at this point to go home with his guy. She quickly punched her digits into his Blackberry and then dragged Chyna to the door.

As they drove back to Lexi's dorm, Chyna kept staring at Lexi in dismay. "I don't want to hear one word," Lexi said pointing her finger in Chyna's direction.

Chyna pulled a zipper across her lips, but raised her eyebrows in further disapproval. A few minutes later as they entered the dorm, Chyna couldn't hold back any longer. "You should have gone with him."

"Yeah, I probably should have, but there will be other guys and other nights."

Chyna scooted closer to Lexi as they reached the top of the stairs and began walking down the stained hallway Chyna had been so uneasy about earlier that afternoon. "Yeah, but he was delicious."

"I guess he was."

"I hope he calls you though."

"I doubt he will," Lexi said coming to a stop in front of the door and fumbling for her keys.

Lexi pushed the door open and immediately veered towards the bedroom. Chyna shut the door behind her and walked towards the lumpy couch. She plopped down allowing her aching feet a reprise from their tormentors. Just as her butt hit the cushion, she jumped up screaming at the realization that whatever she had sat on was not a cushion. And now it was moving.

Lexi darted back out of the room sobering up as soon as she heard the blood-curdling cry echo throughout the apartment. "Chyna, what is it?" she cried unsure what she would find. Lexi gasped in surprise at what appeared to be someone rising from the dead. The figure's head hung limp and arms were stretched out in front like Frankenstein's monster. A low menacing moan escaped the person. Just then the figure's head snapped sideways as Chyna slammed a pillow into the side of his head. Lexi rushed back to the front door, latching on to the handle in the event that they needed to make a run for it, and flicked on the dorm light.

Chyna brought the pillow viscously back down on the intruder several more times. A yell sounded from the person seated on the couch. "Oww, stop that."

"Get out of here! You can't take our stuff!" Chyna screamed smacking him across the face another time.

"I'm here to see Lexi, Goddamn. Chill out," the intruder cried shielding himself from Chyna's assault.

"Chyna, stop," Lexi demanded her feet frozen in place as she stared forward. Chyna paused mid-swing, and then brought the pillow back down to her side. She glanced back at Lexi in confusion. The intruder looked to where she had spoken ignoring the possibility of another attack. Lexi's throat caught at the sight. "This is Jack."

"Jack. *Jack*, Jack. You mean *the* Jack?" Chyna asked stumbling on the name.

Lexi nodded. "Yeah."

"Well then," she mumbled tossing the pillow onto the loveseat, "guess that's my cue. Sorry." She walked to Lexi and gave her a quick hug whispering into her ear, "Let me know if you need anything, sweetie."

"Jack, what are you doing here? How did you get inside? How did you know where I was?" she asked letting loose a string of questions that had flown through her head at the sight of him.

He stared at her in awe. He stared at her like he had never seen her before. He stared at her like she was his lifejacket and he was sinking.

"Jack," she whispered the earlier memories that she had briefly evaded her were clouding her vision once more.

He stood quickly and scooped her into his arms. "I've missed you so much," he whispered sweetly into her ear.

Goosebumps cascaded up her arms as she circled his neck. "I've missed you too," she admitted.

When he pulled back, he rested his forehead against hers and closed his eyes breathing her in. "I'm sorry."

"For what?" She couldn't believe this was happening to her. She felt like she was so drunk that perhaps she had passed out and was dreaming about Jack being here.

"Don't ask that. I'm sorry for everything. I ended it with Kate. All I saw was you when I looked at her."

"Me."

"Yeah. I was an idiot for staying with her. You're what I want."

"Me?"

"Yes, Lexi. You."

"Oh," she whispered breathlessly, pushing her fingers up into his dark, thick, mess of hair and twisting the strands around her fingertips.

"I shouldn't have come like this."

"No, you shouldn't have," she agreed shaking her head.

He pulled back to look at her and her breath caught again as his brilliant blue eyes locked onto her. "I really am sorry for everything, Lex."

She nodded knowing he meant it. She let the memory of him telling her that he loved her for the first time wash over her. It had been so long since she had allowed herself to think of that without tears springing to her eyes. He was here for her. He had come to New York for her.

"I didn't mean to scare your friend."

"Don't mind Chyna. She's probably already asleep. How did you get inside anyway?" she asked her brow furrowing.

"One of your roommates let me in. I told her I was a friend of yours and that I'd wait to see you," he said sheepishly.

"Ugh," she groaned, "you could have been anyone. I'm going to have to talk to them about this."

He pulled her closer against him again. "Aren't you glad they didn't turn me away?" he asked, his mouth turning into his characteristic smirk.

"Very glad," she agreed allowing his lips to fall on hers and savoring the taste of him. In fact, what was going on in her head was how glad she was that she hadn't gone home with Armani Guy, because what she had come home to was nothing compared to what she had found at a club. She applauded herself for her stubborn nature.

"Lex?"

"Yeah?" she mumbled licking her lips.

"I love you."

"I love you, too," she said for the first time, allowing herself to tell him how she really felt. Then she got lost in Jack's kiss once more.

17

PRESENT

"Mmm," Jack grumbled holding onto Lexi's waist tightly, "where ya goin'?"

Lexi sighed back into his embrace loving the feel of him pressed against her. At the same time, her stomach rolled knowing that she shouldn't be wrapped up in him like she was. She had been lying there half the morning, her stomach knotting and unknotting for every thought she had about Jack. They had talked the night away and managed to stay closer to the friend's side of the spectrum, but she knew they couldn't stay there. She knew she didn't want to stay there. Nor did he. In fact, he had been the one that said that he wanted to be with her. Luckily, she had kept her wits about her long enough to tell him she wanted him, but only if she could have all of him.

Yet, it was still nagging at her. If she had really meant that, she would have left last night. She wouldn't have stayed up with him and imbibed a bottle of wine. She wouldn't have woken up this morning with his arms wrapped around her.

"I…I'm going to make some coffee," she whispered attempting to extract his hands from around her middle.

"No. Don't leave me, Lex," he begged nuzzling into her neck and trailing light kisses across her skin.

Her body reacted wonderfully to his touch, forcing her back to arch and head to lean back. "Jack, you can't do that."

"But I wanna," he mumbled obviously still half-asleep. "You taste so good."

She giggled at his slurred speech and attempted to push him away again. That only made him latch on harder to her. "Jack, come on."

"I love it when you talk dirty," he muttered seductively, biting down on her earlobe.

Lexi smacked him playfully on the arm and wiggled out of his embrace. "I'll be right back."

"Don't be too long," he said, his face nearly covered by the covers once again.

Lexi trekked out of the room in nothing but her red boy short underwear and one of Jack's old, D-Bags band t-shirts that was much too big for her. She padded down the hallway and into the living room. Her eyes roamed the maze of candles displayed around the room and sighed at the memory of last night. She had promised herself she wouldn't do this. But the only way to change it was to leave the apartment and return home this minute.

But she couldn't do that. She was not physically capable of leaving him like this. Yes, things had happened in their past that made her angry with him. Yes, he was as arrogant as they came. Yes, he had a girlfriend who he had been thinking of marrying.

Despite all that, she couldn't leave. She had wanted to be with Jack for so long that the thought of leaving him without finding out if they actually could be, would break her heart all over again. She knew that she had probably given him more chances than anyone else would have bothered with, but those women didn't understand what she was going through. If they weren't willing to push through the hard times and savor the good times, then they didn't understand men at all. Everything wasn't always going to be peachy keen, and Lexi knew that, but she had been around Jack long enough to know how he worked. And one thing she knew, the one thing that kept her going through it all, was how she felt about him.

She had never wavered in her affection for him. Six years was a long time to wait for someone. And though times had been trying, Lexi knew deep down that Jack was what she had always wanted. Everything and everyone else had just been a distraction to help her forget him.

Lexi pressed her cold hand to her head hoping to soothe out her concerns. Exhaustion was starting to set in and the last thing she needed was to add a headache to that mix. She fumbled around in her purse until she located her cell phone, then trudged into the kitchen and began brewing a pot of coffee.

She had a missed call from her parents that she knew she ought to return right away. She was supposed to have gone home yesterday, but with everything that had happened with Jack, Ramsey, and Bekah, she hadn't been able to get away. Guilt pushed past exhaustion on the top of her list as she cleared away her parent's number, and punched Chyna's instead. She couldn't face her parents yet.

Chyna picked up after a few rings, and by the sound of her voice, she must have still been sleeping. "Hmmm? Hello?" she mumbled into the phone.

"Morning, sunshine."

"Alexa, is that you?"

"Yep. Sorry I didn't call you back."

"I'm sorry, am I supposed to know who you are?" she grumbled irritably into the phone. "The Alexa I know never forgets a phone call."

"Oh, shush you. It's not like you never forget to call me back."

Chyna yawned loudly. "Fine. What's up? I'm sleeping."

"Actually, you're awake now." Lexi heard rustling on the other line and rolled her eyes.

"I'm only half-awake. Hold on, chica. Let me kick him out. I have no idea why he thought he could stay the night." A loud smacking sound could be heard followed by a howl from the gentleman who had shared her bed the night before. A slur of words in Spanish cut through the line, and Lexi was pretty certain the majority of which were not pleasant. Chyna's voice raised an octave as she insulted him back in Spanish. A smashing sound came next from what Lexi guessed was one of the pieces of priceless china she kept around her room breaking into a million pieces. A second later a door slammed and Chyna returned on to the phone. "Sorry about that. He doesn't speak much English, but he's maddeningly handsome with all that Latin passion. Mmm mmm mmm."

Lexi giggled at her best friend. "I'm sure he is, knowing you."

"Now, spill everything. You went on a date and then didn't have the decency to discuss all the sordid details with yours truly. I'm horrified. Does that mean it went too well and you've been locked in his apartment for two days, or was it so bad you were afraid to talk to me?" she asked waking up at the prospect of sharing dating stories.

"Neither, I suppose. I had a lot going on, but I had an amazing time if you must know," Lexi offered loving how excited her best friend sounded.

"And I must. Tell me everything. Who is he? Where did you find him? What did you do? Where did you go? How good was he in the sack?" she asked adding extra emphasis to the last question. "I can't believe this happens when I'm so far away," she groaned sounding ridiculously sexy.

Lexi shook her head at Chyna's over-the-top personality. "We had a picnic at a laser show outside of the city. It concluded with a gorgeous fireworks display that he arranged with the park specifically for us."

"Ooh la la," she cooed, "Not candlelit dinners and caviar, but we can work with it," she interjected. "So, who is this Mystery Man? And please, do give me details!"

"He's actually…Bekah's brother. His name is Ramsey. Ramsey Bridges," she said cringing as she uttered the words. She bit her lip as she waited for Chyna to erupt on her.

"Bekah. Jack's Bekah? Hmm…well, interesting turn of events, but again we can work with it. What's he look like? Is he sexy?"

Lexi giggled. "Yeah, he kind of is. Tall, really tall with bright green eyes and sandy blonde hair. His body is killer too. David Beckham-esk physique we're talking here."

"Damn! Sexy and wealthy."

"Chyna!" Lexi exclaimed scolding her.

"What?" she asked, pretending to be confused by her friend's outburst.

"You know what."

"Don't act like that isn't important. You'll be in law and he has a trust. After hanging out with me, chica, how can you live with anything else?" she asked bluntly. Chyna never refrained from discussing how important it was to find someone with similar means when you were dating. This went back to her standards of men's clothing as well as to his taste in alcohol, cars, apartments, and down the list. She approved of very few men for anything past the first date.

"Yes, well," Lexi said rolling her eyes, "he is supremely wealthy. And God is he good looking, Chyna. If you had picked him out in a club, you wouldn't have even given yourself time to get a drink from him before dragging him off to your place."

"Watch yourself. I might have to come visit my best friend and do just that." Lexi knew that she was only half-joking. What Chyna wanted, she typically acquired. The only things in life she hadn't been able to control were her parent's separation and the fact that her gorgeous designer friend, Frederick, was one hundred percent playing for the other team. He was the only man she had ever met that was too gay to sleep with her and it bothered her every day.

The delicious aroma emanating from the machine was mouth-watering. Lexi poured two mugs full of the hot brew. Then she leaned back against the counter to finish her conversation and wait for the coffee to cool down. "That's kind of the reason I called you. I need you here this weekend," she said forcing her hair behind her ear several times as she waited for Chyna to as the question she was dreading.

"Before I get onto the subject of *why* you might need me in Atlanta this weekend, you didn't answer my question. How good is he?" she asked for the third time.

"I didn't sleep with him," Lexi admitted reluctantly.

"Oh. So that's why you need me there this weekend," Chyna announced.

"What? No. I don't need you here to help me get with him. I could have if I'd wanted to, but there are a few uh…issues with that. Like a certain someone," she said sipping on her coffee.

"Alexa, what have you done?"

"Oh, Chyna," she cried exasperated with herself, "I just need you here. I went to talk to Jack to get everything clear between us, but it didn't work out the way I had planned."

"Did you sleep with him?" Chyna shrieked into the phone.

"No. No, I didn't."

"Don't lie to me, Alexa Mae."

"I'm not lying. I didn't sleep with him. I promise, C. But he wanted to. And we would have, if I hadn't stopped his advances. Now he's saying he wants to be with me for real this time, and I just don't know what to do, Chyna. He's what I want. Of course, he is. I just don't want things to backfire in my face," she said, confessing all her fears.

"Oh, baby, you shouldn't be doing this to yourself," Chyna cried maddeningly. "You know he's just going to hurt you. That's what he does. He hurts you. He drags you down."

"But he doesn't," Lexi eagerly protested. Though, she wasn't quite as certain about that as she let on. "He makes everything right with me. You've only seen the worst of the situation. You only saw what happened in New York. If I can make it right with us, that's what I want. That's what I've always wanted."

"Shit!" Chyna cursed.

"What?"

"I told you *not* to do that. God, he completely changes you, doesn't he?" Chyna asked sighing heavily. Lexi could tell that she was starting to get pissed off. She heard Chyna take a few calming breaths before continuing. "You are absolutely right, chica. I need to be there. I'll talk to Daddy about using the jet. I should arrive in Atlanta in a matter of hours. I'll have a car pick me up at the airport, and then we can talk this all out together. Possibly a shopping spree to get our minds off of what potential disaster you are creating in your life."

"Chyna, you can't come down here thinking…" Lexi stopped mid-sentence and set her coffee mug down on the counter silently. She thought that she had heard something at the door. She had been pretty sure she had heard something, but she had been so heated in her conversation she had almost missed it. She strained her ears to listen for another potential noise.

"Thinking what?" Chyna asked snippily.

"Hold on one second," Lexi said listening more closely this time. Someone was knocking on the door. She jogged down the hallway and pressed her eye to the peep hole. Ramsey's face appeared distorted and warped by the curved glass, but it was definitely him. "Shit!"

"What?" Chyna cried surprised by Lexi's outburst. "What's going on?"

Lexi rushed back down the hall her heart leaping to her throat as she panicked. "Ramsey is here."

"Here where?" Chyna questioned her.

"Oh shit, shit, shit," Lexi mumbled under her breath pushing her free hand through her messy bed-ridden hair.

"Alexa, calm down. Where are you? I thought you were at your parents," she asked trying to get a grasp on the situation.

"No, I'm not. I really have to go," Lexi told her thinking about what she would have to do next.

"Where are you?"

Lexi hated that she had to admit this to Chyna. "I'm at Jack's place. I'll see you in a few hours, chica."

"Don't hang up…"

Lexi clicked off the line before Chyna could even finish her statement. She paced in a circle, feeling more and more nervous as the seconds ticked by. The knock on the door forced her to spring to action, and she rushed down the hallway to Jack's bedroom. She burst through the door in a panic. Jack's head was buried under a mound of pillows when she walked in.

"You were gone too long. Come lay down," Jack said patting the bed beside him.

"Ramsey is here!" she cried hopping onto the bed beside him and yanking a pillow off of his head.

"What?" he asked jumping up like he had been jolted with electricity.

"Ramsey is at the front door," she repeated. "He's banging on the front door like a freaking maniac. Did you know he was coming over?" she asked frantically brushing her hair away from her face as she looked into his now frightened blue eyes.

"No, I didn't know. What is he doing here?" he asked brushing his hand through his own hair and cursing under his breath.

"How the hell should I know? He's at *your* front door. You have to go get rid of him. He can't see us together. Shit would hit the fucking fan."

"I know. I know. I'll see what I can do. Shit!" he said hopping off the bed and throwing a t-shirt over his head. "What the fuck is he doing here?"

"I don't know, just get rid of him," she said shoving him towards the door.

"I'm going. Just stay in the guest bedroom or the bathroom until he leaves. I'll go find out what he's doing here," he said as he jogged down the hallway. "Don't make a peep," he warned.

Lexi rolled her eyes. As if she was stupid enough to do that. She walked into the guest bedroom leaving the door ajar. She wanted to be able to hear what they were talking about while still remaining hidden. She leaned her head back against the wall and strained to hear what was going on at the front door.

"I'm coming," Jack yelled racing down the hallway and unbolting the door. "Ramsey, hey man, what's up?" he asked casually leaning against the doorframe to block his view of the inside.

"Hey, sorry to barge in on you like this," Ramsey said eyeing him reproachfully as he looked at his ragged appearance, and then glanced at his watch revealing the time to be nearly noon. "Bekah told me that you weren't going into work today, and that you should be home. I just wanted to see if I could talk to you for a bit."

"You know, right now really isn't the best time," he said scratching the back of his head and yawning wide. "I was up all night punching numbers. I'm pretty beat, and since I'll be out all weekend, I really need to get in as much work as I can."

"Oh, it'll only be for a few minutes," he said towering over Jack. "I have a few questions to pass by you."

Ramsey brushed past Jack before he received an answer. "Sure, come right in," he remarked sarcastically shutting the door as Ramsey entered the living room.

"So…" Jack said following him into the room. "Coffee?"

"No, thanks. I just had a few questions," he said leaning back against the sofa and crossing his arms, "about Lexi."

Jack's head snapped to the side at the last statement. "Excuse me?"

Ramsey's eyebrows lifted at Jack's reaction, but he otherwise gave no sign that he had noticed his sharp intake of breath at the mention of Lexi's name.

"I wanted to find out a little more about her. What she's like, where she's from, how ya'll know each other, what she's doing here…that sort of thing," he said easing Jack into the situation.

"Uh…well, why don't you ask her?" he said regretting that statement as soon as he said it. That wouldn't exactly be the best thing for him to do. He could imagine Lexi's phone going off in his room while Ramsey dialed it from the living room. That thought made him cringe. No, that certainly wouldn't go over well.

"I'm just curious about her. I don't want to come on too strong. I've only known her for a couple days. Don't you think it would be strange for me to be asking her all these questions? I know you. You're practically my brother," Ramsey said clapping Jack on the back. "I don't see why you wouldn't share some valuable information with your brother."

"Yeah, man, I would, but I don't feel comfortable sharing her personal information without talking to her first." Jack didn't know what Ramsey's interest in Lexi was, but he didn't like it. He knew he was acting defensive about the situation.

"Come on, Jack. I'm not digging around for personal information or anything," Ramsey said, "I'm talking to you about her. Obviously ya'll were together a long time ago."

"What makes you think that?"

"Have you seen the girl? She's hot. I wouldn't have blamed you for getting with her before you met Bekah. She's a polar opposite from my sister though," Ramsey said falling easily into the playboy persona he exuded around the majority of the people he knew.

"Yeah, that's for sure," Jack agreed. "And, yeah, I mean, we were together back in college, but that was a long time ago."

"And I'm sure she's changed a lot since then, but fill me in," Ramsey pleaded seeing Jack begin to cave under his requests.

"Well, alright," Jack agreed looking across the room at the cracked bedroom door. He remained composed despite the nagging feeling creeping throughout his body. "What did you want to know?"

"So ya'll met in college and dated while you were there, why is she still in your life?" he asked bluntly. He figured it was best to dive in so he wouldn't give Jack time to sugar coat his answer.

Jack's face flushed at the accusations behind his words. "What do you mean why is she in my life? She's a good friend of mine."

"Really?" Ramsey asked nodding his head at the obvious lie.

"Yeah...really," Jack said more vehemently this time. He couldn't help glancing down the hallway again wondering if Lexi was listening to every word they were saying.

"How come I've never met her before? Never even heard you talk about her before?" he probed.

"She lives in New York," Jack said stating the obvious.

"Yeah, but we go to New York on a pretty regular basis. Ya'll never met up while we were out or anything. Bekah or I were with you at all times, and from what I've gathered from Bekah, she had never met her either."

"We've been out of touch up until recently," he admitted hating how much information Ramsey was capable of weaseling out of him. "You don't mind if I get some coffee?" he asked hoping to put some distance between them.

"Not at all," Ramsey said watching him enter the kitchen and reach for an already full mug of coffee. "Why are there two mugs?" he asked curiously, immediately glancing around the apartment as if a stranger were about to jump out at him.

Jack smiled as he brought this coffee back into the living room. "That was from last night," he improvised quickly.

"Alright," Ramsey said not convinced with pretty much anything Jack was telling him, "So, ya'll just recently got back in touch. I'm surprised Bekah's alright with this."

"I'm not sure why you're giving me the third degree. I love your sister. Lexi is just an old friend. That's all," Jack announced to Ramsey.

"Well, that's good to hear especially since we went out the other night," Ramsey added nonchalantly. All the while, he kept his eyes locked onto Jack. The reaction elicited was almost uncanny. Utter shock seemed to sweep his body, starting at this clenched fists and racing up his arms into his tensed shoulders. Jack's jaw tightened with the growing anger that sent through him. His blue eyes were darkening by the second.

"You did what?" Jack asked hoping to keep his voice level, but knowing he was failing.

"Yeah, I took her out for a picnic."

Jack clenched and unclenched his fists a couple times. All he felt like doing in that moment was throwing his fist directly into Ramsey's smug face. He needed to get out of the situation before he did something he would regret. "Well…that's great," he finally said lamely, breathing out as slow as he could.

"Yeah, so anything else I need to know?" Ramsey asked giving him a smug grin.

Jack shook his head. "She's leaving soon. I wouldn't press your luck. I've known her a long time, and she doesn't really go for, well…guys like you. No offense."

"None taken," Ramsey said amused at Jack's reaction.

"I mean with your job and the people you associate with, not to mention that you live in Atlanta, it wouldn't be best for her."

"Of course not," Ramsey said agreeing with him for the hell of it.

"She's different than your other girls."

"How so?"

"Lexi's special in her own way. She's smart…more like brilliant, and motivated. She's going to make something of herself. She'll know if you're playing her like you normally do," Jack told him, his gaze focusing on the hallway where he knew she was listening in.

"I wasn't planning on it, but thanks for the talk," Ramsey said extending his hand out to Jack.

"Anytime. I'll see you around," he said thankful that he was leaving.

Ramsey took Jack's hand in his own and gave his hand a rather firm shake. "I'm not going to play her. She does seem rather special."

"She is."

Suddenly, Ramsey yanked Jack forward so only inches separated them. He set his gaze directly on Jack and growled lowly, "I hear the way you talk about her, and I can see how you feel about her. Don't even try to pretend like you don't know what I'm talking about. Now, if you ever hurt her or my sister, I'll find you." Jack gulped and attempted to avert his gaze. "Did you hear me?" Ramsey asked menacingly still holding his hand in a vice grip.

"Yeah, man, I heard you," Jack snarled back at him.

Ramsey released him shoving him back a little harder than he had anticipated. "Well then, have a nice day, and I'll see you on Friday night."

Jack watched him exit his apartment in a raging fury. He couldn't remember the last time he had felt so infuriated with anyone in his life. First, the son of a bitch had come into his house and interrogated him on his relationship with Lexi. Then, he had decided to share the information that he had a date with Lexi. After all that, he still had the audacity to threaten him.

"Lexi?" he called down the hallway.

Lexi scurried out of the guest bedroom where she had been hiding. Her heart was racing with what had just happened. She couldn't believe all the things she had heard through the door. She completely understood Jack defending their friendship to Ramsey, because the worst thing to happen right now would be for them to get caught all over again. She couldn't fathom why Ramsey would tell Jack that they had gone on a date. She had planned on telling him, but things had been going so well that she hadn't found the right time. Not to mention she had assumed Jack would be angry, and from what she could tell Jack was furious.

"You went on a date with Ramsey?" he bellowed as soon as she was in front of him.

"Well, yeah," she stated meekly.

"Why would you do that?" he asked attempting to control his anger at what had just occurred.

"What did you expect me to do when you ditched me?" she asked him turning the tables on him. "You went off with Bekah and left me all alone while Ramsey was the only person there to take care of me."

"God, I don't know, Lex. Go see your parents or something. I didn't expect you to go out with my girlfriend's brother. This is so fucked up."

"Stop right there," she cried pointing her finger into his chest. "Think about what you said. *You* have a girlfriend. I would hope you wouldn't forget that while you get yourself all worked up over nothing."

"Did you sleep with him?" he asked ignoring her last comment.

"Excuse me?" she shrieked in disbelief.

"You heard me. I just…I just need to know."

"What kind of tramp do you think I am? Is this what you think of me? Do you think I jump into the bed of every available man on the market? How long have you known me, Jack?" she nearly screamed at him.

"Well, you didn't tell me. We stayed up all night talking last night, and you didn't tell me you went on a date with him," he pointed out.

"It's not exactly a great conversation starter with you, especially after how you acted at his party. And anyway, it's not like you were sharing all sorts of details about Bekah."

"Yes, but you know we're together. I don't have to share information about our relationship with you," he said looking her up and down. His blue eyes were blazing.

"You're right, you don't. And since Ramsey and I have *no* relationship, then I don't have to share any information about what we did or did not do with you either."

"So, you slept with him then?" he asked plopping down on the couch in defeat.

"No, Jesus Christ, I did not sleep with him. He kissed me good night. That's all. It was nothing. He practically had to beg me to go out with him in the first place, because I didn't want to. Alright? Are you satisfied?" she asked placing her hands on her hips as she stared at him.

"I'm losing my mind," he said his blue eyes meeting hers. "I realized how much you mean to me, Lex, and I can't help but freak out. I'm sorry." He reached forward and grabbed her hips pulling her into his lap. She snuggled in close to him. "I shouldn't be overreacting like this."

"No, I understand, Jack. I'd probably be freaking out too. I should have told you," Lexi said kissing his cheek.

"I wish you would have," he said turning his face and stealing her lips before they hit his cheek again.

"Jack," she said warningly against his lips.

"Lex," he mumbled back sliding his tongue into her. He wrapped his arms around her waist and pressed her firmly against his chest. She pushed her hands up through his unruly dark brown hair and moved her mouth against his. Being in his arms felt like the most wonderful place in existence. The feel of his lips tasted of heaven, and though she knew deep down she needed to stop him, she was having trouble finding the rationalization as her brain shut down.

Jack stood pulling her legs around his waist, never letting their lips part. She locked her legs behind his back as he supported her weight by placing each hand on her butt and hoisting her up. He pulled back and stared at her flushed face with a smug smirk firmly planted on his face. She could tell by his shallow breathing that he wanted her. His eyes were fiery blue with passion.

"I love you, Lex," he said breathily.

"I love you too," she said, her heart palpitating wildly as he crushed his lips against her again.

He leaned her back against his couch and pressed himself against her. They were both practically naked from recently waking up, and the hardness pressing against her inner thigh made it evident what was on his mind. He pushed up his band t-shirt that she had thrown on and ran his hands down her tiny body. She groaned as he leaned down and began kissing every inch of her flat stomach. From there he moved to her perky breasts. Her body ached for him as he continued his insistent prodding of her upper half. She arched her back in pleasure as the sensations coursed through her body. The anticipation from a year and a half of self-restraint was catching up with them as he retreated back to her plump lips.

"We should get rid of this," he said attempting to yank the shirt over her head. She let him rip the shirt off her, but immediately reached out and grabbed it out of his hand. She covered her bare breasts with the material and scooted to a sitting position.

"We can't…I can't do this," she said sliding the shirt back over her head and removing her legs from around his waist. "I told you how we can be together, and I really have to stick with that," she said, her breathing ragged and body still pulsing with desire for him. It was one of the hardest things she had ever done, but she knew that she couldn't do this. Not again.

Jack groaned and moved to a sitting position next to her. "Yeah, I know. It's just…this is what we're normally like. You're so damn sexy when you get angry. I can't seem to help myself."

"I know. I didn't want you to help yourself either. I *don't* want you to have to help your feelings for me, but this isn't fair to Bekah. We've been here before. I don't want another Kate/Clark situation. It didn't go well the first time, and I have a feeling that it would be just as bad this time around," she told him sadly. Lexi hated so much having to have this conversation. All she wanted right then was to be swept up into his arms and be carried to his bed so they could have hot passionate sex all afternoon. But she couldn't do this again.

"You're right," he said meeting her desirous gaze.

"I'm sorry," she told him shyly. "I do want this terribly bad."

He reached out and caressed her cheek. "I know."

"Well," Jack began awkwardly, "I'm going to go take a cold shower." He stood up uncomfortably adjusting himself. "Feel free to come and go as you please. I really do have a lot of work to catch up on, but I'd love it if you stuck around. I can't seem to get enough of you." He bent down and kissed her forehead sweetly.

Lexi watched him exit the living room. She couldn't believe how close she had come to giving into him. She knew one thing though. She needed Chyna right then. Chyna was the only one who could keep her focused while Jack was taken. She had to give him enough time to deal with Bekah, and allowing him to think that he could have her without doing anything about the situation wasn't going to help her. She needed to stand her ground. But not getting swept up with their desires was a lot of work, and Lexi wasn't prepared for it. That's where Chyna came in. It was too bad Chyna was still hours away, and Jack was currently stripping down naked in the next room preparing to get soaking wet.

18

NOVEMBER ONE AND A HALF YEARS EARLIER

A scraping sound followed by shuffling feet across the carpeted floors made Lexi shift from her otherwise comfortable position. She yawned, refusing to open her sleep deprived eyes to the blinding sunlight. Her hand slowly rose above her head and she stretched languidly across the couch. Her back arched pushing the checkered quilt off of her upper-half leaving her body exposed with only a flimsy, white tank top as a cover-up. She shivered at the near freezing weather and scrambled to cover the rest of her body with the warm fabric. Yanking the covers up to her chin, she snuggled deeper into the plush cushions. Another yawn followed as she wrestled with her own inner turmoil: to study or not to study.

A sharp pain shot across her temples reminding her of the amount of alcohol she had absorbed last night. Memories of shot after shot flooded her conscious, and she knew her answer to that dilemma. There would be no chance she would be studying today. She groaned and shuddered against the pain pulsing throughout her body. Her stomach twisted with nausea and she was certain that she would be sick at any moment. Swallowing down the rising bile in her throat, she groaned even louder this time. A giggle punctuated the early morning air causing Lexi to cringe further into her comfortable niche.

"You gonna get up, you lazy bum?" Rachelle, Lexi's roommate, questioned her in her thick New England accent from across the kitchen through Lexi's open door.

Lexi grumbled angrily into the pillow adding a few choice curse words. "Don't talk so loud, Ray," she mumbled pressing her palms to her forehead.

"It's pretty late, and you know we have that huge Civ Pro reading for tomorrow," she drawled slamming the microwave door shut for Lexi's benefit. Another giggle resounded throughout the space confirming that sentiment. "I wouldn't want to see my genius roomie getting behind in her class work."

If she had had the energy, Lexi would have flipped her off. Under the circumstances, she just griped louder and pulled the covers completely over her head. She let her eyes open and painfully adjust to the feeble amount of light apparent through the blanket. Her mind sifted through the disjointed memories from the previous night focusing in on the high points. Vodka gummis, hot Armani Guy, dancing, leaving with Chyna—Jack. She let her brain wrap around the foreign concept. Had that been a dream?

It felt completely surreal to think that he had been in New York, in her dorm, in her arms. He had come for her. He had confessed his desire—love—for her. He had lain next to her all night.

She shook her head in disbelief ignoring the alarm bells going off throughout her body at the sudden movements. No, she had dreamed that. She drank way too much last night, and out of desperation had conjured up the one person she was always thinking about. She was almost certain she had passed out and Jack had taken over her subconscious...as he typically did.

He wasn't here after all. If he had been real, he would be lying here next to her with his arms securing her in place against his chest. He would be kissing her shoulder and up her neck. He would mumble sweet nothings into her ear and stroke her long unruly hair out of her face in order to get a better look at her warm, dark chocolate eyes. She would melt at the sight of his cerulean irises confessing his affection for her and knowing that they didn't actually need words.

No. Jack was just a dream. A sweet dream, but a dream nonetheless.

That gloomy thought coupled with her ever increasing hangover, Lexi pulled the covers from across her eyes. Her pupils dilated as they adjusted to the extreme change in light exposure. She sat up, still holding the covers tight to her chest in an attempt to retain some heat within her body. After a minute, Lexi shifted her gaze to Rachelle who was studiously seated at the kitchen table with her Civil Procedure book open before her.

"Ray...uh...can I ask you something?" Lexi began awkwardly.

Rachelle flipped the page, not even appearing to hear Lexi's comment. Lexi waited feeling more uncomfortable by the second as she waited for a response. Just when she opened her mouth to speak up again, Rachelle responded noncommittally, "Huh?"

"Can I ask you something?" Lexi repeated.

"You just did, and you can't borrow my book. I need to read this at least four or five more times before tomorrow," she added snappily.

Lexi gritted her teeth, and tried to remind herself that she was at a top five school for a reason. These people were supposed to be bitchy. "I didn't want to borrow your book," Lexi said, "I had a question about last night."

Rachelle glanced up from whatever she was writing furiously into her notepad and snorted. Literally, snorted. Lexi gaped at her in horror.

"Did you uh...let someone in last night?" Lexi asked.

"Are you thick?" Rachelle retorted snapping her pen down on the pad with a little too much force.

"Excuse me?" Lexi asked dumbfounded, cringing away from the loud smacking noise the pen made against the surface.

"I would never let anyone inside," Rachelle stated matter-of-factly, always the epitome of responsibility.

Lexi breathed out a sigh of relief even though it felt more like a sigh of despair. She had been hoping that she was wrong. She wanted so desperately to have Jack here that she was actually badgering her most anal roommate about possibly letting a strange man into their dorm room. How much had she had to drink the night before? She shook her head, regretting the action instantly, and stood to go brew a cup of coffee. Rachelle was some sort of super-human freak that didn't need the stuff, even though she went to bed after everyone and woke up first in the household.

As she prepared the pot, Lexi found her bottle of Tylenol tucked behind three cans of tuna and a crushed package of macaroni and cheese. Dumping out two extra strength pills in her hand, she stuck her mouth under the running faucet, took a too-large gulp, and swallowed them down whole. She hopped up on the cool counter top letting her legs dangle and leaned her aching head back against the wooden cabinets as the coffee pot worked its magic.

After Lexi had filled her mug to the brim with the steaming liquid, she stumbled into her bedroom to get together toiletries for the shower she so desperately needed. Digging through her pockets from last night, Lexi located her cell phone. A text from Chyna stated something about them needing to talk and expressing her feelings about the amazing night. Lexi shrugged off the needing to talk bit and veered towards the shower. The shower was refreshing and seemed to alleviate most of the aches that were permeating her body and completely dispelled any feelings of nausea. Lexi finished off her mug of now lukewarm coffee as fast as she could, changed into some sweats, and ventured back into her living room.

By that time, Lexi's other roommates, Claire and Elizabeth, had returned and were discussing the reading that Rachelle was currently skimming over for the umpteenth time. Lexi tilted her head to the side and ran her fingers through her hair allowing the waves to separate from each other. She moseyed towards the coffee pot and poured herself another mug.

"Did you hear us, Lexi?" Claire asked behind her.

Lexi turned around and surveyed the scene before her. She was the first to admit that she didn't exactly fit in with the other students at NYU. People came in from all over the country to go here, but they at least all had one thing in common: a sense of competition. Her roommates definitely had that feeling, and Lexi simply didn't share it with them. That was why when they were all together in one place. It was very unlikely that they would actually be talking to her. She hadn't heard a single word they had been saying for that exact reason, and told them as much.

Elizabeth upturned her nose at Lexi and mumbled something under her breath. Claire jabbed her in the ribs before responding. "We were wondering how last night went," she ventured barely suppressing a giggle.

Lexi stared at her with her mouth wide open. In the months that they had been living together, she had never been asked about her night. The only topics of conversation they focused on at all had to do with school. Something was up. "Same as usual I suppose."

"I saw your friend. What's her name Asia?" Elizabeth asked knowing full well that wasn't her name. Lexi rolled her eyes at her not enjoying their little game and wondering where this was leading.

"Chyna, actually," Lexi responded wishing she hadn't had so much to drink the night before. If she was going to have to deal with whatever game they were playing, then she needed to be a bit more conscious.

"Oh right, Chyna," Elizabeth said. "What kind of name is that anyway?" she mumbled loud enough for Lexi to hear.

Lexi gritted her teeth and hoped the torture of petty social interaction would end soon. "Yeah, she went out with me last night."

"Did that guy go out with you last night too?" Claire asked giggling into Elizabeth's shoulder.

Lexi froze and stared at the three. Elizabeth's freckled face was nearly masked with the blush that took over whenever she found something humorous. Claire's thin blonde hair had been shaken free of its loose ponytail. Rachelle even let a small smile grace her features at the two girl's ridiculous behavior. God, were they twelve years old? Even though these things were put on Lexi's list of all-time rare behavior for her roommates, what made her body react was the fact that they had mentioned a guy. Yet, how could they know that she had met a guy last night? And was that even what they were talking about?

"Oh, look at her face," Elizabeth said through her giggles.

"She didn't want us to find out. That's why she made him leave so early," Claire announced smacking Elizabeth with her hand playfully. Though, it looked like this scene had been rehearsed.

"Did you see him though?" Elizabeth asked fanning herself.

"Yeah, why would she want to hide *him*?" Claire asked letting the emphasis rest on the final word. "Even Rayray thought he was gorgeous. Didn't you, Ray?" Claire questioned shoving Rachelle's notepad out from under her pen.

Rachelle looked up finally dropping her half-smile as she glared at her roommates. "What does it even matter what I think? I have work to do. Why not harass her somewhere that doesn't involve me?" she asked cattily.

"Um…guys, what are you talking about?" Lexi finally asked, confusion written across her features.

Claire focused in on her assessing the situation. "That guy I let in the apartment last night. He was dreamy and couldn't stop blabbering about you."

"What guy?" Lexi gasped steadying herself on the counter top. Her vision had gone blurry at Claire's words. Had Jack actually been here last night? Her throat felt dry and she reached blindly for her coffee mug. Unable to locate it, she touched her hand to her throat and choked back a cough.

Elizabeth rolled her eyes. "No need to be so dramatic."

"Anyway, he left you a note after you kicked him out," Claire said producing a tiny piece of white paper. "We weren't sure if you wanted it."

Lexi moved forward robotically and snatched the paper from out of her fingertips. "Don't ever touch my stuff again," she snarled narrowing her eyes menacingly.

Claire and Elizabeth looked as if they had never seen Lexi before. Their mouths hung open in shock. Even Rachelle had stopped to stare at her newfound malice. Lexi ignored them all in her anxious desire to read the note, find out if it actually was from Jack, and why he had left so early if it was the case.

She shut the door behind her and fell into her desk chair. She could feel her pulse in her stomach as she held the insubstantial piece of paper in her palm. She ignored her gut feeling that nothing good could possibly come from this and tore open the paper. Her heart fluttered at the text before her. It held one word—one lonely word. The handwriting was unmistakably Jack's, but still he had left her with nothing else but:

Sorry.

She stared numbly at the five letters scratched onto the blaringly white scrap. What was he sorry about? Her stomach sank further. Had she said or done something wrong? She had been blitzed out of her mind last night and couldn't remember a single thing. Only a minute ago she had been certain she had conjured him up in a dream, and now he was leaving her with apologies. She buried her face in her hands a fresh wave of heartache taking over where her hangover left off. A tear trickled down her face and she quickly swiped it out of the way in anger.

No.

She wasn't going to go there again. She had shed enough tears previously and now she needed to get over this. Jack had always and would always have a hold on her heart, but she needed to be smart about it. He was in New York and had found her. That had to count for something. Tossing the paper on her cluttered desk, Lexi rose and located her cell phone once more. After tapping out a quick reply to Chyna that they would have to talk later, she found the number she was looking for and dialed the line.

"Hey, Lex," Jack answered huskily.

She felt her body turn to jello at the sound of his sweet voice. How had she forgotten how amazing his voice sounded in her ears? She sighed contentedly, and then stopped herself. She needed to be frank with him and not get suckered in all over again. "Why the fuck did you leave that note?"

He sputtered, "I...uh..."

"Why did you even come see me if you were going to leave with nothing but a note?" she interrogated him.

"I was pretty drunk," he offered.

"Oh, you were drunk?" she asked not keeping the condescending tone from her voice.

"Yeah, look, I had been meaning to come by and talk to you, but I hadn't been able to work up the nerve. Can we meet up and talk?" he pleaded.

"How long have you been in New York?" she asked her eyes narrowing.

"Come on, just meet me, and I'll tell you everything," he promised his voice taking on an almost desperate tone.

"Just answer the question, Jack," she commanded forcing herself not to break under his sweet talk.

"A couple months," he mumbled.

"What?" she squealed. "A couple months and this is the first I've heard from you?" She couldn't help but feel hurt. He had known all along that she had been around. And there she had been moping about him and feeling like she was seeing him on every street corner.

"I wasn't sure if you were..." he trailed off.

"If I was what?" she asked, her anger flaring.

"Single."

"Oh," she muttered before she had a chance to stop herself.

"Can you please meet with me so we can discuss this? I can tell you've entered full-on freak out mode, and I can't help if I'm not there."

"Then why did you leave?" she spat at him. Lexi was pretty sure that whatever had happened last night, he had to have realized that she wasn't taken. She shook her head furious with herself. There was no way for him to know that. Even if they had done anything last night, past precedent proved that it had never mattered whether or not she had been single. She wasn't even sure why it mattered to him right now, but she didn't ask that.

"I had an interview," he muttered dejectedly.

"For a job?" she asked in surprise.

"Yes, for a job, Lexi. I wouldn't have left your side for anything else," he informed her.

Lexi fell silent after that comment, contemplating her next move. She wanted to go see him and find out what had happened, but she knew what kind of distraction Jack offered. Her first semester grades would be all she had when she was looking for internships for the summer and she needed to stay focused. Rachelle wasn't the only one who had to study in their household.

She shook her head from side to side weighing her option. Biting down on her bottom lip, she realized there was really only one option. "Where did you want to meet?"

*****

Lexi stared up at the mountain of stairs in front of the Metropolitan Museum of Art. She had walked by here on numerous occasions, but had never had enough free time to venture inside. Not that she had ever been a connoisseur of fine art, but she could still appreciate the beauty that lay within the castled walls.

In fact, she had always been intimidated by the outwards splendor that radiated from the building. Chyna had been to a number of benefits and operas at the location, but timing had never been right for Lexi to join her. Now she was stuck staring upwards at the massive construction wondering what she was even doing here.

She felt a light tap on her shoulder from behind. She jerked around caught off-guard by the sudden interruption. "Jack," she said her voice lowering seductively as she caught sight of him.

Her roommates had been right. He looked damn sexy. The afternoon sun gleamed in his eyes reflecting back to the world a bright ocean blue. His shaggy hair, which typically fell into his eyes, had been combed and perfected to rest across his forehead. A worn pair of jeans, that she recognized, hung loose on his narrow hips. A grey long-sleeve t-shirt fit snug across his broad shoulders. Her eyes couldn't help but smolder at the sight of his cut arms and chest which showed countless hours of work. She had never seen him look so built before in her life.

A smile broke out across his face when he noticed her checking him out. She blushed slightly unable to control the feeling of embarrassment. She knew that she shouldn't feel it…after all, it was *Jack*. He pulled her into him wrapping his arms around her waist covered by a purple sweater and long, black pea coat. Breathing in his musky scent made her head dizzy with more than just a cologne haze, and she tightened her grip around his neck to steady herself. Her heart fluttered as he seemed unable to let her go. After a minute of standing there with their arms wrapped tightly around each other, Jack finally pulled back taking a step away from her. Lexi instantly felt like all the warmth from her body had dissipated with the break in contact.

"Can we go inside?" he asked rubbing his hands up and down his chiseled arms. "It's kind of freezing, and I forgot a jacket."

She shook herself out of her trance and nodded, following him up the stairs. Her jaw slackened at the magnificent arched hallway and the crowd of people milling around the entranceway. Jack locked onto her wrist and led her to a more secluded section of the lobby. His hand was hot to the touch despite having just left the frigid outdoors. He gestured for her to take a seat on a hard wooden bench, which she did. She stuffed her hands into the pockets of her pea coat and angled her body to look at him where he sat next to her.

He breathed out a few times into his hands. He obviously thought they were cold even though Lexi disagreed. She waited not wanting to be the first to speak. She wasn't even sure what he was going to say. She was a little scared about what she might find out.

"So," he began averting his gaze to the sleek marble floor.

"So," she agreed not letting her eyes drift from his face.

He cleared his throat uncomfortably. She held his gaze, waiting.

"Lex, I…" he glanced up into her brown eyes and then quickly back down at the floor.

"Yes?" she prodded.

"I'm sorry about last night," he mumbled, but something about the way he said it didn't sound sincere.

"Jack, why don't you cut the bullshit, and tell me what you're actually thinking?" she asked him easily annoyed.

"Ok, ok. I never could get anything past you, could I?"

Lexi shook her head not wanting to take that comment head-on. She could remember a time when he was able to hide many things from her.

He slumped into himself at her reaction. She waited, allowing him to collect his thoughts before speaking again. He straightened up taller than before and met her gaze. "You're right. I'm not sorry for last night. I meant everything I said, and I don't know if you are with someone or not, but I guess…I still wanted you to know."

Lexi blushed at his words. She had been piecing the previous night together in her mind, and could vaguely remember what had happened before she had blacked out. Jack had been there, waiting for her. She remembered his lips against her skin and his voice whispering in her ear. Her heart sped up at the recollection of those three small words they had uttered to each other, and a smile crept to her face.

"You love me," she whispered. She felt something wet on her cheek. When she reached up to brush it off, she was surprised to see that it was her own tears. She chuckled to herself at the absurdity of what was happening. Jack was here, in New York with her.

"You're crying!" he exclaimed. "Did I do something?"

"Yes," she said laughing a little harder.

"Something wrong?"

She shook her head no and threw her arms around him. "Well, yes," she amended pulling back to look at him, "you left without saying good-bye and left me a note apologizing."

"I thought it was in your best interest."

She adjusted her body so that she could get a better look at him. "Did you honestly think I'd ignore your cryptic message?"

He smiled despite himself. "A part of me hoped you wouldn't."

"A part of you knew I wouldn't."

He nodded agreeing with her. "Then, I'm sorry for the message, but I did have to leave and you were still passed out. How much had you had to drink?"

She looked down at her hands twisting in her lap sheepishly.

"That's what I thought," he said running his fingers through his perfectly kept hair. Lexi watched as the pieces fell back into place neatly, only a few stray strands obscured the view of his eyes.

"So are you…are you with someone?" he asked taking her hands into his own, his voice ringing with a note of hope.

Lexi hesitated watching his concerned face before answering him. "No, there's no one."

He breathed out the breath he had been holding and smiled up at her in relief. "That's good." He paused nibbling on his bottom lip as if deliberating his next move. "I never asked over the summer while we were still talking, but what happened with Clark?"

She cursed under her breath extracting her hands from his. She pushed her hair behind her ears several times anxiously. This had been the question she had wanted to avoid.

"Do we have to talk about Clark?" she whispered.

"We don't have to, but you know my end of the story. You were the only one I saw when I closed my eyes," he said bringing his hand up to her chin and tilting her head up to look into his crystal clear blue eyes.

"Then why wasn't I enough when they were open?" she asked another tear welling in her eyes.

"Please don't cry," he muttered wiping away the tear that had fallen down her cheek. "I know I screwed up. We both screwed up, but I'm here now."

As if that solved everything.

She sat up straighter, not wanting to let her emotions take over. She had been down that road before and it was a slippery slope. "Clark and I broke up the day you told me you loved me."

"What?" Jack cried a little too loud for their environment. He drew eyes from the surrounding pedestrians congregated in the hallway to escape the cold. "Why didn't you tell me?"

"Jack, lower your voice," she demanded glancing around at the nosey onlookers.

"No, Lexi, explain," he yelled out his eyes blazing.

Deep down she wished she could have lied to him right then and there. What made him special anyway? She lied to everyone else. She wished that she didn't have to explain why she had done what she did. She had been avoiding the truth for so long. She didn't feel prepared to divulge her actions, but she couldn't lie to Jack. They had decided a long time ago never to do that to each other. Her heart told her that the truth would only hurt him further. That he should leave after everything they had been through. That *she* should run tail-end in the opposite direction, but she couldn't and he obviously wasn't going to either.

"I couldn't tell you, but I couldn't be with him either."

"Why didn't you come to me?" he pleaded with her trying to comprehend what she had done.

"He made me...hurt you, Jack," she finally stammered out. "What I felt for Clark...what Clark thought he felt for me, would never be the same after all that. I'd gone ahead with his plan out of fear. And for what?" she muttered angrily. "For what? Fear of losing him? No, I'd never feared that, but I didn't see that until it was too late. I was afraid of losing you. For what I had with you was more than anything Clark gave me."

"Then why didn't you come to me?" he repeated interrupting her stream of conscious. "Why didn't you tell me?"

"Can't you see? I did it, because I loved you. Though you said the words first, I didn't believe you," she told him breathlessly, her face paling after finally telling him everything she had been holding in.

His features morphed at the shock of her words. She could tell he wasn't pleased with what she had said. "You think I'd tell you I love you, if it wasn't true?" he growled.

"Your girlfriend had just told me you had held out on sex with her for over a year and a half because she was a virgin. You obviously respected her. You couldn't even wait two days at a beach house while our significant others were a couple hundred yards away. What does that tell you?" she asked her face regaining a little bit of color with the vehemence in her voice.

He leaned back hard against the bench and ran his hands through his thick hair again. Lexi's eyes were drawn to the movement, and she wished he would stop doing that. It kept making her heart flutter. "Yeah, I really respected Kate by *not* sleeping with her," he stated sarcastically shaking his head. "Is that what you think?"

Lexi looked at him helplessly. It had been what she thought at the time, what she had thought for a long time, but now staring into his defeated face, she was beginning to second guess herself.

"It was the opposite," he told her taking her hand out of her lap once again as he regained composure. "I didn't respect her at all, because I slept with you. She was easy to handle and convenient. Nothing more to me than that. I cared for her, but when you walked away from me that day, our relationship turned hostile and almost pathetic. I stayed with her more out of boredom. And to find out you weren't with Clark after all that, I just…I don't know what to say…" he trailed off.

They sat in silence both milling over the new found information that miscommunication had deprived them of so long ago. Lexi sighed, itching to find out what this meant for them in the present time.

"I guess we both thought we were doing what was in the other's best interest," Jack told her.

"Where do we go from here?" Lexi asked tentatively looking up into his blue eyes. What she saw gave her more hope than she thought she deserved. His eyes were lit up and the smile that crossed his face took her breath away.

"I have a thought," he began leaning forward and pressing a kiss to her cheek. She was unable to believe he had just kissed her after all that.

"What's that?" she asked nudging him along.

He scooted closer on the bench so that there wasn't any room left between them. "I'm going to be in New York for a little while so why don't we try this out?"

"You mean date?" she asked in disbelief.

He scrunched up his face. "You think that we can really be normal enough to date?" he asked sarcastically.

"Oh shush," she said smacking him playfully, "I just mean that we're a little bit past that point and we're not exactly normal."

He nodded agreeing with her. "Okay, so, we don't date. Let's not be a couple since we're pretty good at that at least."

"Then what are we?"

"We're working on making this right," he said bringing his lips to hers gently.

"I like the sound of that," she said against his soft lips, her breath quickening instantly.

He drew back from her, a cocky smirk played across his features. "I forgot how much I love your reactions to everything."

He trailed a hand down the side of her face and on to her neck. "Jack, we're in public," she reminded him. He retracted his hand seeming to realize that they were in a crowded place for one of the first time. Lexi glanced around at their surroundings to make sure that they hadn't drawn any more unnecessary attention towards themselves. When she was satisfied, she turned back to Jack taking in his beautiful features and feeling giddy and light-headed all at once.

For the first time, she was hearing the words she had always dreamed of hearing. Maybe not in the exact way she had expected, but it was an improvement. So they weren't a couple, but since when was that new? They had never been a couple. They had never had that kind of relationship. This was probably the best thing for them anyway. She couldn't imagine them as a serious couple. Every other person they had dated that way had ended in disaster. She didn't want them to end up like that. She wanted what she had always envisioned with Jack.

"Where are you staying in New York?" she asked not so subtly. She bit her bottom lip and stared up at him under her long black lashes.

"I'm guessing your dorm room only has a twin," he said smirking as he stood hauling her up off the bench and leading her out of the building. "You know, I had planned on taking you through the museum."

She smiled up at him as they entered the cold afternoon air. "I'm going to assume there will be time for that later."

"Not if I can help it," he said with a wink as he laced his fingers with hers. They trotted down the stairs together. He hailed a cab that drove them across town away from Central Park, Washington Square, and Park Avenue, to a rundown building with dilapidated paneling and a slew of broken windows. Lexi cringed at the sight, unfamiliar with the more unpleasant side of town. She followed him up four flights of stairs and stood before a door with three layers of off-white paint chipping from the frame.

He flashed an apologetic smile before entering the apartment. Lexi breathed a sigh of relief at the interior. Despite the disgusting outwards appearance, the inside was clean and well furnished even if nothing in the apartment seemed to match. "Sorry about this. I was staying with some family friends for awhile, but they ended up having their parents move back in with them so they could keep a better eye on their health conditions. That put me out of a place to stay, and I ended up here with this girl I met at my last job. I'm not sure if she's around," he said looking around the apartment warily.

"How many jobs have you had?" she asked curiously.

He squirmed under her question. "A few more than I would have liked."

"Oh," she stated unsure of what to say. "What are you doing now?"

"Uh…I'm a waiter, but I feel more like I'm in between jobs. I was working at this amazing job off Wall Street," he told her his eyes glossing over with pride, "but they had to let a whole bunch of people go because of the economy. I moved up here for the job, and then it was taken out from under me. I've been talking to a lot of companies though. It'll pick up."

Lexi empathized with his pain. She had heard of so many people losing their jobs due to the economy. She was avoiding the real world as long as she possibly could and hoping everything would turn around by the time she was out of law school. Lexi reached out and touched his arm bringing him out of his bad mood.

"Oh, yeah, sorry," he apologized guiding her towards a door. "This is where Stella is letting me crash until I can get on my feet again."

He pushed open the door and revealed a room just large enough to fit a double bed, dresser, and TV. Not that he needed much else at the moment. He closed the door behind them as Lexi climbed onto the bed. She snuggled into the green comforter surprised at how comfy the mattress was. Jack crawled onto the bed after her, tucking his arm underneath her shoulders, and pulling her into him.

She let his kisses travel down her face, to her neck, and across her collarbone. It was a different feeling than she was accustomed to with Jack. He wasn't in a hurry with her. It had been a long time since they had been together, and he wanted to savor every inch of her body. He paused at the base of her throat running his hands across the smooth skin left exposed by her sweater.

"Don't take this the wrong way," he said pressing his lips to her skin, "but this is the palest I've ever seen you."

She laughed deep into her diaphragm. "There's not as much sun here."

Jack straddled her legs and reached for the purple sweater that was covering her pale form. He slid his hands up under the material dragging the flimsy tank top with it over her head. Trailing from her bellybutton across her ribs, up between her breasts, and then back to the hollow of her throat, he hummed softly, "Pale, pale, pale. Do, do, do." Lexi couldn't keep from giggling at his adorableness.

One hand snaked under her body and unsnapped the sheer lace bra she was wearing. He tossed it to the ground and yanked his own shirt over his head in one fluid motion. Lowering himself back down to her body, he made work with her breasts until she was squirming under him. The rest of their clothes followed and each took their time exploring and reacquainting themselves with each other's body. She could tell he was getting close to going over the edge as she gripped him in her hands and used her mouth to pleasure him further. He shuddered and seized her shoulders pulling her on top of him. She gasped surprised by his forcefulness.

"You don't want me to finish?" she asked wiggling her hips teasingly.

He smirked. "Yeah, I do," he said as he pushed her hips down sliding inside of her. She groaned at his touch. Jack let loose a low moan at the feel of her encircling him. Lexi squeezed her muscles and felt him quiver underneath her. She leaned forward resting her hands on the bed and gave him a loving kiss before he started moving slowly inside of her. They both enjoyed alternating between who took control of the situation, the speed, and tempo that the other employed. As they both were getting close, Jack shoved her upwards and off of him. Without even giving it a seconds thought, he flipped her over grasping her hips in his hands and started where they left off doggie-style. They finished together, both spent from the physical and emotional rollercoaster from that day.

After cleaning up, Lexi fell back into Jack's arms letting him hold her tight. He fanned out her hair letting it run loose between his fingers. "Better than the museum?" she asked playfully.

"Much better," he said leaning down and kissing her on her temple. "Everything is better when I'm with you."

She sighed heavily unable to believe that after everything they had been through and all the heartache and tears she had endured, she was finally getting the chance she deserved with Jack. So maybe they weren't officially a couple, but at least they were something. She could deal with whatever came next as long as he was around. That would be good enough for her…for now. Then they could go past this, and work towards a real future together.

But right now, she was ready for round two.

19

PRESENT

Lexi bounded into Jack's room and quickly stripped off the D-Bags band t-shirt he had loaned her. She looked longingly at the cracked bathroom door where steam was currently streaming from. She took one step forward, her heart racing with desire knowing that Jack was naked on the other side. She cautiously approached the bathroom door and peered into the room. Lexi could just make out Jack's figure through the glass.

She had been so determined to barge in there even though she had just kept them from making the same mistake. She leaned her head against the doorframe and shut her eyes attempting to reason with herself.

Yes, Jack was naked in the next room.

Yes, he probably looked freaking amazing as the water ran down his body.

Yes, she wanted him.

All of these things were obvious to her, but she needed to keep a lid on her emotions. Just because she wanted Jack didn't mean that she should have him. He was taken. Though she had never respected that in the past, she liked to think that she was a different person now.

As she was about to walk away, she heard soft humming over the drum of the water hitting the glass. The humming turned into a melody and eventually, Lexi could put the pieces together and make out the lyrics to Mae's song *The Ocean*. She left her eyes shut tight allowing the lyrics to flow over her. She could have stood there indefinitely just listening to him sing so clearly over the water. His voice was mesmerizingly smooth and took her back to times when things had been easier. Or at least, she had thought they had been easier. In fact, they had been the calm before the storm.

She knew that if she rushed into that bathroom right now, it would be exactly the same. Jack would have all the control. It was hard enough turning him down twice in a twelve hour period. She wasn't sure she was capable of doing it a third time.

The final note of the song sounded in her ears and the shower cut off. Lexi jumped from where she was standing, not expecting them to be timed together. She grabbed her clothes from his dresser and rushed into the guest bedroom. Scrambling into last night's clothes, Lexi dashed for the exit. She didn't want to be here when he got out. She didn't trust herself enough not to succumb to his wiles.

Lexi hailed the first cab that she saw and had them whisk her to the airport. Flight time from JFK to Hartfield-Jackson was only two hours, and since Chyna was flying private jet it might even be less time. Lexi didn't care how long she would have to wait. She couldn't be around Jack right now. She needed her best friend. She needed Chyna to tell her that she was doing the right thing, because Lexi had never been good at that. And all she wanted to do was turn around and be back in Jack's arms.

The cab stopped in front of the airport terminal. She threw some cash over the front of the seat and quickly exited the vehicle. The cabbie rolled the window down and called out to her. "Change?" She turned around and shook her head at him.

The wait was shorter than she had expected. She had passed the time sitting with her feet propped up across three chairs, listening to whatever was blaring through her earbuds, and people watching. New York was bad enough. She couldn't believe what she had seen coming to and from an international airport. She shook her head at the remembered images and deposited the iPod back into her purse. Chyna had employed some poor sap to wheel her luggage through the airport for her. Lexi shouldn't have expected anything less from her gorgeous friend. When Chyna caught sight of Lexi, her feet moved double time as she nearly ran in her rather impractical four inch heels to greet her best friend.

"Alexa, I'm so glad I'm here," she squealed wrapping her arms around her neck.

"I'm glad you're here too, Chyna," Lexi told her.

"Let's hope my town car is waiting," Chyna stated grabbing Lexi's hand and whisking her out of the airport.

A black town car was indeed waiting for Chyna's arrival outside of the airport. After the baggage was secured in the trunk and the girls were in the backseat, the car whisked them away to the hotel in which Chyna already had a penthouse reserved in her name. Once the two were safely in the hotel accommodations, Chyna immediately went on a rampage. Lexi was only half listening to what she was saying as she stared in awe at the hotel room. She had seen impressive residences. Chyna obviously had a remarkable suite, but Lexi had been there so often she had become desensitized to its beauty. This place was completely different. Everything about the room was classy and elegant, drawn out in soft golden hues. An exquisite den area was set in dark oak and brown and cream suede. Through colossal double doors revealed a four-poster bed draped with an intricately detailed quilt comforter and at least a dozen throw pillows of varying shape and size. The sheer, gold-trimmed curtains opened to a sprawling balcony overlooking the city. From several dozen stories up, Lexi could really see the splendor of the place she had grown up.

Chyna cleared her throat. "Are you listening to me?" she asked grabbing Lexi's wrist.

"Huh?" she asked turning away from the decorations to look at her friend.

"I was talking about what's been going on with you," Chyna told her unceremoniously.

"Yeah," Lexi mumbled falling backwards in a large chair that she sank into on impact. "Things aren't exactly going as planned."

"You think?" Chyna asked sarcastically. "You were supposed to tell the girlfriend what happened between you two, and let that be the end of it. What about that was complicated?"

Lexi buried her face in her hands. "Everything," she grumbled.

"No, it's not. That's what I was saying earlier. You get *way* too attached. Clean break is what you need. Just forget about him. Forget about whatever happened between you two. That's what you were supposed to be doing here, Alexa. Tell me what happened to change that. I cannot fathom why you'd want to have anything to do with this scumbag again after what he did to you. I kind of want to go find him myself and cut off his you-know-what," she exclaimed angrily. "He doesn't actually deserve to have balls after everything that went down. I can't believe I actually convinced you to come see him. I should have seen this coming. What was I thinking? He's obviously the same pig-headed asshole he always was. He thinks he can waltz right in, take over your life, and leave you in pieces all over again. Well, I'm not having it alright? Do you hear me?"

"C, chill out. That's not how it's going to be."

"You're damn right that's not how it's going to be. Wanna know why? Because I'm not letting you near him again. I don't care what you say, Alexa Mae."

"You've got it all wrong," Lexi said through her teeth.

"And you're brainwashed by him," she cried.

"I'm not brainwashed, alright?" Lexi yelled back. She stood forcefully and stared at her friend. "I know what happened with Jack, and I swore I would never let that happen to me again. I know what he is capable of, but it's not going to happen this time."

"I hope it's not going to happen, because you're not involved with him," Chyna retorted staring back at her friend.

"I could have slept with him. I could have given myself up to him all over again. I could have torn down all the walls that I had placed around myself against him, but I didn't. Do you know how hard it is to say no to him? No! How could you?" she cried, anger that she had bottled up threatening to overflow. She was even beginning to make wild accusations against her best friend…the one person in New York she told everything. Well…almost everything.

"Watch it," Chyna warned.

"You are just given everything you want. You take everything that you want. You have no concept of what it means to say no to someone that you truly love, because you don't love anyone," Lexi uttered viciously.

Chyna's mouth dropped open in shock. "Excuse me?"

"You heard me," Lexi growled. "You have a silver spoon shoved up your pretty little ass, and the world jumps at your beck and call. You've never loved anyone, because you've never put yourself out there to be loved. You just sleep with guy after guy after guy."

Chyna's jaw set at the accusation. "And you're much better?" she asked shaking her head. "You do the same thing, but at least I know where I stand with them. You…you're just using them, because you can't *have* the one thing that you want. The one person that you want doesn't want you, and you're right, I don't know what that's like. Everyone wants me."

"Yeah, they want to fuck you and be gone by the morning," Lexi said maliciously.

"That's better than wasting a life on someone who will *always* choose the *other* girl over you. I'd rather be in control, using them rather than have them use me, because that's all he's doing. He's using you, and when he's done, he'll throw you out with the trash like he always has," Chyna snarled letting her words cut straight through to Lexi's core.

Lexi couldn't believe what she had just said. Was this what Chyna had been holding back all those years? Was this what it was like to get the full blow of Chyna's anger? Suddenly, Lexi felt like all the air had been sucked out of her body. Her chest was seizing up with the lack of oxygen, and her head was spinning in the oxygen deprived environment. She could feel her face lose its color as the blood flow weakened. She gasped out hoping to breathe in some precious oxygen, but nothing happened. Then she was in darkness.

*****

When Lexi finally began to stir, the first thing she noticed was that she was no longer in the same place. Her fingers spread apart as she felt the silky material caress her hand. Her eyes fluttered open as the reality that she was lying in the hotel bed came to her. She turned her head to look around and found that there was a crowd of people whispering inside the double doors. A searing pain shot through her head at the movement. She reached her hand up to her aching head. Her hand pushed into her tangled hair and found a large knot on the backside of her scalp. She groaned at the slight feel of her fingers brushing the spot.

The noise must have alerted the room as Chyna immediately scrambled to her side. Her face was tear-stained and the most imperfect Lexi had ever seen her. It was a relief to see her this way. And though she knew this had something to do with her, she couldn't remember what had happened.

"Oh my God, you're okay," Chyna gushed, a fresh wave of tears threatening to break loose. "I was so worried. Oh my God. Oh my God." She was fanning herself with her hand as she perched on the side of the bed. Her face was stricken with worry.

"C, what happened?" Lexi asked weakly attempting to sit up in bed.

"Whoa there," a man said rushing forward and pressing her shoulder gently back into the bedding. "You'll want to stay lying down for a little while longer. Looks like you had quite a spill."

The wave of nausea that hit her when she tried to get up was the only reason she hadn't fought this man. "Yeah, I guess so," she said turning her face to look at Chyna again. She wanted answers.

"Oh, this is *all* my fault," Chyna muttered covering her face with her hands. Lexi glanced back to where the crowd had been, and saw that everyone else was beginning to exit the room. She figured it must be hotel staff of some sort.

"Ma'am, I'm sure this was not your fault," the man said putting his hand reassuringly on Chyna's shoulder. "People faint for all sorts of reasons," he stated calmly. His hand rubbed down her arm gently in an effort to halt any further bouts of despair.

"I fainted?" Lexi asked trying to put the pieces together.

The man reluctantly stepped away from Chyna. He was a bit older with graying across his temples, but with a look that showed he must have been very attractive in his younger years. Lexi didn't miss the glance he sent Chyna's way before focusing his attention back on Lexi. "Yes, as far as I can tell, you just fainted. I'm Dr. Mike Cutler. You can call me Mike if you like," he said flashing Chyna another brief smile.

"Will I be alright, Mike?" Lexi asked using his name to snap his attention back to the person who was bed ridden.

"You took a pretty nasty fall and managed to smack your head into the side of the coffee table. There is a large knot on the back of your head, but that should be gone in a matter of hours. You'll have some tenderness over the next couple days, but nothing to trouble yourself over. No concussion or any serious damage. You'll need to take some ibuprofen for the pain. Seems to have frightened your friend here quite a bit though," he said readjusting his focus again. Lexi rolled her eyes. "If either of you need anything further, give me a call," he told Chyna as he handed her a business card.

Lexi was almost certain that his cell number would be scrawled on the back side. Even in her darkest of hours, Chyna continued to get hit on.

"Thanks, Mike," Chyna muttered not paying him much attention.

He gracefully exited the room leaving the two girls alone once again.

"Did you get his number?" Lexi asked pointing at the business card.

"What?" Chyna asked oblivious. Then she glanced down at the tiny piece of white paper. She flipped it around experimentally in her hands a few times before noticing that, indeed, there was a number scratched onto the backside. "Yeah, I guess I did."

Lexi couldn't hold in her giggles. Chyna looked aghast at her sudden onset of laughter, but quickly joined in. Soon they were both laughing uncontrollably. Lexi put her hand on her head and groaned as the pressure of her laughter cut across her injury.

"Oh, Alexa, I really am so sorry. I didn't mean to be so…so mean. I had no idea you would faint," she muttered vehemently, her emerald eyes wide.

Lexi chuckled. "Me either. I've never done that before." She gingerly scooted up to rest against the headboard, wincing as her head protested the movement. She could hardly believe that this had happened to her. When Dr. Cutler had told her that she had fainted, the memories had flooded back to her. She remembered the argument with Chyna, and the sting of Chyna's words still rang in her ears. She knew she had overreacted, but thinking about what Chyna had said made it difficult to breathe.

"Does he mean all that to you?" Chyna whispered wringing her hands.

Lexi sighed and turned her head to look at her friend. She pushed her hair behind her ears several times before answering. "He's always meant everything to me."

"But he's with someone else now," Chyna stated hesitantly. She was afraid to set her off again and have a repeat of what had just happened. She had never been so afraid for anyone in her life.

"I know. I know. He said he wants to make things right with me. I told him we could only be right if neither of us are attached. I need to give him the time to become unattached."

"And how do you know he'll do that?" Chyna asked. "I mean, didn't he call you down here because he was ready to commit in the first place."

Lexi bit her lip. "Not exactly. It was more for her benefit. It just seemed to backfire on her. He realized that he knew what he really wanted when I was around. That he wants me. You should have seen his jealous face when he found out that I went on a date with Ramsey," she said smiling fondly at the memory.

"And what about him? Just one date? You told me that you kind of liked him," Chyna mentioned hoping that something…anything would snap her friend out of this.

"Ramsey's…ya know. Whatever. I had a good time, but he's so…all in your face. His personality is all encompassing. I can't breathe around him," Lexi told Chyna, surprised by the reality of her words.

Chyna cleared her throat. "Some people think these are good qualities. It's called passion," she mumbled peaking at her friend from under her thick dark lashes.

Lexi scowled at her friend. She didn't want to think about Ramsey, mostly, because she didn't know what to do about Ramsey. He wasn't like the other people she had dated. She had thought that he would be easy to figure out, a cookie-cutter sort of character. Yet, she couldn't deny that she had enjoyed herself on their date, uncharacteristically so. She had lost herself in his strange, in-your-face personality for a time. She had even forgotten about Jack. It had surprised her that she had been able to forget such strong memories while with another man. She had become so accustomed to measuring up every guy to Jack that, if she was honest with herself, it had been a pleasant reprieve from the tireless drone of unimpressive desperation that most guys wore like cloaks.

"I don't know about that," Lexi replied biting her teeth and averting her eyes.

Chyna chewed on the inside of her cheek to keep from smiling at her friend's reaction. It was the same disbelieving tone she had used on the phone when talking about this Ramsey character. Chyna simply couldn't wait to meet him to find out what exactly was so special about him. "I think you do."

"Well, it doesn't matter. I can't go out with him again when this stuff is going on with me and Jack," Lexi told her.

"What? Why not? He's going to be with Bekah!" Chyna cried forgetting her promise to herself that she wouldn't get too excited while talking to Lexi. She bit her lip waiting for Lexi's reaction.

"Shit!" Lexi cried, her eyes lighting up with worry.

"Oh God, I'm sorry. I didn't mean to bring it up again."

"No, not that," she cried closing her eyes and smacking her head backwards against the headboard. She cursed again, louder this time, with the pain of slamming her head.

"Don't do that," Chyna cried reaching for her friend.

Lexi staved Chyna off. "I forgot I'm supposed to be going with Ramsey to Jack's birthday party on Saturday."

"Oh!" Chyna said her mouth popping open.

"What am I going to do, C?" Lexi asked tears welling in her eyes from the pain in her head and the sudden realization that she was in quite a pickle.

"That's easy, sweetie," Chyna told her reassuringly. "You show up with that hunk of a man on your arm and revel in the jealousy that will flow freely from Jack. It's too easy honestly."

"I don't need to make him jealous," Lexi said her brows furrowing.

Chyna rolled her eyes. "It's a reminder that if this is what he wants," she gestured towards Lexi, "then he needs to make up his fucking mind."

*****

That is how Lexi and Chyna ended up three days later in a black stretch limo escorting them to Jack's birthday extravaganza. Ramsey had dropped off Lexi's purchases at Chyna's penthouse suite. The two had instantly hit it off while Lexi glanced anxiously between the two. For some reason, Ramsey never passed more than a fleeting glance in Chyna's direction. It was unlike anything Lexi had ever seen. Most guys openly ogled her gorgeous best friend, but Ramsey managed to make pleasant conversation without flirting and without coming onto her. Lexi was amazed by the end of the encounter, and didn't know what to think about it.

After that, Lexi visited her family for the remainder of the week. Chyna came down for an afternoon to meet the family, but otherwise had occupied herself as she always had with guys and nightlife. The time at home had been refreshing and grounded her unlike anything else could. The reality of the past week was setting in, and she needed to get a grip on herself if she was going to survive the weekend. Her parents hadn't badgered her with questions about herself. They had just seemed genuinely happy to have her around, even though it was a shorter period of time then she had promised. They did seem to like the prospect that she might take the Georgia Bar, and practice law a little closer to home. She didn't want to get their hopes up though and felt bad when they continued to bring it up.

Regardless, Lexi was more nervous about the upcoming night. Ramsey looked smashing when he entered Chyna's penthouse. He wore an amazing Armani tux that was tailored to perfection. His blonde hair was spiked and something about his green eyes sparkled when he entered the room. Lexi had to remind herself to breathe when his gaze met hers. He had commented on how beautiful they looked, and Lexi had to admit that both of them had *really* outdone themselves.

Chyna's shiny black hair flowed out across her shoulders and down her back, just above where the back of her lacy black dress came to a point. The halter dipped low enough in the front to show off the tops of her perky breasts and hugged tight to her body flowing out around her calves.

A red, strapless, sweetheart bodice clung to Lexi's tiny form giving her curves that even she was surprised that she had. The dress fell to the top of her knees revealing the chiseled muscles in her calves that were only more prominent from the black stilettos that adorned her feet. Her chocolate curls were expertly held up off the back of her neck into a messy bun creation with tendrils falling around her face. Ramsey's mouth parted at the sight of her, for once, speechless.

Lexi lounged back against the leather interior, a smile playing across her face at the memory of the look on his face.

"What are you all smiley about?" Ramsey asked not able to keep from speaking for very long. His arm was rested precariously over the back of her seat, a champagne flute held loosely in the other hand.

"Um, what?" Lexi asked jumping in surprise. She hadn't expected to be caught.

Chyna's eyebrows lifted on the other side of the car. A smile crossed her face when she looked upon the couple, even though she could see Lexi flinching.

"You're all smiley," he repeated trailing his free hand across her cheek.

Her eyes bulged slightly at the light contact. She sure hoped this wasn't going to be one of those nights where she couldn't keep control of her emotions. Ramsey was…well, he wasn't Jack. Of that much she was certain, but that didn't mean she didn't enjoy his company.

Lexi tried to push Chyna's words about Ramsey out of her head. She didn't want to *use* him to make Jack jealous. She didn't really want to think that she was using anyone.

"Just smiley," she told him as she dipped her head backwards leaving his hand caressing thin air. He didn't seem affronted by her rejection and rested his hand against the back of the seat once more. "Where are we going?"

Ramsey turned his brilliant smile on her, and she gritted her teeth to keep from sending him a girly smile in return. "It's a surprise if you don't already know," he said confidently.

"You and your surprises," Lexi griped.

"You seemed to like the last one," he huskily whispered.

This time Lexi couldn't keep the smile from her face. "Yes, well…" she stammered.

Chyna giggled in the corner, quickly brushing her hand up to her mouth to contain her laughter. Lexi's eyes darted to Chyna, glaring in her direction. Chyna winked back unable to control her euphoria.

The car continued forward, and Lexi tried to piece together the direction they were driving through the city in an effort to determine their destination. Lexi recognized the buildings as they passed the Georgia Tech and Georgia State campuses. They were going in the opposite direction of Buckhead. So once again, Ramsey had surprised her. Though she wouldn't let him know. She wasn't certain where they would hold a birthday party around here though. Even when she had been with Bekah searching for formal dresses, she hadn't been quite certain where they were going that required something so formal. Now it appeared that they weren't even going to be in the city.

As the limo took the next exit off of the interstate, Lexi's eyes lit up with excitement. She had spent dozens of evenings inside the walls of the place they were about to be dropped off. Turner Field, home of the Atlanta Braves baseball team, appeared before them. The parking lot was near empty which signified that there must be an away game. The limo dropped them off at the front entrance of the stadium where they were immediately escorted inside.

Even Chyna seemed impressed by the extent that had been put into a simple birthday party. She had thrown her fair share of impressive parties, but this was altogether different compared to the things that occurred in New York.

Lexi, Chyna, and Ramsey followed the usher inside and as they rounded the corner the 755 Club came into focus. Ramsey thanked the guide and sent him on his way as he stepped forward to the hostess. The tall, buxom blonde standing behind the desk smiled pleasantly as Ramsey approached her. They shared a few words that showed they were acquaintances. Lexi's stomach knotted as the woman turned what appeared to be the full force of her charm on Ramsey. She knew it was irrational to feel anything, and honestly, she didn't even know what this feeling was that was taking residence in her stomach.

Ramsey gestured towards Lexi and Chyna, and the woman's face soured slightly at the indication that he had brought two dates. The woman motioned for them to enter.

"What was that all about?" Chyna whispered to Lexi. She shrugged her shoulders not really wanting to know. Lexi had too many of her own issues to deal with, without thinking about someone else's.

The room they entered was large enough for a party to fill, but not too big that everyone would be so spread out they wouldn't enjoy themselves. The space was already beginning to crowd in.

Lights were dimmed and music was playing evenly through the speakers at a volume just loud enough that no one had to speak over the music to be heard. Hors d'oeuvres were being carted around the room on silver platters. There was an open bar along one side of the establishment and another that opened up to a stunning view of the Braves field. The sun had set across the veranda, and the last hints of pink and orange hues lit up the building before diminishing into darkness.

Lexi's eyes followed the crowd of formally dressed do-gooders noticing a distinct pattern. She set her gaze on the swarm surrounding one end of the bar. Through the crowd a pair of blue eyes seemed to catch sight of her across the room. His mouth opened slightly when he took in her breathtaking beauty, all concentration lost on his eager subjects. He was king for the night, and the room full of jesters were keen to do his bidding. The queen at his side appeared elegant and serene in her flowing, gold, silk dress. She upturned her nose as the king extracted himself from her grasp and volleyed himself across the floor to his mistress in red.

Bekah followed quickly behind, speaking before Jack could reach Lexi. "Ramsey," she cried wrapping her arms around her big brother. "What took you so long?"

Ramsey smiled down on her. "I had two gorgeous ladies to escort," he said wiggling his eyebrows up and down and moving to wrap his arms protectively around Lexi and Chyna.

"You came with *him*?" Jack asked them even though it was pretty obvious to anyone involved with the situation that he was talking directly to Lexi. After the conversation she had had with Jack about her date with Ramsey, she was amazed this was all the reaction she had elicited from him.

"I did tell him that I would go with him, and I wouldn't want to go back on my promise," Lexi stated pointedly. Jack's eyes blazed at the implications behind the statement, but before he could react, he was shouldered out of the way from behind.

"What the…" he trailed off.

"Lexi, baby, oh dear God. Please tell me you are single. Please, oh please, oh please," Seth cried running his hands down her sides.

Lexi couldn't help but giggle as he scooped her up into his arms. "Seth, put me down," she cried as he twirled her around in place, knocking her legs into the unlucky few who didn't get out of the way.

"I'm never letting go," he said setting her on his feet, but dropping his head so that it rested on her breasts. Lexi let out a peel of laughter at the absurdity of the situation.

"I haven't seen you in forever. The least you could do would be to give me a legitimate hug," she told Seth.

Just then someone stood behind Seth and smacked him hard against the back of the head. "You get off her this instant, you pig," Sandy cried grabbing at his arms.

"Oh, sweetie, it's just Lexi," he said letting go and turning to his wife.

Sandy nudged him out of the way and reached out to hug Lexi instead of continuing her scolding. "I'm sorry, Lexi. It really is good to see you. When Jack told me you were coming, I flipped my shit. I was so excited."

"I can't believe you're here either. Jack didn't tell me you two were coming up," she said glaring over at Jack.

"Don't blame him," Sandy replied swatting at her husband's wandering hands. "Seth didn't think he'd be able to get away. It was kind of last minute."

"This is a touching reunion, but I need a drink," Chyna said as she wandered away towards the bar.

"I should probably follow her. You never know what…or who is going to happen to Chyna when she is alone," Lexi said extracting herself from the group. As much as she loved Seth and Sandy, it just brought back too many painful memories to be around them, especially with Jack only a few feet away. She took one brief glance backwards and saw him staring at her behind as she walked away. She knew that look. It was right before his eyes turned crystal clear blue and his desire began to peak. He wanted her. Right now. It didn't matter where he was at the moment. He just wanted to have her.

One more reason for her to back away from him. She wasn't sure how well she would be able to resist him when he looked so damn good, and was looking at her like he could devour her whole.

"C, what am I doing here?" Lexi asked as she reached Chyna and latched onto her elbow.

"Because you want him," she stated simply, ordering a round of dirty martinis for them. The bartender almost instantly had the drinks before them. He was cute, roguish looking with a strong jaw line masked by stubble and dark hungry eyes. She smiled at him taking in the way his large, calloused hands poured the drinks into triangle-shaped glasses. He pushed the drinks towards her on blue and white napkins. Chyna produced a twenty from her billfold and tossed it into the blue glass tip container. He winked at her. Lexi knew Chyna could have his number any minute now.

"Yeah, you're right. That is what I want," Lexi agreed reaching for the martini.

"Did you say you wanted something?" Ramsey asked coming up next to them. He raised two fingers and nodding at the man behind the bar.

"Uh…yeah. Well, I already have my drink," Lexi replied.

"Steven," Ramsey said in greeting. The two men shook hands across the bar. "Good to see you. It's been awhile. You here now?"

"A couple places now," Steven replied pouring a drinking for Ramsey and sliding it across the table.

"I was wondering where you had gone."

"Wherever the money is."

"Well, if you need anything, you let me know," Ramsey told him.

Lexi analyzed the situation before speaking. "Do you know everyone?"

Ramsey chuckled. "Pretty much. It's my job to know everyone."

"Uh huh," she humped. "And what do you do?"

His face paled at the question, but he quickly recovered. "I know people, that's what I do," he said sending a full-watted smile her way. Her eyes narrowed at his backhanded way of telling her to back-off. But her curiosity had been peaked, and now she really wanted to know what he did.

For tonight, though, she needed to focus on Jack. It was his big night after all, and she needed to find out what he was actually going to be doing about Bekah. She would be leaving on Sunday for New York, and she needed a more definitive answer about their situation. They had talked a few times on the phone since she had fled his apartment, but she hadn't gone to visit him again. Too much temptation in one week wasn't good for her. He had respected her wishes thus far, but she wasn't going to hold her breath that it would continue.

Lexi gritted her teeth as she watched Bekah saunter across the room with a trio of other blonde-headed bimbos. "You know them?" Lexi asked Ramsey nodding her head in their direction.

"Ahh…yes. The fearsome four was what my friends used to call them in high school. They've been inseparable since then too. They all went to Duke, spent four years there, and came back to Atlanta together," he told her knocking back his drink.

The girls stood a few feet from Lexi as they ordered drinks. She heard them giggling and then eventually began to pick out the voices from each other. She didn't glance their way, but soon learned the gist of the conversation. They were talking about a guy…Jack.

"I wish I could find one like him," a mousy voice squeaked.

"He is so handsome and charming," another girl spoke up. Her voice was more of an alto compared to the last girl.

"And I bet he fucks great," the last one drawled, her thick southern accent marring her voice and grating on Lexi's eardrums.

Out of the corner of her eye, Lexi could just make out the devilish smirk that played across Bekah's innocent-looking face. "Oh God, he is amazing. Girls, I don't think I can delve into it enough, but last night was unlike anything I've *ever* experienced."

Lexi blanched at the words. Jack had been with Bekah last night. She hadn't thought he would stop seeing Bekah, but she certainly hadn't thought he would sleep with Bekah after what he had promised Lexi.

"The way he fucks me," she cooed, "it's better than any other guy I've been with."

"No need to be so crude, Bek," the mousy girl retorted giggling.

"I like it," the southern drawl sounded again. "Is he fast and wild? Does he just pound into you? Or is he gentle and smooth, pushing his cock in and out of you forcing you to scream with pleasure?"

"Amber," the mousy girl shrieked, "think about where we are!"

"I was just wunderin'," she replied her accent getting deep and throaty.

"I don't mind talking about it since he does all of the above. Last night he just took me fast and wild like you were talking about Amber. He took me as if I was the only person he ever wanted to be with, as if he was claiming me for his own."

Lexi leaned forward away from the bar feeling all the blood rush to her face as nausea took over her body. This couldn't be happening. Had she been this stupid? Could he have done this to her? She hated that the answer was yes. He wasn't exactly strong on keeping his promises. The only exception being that he had never lied to her, and sometimes she wished that he did.

"Whoa, are you okay?" Ramsey asked wrapping his arm around her shoulders and hauling her back to a standing position.

"Um, yeah, I'm fine," she mumbled putting one hand on her stomach and the other over her mouth.

"You don't look fine. Chyna, look at her," he commanded.

Chyna pulled herself away from the hot bartender to give Lexi a cursory glance. "Oh, you do look sick. Maybe you should go get her some air," Chyna suggested.

"That's a great idea," he said supporting her as they began to cross the room towards the open balcony. The farther away she got from Bekah the easier it was to walk and not feel like her stomach was about to erupt. But dwelling on Bekah's words was completely counterproductive to any ease she might have been feeling.

"Ladies and gentleman, if you will join us over here, we have a bit of a tribute to the birthday boy over the years," Seth announced into the microphone. The crowd began to reassemble in front of a projection display.

"Will you be okay to watch this? I don't want you to get sick," he said anxious about her well-being.

Her curiosity stalled the feeling in her stomach. She stepped forward with Ramsey clearing the way for her to pass through. A series of pictures began to flash across the screen in quick succession. The first few she didn't recognize. She figured, from the looks of them, that they were bachelor party pictures. Coveted images that girlfriends were never supposed to see. As the slideshow progressed, Lexi started noticing more and more pictures. Suddenly, the film stopped on a close-up of her and Jack huddled together on the beach. They were showing off their tanned bodies. Lexi could vividly remember them goofing off that afternoon. It was the day before they had made love for the first time.

She didn't know that there were still pictures from that time of her life. Another series of photographs shot across the screen of her and Jack along with dozens of other friends. She was as much of a constant through the pictures as he was.

Her eyes scanned the room and landed on the baby blues that had already located her. The emotion that welled inside of her was completely different than what she had earlier been feeling. She was still angry, but with her past flashing before her eyes all she could see was Jack. Jack had been as much of a constant in her life as she was in his. And they would get through this…whether or not he was currently sleeping with his girlfriend. They had gotten through everything before, and they would get through it now.

Lexi watched Jack snake an arm around Bekah's waist and pull her in close like she had felt him do to her so many times before. She smiled lovingly up at him, and the same feeling began to creep over Lexi.

The only way things could be okay now is if she didn't watch them together like this. She grabbed Ramsey's hand and pulled him back towards the balcony. "Maybe I'm not feeling as well as I thought. I'd rather not be in here," she whispered to him.

"You don't want to watch the end? I think you're in the end," he told her.

She shook her head fiercely. "I think I better not."

"Alright," he said guiding her to the outside.

This time when she took one glance over her shoulder, Jack wasn't there, and he wasn't watching.

20

DECEMBER ONE AND A HALF YEARS EARLIER

"Shush," Lexi cried for what felt like the hundredth time. "Guys, you have to cut it out and be quiet. He'll be here soon, and then you'll just be embarrassing me...again."

Rachelle gave her a half-smile. Elizabeth's freckled face darkened, but she couldn't keep from giggling. Her red hair was flying as she let her head tilt backwards with the laughter that was overtaking her. Claire, never too far from Elizabeth's state of emotions, ran her fingers through the thin blonde strands that curled under her chin. Her answering giggle only egged Elizabeth on.

"But I can't wait for him to get here," Elizabeth muttered.

Lexi's eyes narrowed. "He's here all the time. There's nothing special about tonight."

"Ah, ah, ah..." Rachelle interrupted. "Tonight is special. Finals are officially over."

"And we're going out with you," Claire added her dull grey eyes searching Lexi's face for a reaction.

"And Jack will be all dressed up," Elizabeth mumbled closing her eyes and imagining him in much less clothing.

The two girls had been badgering her about Jack since he arrived. Even though they saw him nearly every day for the past month, they couldn't stop their endless discussion of him. Lexi was beginning to think they did it just to get a reaction from her. And they hated that, despite their horrible finals preparation for the past couple weeks, Lexi had been in a constant state of euphoria.

Jack and Lexi had held to their word. They were not a couple. They were lovers and most definitely in love. Yet, they weren't together. It was easier that way so far. She was busy with law school, and he had been desperately searching for a job where he would be able to use his degree. With all that, he still had to work as a waiter and sometimes performed with a piano or guitar to make money to pay the bills that were piling up in the tiny broken-down apartment.

It made the time they were afforded together that much sweeter. And somehow they had formed a friendship different from any they had ever had before. Now they spent long, late afternoons in Central Park discussing anything that came to mind. In their past, they had been careful with the precious time they were allotted and even more careful with the time they shared around others. They never wanted to appear too friendly.

But now they could lounge around each other's apartments all afternoon, hanging with their roommates, or other times they sat alone watching movies snuggled together. But beyond all that, their passion rang through it all. They made love nearly every day. As often as she could afford to put off studying, they would spend all afternoon in his bedroom trying out new positions, volumes, and heightened climaxes. Lexi could live like this forever.

Well, as long as she could get her roommates to shut up.

A knock sounded from the doorway, and Lexi shot her roommates a fierce glare. Elizabeth and Claire, giggling into their hands, took a seat next to Rachelle, who admonished them with a look of her own. The two girls dropped their hands and tried to divert their attention from the visitor in their doorway.

Lexi pushed her hair behind her ears once before opening the door. Lexi gasped and clutched the doorframe for support, when her eyes landed on the form in front of her.

"Clark," she gasped, shock written across her face, "What are you doing here?"

Her heart was pounding in her chest. Clark had never forgiven her for what she had done to him. And she didn't blame him. If the situations were reversed, she wouldn't have been able to forgive him for his treachery either. He had slandered her name, and forced her out of their circle of friends. It was like she had lost everything in the divorce. The only thing that had kept her going was the knowledge that she would be in New York soon enough, and away from it all. Which did nothing to explain why he was here on her doorstep.

Always confident, he didn't even flinch. He smiled politely and let his green eyes work their way down her body. She instantly felt self-conscious in her skimpy black dress. The tiny spaghetti straps ended in a v-neck front and the polyester material hugged her curves in all the right places. Lexi hugged her arms across herself only increasing the amount of cleavage visible.

"I came to see you. You look beautiful," he told her, his voice rich with emotion.

Lexi gulped hard. She couldn't believe this was happening to her.

"Can I come in?"

Lexi bit her lip unsure of whether or not she should let him in. On the one hand, she hadn't seen him in a very, very long time, and so it was nice to have him here. On the other hand, Jack would be here any minute. She couldn't even imagine that.

"I don't know if that's such a good idea," she muttered her eyes on the floor. She could hear whispering behind her back, and knew that her roommates were trying to decipher who the mystery man was.

Clark downcast his eyes. She could tell his mind was working overtime. "I haven't seen you in a long time. I'm all the way up here. Are you sure I can't come inside?"

Lexi glanced over her shoulder and saw that, indeed, her roommates were very curious about the man standing before her. She felt like she had been a spectacle on display for them for the past month. When she looked back up at her ex-boyfriend, her heart skipped a beat. There were so many things wrong with this reaction that she didn't even have time to process them all. "I...I can't let you in. I'm sorry, Clark."

He nodded slowly. "Well, I guess this was a mistake," he grumbled. "Have a Merry Christmas, Lexi."

Clark turned and began to walk back down the hallway. She stepped one foot over the threshold and watched his slumped form trudge away from her. She hated that she was hurting him. Why did she always have to hurt him? The things that she had done to him within the past year should have been enough. She couldn't let this go on. He was here for a reason, and she owed him at least some of her time.

"Who was that?" Claire called unable to control her curiosity.

"Just a friend," Lexi told her before slamming the door behind her. "Clark," she called tip-toeing down the hallway in her stilettos. He stopped before he reached the stairwell and turned to face her. She raced the rest of the way down the hallway. "I'm sorry. I should have let you come inside. I was just...just so surprised."

"I guess I should have called," he admitted, a smile playing across his features.

"Yeah, I think that would have helped." Her face was flushed and hands trembling. She hadn't been this nervous in someone's presence in a long time, and she was in law school! Mostly, she didn't know what he wanted, and that terrified her.

Did he somehow know that she was seeing Jack? Had he come for revenge? Could he have gone to the dark side?

"Why don't we just talk here?" she gestured for him to take a seat on the cold stone step.

His eyebrows furrowed together. "If you'd prefer that. You look like you're freezing," he commented reaching forward to warm her arms.

She scurried back a step not allowing herself to get in contact with him. That could be bad. She had never had this issue with anyone other than Jack, but then again she had never been in a relationship with Jack…or whatever it was.

There was no need to be like this around Clark. They had their chance, and she had blown it. There was no way they could ever be together again. She didn't want that. She had what she wanted already. With that comforting thought, she took the seat next to him, shoulder to shoulder. He didn't make a move to warm her again, but allowed her slight shoulder to brush against his own.

"Can I repeat my earlier question?" she asked glancing up at him through her black lashes. "What are you doing here?"

His strong hands fiddled with the white button on his blue, plaid, long-sleeve button-up. His arms rested on the dark designer-cut jeans where they faded at the knee. Seemingly realizing that she was observing him, he dropped his habitual buttoning and unbuttoning and met her gaze. "I'm here on vacation…" he paused.

Lexi could tell that there was more to what he wanted to say, but she wasn't sure what it was. He seemed somehow reserved about what he wanted to tell her. She had been with him long enough to know when he was holding something back. She didn't want to push him though. He could tell her whatever part he wanted to tell her. She hoped she could keep herself from prying. She would rather die than have him pry and find out about Jack. With his intuition, she knew it would only take a couple questions to come up with that answer.

"How did you know where to find me?"

"I called your mom before I left to ask her where you were located on the NYU campus," he admitted cringing at his own snooping abilities.

"She didn't tell me that," Lexi muttered angrily.

"I asked her not to tell you, because I didn't know if I would come visit you," he responded quickly. A curly lock fell into his eyes and he reached up and brushed it away. Strong memories of doing just that overwhelmed her. She reached up and swept her own hair behind her ears several times to try and still her thoughts. He smiled at the familiar movement. "Well, at least you haven't changed much."

Lexi couldn't admit how true that sentiment was.

"Uh…so you didn't think you'd come see me?" she asked trying to keep him on track.

"We ended…so abrupt…so wrong," he responded sounding wounded. "And I know part of that was my fault."

Lexi felt like she had swallowed a bag of cotton balls her mouth had gone so dry. She didn't want to talk about their break up. Yes, they had broken up, but that had been quite some time ago. Why did he want to talk about that now? "Yes and everything else was my fault," she murmured broken and dejected.

"Lexi," his voice silky, "the way I treated you was completely uncalled for, and I don't know if there is any semblance of a friendship…of more," he whispered. "But if there is, then I want to find it."

"Why are you saying this to me?" she cried angrily springing from her seat. "I don't need to hear this from you, Clark."

"Lexi, sweetie, I'm trying to apologize," he said rising alongside her.

"And I appreciate that, but we can't do…*this*," she said, the thought sickening her. "How could you even want that after everything that we've been through?"

"You were always what I wanted. Don't you see that? I was going to give you a second chance after you cheated on me for nearly a year with one of my best friends. Can't you see that you were what I wanted? Then you threw that in my face."

"You made me hurt him," she whispered.

"He deserved to be hurt, and Kate stayed with him anyway. I hear they're still together," he told her. He took a step towards her.

She didn't take the bait. Her brain told her that if she announced her secret then this would quickly turn into an all out shouting match. She didn't need that. "You'll never get over it," she cried angrily pushing him backwards out of her face. "It's been a year, Clark, and you're still not over it."

"God damnit, Lexi! I hadn't even thought about this in such a long time, and now here we are arguing about it again."

"That's because you won't let this go. You come to see me on your vacation, or so you say, and then bring this shit up?" she cried.

"Look, I *am* here on my vacation, but I didn't come here to fight with you. I came to try and make amends. Obviously we're amazing at this," he stated sarcastically. "Can we try and start over, even just as friends?" he asked her.

"I'm not sure how well that would work," a voice called from the stairs below them.

Lexi stomach turned as the familiar voice hit her ears. She turned slowly and found Jack walking up the stairs towards them. She knew that he had been on his way over, and had hoped to get Clark out of here before he arrived. Somehow they had got to arguing and that just hadn't happened.

Jack's fiery blue eyes met her own eyes, and her heart swooned. She had forgotten that he was supposed to be dressed up for their evening out in celebration of the end of first semester finals. He looked amazing and she couldn't even break away for long enough to see Clark seething at the sight of Jack.

"You've got to be fucking kidding me," Clark muttered upon Jack's arrival. "Lexi, tell me you're kidding," he cried reaching out and grasping her arm.

Jack was there in an instant. "You should let her go," he said enunciating each word clearly. The two met eye-to-eye, Clark was only an inch or two taller than Jack, but he released her nonetheless.

Lexi moved between the two guys in an effort to put distance between them. This was the last thing she had wanted to happen when she had agreed to talk to Clark. "Guys, just chill out," Lexi said her voice lacking conviction.

"I can't believe I even came by," Clark stated glaring menacingly at Jack.

"Me either," Jack said putting his arm protectively around Lexi's shoulders.

"Can you both back off, please? This is all one big misunderstanding," Lexi muttered frantically.

"Oh no, I don't think it is. I was standing in this stairwell long enough to hear the majority of ya'll's conversation. I think I understand completely what is going on here," Jack announced.

"Fuck off, Jack. What they fuck are you even doing here? Aren't you and Kate still together?" Clark snarled.

"No, we're not still together," he cried vehemently pushing Lexi out of the way and shoving Clark against the wall. "You want to know why I'm here?"

"Jack!" Lexi cried rushing back towards him and yanking at his arm.

Clark glared evenly at Jack. "I'm here, because we're together. *Lexi* and I are together."

"Right," Clark drawled rolling his eyes.

"Clark, don't egg him on," Lexi yelled trying to pull at Jack's hard muscles.

"Do you have something to say?" Jack asked pounding his fist into the wall next to Clark's head.

"Jack, just stop!" Lexi yelled again. Suddenly, Clark tilted his head back against the stone wall and laughed. Lexi stared open mouthed at him. "What is so goddamned funny?" she asked her southern accent slipping out with her anger.

Clark shoved Jack's arm away, forcing him to take a step backwards. He laughed again deep in his diaphragm and stared between the two of them.

"You two are funny. Maybe I was wrong about you, Lexi. You two *deserve* each other," he spat.

The words came out like an insult. He meant that they were two of the same kind of people. That no matter where Jack and Lexi ended up, they were destined to hurt someone else. Maybe even continue on a never-ending path of hurting each other.

Clark brushed past the two of them and stumbled down the flight of stairs. Lexi watched him go, her heart wrenching with his departure. How had this veered so far off course? She ran her fingers through her long locks. She tried to hold back the tears that were threatening to escape the ducts of her eyes.

It wasn't so much what Clark had said, because a part of her had always believed his words. She had known all along that her and Jack were meant to be. They were cut from the same mold, which is why they had always worked so well together. He was the other half of her whole.

The situation in its entirety is what had gotten her riled up. She thought that these moments were over in her life. She had been blinded by her happiness with Jack. Sure, she thought about the bad times, but she hadn't allowed herself to dwell on them. There was no need. But now, with Clark's recent reappearance into her existence, the memories rushed back into her mind like a flash flood. And this time her mind was raw. It hurt worse than she had remembered.

"Lexi?" Jack asked as she collapsed into his arms. "Are you okay? Don't listen to him. Just don't even think about it. He's such an asshole. I could kill him for hurting you."

Lexi shook her head. Her body was trembling as he wrapped his arms around her waist lifting her from her feet as he stood straight. She wouldn't let the tears fall. She simply couldn't let the tears fall. As Jack held her closely, her breathing slowed and her trembling eased. His embrace was more comforting than anything else could be. It let the memories be pushed back into the box that encased them in her mind.

After a minute, she spoke, "I'm fine, Jack. It's not what he said. It's what he made me remember."

He set her down on her feet resting his forehead against hers. "I know."

"It's okay," she murmured.

"It's not okay," he uttered wrenching back and looking into her dark brown eyes. "Lex, it's *not* okay."

Lexi sighed heavily and took a step backwards. "You're right. It's not okay. We've moved on. So…let's just move on," she said yanking the stairwell door open and walking through it without waiting for his response.

She heard Jack's footsteps behind her, but he was smart enough not to come any closer. When she reached her doorway, she strolled inside. A chorus of questions bombarded her upon entry. The cacophony pained her fragile eardrums, and she held her hand up to silence them. Surprisingly, the girls stopped at once. Their dramatic gossip before she returned must have made them realize that something had gone on, and with Jack in tow, they didn't care to embarrass themselves.

"Jack is here now," she murmured, "Feel free to ogle him. That's much more normal than the rest of my life," she said walking into the only bedroom and shutting the door.

She heard whispers on the other side as the girls hypothesized what had occurred. Then a knock sounded on the door. "Lex," Jack smooth voice called out to her.

"Just give me a minute," Lexi told him taking a seat on the cold tile floor and hugging her knees to her chest. She just needed a second to let the waves of emotion fall off her shoulders. A few deep healing breaths later, Lexi stood up and looked at herself in the mirror. Beyond the wild look in her eye, she didn't look any different than before. Her make-up hadn't smudged and since she hadn't allowed herself to cry over the pain, she didn't have any mascara streaks. Pleased with her appearance, Lexi plastered a smile on her face and exited the bathroom.

"Are you guys ready to party?" she asked tucking a loose strand of hair behind her ear.

The faces before her did not look as convinced that they were ready to party as she had hoped they would be. Claire and Elizabeth weren't even eyeing Jack as they had promised. Jack's face was ashen with worry for her, but she could see something else in his eyes. She wasn't quite sure what he was feeling at the present moment. And all she wanted to do was get this night over with so they could crawl into bed together. Rachelle was the only person who hopped up out of her chair at Lexi's announcement. She smiled politely, meeting Lexi's eye and winking.

The two girls hustled everyone out of the apartment and into the awaiting cab. Claire and Elizabeth seemed to regain their typical bubbly personality, and kept the ride interesting. Luckily, neither Jack nor Lexi had to participate much in the conversation to keep them talking. Jack paid the cab as the girls climbed out of the backseat and onto the sidewalk.

"Miss Lexi," Bernard, Chyna's doorman, said tipping his hat and smiling brightly.

"Hey, Mr. B, it's good to see you!" she told him sincerely. "You must be pretty busy tonight."

He shrugged. "You know how Miss Chyna can be with her parties." Lexi nodded. She sure did. "Well, you have a good time. Try and keep her under control." He swung the door open and allowed them to enter Chyna's building.

They could hear the loud music before the elevator doors dinged open on the top floor. Chyna had really outdone herself in celebration of the end of Lexi's first semester. All of the lighting had been replaced with black lights. Strobe stage lighting hung from the ceiling reflecting off the blank walls and the mass of bodies grinding to the techno beats blaring from studio speakers. The sunken-in living room had been emptied of furniture and converted into a dance floor. Lexi couldn't differentiate one person from another in the room.

Jack reached out and took Lexi's hand in his own. His touch momentarily dispelled her earlier apprehensions. She led them through the crowded apartment amazed at how few of the people she actually recognized. A path cleared for them and they moved forward into the swinging double doors that led to the kitchen where a full bar was in service for the guests.

When they walked in, they found Chyna seated at the kitchen table, her head tilted backwards, an upside down margarita being poured into her mouth. She gulped down the tequila and stood. The crowd surrounding her cheered and she pumped her fist in the air in victory. Another girl took her place and Chyna bounded over to the group.

"Thank goodness you are here!" she cried wrapping her arms around Lexi. "My Alexa is that much closer to being a lawyer. Which is fabulous, because you never know when I'll need one," she said wiggling her eyebrows suggestively and bumping hips with Lexi.

"Lord I hope you never need one," Lexi mumbled.

Chyna giggled hysterically, already beyond wasted for the evening. Lexi smiled letting Chyna's infectious personality wash over her. Lexi settled into a corner of the kitchen with the rest of her entourage taking shots of varying colors. Rachelle, who never drank, even participated for the special occasion. After a few rounds, Claire and Elizabeth ran off to the living room claiming that they needed to get their groove on. Chyna hadn't been able to suppress her laughter.

"Are you sure they are in law school with you?" she asked turning back to face Lexi.

Lexi giggled. "Yeah, my sentiments exactly," she yelled over the music.

"They are a bit much," Jack agreed lounging back in his chair. He threw an arm over the back of Lexi's seat and propped his leg up on his knee.

"They are absu…fucking…lutely ridiculous," Rachelle slurred resting her head on the table.

"Are you alright, Ray?" Lexi asked placing her hand on the girl's shoulder in concern.

"I don't understand them. I don't know how they got in, and I don't know how they survived!" she cried leaping up unexpectedly.

Lexi wasn't sure how Rachelle had survived with how high strung she was and the amount of Adderall that passed through her system. "Who cares, Ray? We made it! That's what matters."

"I'm going to go celebrate," Rachelle announced, "with him." She pointed towards a guy standing against the wall waiting for his beer. And with that she sauntered off leaving Lexi, Jack, and Chyna alone.

"That was interesting," Chyna said, "but I need more booze. You love birds have fun." She fluttered her fingers at them as she disappeared behind the kitchen doors.

"Just you and me," Lexi said turning towards Jack and licking her lips seductively.

"Finally," he murmured capturing his lips with hers.

She groaned deep in her throat and shifted from her seat to his lap letting her legs face towards the wall. He wrapped his arms around her waist pulling her tight to his chest. He deepened the kiss letting his tongue brush across her lips and into her mouth. She sighed with pleasure and met his tongue. Her hands pushed up into his thick dark hair and gripped the strands causing a moan to escape his mouth. She felt his wandering hands sneak under her dress, trail across her inner thighs, and tease the flimsy lace material.

Lexi jerked back from his mouth in surprise. She couldn't believe he wanted to do this here, with all these people around. Not that anyone would really notice. There were dozens of people filling the rooms and the lights were all but extinguished. His demanding fingers pushed the thong aside and began to gently rub from her clit down to her hot, wet opening. A smirk played across his features as he watched her surprise shift to desire.

"Oh, Jack," she whispered not even sure if he could hear her over the music.

Her eyes fluttered closed, but he leaned forward and whispered in her ear, "Don't close your eyes. I want to see everything."

Her eyes shot open at his command. His breath was hot on her neck as he moved his mouth to the soft spot under her ear. He trailed kisses down her neck as his hands continued to stroke her until she was trembling. Then, when he didn't think she could hold back any longer, he inserted his finger gently inside her. She gasped clutching on to him as waves of pleasure rushed over her.

She slumped forward resting her head on his shoulder. He pulled back from her and reached for a napkin to clean himself up.

"Let's get some privacy," he said gesturing for them to exit the kitchen. As they stood, Jack paused and fished around in his pockets. "Hello?" Jack answered the phone pressing it firmly to his ear to try and drone out the background noise. "Yes sir, this is Jack Howard." After a pause, Jack spoke up again. "I am still interested. I am definitely interested," he said enthusiasm creeping into his voice.

Lexi looked up at him, her eyebrows rising in curiosity. She mouthed, "What?" to him.

He held his hand up a huge smile on his face. "Sure. Absolutely." The smile faltered. Lexi really wished that she could hear what was going on. First, he was ecstatic. Now he looked a bit hesitant, and she didn't even know who was calling. "Tonight? Yeah, no, that won't be a problem. Yes, sir. I'll be right there."

Jack hung up the phone. His face was apprehensive as his blue eyes turned to Lexi. "What's going on?" she asked smiling brightly.

"I got an interview!" he said leaning down and kissing her on the mouth.

"That's awesome," she cried.

"But I have to go tonight…now," he muttered looking away from her.

"What? Why? Isn't it kind of late for an interview?" she asked realizing why he had looked anxious.

"Last minute kind of thing."

"Oh, well, go! Get out of here! Good luck!" she cried throwing her arms around his neck.

"You aren't mad?" he asked his brows coming together.

"Of course not. I want you to do well."

He looked a little suspicious of how well she was taking the news, but didn't want to question her again. "I'll make this up to you. We'll pick up where I left off. I promise."

"No need," she said waving him off.

"Oh, there's need," he murmured raising his eyebrows. "I'll call you when I know something."

Jack leaned down and kissed her deeply once more before rushing out of the room. She exited the kitchen in search of Chyna. Without Jack, she was missing her source of sunshine, her ability to forget what had happened earlier that evening. Her heart was aching from the memories and she needed someone to fill that void.

"I just saw your hubby leave the building," Claire slurred coming up out of nowhere and grabbing onto her arm. "He was escorting some blonde outside." She wiggled her eyebrows up and down suggestively. "She was fucking drunk."

"I think you're fucking drunk," Lexi told her snatching her arm away from the girl. "And I know he left, because he has a job interview. They just called him."

"Whatever you wanna believe," Claire said falling backwards into a tall guy who jostled her back in the other direction. She stumbled a few feet before crashing into another unsuspecting partier sending a ripple effect through the rest of the dancers.

Lexi turned from the angry drunken mob to restart her search for Chyna. She didn't particularly care what happened to Claire. She had too much alcohol in her system and normally got on her nerves without the extra effect. She was literally grating on her just by being in her presence right now.

She spun in place scanning Chyna's penthouse suite. It was going to take forever to locate her friend who literally could be anywhere. More people continued to stream in through the front door while others were devastating the premises. Lexi searched the apartment as fast as she could unable to locate her lost friend. Finally, as she was about to step into Chyna's bedroom, the door popped open and a fuming beefy man stalked out of the room. His nose had blood running freely from it and he seemed to favor his right side. Lexi heard him mutter a string of curses as he exited.

She staggered backwards out of the man's way. He didn't even seem to realize anyone was in front of him. A peel of laughter broke free from the bedroom, and Lexi peeked her head around the corner into the room hoping to find out what was going on. Chyna readjusted her bra strap which seemed to have been pushed out of place.

"You okay, C?" Lexi asked concerned that perhaps the laughter hadn't been pleasant.

"Yeah, had to get rid of some asshole," she commented yanking her skirt back to its appropriate length.

"Did you do that to that guy?" Lexi asked unable to keep the humor out of her voice. Chyna nodded a smug smile across her face. "He looked pretty messed up."

"I've been taking self-defense classes for as long as I can remember. He got too friendly too fast and I didn't want it. So I jabbed my palm into his nose. Then rammed my elbows into his kidneys until he squealed like girl and ran out of here," Chyna said grabbing her hair and pulling all to the right side of her body.

Lexi doubled over with laughter. "That's impressive. You'll have to teach me a thing or two."

Lexi leaned back against Chyna's bed. Chyna eyed her for the first time. "So, where is your man? Aren't you supposed to be sexing it up by now?"

Lexi cringed. "He got called away for a job interview."

"Uh huh…" Chyna said coughing into her hand. "A job interview. At this time of night."

"Don't tell me you don't believe him either," Lexi cried throwing her hands up into the air.

Chyna threw her own hands up in defense. "No, I believe you if you say so, but it does seem just a little suspicious."

"Well, you weren't there so you didn't hear the conversation," she said trying to dispel the feeling of foreboding coming over her. Jack wouldn't do that. They had been about to have sex. There would be no need for him to run off for anything else unless it was important. That is what he had said the very first night she had seen him back in town. He wouldn't leave her side for anything else.

It's not like he had been acting sketchy anytime recently. It's not like he had a reason to do anything when he had her. They had been almost too happy. She had kept him too…satisfied for him to want anything else. She couldn't even think about that possibility. He said he would never lie to her again and she had to believe that was the truth. She couldn't let old fears win out.

"No, you're right," Chyna said not convinced. "Let's just forget about it. You've had a long couple of weeks and we're here to party."

Lexi took a deep breath and let it out slowly. "You're right. You're always right. Let's party!"

And so they spent the remainder of the night doing just that. Neither thought about their worries, complications, or futures, they simply enjoyed the company of a crowded room of strangers. Lexi tried to keep the drinking to a minimum, but she danced until her heart's contentment. Her roommates were slumped all around the room making out with random guys. Lexi would have never believed it if she hadn't seen it with her own eyes. Without her own guy to be affectionate with, she decided to call it an early night.

She realized at that point that she hadn't even checked her phone since Jack had left. He could have called and she might have missed it. Anxious to find out what had happened, she quickly kissed Chyna on the cheek and told her good-bye.

Once she got in the cab, she pulled out her phone to check for any messages. Her heart fluttered when she saw that she had a missed call from Jack and a voicemail waited for her.

After the annoying woman informed her of her options about the voicemail, Jack's clear voice rang in her ears. "Hey Lex, interview's over. It was just bs…just fucking bullshit. I…I don't really want to talk about it. I'm just gonna go home and crash. I'll talk to you in the morning. Have fun."

The line went dead in her hands and she snapped the phone shut. She slid the phone back into her purse feeling dejected. Something had gone wrong at the interview, but he didn't want to talk to her about it. She knew that it was a completely rational reaction for him to not want to discuss his feelings. Guys were like that all the time. She just thought that they were beyond that point. They had known each other for a long time. But she didn't want to think about any other option for him not wanting to talk tonight. Chyna and Claire had planted a seed in her mind, but she couldn't believe them.

The only thing that she could think about right now was that after all that work she had put in for the school year, she was the only one left all alone for the night.

Somehow she wasn't sure how this night could get any worse.

21

PRESENT

The stadium lights that were illuminated for the occasion stretched out across home plate, through the gritty dirt to the pitcher's mound, splayed out through the evenly cut emerald green grass, and further down the endless rows of bleachers. City traffic could be heard as hundreds of cars traveled across the series of roads and highways that mapped the terrain. Twinkling stars were faintly visible overhead despite the perpetual lighting that whitened the black night.

Lexi's heart stuttered as she attempted to compose her features. She folded her arms one over another and leaned onto the cool, black railing. Ramsey rested against the railing keeping his body angled towards her. His green eyes never left her face to survey the beautiful manmade structure below them.

"What's going on?" his deep, husky voice asking several things with his one question.

"I..." Lexi sighed trailing off. "I don't know."

Ramsey smiled, nodding along. "You're not sick."

It was more of a statement than a question, but she nodded anyway. No, she wasn't sick. She was coming to a crossroads in her life, and she didn't know which road to take. She wanted to be with Jack. After all the shit she had put up with, he was still what she wanted. But could she handle this in-between time? Could she handle him being with someone else while she waited like an idiot all over again?

"I didn't do anything," he stated attempting to get all of the possibilities out of the way as to her illness.

"You?" she asked a little taken aback. "No, you haven't done anything." Of course she had thought about Ramsey, but there was too much other stuff going on in her head that she hadn't allowed him much room. He was aggravating to no avail. Even now he was much too close for her level of personal boundaries. She could feel the warmth of his hand as it nearly grazed her elbow resting on the railing. His body tilted forward resting a mere six inches from her face. Such closeness should be reserved for intimacy, but she was coming to realize this was just Ramsey...or maybe he did want that intimacy. She cleared her thoughts. That was the last place she needed to let her mind wander. Even though, it wasn't a bad alternative while she waited for Jack.

"Then it can only be one thing," he told her. She turned to meet his determined gaze waiting for his guess. "Jack and Bekah."

Lexi's heart, which had stilled as she let the light breeze calm her mind, kicked into overdrive at Ramsey's statement. Sure she knew that Ramsey had an idea about her and Jack from the conversation at Jack's apartment. As far as she knew though, he had no idea about her actual involvement with Jack. He had no idea of Jack's hold on her. He certainly had no idea that she had listened in on his threatening conversation with Jack.

But she knew she shouldn't assume anything. Who knew if Bekah had told him or if Jack had spilled the beans about their past to him while she had been at home. She didn't want to think about that either. The last thing she wanted to do was have anyone else know about her relationship with Jack, and Ramsey was getting dangerously close.

"What about Jack and Bekah?" she croaked running her fingers through the loose strands that had fallen out of her bun and threading it behind her ears.

"I'm not sure, but it's something," he admitted leaning in even closer to her.

Lexi breathed out a sigh of relief. He didn't know. That was comforting. Him invading her personal space further was not. "You're um...," she gestured between them, "in my space again. We've talked about this."

He nodded not backing up an inch. "Tell me what's going on," he gently asked bringing his hand up and stroking her face. His hand trailed down from her temple and tucked a loose strand of hair behind her ear.

"I'm pretty sure the only thing going on has something to do with you and me," she muttered huskily feeling her body turn towards him. His hand wrapped around her tiny waist bridging the distance between their bodies.

"Maybe you're right," he whispered towards her. His lips were so close to her, when she licked her own lips, she brushed up against his as well. A groan escaped him with the light, teasing contact, and he hesitantly brought his lips down upon hers. The first touch was smooth and gentle as if he was testing the water. His lips were amazingly soft and she could taste the sweetness of peppermint on his breath.

Warning alarms went off in her mind. All she wanted to do was ignore what her mind was telling her and get lost in the here and now. Forget everything that was keeping her stressed out and relish the beautiful moment of a man wanting her.

Her hands moved from their place on the railing and pushed against his hard, muscled chest. As much as she wanted to, she couldn't let this continue. It would end up hurting everyone.

"I don't know if…" she trailed off again. He didn't let her finish her statement before pressing his body more firmly against her. Her mouth popped open in surprise leaving him with the advantage. He leaned his head down and kissed her bottom lip, gently sucking it between his teeth. Her eyes fluttered closed. Ramsey's hand reached up to twine around her hair, tugging softly on the strands, and tilting her head back. He pressed his lips firmly against her own. It only took a second for Lexi to react and relax into him.

A loud coughing sound came from behind them. Ramsey and Lexi hastily broke apart, straightening themselves out as they faced the intruder.

"I figured I'd find you out here," Chyna said cocking her weight to her right hip. She threw both hands up to her hips, leaning the left shoulder forwards, and tilting her head up defiantly.

Lexi ran her fingers through her mussed hair and smiled hesitantly at her best friend. "Well, you found me."

"Oh no, I wasn't looking for you," she announced letting her eyes shift to the man standing next to her.

"How can I be of assistance?" Ramsey asked politely stepping away from the railing.

"Apparently, there is a birthday going on inside," Chyna commented dryly. "You have something to do with that?"

Ramsey looked a bit sheepish as he took on Chyna's confrontation. "Indeed I do."

"Then perhaps you should run inside and check on what's going on," she suggested. "There's some kind of catastrophe happening with the cake. Everyone's looking for you."

Ramsey apologized to Lexi, and quickly excused himself. He flashed Chyna a smile as he walked by, but she didn't return the gesture.

Chyna stalked right up to Lexi standing exactly where Ramsey had been only seconds earlier. "What are you thinking?" she cried leaning back against the railing and pressing her hand to her forehead.

"Not now, please," Lexi murmured feeling even more confused than earlier.

"I think we should get out of here," Chyna told her. "You're a mess. I'm not even sure *you* know what you are doing anymore."

"We can't leave," Lexi said shaking her head. "I can't leave yet."

"I don't know why we should stay. Now, I wasn't going to bring this up, but I can't stay silent, chica. You're my best friend and I know you're hurting. Jack is here with his girlfriend and despite what just happened, I know how you feel about him, and it has to hurt like hell. Why would you want to go through that? Then…Ramsey?"

"Well, I don't know what I was doing with Ramsey, but I do know that I need to stay and see this through. Please…for me, C," she begged her eyes swelling in size.

Chyna shook her head contemplating the decision before her. As Lexi's best friend, she felt obligated to get her out of this situation. Lexi had been there for her more than anyone else in her entire life. How could she let her friend walk into the fire pit? She saw no alternative though. Lexi was determined. "Fine, but can you please be careful?" she pleaded.

After the girls agreed, they trudged back into the club where a loud chorus of Happy Birthday was being sung by the guests. Lexi and Chyna joined in with the celebratory tune weaving their way through the crowd to the birthday boy. Before they broke through, Lexi glanced up at the screen where the slideshow had been circulating pictures of Jack's past. Her heart froze on the final image.

A high resolution photo taken within Ramsey's house this past weekend was displayed before her eyes. Jack stood next to Bekah with his arm around her waist. Bekah's head was tilted sideways comfortably resting against Jack's shoulder. Ramsey had an arm slung over both Bekah and Lexi's shoulders. Lexi was leaning back against Ramsey's chest. The signs that she was too drunk to stand straight were already evident. All eyes were bright and smiling. Their faces were flushed from dancing.

But what caught her eye was the look on Jack's face. He looked happy, buoyant even, but there was something different about his expression than the rest of the group. His eyes were diverted, cutting across his girlfriend and her brother straight to Lexi. And the look he was pressing towards her was very familiar. His eyes were crystal clear blue with desire. He only had eyes for her, and he wanted her. Even though his girlfriend was in his arms, he still couldn't seem to take his eyes off of Lexi.

She glanced around the room transfixed by the image before her. How could no one else see what she saw in the picture? How could anyone think of including this very recent picture with him looking at her in such a fashion? But no one else seemed to be looking at the picture. At least no one was analyzing it quite like she was. She couldn't believe it. Was everyone momentarily blind?

"What are you doing?" Chyna hissed latching onto her hand and pulling her through the crowd. Lexi stumbled the few feet forward right into Ramsey. He reached out and slung his arm across her shoulder bringing her closer to the action. She glanced from him to Bekah to Jack. At the center of the table was a large sheet cake with blue frosting announcing Jack's birthday. He had both hands on the table poised to blow out the flickering candles. Everyone was yelling for Jack to make a wish in the background, but all Lexi saw was the way the group was entwined. They were practically set up for the picture again, but this time when Jack's head swiveled to the side, he locked eyes with Bekah before releasing his breath.

The crowd cheered as the lights went out one by one relinquishing the room into darkness. Lexi felt as if she were about to combust. Way too many emotions kept clouding her mind. The rollercoaster seemed to be dragging her around each loop and bend without care. How could Jack be so secure in Lexi only a few nights earlier, but at the same time be here, like this, with Bekah. She knew what he was capable of…of course she knew. She was trying to be smarter about the whole situation by staying away from him, but she couldn't stay away to her own detriment. She needed to talk to him. She needed to find out if he had been lying to her when he had said all those things about wanting to be together. She knew Jack wasn't a liar, at least not to her, but something about the whole situation felt wrong. Well, everything about the situation felt wrong, and that's what really worried her.

The lights flickered back on and suddenly the entire atmosphere of the party began to change. Loud music filtered through the club speakers, the bar instantly became crowded with eager patrons ordering hard liquor drinks, and dancing took up the majority of the room. More people trickled in as the party began to roll into full swing. All of them seemed to know either Jack or Ramsey in some capacity, not that Lexi could keep up with any of their names. Her mind was filled with other more pertinent conflicts.

She let Ramsey lead her through a few dances despite her better judgment. He was such a good dancer, and she couldn't help but stay on the floor with him longer than she had originally anticipated. Her plan had been to dance a number or two with Ramsey, cut in with Jack, and then somehow get him alone so she could speak with him about what was going on. So far that plan was falling to pieces.

Ramsey was such an excellent diversion that she had completely lost track of where Jack had gone. Lexi's gaze had followed him as he had the bartender pour two drinks filled with dark liquid. Then she watched as he finished the contents of one and brought the other to Bekah who was chatting with her bitchy friends. She giggled as he nuzzled into her neck and whispered something into her ear. When she turned to face him, he led her out to the floor where they danced together like the perfect couple everyone thought they were. The sight of them rubbing up against each other in such a manner made Lexi gag and turn her focus away for a split second, and then they were gone.

She cursed under her breath for losing them. It was getting late and she really needed to speak with him before she left. She would only be in the state for two more days, and if she didn't speak with him now, she had no idea what would happen. Would all this time she had spent here and everything she had gone through be for nothing? Or would she finally get the happy ending she deserved?

She couldn't stand around and wait to find out any longer. She needed to take action.

Lexi leaned forward on her tiptoes facing Ramsey. His eyes traveled down to her lips staring expectantly as they moved closer to him. She whispered, "Will you get me a drink? I have to go to the powder room."

"Sure, what would you like?" he asked wrapping an arm around her thin waist to hold her tight against him.

"Surprise me, but no Jack Daniels," she prompted immediately.

"Or a Sex on the Beach," he responded.

Lexi stepped back automatically her mouth popping open in surprise. She couldn't remember ever telling him that she didn't like those, yet that was always her next response. "Did I mention that to you?" she couldn't help asking.

He smirked, his green eyes sparkling. "Intuition, darling." He reached down and cupped her cheek sending chills down her heated body. His head dipped and he lightly brushed his lips across hers before disappearing to get her a drink.

Her head was spinning. Where had that come from? And why did it suddenly feel familiar?

She stared after his retreating back for a second before someone collided with her sending her stumbling back a few feet. The guy attempted to apologize, but Lexi brushed him off. She rushed away from the man and began searching for the birthday boy. It really shouldn't be that hard to find him since the entire party was thrown in his name. Lexi's only concern was that she was going to find him in a precarious position. That was the last thing she needed to happen. She couldn't imagine what that would do to her in that event. She wasn't sure how much more she could take from Jack, and didn't want him to tip her over the edge.

The space wasn't that large and she quickly realized he wasn't anywhere noticeable. About to give up, she relieved herself, since that had been her excuse in the first place. As she was coming out of the women's restroom, Jack exited from the men's. A group of men called happy birthday to him as he began to walk back towards the party unaware that Lexi was directly behind him. She pushed past the other men, her high heels clicking against the tile as she approached him. Lexi reached out and grabbed his hand before he entered the club again.

"What the…" he said turning around sharply.

"Jack," she cried stopping him in his tracks. His expression shifted quickly from surprise to delight to anger and then settled at indifferent. It all happened so fast that, had she not known him as well as she did, she certainly would have missed what was going on in his head.

"Lexi."

"Can we talk…privately?"

"Now isn't really a good time," he said pulling her closer to him so they could speak without anyone else hearing. She hovered inches away from him.

"I think now is the only time," she muttered staring up into blue eyes.

"Why would you say that?" he asked his brows furrowing together.

"Jack, I'm just…confused. Please," she begged.

He glanced around the hallway checking to see who might notice them leaving together. He was an expert at becoming invisible, sneaking around, and not getting caught. These were all things she had been a source of in his past and now, she reluctantly realized, she was forcing him into it all over again. "Fine. Follow me."

Lexi followed him around the corner and through a side door that led to a long concrete walkway. She had never been here in the past, but she assumed this must be the staff exit or even an exclusive exit VIP members used while within the private 755 Club. Jack closed the door behind them and led her away from the door.

"Lexi. It's my birthday. This couldn't have waited until tomorrow?" he asked crossing his arms over his chest and standing before her. His stance made him appear distant and unapproachable…not the way she typically viewed Jack.

"No. I don't think that's such a good idea," she told him hesitantly.

"Well, I do. I don't have time for this right now." He spoke the words, but he didn't move.

"Well, make time. I need to ask you some questions," she told him firmly.

"Now?" he whined. "It's my birthday."

"It's past midnight," she told him checking her watch to verify. Actually, when she looked down, she noticed that it was twenty minutes until midnight, but she didn't mention that fact.

He rolled his eyes. "Fine. Ask away."

"Is this still what you want?" she asked her voice trembling.

"Lex, baby," he murmured hugging her against him, "didn't I tell you that you are what I want?"

She sighed against his body. She didn't like that he was evading her question with another question. Why couldn't he answer straight up? "That's what you said three days ago, but, Jack, I'm leaving in two days. What are we going to do after that?"

"We'll work it out. I just need time. You have to understand. Bekah and I," he sighed trailing off.

"I do understand that you have been together for some time…without my distraction. But how can I be sure that I'm not just that…a distraction?" she asked, her eyes pleading with him. She had never felt so rigid against his body. He wasn't calming her as he usually did. Even his baby blue eyes, which normally held so much warmth and desire when cast upon her, were almost icy. She didn't know what was going on.

"You have to trust me. I've never lied to you before," he muttered glancing towards the door.

"Jack, what's wrong with you?" she whispered staring up into his blank face.

When he next looked back at her, the Jack she knew and loved had returned. His eyes looked hungry. It was a look she knew well. His body had relaxed into her even pressing her closer.

She didn't know where his emotions would go next. One minute he was icy cold and the next he was on fire. She couldn't keep up.

"Nothing is *wrong* with me," he spat the words out.

"I mean the way you were looking at me…" She shuddered.

"Lexi, I don't have time for this," he said eyeing the door again. "I really need to get back inside." He started to walk away from her. She knew she had kept him out here too long, but he hadn't answered any questions. He hadn't done anything but shift moods too frequently for her to count.

"I thought things were going to be different," she muttered stopping him with his hand on the door. She needed to know what was going on, and if the only way to do that was to elicit a reaction from him, then so be it.

He turned and faced her. "Things *are* different."

"It doesn't feel like it. It feels like every other time." Hurt crossed his features at her accusation.

"Get off my case, Lex" he said turning back towards the door.

"You can't even look at me," she cried knowing she was being completely unreasonable. She felt as if she were about to burst. She couldn't think of another way to get through to him. All she needed was some sort of answer one way or the other. A part of her knew that she wasn't being fair. He deserved time to figure out what to do about Bekah. Another part of her thought she had given him enough time over the past six years to figure out if he wanted another girl or not and that she needed an answer.

He turned around and walked slowly back to her, standing only inches away, but not touching. "There. I'm looking at you," he said his blue eyes staring purposely into her brown ones.

"You'll never change," she snarled. She couldn't believe the words had come out of her mouth. She had been thinking them all along, but the words struck too close to home for their relationship.

"Maybe I already have," he growled back walking forward and pushing her forcefully against the cement wall. His hand reached down, hitched her left leg up around his waist, and he pushed himself against her. She could feel his erection jumping to life as the adrenaline pumped through their bodies. Her black silk thong brushed against the crotch of his charcoal suit pants causing both of them to shudder with desire.

His blue eyes thawed upon catching her gaze. He leaned forward, pressed his free hand against her bare neck pulling her head away from the concrete barrier, bringing her face less than an inch from his own.

"Uh, Jack," she whispered unable to break his steady gaze. He leaned forward his breath hot on her face. For a split second, she could see herself giving into him right then and there. She could break down all those walls of sexual tension and give him back the control he so obviously desired. It would be so easy to let go. He was what she wanted after all. Why did it have to be wrong to get what she wanted?

"Shh," he said covering her mouth with his own. The kiss was soft, yet urgent. She sighed against his lips letting them part and his tongue to enter her mouth. The kiss turned feverish, and she found that she had pushed her fingers up through his thick hair pulling him closer to her. Her desire was growing every second she stood with him close to her. She couldn't even think properly with the way he had her positioned. His hand pushed the red material of her dress away from her thigh, cupped her bare ass, and hoisted her other leg up around his waist. He pushed against her then slowly, almost teasingly, rubbing himself against her.

Lexi groaned not sure how they had ended up in this position, but she didn't care. She had resisted him so long, and it was painful to stay away from him. Even when her mind allowed her the moments where she wasn't thinking of him, he was always there in the back of her mind. And here, in the present, she couldn't imagine anywhere else she wanted to be.

He bit her lip a little harder than intended, and she knew she would have a bruise the next day. Right now she just enjoyed the pain mixing with the pleasure of his hands running across her breasts and fluttering across her erect nipples. Lexi reached between them unfastening his belt, popping the button open and shaking the zipper to the bottom. Her hand trailed the length of him through his cotton boxer briefs. He shoved himself against her harder than before when she touched him.

She reacted instantly, reaching into his pants and grabbing a hold of the shaft. It lengthened in her hand and he groaned deep in his throat. His hand fumbled for her underwear, ripping the gentle material in his haste to slide them to the side, and pushed his thumb against her clit. He moved his mouth from her lips to her ear and throat roughly biting, sucking, and nibbling as she squirmed against his chest.

Convulsions were overtaking their bodies, their desire heightening as each second of public fornication dragged on.

Jack abruptly stopped his kneading of her, grabbed his dick in his now wet hand, and forcefully pushed inside of her. Lexi's head snapped back against the cement wall not even feeling the pain as his erection filled deep inside of her. She clenched her muscles around him unable to believe how incredible he felt. He let his head fall between her breasts breathing a few deep breathes of desire. Then he lifted his head up and began thrusting inside of her. She gasped at his forceful demeanor. He refused to take it slow as he vigorously pounded into her body. He filled her over and over again. His movements were unrelenting, and she almost cried out. She wasn't sure if it was with pleasure or pain, but he covered her mouth with his hand. Lexi felt the orgasm take over her body. She tightened around him, her body shaking with pleasure, but he never let up. Even as the waves of passion took over her body, he continued inside of her holding out on his orgasm so she could have another.

When she finished, he shifted his hands to a position where he could haul her up and slam her back down onto him. She moaned into his ear as she felt all her weight pushed against his dick as he invaded her deepest core. Her back was chafing against the wall, but she couldn't care less. She wasn't the one who had spent several hundred dollars on the dress. Lexi couldn't believe he was holding out so long, she was almost ready to go again, and his determined, beautiful face looked as if he could go all night.

Just when she thought she might explode again, he abruptly stopped with just the head hovering over her opening. She felt her body react with yearning, and she got even wetter. He smirked at her and reclaimed her lips with his own. She volleyed with his tongue whimpering as he paused over her. "Jack," she groaned, wiggling her body hoping and praying that he would move.

He pushed in a fraction of an inch before pulling back out. She whimpered again breaking contact with his lips and glaring at him. His smirk turned into a full on smile as he leaned into her, pushed the head in, and stopped. "Did you want something?" he asked the words coming out breathy and desirous. It was obvious that he wanted it too.

She nodded.

"I can't hear you," he responded pulling back out of her and moving around in a circle over the sensitive lips.

She moaned deeper trying to push her body against him, but he had her hips firmly between his hands and wasn't letting her have any control. "I said I can't hear you."

"Jack," she moaned as he dipped in and out of her again. She didn't want to beg, but she needed him to finish. She was on the brink of a sky-rocketing explosion. He waited, teasing her endlessly until she spoke again. "Get inside of me…now," she commanded.

Her words worked like magic, and he couldn't hold out any longer. He forced himself back into her and continued his insistent pulsing. She felt like she was going to burst at any second. Her lower half was throbbing with pleasure, and her chest was heaving as her heart raced along ahead of the rest of her body. She closed her eyes and arched her back against him allowing the deepest angle he could reach.

"Cover my mouth," she murmured feeling a scream bubbling up in her chest.

He complied easily. As his hand came up to cover her mouth, they both exploded. He shoved her body down onto him one last time. His eyes rolled back into his head as they came together. By the time she was spent, she found that she was gasping for air and her body trembling.

After a minute of recovery, Jack pulled himself out of her and quickly readjusted his pants. Lexi slumped against the wall. Her shaky hands yanked her dress back down to its rightful length. Her underwear were ruined beneath the material.

"Jack that was…amazing," she whispered into the night air. She brushed her sweaty curls off her face. She watched as he wiped his hand across his forehead taking the thin layer of sweat with it.

"Yeah, it was," he said walking towards the door. "But I have to go."

"That's it?" she asked her voice wavering uncertainly.

"What? That wasn't good enough for you?" he asked his voice echoing a hint of humor into every syllable.

"That's not what I mean."

"This doesn't change anything, Lex," he said turning to face her but staying a good distance away from her as if he couldn't control himself not to take her again.

By the way he said it, it sounded as if it changed everything. She was his again, his for the taking. "I think it changes things. You can't go back to her after that," she squeaked.

"I'm not sure what I'm going to do."

Lexi gasped. "You mean…"

"Look, I don't know what to do yet. I just knew that's what you wanted," he saying eyeing her mussed appearance.

"That's not what I wanted."

"If it wasn't, you wouldn't have let me do it," he told her simply.

"I wanted answers."

"And I don't have any."

"So, what was this?" she asked tears welling in her eyes. How had this gone south so fast?

"This was fucking, Lexi. You should know that. You're really good at it."

His words were cold and calculated as if he were trying to hurt her. It was working. "Fuck you, Jack."

"Whenever you want."

"So, this is over?" she croaked.

He seemed utterly surprised by this conclusion. "No, baby," he said striding towards her and taking her face between his hands. She didn't even have the energy to push him away. "I just need more time. This was…great, but it doesn't change the things I still have to deal with. Now, I really have to go." And with that he strode out of the walkway and back to his birthday party.

Happy birthday to him.

Lexi stayed outside for a minute contemplating how she had allowed things to get so out of control. She had promised herself she wouldn't let this happen, but when push comes to shove, literally, she couldn't say no to him. If she were to do it all over again, she would make the same goddamn mistake. That was the part that miffed her the most. She knew that she should look at it as a mistake, but she couldn't. He had said that it didn't change anything, but she knew deep down that it changed everything. If he could have her like this, would he want her any other way?

She bit her lip in her consternation and cursed loudly forgetting that Jack had bit down hard on the sensitive tissue. The one thing she did know is that she needed to get away from this place. She didn't care where she went as long as it was far away from here.

Lexi darted back into the bathroom, shimmying out of her sodden, destroyed underwear and chucking them into the trashcan. She pulled her knot of curls out of the messy bun that looked like a disaster after having been scrapped against a cement wall. She applied a thin layer of clear lip gloss hoping that would cover the bruise that was forming, but she doubted it. She assessed her neck noticing a few red marks beginning to form where Jack had been too violent, but she didn't have any concealer and hoped no one would notice as she snuck out.

There was no way she could atone for her dress though. The back looked like, well…like it had been dragged across cement. Some strings were hanging free from the material. The silky fabric was dotted with scuffs that resembled a bathing suit bottom after sitting on the edge of a pool for too long. Not to mention the scratches that covered her upper back where her hair had been held high. She would never be able to explain those. Luckily, her back hadn't bled, but some of the scrapes were so red she was certain had he gone on any longer, they would have. She hoped her long hair would hide as much as possible.

After deciding nothing more could be done, she snuck back out of the bathroom and made a beeline for the exit. When she got there, she ducked through the double doors and stopped as she almost ran smack dab into Ramsey. She didn't even know how long she had been gone.

"Where have you been?" he asked concern evident in his voice. "I've been searching for you everywhere. I had just decided to see if any cabs had taken you home, but no one knew anything. Are you alright?"

His green eyes were wide with worry. She knew she should feel guilty, and maybe a small part of her did. Ramsey was starting to grow on her and he seemed so genuinely concerned. But this was the last thing she needed after what she had done.

"Uh, yeah…" she trailed off not meeting his gaze. "Sorry."

"It's fine. I'm glad you're alright," he said scooping her up into a hug. She bit back a cry as his hands brushed against her red, swollen back.

"I have to get out of here," she muttered abrasively. "Can you call me a cab?"

"Where are you going?" he asked hesitantly trying to meet her eyes.

"Back to the hotel."

"Alright. You have a key right?" he asked. He snapped his fingers at the concierge to begin to make arrangements.

"Oh, shit!" she cried. "Chyna lost the other one and I gave her mine. I have to go find her." She turned to make an embarrassing reappearance into the club.

"She already left," he muttered stopping her from leaving. "I think she is going to his place."

"Fuck!" Lexi could not believe her awful luck. She couldn't stay here any longer, but there was no way she could go back to the hotel. "I guess I can see if they'll make me a new one," she muttered hopefully.

"Come with me," Ramsey said stepping closer to her. She did not want him to be in her personal space right now. He would surely notice her bumps and bruises, and she didn't want him to ask questions.

"I can't," she muttered.

"You can stay in the guest bedroom…if you want," he added for his own benefit.

"Do I have any other choice?" she grumbled wondering why the universe hated her so much.

He shook his head. "Tell them to pull the limo around," he commanded the woman as he escorted Lexi out of the building.

22

DECEMBER ONE AND A HALF YEARS EARLIER

The next morning was the gloomiest of any Lexi had witnessed since moving to New York. Snow had fallen the night before, and in typical city fashion, the streets had been cleared of the white flurries by daybreak. Brown slush took its place on the sidewalks and gutters creating a hazardous environment for any who traversed the city. Dreary, charcoal clouds covered the sky casting a depressing aura across the metropolitan area. A heavy fog mixed with the ever increasing quantities of pollution hanging thick in the morning air.

Under these conditions, most normal people would have avoided leaving their apartment at all costs on a Saturday morning. Lexi was not one of those people. She thought she had switched off the alarm set for finals, but it still managed to go off at eight in the morning. Her sleep had been restless and no matter how hard she tried to go back to sleep, it would not come to her. Instead, she made the mistake of pulling on a t-shirt, black track suit, and running sneakers to take a brisk jog around the park before the city livened up.

The wind viciously whipped her hair around her face, cutting across her delicate skin and stinging her eyes. Tears streamed from her eyes as she sprinted the last leg of her run before exiting Washington Square Park. She doubled over clutching her hands to her ribs as her breath came out in spurts. The wintry air filled her lungs causing her to wheeze in pain at the assault. Her heart was still working overdrive thumping away in her chest from the physical exertion. She attempted to wiggle her toes which felt near frozen in her soggy socks and snow-coated tennis shoes. The movement was painful as life came back into her lower extremities.

She straightened brushing her hair out of her face. The gloves she wore hardly kept the cold from reaching her fingers. Now that she had stopped jogging, the sweat she had built up was settling onto her skin making her entire body shiver. The wind picked up in velocity pushing and pulling her the rest of the way to her apartment building. She stumbled into the high-arched enclosure letting the wind break past her. A low whistle could be heard as it rushed through the streets. Lexi was just happy that she was out of that. She didn't know what she had been thinking going on a run with the weather in such precarious conditions.

Well, that wasn't true. She knew the real reason for her early morning jog. The message from Jack kept replaying in her head, and despite herself, she couldn't shake the feeling that something was wrong. She knew that she should be reasonable. He probably went through another rejection and wallowed in his own pity. It had happened frequently enough, and she knew he shouldn't get worked up about it, but he *had* gotten worked up about it. She could tell from the tone of his voice that he was upset.

All she wanted to do was be there for him.

She wrapped her arms around herself as she strode past the security guard. He recognized her and waved, not even checking for her identification card. She was lost in her thoughts as she took the stairs back to her apartment.

Lexi knew that she wasn't Jack's girlfriend. They weren't officially together or anything. They had made that perfectly clear in the beginning.

Yet, something was nagging in the back of her mind. When he had been threatening Clark, he had claimed they were together. She wasn't naïve enough to believe that they were automatically going to jump into something that they were unaccustomed to. She knew how they worked, and thus far, it had worked out surprisingly well. But it was a step in the right direction. If he could speak about them being a couple, even if it was out of blind jealously, then she saw that as a positive.

Her teeth were chattering as she slid into her dorm room. She clenched and unclenched her fingers hoping to accelerate the blood flow. Sliding her gloves off Lexi brought her hands to her mouth and blew on them as she rubbed them together.

"Where have you been?" Lexi heard someone call anxiously from a bedroom.

Startled from warming herself up, she glanced up and saw Rachelle silhouetted in the doorway. "I went for a run."

Rachelle peeked back through her window as if to confirm that it was, in fact, miserable outside. "In this weather?" she asked condescendingly.

"Uh...yeah. I needed to clear my head."

"Did it work?"

"Not really. I'm kind of frozen," she told her a chill running down her back at the mention of the cold.

"You Southerners," she scoffed, "this isn't cold."

"Feels pretty cold to me," Lexi said wrapping her arms around her body.

"Whatever. Why didn't you take your cell phone with you?" she asked disapprovingly.

Lexi cringed realizing that she had forgotten her cell. She knew when she was out in the city, especially when she was alone, that she should have it with her, but she hated carrying it with her when she was running. She felt weighed down by technology. But Rachelle was looking at her expectantly. "Uh, yeah, sorry. I guess I forgot it."

"Yeah, I know. It has been ringing off the hook all morning...on loud," she grumbled crossing her arms over her chest.

Lexi gulped, taking a sideways look towards her room as if her phone was going to start ringing again at any moment. "Sorry 'bout that."

"You should call Jack back. I finally had to answer and tell him I'd give you the message, but that you weren't home."

"You told him I wasn't home?" she squeaked.

"What was I supposed to do? You weren't in your room. Your phone was still on your desk. Your purse was missing. You had to be somewhere. I told him you were out. What's the big deal?" Rachelle asked.

Lexi groaned. "My purse is missing? Great, just great. What a fantastic morning."

"Just call him back," she said slamming her door angrily.

Lexi sighed and trudged into her room. All she wanted to was shower. She did not want to have to deal with this right now.

She glanced around noticing that her purse was still exactly where she had left it safely tucked under her desk. Rachelle must have missed it when she answered the phone. Lexi breathed out a sigh of relief that nothing had happened to her purse. She unplugged her phone from where she had left it charging the night before and turned it on. Eight missed calls showed up on the phone and she had four text messages, and that was before Rachelle had gotten to her phone to turn it off.

Even though all she wanted to do was take a shower and not think about anything, she reluctantly opened the phone and dialed Jack's number. As she waited, she peeled of her running jacket and hung it on a hook on the back of her door. Her t-shirt came off next followed by the black, long-sleeve, Under Armour shirt. Her track pants hung low on her hips and her black sports bra hugged tight against her chest.

"Lex," Jack breathed into the phone, "where have you been? I've been calling all morning."

"Yeah, Rachelle told me. Sorry about that."

"What were you doing? Who were you with?" he asked accusing her with every word.

"I was out for a run."

"In this weather?"

She wanted to curse. Why was it so hard to believe that she would go out for a run when it was nasty outside? She needed to clear her head. It wasn't the end of the world. That didn't give everyone the right to accuse her of anything. "Yeah."

"Right."

"What? Do you not believe me?" she asked, her earlier anxieties making her jumpy.

"Sure, I believe you. If you say so."

"Why don't you sound like you believe me?" Her voice couldn't hide the hint of annoyance at his tone. He was the one who had dipped out of the party, and then left a sketchy voicemail telling her not to come over to be with him. She should be the one accusing him of not being around.

She took a deep breath and let it out slowly. He had a rough night with the job interview. He was probably just irritated with that. There was no need for her to make it worse for him. "I'm sorry. It was just a rough night."

"I know what you mean," he whispered.

"Sorry, I didn't bring my phone. I'll remember to take it with me next time," she apologized.

"Actually, we need to talk."

Warning signals began blasting off in her brain even worse than this morning. Those words were never a good sign. Nothing good could come from saying that. "About what?" she managed to get out.

She could hear him take a deep breath. "Can I come over?"

"Of course you can come over. You're here all the time," she mumbled knowing it had to be bad, if he had to ask to come over.

"I have to take care of some...stuff here, and then I'll be over so we can talk. Alright?"

She nodded swallowing heavily. Then she realized he couldn't see her and said, "Yeah, that's fine."

"Bye," he said hanging up the phone quickly.

Lexi shut her phone and tossed it back into the mess on her desk. She yanked her hair out of the ponytail on the back of her head and let her mass of curls fall around her face. Brushing them out of her face with her fingers, she could feel some of the tension release from her body.

The events from the past twelve hours were replaying in her head. Where had things gone wrong? They had been perfect at the party. God, they had been about to leave to have sex…make love until they had been interrupted.

The interruption.

What had Claire said about him leaving? That she had seen him exit the premises with some drunken blonde chick on his arm. Lexi could remember the look of disbelief in Claire and Chyna's eyes when she had explained about the interview. They both had the same expression.

She shook her head not wanting to think about that. Her body hurt from running, lack of hydration, and chronic worrying. All she needed was a long hot shower and to chill the fuck out. No use worrying over something that she had no idea about. Everything her imagination was conjuring up was only successfully making her more worried about what had happened last night, and why he now so desperately needed to talk to her.

Taking the time to thoroughly wash away any lingering doubts, Lexi took extra long in the shower. She scrubbed every crevice washing away the sweat and grime from her run twice with her cranberry body wash. She lathered and rinsed her hair until it was silky smooth. When she cut off the water, the bathroom was thick with steam and the mirror completely obscured by fog. Typically, Lexi wasn't the type of girl who primped, but today was not like other days.

After towel drying her hair, she blew it out until every long strand was dry. Then she pulled a straightener down until all the curls were gone and her hair hit her lower back. Black eyeliner rimmed her eyes and a layer of mascara touched her lashes. After adding a hint of rouge to her pale cheeks, she figured she had spent enough time in the bathroom. She was amazed that no one had bothered her already. With only one bathroom between four people, it was usually only a matter of time before someone came banging on the door.

As Lexi walked out of the bathroom, she did hear a knock coming from the door. She wrapped her skimpy white towel tightly around her body and scrambled towards the front door. "Jack," she cried as she opened the door. "I thought you had stuff to do."

He looked at her as if he were looking at her for the first time. The way her silky hair shone as the hallway light hit the strands. The way her side swept bangs fell neatly into her enormous brown eyes, which only looked larger and more beautiful from the make-up she had carefully applied. Her skin contrasted with the bleach white towel giving her a sun-kissed look. A smile broke out across his face as he took in the sight of her partly exposed body.

"It's been over an hour," he commented.

"Oh, has it?" she asked embarrassed even further. She couldn't remember ever taking over an hour in the shower. "Are you going to come in?" she asked stepping aside and hugging her towel tight to her chest. She could feel it slipping out of place.

Jack stepped through the doorway allowing Lexi to close it behind him.

"I'll just go change," Lexi said walking swiftly towards her bedroom. Jack followed behind taking a seat in her desk chair. She turned to face him without moving to get clothes out of her closet. "So, what uh...stuff did you have to do?" she asked leaning back against her desk.

Jack averted his eyes to the floor. "I had to get things taken care of. It's no big deal."

"Oh," she said lamely. Lexi sucked her bottom lip into her mouth biting down lightly. She could tell that it was a big deal or he wouldn't have to be so secretive about it. But she was already afraid of what he might say. There was no need to bring anything else up until he was ready.

Lexi sat back against the desk, scooting over a few coffee mugs and class notes. "I thought you were going to change," he noted once he finally spoke up. His eyes roamed her body.

"I was, but you wanted to talk to me."

"I didn't expect to speak to you naked," he murmured.

"I'm not naked," she told him pointing towards her tiny towel.

"Close enough."

"No, it's really not. You've seen me in less."

Jack cringed away at her words. Not a good sign. "Just...change."

"I'd rather we talk," she told him standing her ground.

"Fine," he muttered standing swiftly from the chair and knocking it back against the wall. Lexi jolted from where she was sitting. "So, let's talk."

Lexi waited. "I don't know what you want to talk about," she whispered her eyes cast to the floor in anticipation.

"I don't really know how to begin this."

"Are you," she choked on the words, "are you breaking up with me?" She felt tears welling in her eyes at the prospect. The way he was talking that was the only conclusion she could come to. He had realized he didn't want her after all and they were not going to be working towards that relationship. It didn't make sense. It didn't make sense at all after what he had said to Clark, but she couldn't see an alternative. She had been through break ups before and he was about hitting it on the nose.

"What?" he asked. "No. Well, I couldn't anyway. We're not in a relationship. I mean we're together, but we're not...you know...*together*."

Lexi really could not tell the difference anymore. They had been doing everything together for over a month, and they had been intimately involved emotionally for nearly four years. How much more could he want?

"So, we're not breaking up then?" she asked feeling pitiful.

"No, well, I dunno," he muttered.

Lexi coughed running her fingers through her stick straight hair, and trying not to cry. "Why don't you know?"

"It all depends on you."

"I don't want us to break up."

Jack smiled a true genuine smile reaching all the way up to his beautiful blue eyes. "Yeah?" he asked his smile beginning to wane. "You might change your mind."

"I don't think so. I've made up my mind."

"Look, Lex, I don't want to lie to you. I told you I never would, and I want to stick by that."

Lexi's heart was beating out of her chest. It was almost painful as the weight of it slammed forcefully back and forth against her ribcage. He had lied to her as she had feared. She didn't know what it could be about. Was it the blonde girl? Did he not go to the interview?

"Then don't lie to me."

"I don't want to," he said stuffing his hands in his pockets. "I have to tell you something."

"What do you have to tell me?" she asked impatiently. "Is this about the girl Claire saw you leaving with last night?"

"Girl?" he asked confused. "No, it has nothing to do with that. She was just drunk and I was helping her out of the party and into a cab."

"Is this about the interview?" she couldn't help asking.

"No...well, yeah, sort of, but please Lexi let me speak," he finally commanded her. Lexi waited expectedly. "I...I slept with someone else last night."

It was Lexi's turn to shoot up from her seat. "What?" she screeched nearly dropping her towel. She grappled for the loose material pulling it up to fully cover her body.

"I...yeah. I didn't get the job. I wanted to go home and crash, but then there was a huge party at my place. I couldn't get any rest so I got hammered instead. One thing led to another and..."

"So you just *slept* with someone?" she asked in horror.

"Yeah. I'm sorry. I just fucked up. It didn't mean anything."

"Is that supposed to make me feel better? Oh, I'm sorry, Lexi. It was just a meaningless fuck! How do you think that could help me? What the fuck were you thinking?" she questioned him pulling out a t-shirt and gym shorts from her dresser and hastily yanking them on. She felt exposed in her towel and realized now why he had wanted her to change.

"I wasn't thinking. I was drunk, and it just sort of happened," he yelled back.

"You're absolutely ridiculous!"

"Stop getting so riled up. I came here to tell you because I couldn't keep it from you. Isn't that worth something?"

Lexi's eyes narrowed as they zeroed in on him. "A very small something."

"Oh come on."

"Did you somehow think this would be okay? I don't understand your motives at all."

"Lex, I didn't have a motive. It just happened. You of all people should know what that feels like."

"No, I *don't* know what that feels like! I never slept with someone without forethought."

"You're such a liar. When we first slept together you had no intention of sleeping with me and then we did."

"Whatever. That was us though, Jack. We're...different." She so desperately wanted to make him understand.

"You're such a hypocrite," he cried throwing his hands up in the air. "What do you think we were doing the whole time we were with other people? We were cheating on them. We were the bad guys."

"I know that," she yelled back forcefully.

"Then why the fuck are you getting so pissed off about what happened? I fucked up alright. We've done that before," he said pushing away his feeling towards his actions.

"Don't even go there with me, Jack. You know that's not true. We both know what we are. We cheated on other people, and that was what defined us. That was what defined our connection for quite some time."

"Then why are you freaking out?" he asked exasperated.

"I thought that by finally being together this would stop," she mumbled.

"You thought we would change being the people that we are, because we're together now? Or not even really together actually."

Lexi cringed at his words. Those had been her words. She had been just as afraid of any sort of commitment as him. "You told Clark we were together," she whispered.

He looked away from her. "Well, we're not together. We never have been. So please, Lex, stop freaking out. I told you what happened because of what we are."

A small part of her wished that he had lied to her. That would have made things easier, but she knew that she wasn't thinking rationally. Honestly, she should have known this was going to happen. She should have seen it a mile off that she wasn't anything different to him. She would never be anything different to him. But she hadn't seen that. She had blinded herself to his easy charm and comforting ways. She had been suckered in and left hanging out to dry all over again. Except this time it was worse, because this wasn't happening to some poor sap that happened across his path. No.

This happened to Lexi, and she knew better. She had been there when every other girl had been defeated.

Instincts sent sparks throughout her body pleading with her to stay away or else, but she didn't listen. How could she listen? This was Jack. He was all she had ever wanted. He had always been the thing that she had wanted.

"I shouldn't have thought you would change," she grumbled pushing her hair behind her ears angrily. "I should have known you wouldn't respect me anymore than the rest."

"Come on, Lex. It isn't like that. You know you aren't like anyone else," he pleaded.

"What do you even mean by that? Did you think you could just che…" she caught herself before finishing the words, not wanting to instigate another round of we're-not-even-together conversation, "sleep with someone else, and I would be okay with it? Is that how you thought I was different?"

"Well…" he ran his hands back through his long shaggy hair, his blue eyes lighting up with the energy in the conversation. "I didn't know you'd freak out like this. After what happened with us, I don't know…" he said trailing off.

"See, I knew what we were. I knew that we had cheated on other people with each other, but I guess I never thought I'd be on the other end of this…this hurt. I ignorantly thought now that we're something, that wouldn't come between us. We're meant for each other, Jack, and you just went and ugh," she shrieked angrier than before at his apparent ignorance of the gravity of the situation.

"I'm sorry, Lex, but I don't see why you'd freak out about this after everything."

"And there in lies the problem," she mumbled slumping down to the floor. "I thought you only cheated on other people, because it was me. After all, I never cheated with anyone else other than you. But it wasn't me all along, was it, Jack? There were probably others, and the connection I thought I was feeling was all a lie."

"What?" he asked shocked. "No, that's not the case at all. I didn't lie to you."

"So you didn't sleep with anyone else while you were with Danielle or Kate?" she accused.

"You mean besides Danielle and Kate?" he asked pointedly.

Lexi choked on those words. "You slept with Kate?"

He looked down sheepishly. "Uh…yeah. Did I not mention that?"

Lexi shook her head trying to wrap her mind around that. The virgin had given up her virginity to the man who had cheated on her on numerous occasions. And for what reason? To be left behind. Lexi couldn't process the information. She just couldn't deal with it right now…not with everything else. "Yes, besides them."

"No, it was only you, Lex. I meant everything I said to you. I just," he sighed heavily, "fucked up. I fucked up, Lex. How many times do you want me to say it?"

"How can I even believe you?" she asked, her brown eyes were cold when they looked upon his face. She couldn't express emotion properly right then. All she could imagine was him sleeping with someone else the night before. He had done it without any emotion or any forethought for how she would react or take the news. He had somehow in his conscious, even if he had been drunk, thought that she would be okay with this. Their relationship, or whatever you could call it, was completely off-base if that was what he thought.

"I haven't lied to you. For Christ's sake, I came to you and told you that I slept with Stella," he confessed.

"Stella?" she asked her eyes hardening. She stood back up. "You didn't tell me you fucked your roommate."

"I…uh…are you sure?" he asked his face shifting away from his confident air.

"No, you didn't," she replied biting her lip to keep from lashing out at him with all the expletives she wanted to send his way. After taking a deep breath she spoke again. "How many times have you been together?"

"What? Last night was the first time."

"Right." It was her turn to be disbelieving.

"What are you trying to say?" he asked regaining his earlier composure.

"I find it hard to believe that you've only slept with that girl once," she cried. "You worked together. She lets you move in with her. I mean, I'm not stupid. This can't be the first time."

Jack walked across the room bridging the distance between them. "I have never slept with her before," he said emphasizing each word perfectly. "She was a mistake. It wasn't supposed to happen. She just happened to be there."

Lexi looked up into his beautiful blue eyes unable to believe some of things that were coming out of his mouth. Did he think that he was somehow improving his case?

Her breath hitched as he took one last step entering her personal space. She could feel the heat radiating off of his body. His hair fell into his eyes as he tilted his head to look into her face. She wanted to scream, yell, and run in the opposite direction, but her feet seemed to be shuffling the wrong way. His hand came up and cupped her chin tilting her head further so he could bend down and press his lips gently to hers.

Wrenching free from his touch, she stumbled across the room. She couldn't believe how easily he overpowered her senses. Her heart was racing, but surprisingly not from the feel of his lips. She had never felt such anger over a kiss from Jack. He knew what he was doing and how she completely lacked composure around him. Except this time Lexi wasn't going to let him win. She needed to talk to him and she needed answers.

"Who is going to happen to be there next time?" she spat at him, her eyes narrowing. "Stella happened to be there when you needed someone, but you could have easily called me and I would have come to you. I would have been there, but you didn't *want* me there. You wanted to fuck something meaningless because you are too fucking afraid to let me in."

"Lexi," he interjected hoping to reason with her. He took another step forward nearly cornering her.

"Goddamnit, Jack! Don't you take one more step towards me," she yelled, her arms extending to push him away from her if necessary. "I need to have this conversation with you, not get lost in your stupid blue eyes."

He smirked despite her seriousness. "Stupid blue eyes? I thought you liked them."

Lexi glared. "Cut it out."

"Fine. Sorry," he mumbled.

They both stared at the floor not sure what the next course of action should be. Lexi felt numb from everything she had heard. Her body, which had already been aching from her run, hurt all over. She just wanted to cry, but at the same time, she felt as if she had no more tears left. Maybe if he had broken up with her, she could have cried. But not over this. She just hurt from this.

"Where do we go from here?" she asked him afraid of the answer.

"I was going to ask you the same thing."

Lexi raised her head and stared at the man she had loved for close to four years. Could she give up everything over a one night stand? Was she really a hypocrite for being angry at him for sleeping with someone else? It's not like they had set any boundaries, any rules. She had assumed that was a given. But then again, she had been on the other end of this scenario with his last two girlfriends. It only made sense for him not to know what the rules were, especially if he still had it in his mind that they weren't officially together.

But that did not excuse how he was treating her.

"I think you should leave," she finally said.

"I told you it was up to you whether or not we kept this going," he mumbled crossing the room to the doorway.

"I didn't say that I'd made a decision," she said stopping him with his hand on the knob.

He turned around and looked at her wistfully. "You mean..."

"I mean you should get the fuck out, because I don't want to see you for the next month or so, I'm so angry at you." He hung his head. "But I doubt I'd ever make it a month after what we've been through." His blue eyes looked up at her, hope apparent throughout the irises. "But I can't look at you right now. I feel sick to my stomach at the sight of you. You don't care about me, Jack. Or at least not enough to ignore a girl when she spreads her legs for you. I don't know if that is enough for me. Don't come back until you have something better to tell me."

When Jack left her dorm, Lexi felt as if all the air had been sucked out of the room. She collapsed back against the couch and stared at the door he exited until her eyes stung from not blinking enough. What had she done? What had he made her do? How could he force her hand in such a way? So many questions ran through her mind. She didn't know which to focus on first.

What she did know was that he had hurt her...he had hurt her worse than ever before.

And she had meant what she said. She couldn't look at him right now without hurting. She felt betrayed because of him sleeping with Stella, but she was just as angry with herself. When he had given her a chance for them to be together, she had been scared and thought it would be safer to try it out without an official title. Look how *that* had back fired in her face.

What pissed her off the most was that she hadn't truly wanted him to leave. He was a part of her now. She had told him not to come back unless he had something better to say, but she was terrified that he never would.

She had made up her mind a long time ago that Jack was the only man for her. If they had gotten through this far, then they could make it through anything. But he had been with Stella, when he had *known* he could have her. What kind of guy does that?

She shook her head. She had been in that exact position on a number of occasions with Clark. She knew how easy it could be to escape with Jack when she couldn't be around Clark. As wrong as she knew it was, she hadn't been able to stop herself. She had always thought that desperation came from wanting Jack. Perhaps he had always done it because he enjoyed the cloak and dagger effect of hiding and running away from his life with her.

Was that all she had been for all those years?

She couldn't be sure.

Lexi wasn't sure how many hours had passed as she sat rooted to her place on the sofa. Claire and Elizabeth moseyed in at some point chatting about how amazingly wild Chyna's party had been. They attempted to coax a response out of her, but she sat like a statue as they carried on about their night. Rachelle eventually resurfaced and, after seeing the blank look on Lexi's face, ushered the others out of the living room. Lexi didn't even have a smile for her, though she did appreciate the gesture. She did not, however, appreciate Rachelle's own efforts to find out what had happened between her and Jack. Lexi just glared at her as she rattled off outrageous scenarios.

"Get the fuck out of here, Ray," she growled speaking for the first time.

"This isn't healthy. I wasn't sure if you even could speak. If you won't speak to me, I'm calling Chyna and getting her over here. Maybe she can talk some sense into you," she grumbled stomping into Lexi's room.

Lexi didn't even have the energy to stop her. What did it matter if Chyna came over? That wasn't bringing Jack back to her and if it did, it wasn't going to take back what had happened last night. She continued staring forward at the TV which, at some point, had been switched on to a terrible Soap Opera. She didn't recognize what was going on and after a couple minutes all the colors began to blur together. She knew her roommates were talking about her in the other room, but she couldn't concentrate enough to make out what they were saying. It didn't matter anyway.

"Oh, honey," Chyna cried as soon as she burst through the door. She rushed across the room and sat on the couch next to Lexi. "What happened to you?" Lexi felt her wrap her arms around her and squeeze. She let her, but it still didn't matter. "How long has she been like this?" Chyna anxiously questioned glancing over the couch at her worried roommates.

Claire shrugged and glanced towards Rachelle who answered, "I'm not sure. Jack left around eleven. I heard the door slam. I guess since then."

"Eleven in the morning?" she screeched. "And you're just calling me now? Why it's nearly six o'clock."

That surprised Lexi. She hadn't realized she had been here that long...an hour at the most. Where had the time gone? Had Jack called? She didn't ask any of these questions, just remained seated staring blankly ahead.

"Sorry," Rachelle mumbled. The other two girls didn't even respond, just huddled behind their friend. "I didn't know what was going on with her."

"Whatever," Chyna stated dismissively. "Alexa, hey, look at me." Chyna gently turned her head to face her. Lexi's brown eyes were blank and bloodshot as if she had been crying, but every other indication was vacant. "What happened?" Lexi stared at her friend. "It's okay. You can tell me if you want, but you don't have to."

Lexi could tell she was worried. Chyna's voice was cracking with concern. She had never seen Lexi this way. That's because Lexi had never felt this way. She felt comatose, as if she no longer needed anything to sustain her body. She could stare off into open space indefinitely and nothing else would matter. Maybe nothing else did matter.

"Chica, can you even hear me?" Lexi hadn't noticed that she had still been talking. What was so important? She wanted to drift away...far away from this time and place. "Alexa, wake up. What has gotten into you?" she asked shaking her shoulders gently. She felt her head loll back and forth as her neck lost control of keeping her head upright. She still didn't make a move to speak up. Chyna looked to be near to tears and there was nothing Lexi could or would do about it. She wanted to be left alone. "I just...I don't know what to do with her," she murmured standing and speaking to Lexi's roommates. "What could have happened to her?"

Chyna jumped backwards as a knock sounded from the front door. Rachelle crossed the room swiftly and gasped as it swung open.

"You son of a bitch," Chyna cried stalking across the space. "What the hell did you do to her, Jack?"

"I...Lex," he murmured softly glancing around Chyna at Lexi's near statuesque form.

Lexi glanced up for the first time feeling as if she had been awakened from a dream. She hadn't expected to ever hear her name uttered by his voice ever again. "Jack."

He attempted to enter the apartment, but Chyna blocked his way. "How dare you think you can walk back into her life like this! She's been sitting like a completely unresponsive rock for the past seven hours because of you...and you think..."

"Chyna, cut it out," Lexi commanded her voice weak but controlled. "Let him in."

"Are you sure?" Chyna asked biting down on her lip. It looked like the last thing she wanted to do in the whole wide world.

"Yes." That settled it and she moved away letting him enter the dorm. Rachelle shut the door behind him and quickly made her, Claire, and Elizabeth *very* busy. Chyna stood by ostensibly, ready to pounce at any second in the event that he hurt her friend again. Lexi sighed. "I'm alright, Chyna. You can go. I know you're supposed to be meeting with Frederick today. He hates when you're late."

"He can deal," she grumbled not budging.

"Go. I won't have him angry with me. I'll call you if I need you." Chyna looked anxious about the situation but, eventually, nodded and left.

Lexi noticed how bad she ached all over for the first time since that morning. She had never fixed her dehydration problem and every muscle in her body was crying out from thirst. Her eyelids were heavy and pink lips chapped. Her back ached from sitting ramrod straight for seven hours. Most of all, her heart hurt terribly. She had closed off her emotions when he had walked out the door, but now with him standing in front of her, it all came back in a wave. Her heart was tearing, breaking, being shred to pieces, and it was unlike anything she had ever experienced. She wanted to gasp out in pain, but she kept her mouth closed and held in her aches. Jack had come here for a reason, and she wanted to know what that reason was.

"You said if I had something more to talk to you about…anything better that I should come back," he told her speaking quietly as he sat next to her on the couch.

"It took you seven hours to think of something good enough to say to me?" she whispered, her voice raspy.

"Please, Lex," he pleaded his blue eyes boring into her.

"Go ahead."

Jack took a deep breath before speaking. "I've always been the kind of person who believed that I'd never find someone I wanted to commit to. That after all the shit I went through with my parents' divorce, I'd never want to be with someone indefinitely. I'd never see another person as anything more than a divorce waiting to happen. I pushed every person I've ever been with away from me, and for what?

"I did it, because I was scared. I did it, because I was selfish. I wanted everything and really all I was doing was accepting nothing. And you…you, my dear," he said his hands reaching for her cheek but dropping before he reached her. "I hurt you more than all of them. I lied, cheated, and took you for granted. You were it for me, and I managed to even fuck that up.

"I fuck up, because I don't know how to do anything else. I'm worthless. I'm less than worthless. I should never have been in a relationship in the first place. If anyone had known what I was capable of, they would have run. But you knew and you stuck by me. You put up with me even when you had no reason to. I know I'm terrible at showing it but I do love you. I want you to know that you have my heart. You always have and you always will."

"Jack, how can you say that to me?" Lexi asked fighting back tears.

"Because it's the truth," he murmured.

"But you've never been able to show that to me."

"I might be able to." Her eyes narrowed suspiciously. Jack's hand went to his pocket and dug around for a second before retrieving a tiny black box. Lexi gasped as her eyes took on the shape of a jewelry box.

"What…what's in there?" she asked her voice shaking. Her eyes were wide with wonder and a hint of fear.

He cracked the box open revealing an exquisite princess cut diamond with a string of matching diamonds on either side. The band was pure white gold. It had an old timey feel to it, but Lexi had never laid her eyes on a more beautiful ring. "This was what I was going to give to you to prove that you have my heart."

Lexi hand flew to her mouth in shock. She couldn't help shaking her head in disbelief. No. Not now. Not after everything. She couldn't drag her eyes away from the amazing diamond.

"No," she murmured.

He nodded picking the ring up out of the box and twirling it around between his fingers. "I know I don't deserve you, Lex."

"No," she muttered again.

"I know," he said nodding. "This was my grandma's ring. My mom gave it to me over my brothers, because she knew that I would choose someone who really mattered to me, not just the first person who came along."

"Jack, please, just stop."

He seemed to ignore her. "Now I wasn't planning to show this to you, but," he looked up from the ring into her wide-eyed brown orbs, "this was meant for you. Only you."

"No."

"But either way, that was what I had to tell you to show you my heart," he whispered.

"How could you do this now?" she murmured, tears forming in her eyes even though she had told herself over and over that she wouldn't cry.

"It was the only thing I could think of," he said snapping the box shut and stuffing it hastily back in his pocket.

"What does this mean?" she couldn't help asking.

"I took a job in Atlanta. I won't be a burden on you any longer. I can see what I did to you, what I continue to do to you, and I won't let that continue to happen. I fucked everything up by sleeping with Stella, and I know that. I'll never forgive myself, and I don't exactly expect you to forgive me."

"Atlanta?" she asked her voice coming out strangled. "I thought you got turned down."

"The man that I interviewed with last night suggested me to a friend and as long as I'm in Atlanta by tomorrow night I have the job. It was a last minute kind of thing," he told her.

"All of this was for nothing?"

"No, it made me realize what I did to you. And I'm not going to do it again. So this is good-bye. I'll try not to bother you again. I love you, Lex," he said planting a sweet kiss on her lips.

She could barely function right now. He was leaving her after all. They weren't going to be able to get through this. Even though she thought they would be able to work it out, they would never be given the chance. And as she watched him walk out her door, she truly knew that she would never ever hear from him again.

23

PRESENT

Lexi slipped inside Ramsey's town house carefully positioning herself where he couldn't get a look at her back. She sucked her bottom lip into her mouth wincing at the extreme tenderness. Ramsey glanced in her direction, and she instantly moved to cover her throat with her hair. No need for him to ask questions. It would really just be an unnecessary hassle. And, in either case, it wasn't something she could explain.

She stood by the stairs and waited for him to go first. She followed behind closely ducking into the guest bedroom where he stood against the doorframe.

"I'll get you something to sleep in," he told her a smile playing across his features.

"Uh…thanks," she stated awkwardly turning to face him in the doorway. She liked the smile he was sending her way. It was very…sincere. He looked as if he genuinely did not want to be any place else in the world at that moment. He would be content standing in the doorway staring into her face for eternity. He wasn't even pressuring her to feel anything more, just to look at him. And, man, was he attractive.

Lexi's stomach twisted at the thought. She did not want to be thinking these types of thoughts around Ramsey. He disoriented her in a completely different manner than she was used to. Jack tilted her completely off balance. She couldn't think…she could hardly breathe around him. It was as if her orbit shifted around him.

With Ramsey she could feel a sense of equality about their movements as if the world was in the right place again. He revolved around her, and she matched his movements. It was a completely new experience. And also terribly frightening to know that she could have such a connection to someone she had just met…to someone she hadn't even particularly liked up until tonight. She couldn't think about that right now. Tonight, of all nights, she needed to keep her wits about her.

She stood motionless in the doorway as Ramsey fetched her clothes. She couldn't help thinking about the events of the night and how they had unraveled.

The sex was never supposed to happen. She just wasn't capable of controlling her actions around him. Turning Jack down was the hardest thing she ever tried to do. No matter how many times they had fucked up together, she never found it easier to break free from him. There was always Jack. Even after the crazy sex and horrible things he had said to her, she couldn't think about giving him up. He had told her that none of it mattered, and it didn't change anything.

How could none of it matter?

How could the sex not alter his decision in the slightest?

Lexi couldn't wrap her mind around that concept. Sure she had been sleeping with Jack for years, but it's not like the sex never mattered. She had held out on him for a year a half, granted they hadn't been together the whole time. No, they had never been together. He had made that perfectly clear when he walked out that door…when he ran.

Her face darkened at the painful memory. She typically kept it under lock and key where no one could access it. But with everything that had gone on tonight, she couldn't hold it together. Her jaw was clenched tight and her eyes had the remembered look of agony. All she wanted to do was keep from crying until Ramsey brought her something to change into.

Just then he walked around the corner and down the hall. Lexi quickly recovered hoping that her expression was as neutral as possible, but she could see that he wasn't fooled.

"Thanks," she muttered yanking the clothes out of his hand and slamming the door quickly.

Lexi smacked her head back against the door instantly regretting her actions. Reaching her hand back to touch her head, she found a small knot forming where it had been knocked against concrete. As if her problems weren't enough, now every bump and bruise would remind her of Jack. Great!

She groaned as she forced her body to stand back up. Hugging her arms tightly around her body, she moved in front of the full-length mirror pinned against the wall. Lexi gently pulled down the side zipper on her now ruined dress. The silky material slid off her narrow hips and pooled at her feet. She unclasped her black, strappy, high heels and kicked them off. Her strapless bra followed. Lexi turned from side to side examining the damage. She could see little bruised indentions in her thighs where Jack's hands had held her up. Her lip was turning a slight shade of purple, but her neck wasn't quite as bad as she had anticipated. Her back was scratched, but not red and puffy like before. In the dim lighting, the rest of her body looked nearly normal.

This allowed a small smile to cross her face. Their indiscretions wouldn't be as noticeable as she thought. Her aches were at a minimum, and she would be as fit as ever in a couple days.

The smile dropped off her face and the tears began to well in her eyes. She allowed them to flow freely down her cheeks, cursing herself for feeling the emotions she was encountering.

This might be her last reminder of Jack.

He had said that he still needed time to think, but didn't she, of all people, know better? Jack didn't think. He acted. He did exactly what he wanted when he wanted to, and since he had done that with her, he had received everything he had endeavored towards.

She collapsed, naked, in a heap to the floor. Her hair cascaded around her face. She felt something wet on her knees and she realized, suddenly, that it was tears. Lexi swiped at her eyes. She glanced up into the mirror and recognized the trail of black flowing down her cheeks. She vigorously scrubbed the mascara tears away leaving her cheeks raw and splotchy.

Her head tilted to the side as she stared onwards at her reflection. She tucked a loose strand of hair behind her ear once out of habit. The movement reassured her, and she did it again until the curly strands were maintained neatly behind her ears. It was the least she could do to keep from crying again.

This was the last time she ever wanted to cry for Jack Howard.

Her head snapped to the side at the sound of the door creaking open. Ramsey stood silhouetted in the doorway in nothing but a snug pair of maroon boxer briefs. For a second as she stared at him, she lost all thought of being naked sitting on the floor. He looked so delectable. She had never seen him with his shirt off, and damn was her first impression right. He certainly had to have a personal trainer.

"Oh, sorry," he said his eyes sliding down her near naked form. She could tell he wasn't sorry, and she was too broken and dazed to say otherwise.

"Did you need something?" she asked, her voice cracking with the effort to keep from crying.

"I was coming to check on you."

For once, he kept his distance. Lexi let her head drop wishing she could erase this entire night. She had been stupid to think that she could be a part of Jack's life. And in that moment, she felt more used than she ever had in her life. Even if that hadn't been Jack's original intention, after he left her standing there bruised and broken, she couldn't help but feel that he had used her. And she wasn't even sure what had fueled such anger from him. The sex was amazing, but there was an undertone of hostility in his movements. Not to mention his abrupt goodbye. When he said that it didn't change things, she was really more afraid that he meant it.

"Is there something I can do?" he whispered into the darkness.

She shook her head back and forth. All she needed was to be alone.

"Are you sure?" he asked taking a few tentative steps into the room.

"I'm fine," she murmured. It wasn't believable though. She was naked sitting in a crumpled heap on his floor looking as if she had been crying.

She glanced back up and met his worried gaze. "You don't look fine." He took another step forward.

"Thanks," she muttered sarcastically.

"I didn't mean it like that. I just meant…" he trailed off.

"I know what you meant."

He cleared the space between them in a quick stride and squatted in front of her. "Please let me make it better. I hate seeing you this way," he whispered reaching out to her.

"Then don't look at me," she said pulling herself away from his touch.

"I can't help but look at you."

"Yes, you can."

"No, I can't," he said leaning in closer. "You are the most beautiful thing I've ever laid eyes on."

"Beauty is only skin deep," she quipped not letting herself get suckered into his sweet talk.

"Not on you."

"You don't even know me."

"And you don't know me. Yet, we've gone on two dates and we've kissed. I know you feel something for me. You just don't know what it is yet," he told her sitting next to her on the floor.

Lexi shook her head. "You're right. I don't know you, and I don't know what I feel."

"Then let me show you," he said leaning forward and capturing her lips in his own.

Lexi groaned deep in her throat wondering how she had gotten herself into this mess. Here she was going back and forth between two guys. This, being here right now, was so wrong.

Misreading her groan, Ramsey took this as encouragement and deepened the kiss. He let his tongue slide into her mouth and flick against her tongue. His hands buried themselves into her thick mass of curls pulling her face closer to his. She couldn't stay unresponsive as he expertly maneuvered against her mouth. It was as if some kissing instinct had awakened in her, and she tilted her head giving him a better angle.

Her mind was so frazzled from the events of the night, but still she knew this was wrong. "Ramsey," she muttered against his lips.

As soon as it came out of her mouth, she knew he would take it as further encouragement. His name had come out breathy and seductive when she had been going for questioning.

"Mmm," he moaned against her lips, letting one hand trail down her neck, across her slight shoulder, and gently grazed the side of her breast, before resting strongly on her waistline. She couldn't keep her breath from hitching as his large hands staked a claim on her body.

She knew she should stop him from continuing. Her mind went into overdrive as she thought about how wrong her actions were in that moment. But before she could even push him away, he snuck his arm up under her legs and effortlessly hoisted her into the air. The sweet taste of peppermint lingered on the tip of her tongue as she broke away from him.

He carried her to the foot of the bed and gently laid her back against the soft down comforter. She was distinctly aware of her nakedness as she stretched out across the bed. There was so little clothing between them leaving her in a very precarious position. From her angle, she could see the bulge in his boxer briefs growing at the sight of her. She couldn't help but smile at his reaction. Of course, she knew it was the *wrong* reaction. All she seemed to be doing was sending him wrong signals, but she couldn't help it. Very few women wouldn't have smiled at that moment.

His hands moved forward and clutched onto her hip bones. Then he dipped his head down and began kissing upwards from her navel. Slowly but surely he moved around her belly button, up between the curves of her breasts, to the base of her neck, across her jaw line, and then, finally, back to her lips. She felt him press against her as he coaxed a reaction out of her tender lips. His hands roamed her body taking in every curve of her skin. She could feel him urging her on, aching for her body. He interlaced their fingers and pressed her arms above her head leaving her completely vulnerable. He began a slow grind against her ,never letting up on his amazing kisses.

Ramsey left her hands above her head and began to roam lower and lower until his fingers were feather light against her inner thighs. "Ramsey, I…" she got out before he was kissing her again. His gentle hands began making circle motions against the sensitive skin, trailing closer to her most sensitive area.

Fire alarms were going off in her head at his advances, and she knew she needed to stop. In fact, she really *wanted* to stop. After everything she had been through tonight, she could not add this to the list of stupid things for the evening. She pushed against his chiseled chest, but she might as well have been pushing on a brick wall for all he noticed. One finger moved closer and pressed against her opening. He didn't do anything more than rest there, but she was already wet with anticipation…an anticipation that she would never let come to fruition.

She turned her head to pull away from his demanding kisses. "Stop," she whispered lacking the conviction she felt.

"What did you say?" he asked expertly inserting two fingers deep inside of her without allowing her enough time to answer. She couldn't believe how amazing this felt, and it was just the foreplay. She needed to stop or she was going to regret her actions.

"I said stop," she murmured attempting to wiggle away from him, but he had his other hand locked securely against her hip preventing her from moving.

"But you like it. You're enjoying it."

"No," she said shaking her head as her lower half convulsed with pleasure.

"Your body is telling me otherwise and I haven't even gone any farther."

"You can't…go any…farther," she gasped out.

He sighed letting his head fall forward but halting his movements inside of her. His hot breath gave away his already heated desire for her. "Are you sure?" he asked wiggling his fingers playfully.

She gasped. "Yes…"

"You want me to stop?"

"Yes."

He sighed against her, heavier this time, but extracted his hand from her lower extremities. He rolled over and laid next to her, his chest heaving up and down with the effort of following her orders. She could tell he was expelling a good deal of exertion keeping himself from her, when he was already hard and ready for her.

Lexi hopped up off the bed and shimmied back into her ruined dress forgetting that Ramsey had given her new, clean clothes to change into. "I have to get out of here," she said reaching for the door.

"What?" he cried hopping off the bed in surprise. "You just got here."

"I know, but I have to leave."

"Don't go. I won't do anything else," he pleaded with her, meeting her at the door.

"This isn't about you," she muttered wrenching the door open.

"Then, it's about Jack," he said catching her off guard.

She stumbled catching herself on the door frame. "It doesn't matter what it's about. I just have to leave."

"Where are you going to go?"

"I'll figure it out," she said walking out of the room, through the hallway, and down the stairs. She could feel him following her, but she didn't look backwards.

"You shouldn't go running off in the middle of the night."

"I can do whatever I want," she cried striding across the living room.

"I know you can. I just want you to be safe," he said quietly.

She bit down on the inside of her cheek to keep from saying anything she might regret. He was looking out for her, and she knew that. However, getting into any sort of physical relationship with someone else right now was plain wrong. She had too much baggage. She needed to clear away some of that before anyone else got hurt. "I will be safe," she told him turning and facing him.

"Promise?"

"Yes," she said twisting the knob behind her back and pulling the door open. "Sorry."

Lexi rushed down the stairs and out onto the dark city streets. She had forgotten how different New York and Atlanta were. At any given second in New York, she could hail a cab to take her to any destination. Here people had to call for a cab and wait for it to pick you up. In New York, people were constantly on the streets and, where Lexi frequented, she could walk anywhere. In Atlanta, she rarely felt safe walking in even the classiest areas of the city during the day, let alone at night.

She took a deep breath and dialed the number for a cab service. After a few minutes, the cab arrived and carted her to Chyna's hotel. Lexi had the concierge ring for Chyna, but found that no one was in the room or else Chyna was incapacitated. Either was just as likely. Since she had no proof that she should be in Chyna's penthouse, they refused to give her a key to the room.

"If you won't give me a key, can I stay in your lobby until she gets back?" Lexi asked exasperated.

The woman looked at her condescendingly, taking in her smeared make-up and torn dress. "That is not typically permitted."

"Do you really want one of your A-list clients angry at you when Chyna finds out that you treated her best friend this poorly?" Lexi asked smoothly.

Her face shifted into a line of worry. Individuals who came to the hotel and rented the penthouse suite were few and far between. "Very well. When Ms. Van der Wal returns and we can confirm your identity, then we can allow you into her room. If you would like a room of your own, we could arrange that. Otherwise you will have to wait."

Lexi sighed heavily and wandered over to a loveseat. She pulled her feet up onto the cushion and rested her head against the arm of the chair. All she wanted to do was forget that tonight had ever happened.

A short while later she someone was shaking her awake and calling her name. Lexi's eyes fluttered open and she realized, somewhat unbelievably, she had fallen asleep. Her neck was sore from the uncomfortable position, but her mind, at least, was still. She must have been exhausted to have fallen asleep that quickly.

"You alright, chica?" Chyna asked looking at her anxiously.

"A little sore." *What an understatement.* "But I'll be alright. Can we go upstairs?"

"Yeah, sure," Chyna agreed helping Lexi to her feet. "Did they give you any trouble?" Chyna asked staring daggers at the concierge.

"No, they were fine. They did exactly as I expected," Lexi replied following Chyna to the elevators.

The two girls took the elevator to the top floor and Chyna let them into her suite. All Lexi wanted to do was to crash for the next several hours. She was both physically and mentally exhausted. Chyna had other ideas though. She obviously had all the energy from just getting laid that Lexi was lacking. And even though she needed her mandated seven hours of beauty sleep, she didn't seem ready for that to begin.

"Can you spit it out so I can go to sleep?" Lexi asked resting her head back against the couch.

Chyna bit down on her bottom lip as she stared uncomfortably at her friend. "What the hell happened to you? You look like a train wreck. You should have seen the way those people were looking at you downstairs. God, you could have been a hooker for all they knew. A hooker wearing amazing clothes, but still..."

Lexi rolled her eyes not caring much what others thought about her. "I had a rough night."

"I'll say. Just look at you."

"Thanks, C. I got it," she mumbled irritated.

"Then what happened?"

Lexi sighed wavering between a lie and the truth. "Jack and I slept together."

Chyna's mouth dropped open. "No! When?" Lexi lowered her eyes to the floor. "Tonight?" Chyna squeaked. "How could you?"

"You know the answer to that."

"You said you weren't going to."

"I hadn't planned on it. This obviously wasn't planned," she said gesturing around her.

"But, Alexa," Chyna scolded.

"Don't use that voice with me," she growled. "Things didn't go as planned anyway." Things definitely did not go as planned. She hadn't planned on sleeping with him. She hadn't planned on falling for him...again. She hadn't planned on her night with Ramsey. She hadn't planned on any of it.

"Did he hit you?" Chyna asked fear obvious in her voice. "You look like shit."

"What? No! God, no," Lexi exclaimed running her hands through her hair. "He just…he was really cold to me afterwards."

"Like how?" Chyna asked concerned.

"I don't know. He said this didn't change things," Lexi attempted to explain.

"What does that mean?" Chyna asked aggravated.

"I think it means he needs more time to decide what he wants. It just came out wrong," Lexi said trying to convince herself too.

"I doubt it."

"Chyna," Lexi said warningly.

"No, you listen to yourself. He fucked you then pretty much told you that you didn't mean anything to him. How could you think otherwise?"

"He said he still needed time. He told me he wanted to be with me. Chyna, they can't be together. I have to stop this. He can't do what he did to me and expect not to have to make a decision," she told her vehemently.

"Alexa, stop. You can't think like that. You cannot break them up."

"But he wants to be with me. A part of him still wants to be with me."

"You don't actually believe him, do you?" Chyna asked scrunching her perfectly waxed eyebrows together.

"He's never lied to me before," Lexi said but doubt was in her voice.

"Are you sure?"

"He hasn't lied to me in six years. Why would he start now?" Lexi asked trying to force a sense of determination.

"I just…don't know," she said biting her lip and looking away.

"What are you getting at, Chyna?" Lexi couldn't keep the venom out of her voice.

"Look, maybe he never lied directly, but that didn't mean that he was telling you the whole truth," Chyna told her.

Lexi sighed. She had thought of that. In fact, a part of her wondered if maybe everything he ever said had been in some part a lie. But she couldn't let herself get caught up on that. He was the same Jack she had always known, and he loved her. No matter how difficult the past week…the past year and a half had been there was a part of him that would always love her. She needed to harness that affection and make him realize that was what he had always wanted…what he still wanted.

"Did you forget that this was all *your* idea in the first place," Lexi asked evading Chyna's last statement.

"Goddamn, chica, I sent you up here to get over the fucking douche bag, not to fall in love with him again."

"Well, I'm not sure I ever stopped loving him."

"You don't know what you're saying," Chyna said shaking her head miserably.

"I know perfectly well what I am saying. I know exactly how I feel about Jack."

"You're acting like a teenager. Pull yourself together. You don't need this guy to feel loved. There are plenty…"

Lexi interrupted, "Don't feed me the there are plenty of other fish in the sea line."

"But there are!" Chyna cried. "Have you not seen the way Ramsey looks at you?"

Lexi rolled her eyes, but her heart was aching at the admission. She couldn't tell Chyna what had happened between them. The news that they had almost slept together would only fuel her passion. And she was stuck with Jack. No matter what he had done or how confused he was. He held her heart, even when it was breaking. "Don't talk to me about Ramsey."

"Then don't act like Jack is the only person who has ever looked at you like you're a goddess."

"Just because Ramsey feels this way about me doesn't mean it is reciprocated," Lexi cried back.

"Then explain what happened out on the balcony."

Lexi blushed. If Chyna knew the rest of what had happened, she would never hear the end of it. "That was a mistake."

"It didn't look like it."

"I slept with Jack right afterwards. What does that tell you?"

"That you are a very confused person!"

"I'm not confused. I know exactly what I want."

"I didn't want to have to tell you this," Chyna said shaking her head fiercely.

"What?" Lexi asked barely listening to her. All she wanted to do was get this conversation over with and sleep.

"I heard some of Jack's friends talking about him and Bekah," she trailed off.

"And?"

"There are rumors of them getting married."

"Yeah. Isn't that why I'm here in the first place?" Lexi asked dumbfounded as to why Chyna was even bringing this up to her again. She was here to convince Bekah that Jack was ready for commitment. Well, she certainly hadn't done that. If anything she had confused him more.

"I know, but I think he's going to do it."

"What?" Lexi questioned staring at her like she was a Martian.

"The guys were talking about planning a bachelor party," Chyna whispered hating that she had to break the news to her.

"It could have been for any of them," she said but she hardly convinced herself. Doubt had crept into her voice.

"I think they were all married," she murmured.

"No." She shook her head and pushed a loose strand of hair behind her ears. Her sleep deprived brain couldn't process what Chyna was saying. Jack couldn't be marrying Bekah. He didn't love her. He didn't feel for her what he felt with Lexi. There was no way this could be happening. "No. No, he's not," she said the weakness in her voice evident. She felt as if she had been punched in the gut. She was receiving just enough air to keep her upright.

"What did you say? Alexa, you have to believe me. I'm looking out for you."

"No. I won't believe it," her voice coming out in a monotone.

"I'm sorry. I didn't want to tell you. I didn't want this to happen to you," Chyna said feeling like the shittiest of shitty friend's right then.

"This cannot be happening to me."

"I'm sorry, sweetie," Chyna said moving to her side. "Do you still want to be with him?"

Even after that admission, even after Lexi's first realization that Jack might marry someone else, she still wanted him.

"Is Jack really what you want after everything?" She reached out and grasped Lexi's hand affectionately.

"You don't understand," Lexi said yanking her hand out of her grasp. "You never understood." The feeling of losing Jack overwhelmed her body. The feeling was so familiar, that it could only be associated with *him*. Her heart felt as if it were being fed through a shredder, and then played back in reverse.

"How could I understand?" Chyna asked vehemently. "Do you even see yourself? You're a wreck. You look exactly the same as last time. You're shutting down and shutting everyone out. You can't let him do this to you every time he comes back into your life. Can't you see that this boy has done a number on you that can never be undone, unless you let him go? You have to let him go."

"How can I let him go?" she asked her breathing coming out shallow. "How can I let him go, if he won't let me?"

"You have to find a way to be strong."

"No, I can't be sure. I have to go to him and find out what the truth is."

"You think he's going to tell you the truth?" Chyna asked dubiously.

"He damn well better!"

24

PRESENT

Chyna managed to talk Lexi into getting a few hours of much needed rest. She needed to be of the right state of mind to talk with Jack. And, anyways, he would probably be sleeping at six o'clock in the morning, when Lexi was ready to burst into his apartment and confront him. The exhaustion that had crept up on her that whole night suddenly evaporated with the prospect of finally coming to a conclusion about her relationship with Jack. Restless sleep eventually overtook her, but it did very little to stem her anticipation.

The thoughts swirling around in her brain only managed to make her more nervous about her upcoming appointment with disaster. She couldn't fathom that Jack had lied to her. They had always been up front about their feelings and how they were going to work…no matter how dysfunctional everything else turned out to be.

When she finally awoke the next day, she found that somehow she had managed to sleep through a good portion of the day. She wasn't certain how that had happened, but was grateful for the break from her earlier thoughts. Except that left her with only a few brief hours to accomplish everything she needed to get done. She canceled her flight that Jack purchased for her earlier that month, reimbursing those funds to his card. With Chyna's arrival, Lexi decided to leave on her private jet. A flight that would leave that very night. A flight that Lexi was not certain she was ready to get on.

She groggily got out of bed, reaching for her phone. Beyond the two messages from Ramsey making sure she had made it home alright and apologizing for his inappropriate behavior, there was nothing else. Jack hadn't called. He hadn't texted. He had made no effort to get in contact with her after their escapade.

Lexi lazily tossed the thing back into her purse and strolled into the bathroom. After a scalding hot shower to clear her mind, Lexi did some extra pampering. She needed to look her best when she spoke with him. If she looked as shitty as she felt, then she would lose a good deal of the confidence that she needed. She let her loose curls go about their business and applied some make-up to highlight her golden skin and large brown eyes. Her hair covered the damage done to her back, but she had to touch up her neck where a few hickeys were beginning to show. A thin layer of lipstick hid the bruising on her bottom lip. A purple dress that was simple yet appealing was her first choice. She paired it with black strappy sandals. She hoped it was enough.

Her first instinct was to go by his apartment, and with Chyna's approval, she took the town car across the city. As she approached the entranceway, the attendant who had been on duty when she had stayed the night at Jack's less than a week ago was exiting the building. "Oh, excuse me," the attendant said almost running into her.

"No problem at all. Hey, I think I know you," Lexi said.

"Oh, yeah," the girl said pointing her finger at Lexi as if she were placing her. "You know Jack, right?"

"Yeah. Do you know if he's in right now?" Lexi asked taking a step closer to the doorway.

The girl seemed to mull it over. After a second of contemplation she answered, "I don't think he is. I remember him leaving this afternoon."

"Do you happen to know where he was going?" Lexi asked knowing she sounded snoopy.

"Look, I don't really like to get involved," she said crossing her arms across her chest uncomfortably.

"Oh no, I totally understand," she said immediately. She had to be quick on her toes or else she wouldn't get any information. "It's just his girlfriend is freaking out, because he won't answer his phone, and she asked me to come by since she couldn't."

"Well," the girl began tilting her head sideways.

"I swear I wouldn't bother you if it wasn't an emergency," Lexi said lathering on the desperation.

The girl sighed and tossed her hair over her shoulder. "He came down earlier and looked a bit bummed out. Said he needed to get some things accomplished at the office, but don't tell him I told you so," she said racing down the remaining stairs, across the street, and into a parked Civic.

With more direction than when she had woken up this morning, Lexi piled back into the town car to make her way to Bridges Enterprise. She knew the building well from her long history in the city, but had never ventured inside. All she knew about the business was that the Bridges name had been around for a long time. It comprised of attorneys, accountants, and any other form of business that could assist you with your troubles, and they charged a fortune for their rather successful services.

The town car dropped Lexi off at the base of the monumental staircase leading up to the building. After climbing the flight of stairs, she stepped into Bridges Enterprise, an enormous, emasculating building covered almost completely in glass. The high-arched, sleek entranceway opened into a clean, marble tiled lobby with forty foot ceilings, plush leather sofas, and high-glossed counter space. Every person was impeccably dressed in the latest fashions as well as physically fit and attractive. The women all wore knee-length skirt suits with high heels while the men wore suits each with a different color tie. It was terrifying being in a room with so many well-groomed individuals. Lexi's simple dress suddenly felt out of place, but she held her head high regardless.

She cautiously approached a tiny Asian woman working behind the reception desk. People milled around the lobby. Some entering and exiting elevators, stopping to chat with an associate, or waiting patiently for their important meeting. With a company this large it was necessary to have the office available to clients seven days a week.

"Thank you very much. Here at Bridges Enterprise we do everything we can to bridge the distance between you and your troubles. Have a wonderful day," she said hanging up the phone before looking up at Lexi. "May I help you?" the woman asked, a genuine smile crossing her face.

"Yes, I am here to see Jack Howard," Lexi told the woman hoping to make it see more of a demand than a request.

The woman smirked and glanced down at the monitor in front of her. She clicked a few buttons before returning her eyes to Lexi. "Do you have a meeting with Mr. Howard?"

"Not exactly," she admitted, "but I do need to see him."

"Mr. Howard is a very busy man. I hope you understand when I say that you would have to have an appointment to see him," she stated firmly.

"Right, well, does he have a full schedule today?" Lexi asked attempting to peer over the desk.

"He has the day marked off to be with Ms. Bridges."

"But he is in the office today," Lexi badgered anxious to get this over with.

"Is there anything *I* can assist you with?" the woman asked dodging the question effortlessly.

"Not unless you can tell me what office is his," she said deliberately.

"Ma'am unless you have an appointment, which you do not, then Mr. Howard is unavailable to you. However, there are more trained professionals in his department that are free this afternoon, if you would like to make an appointment with one of them."

"No, thank you," Lexi said gnawing on her bottom lip. What a waste of time. This woman would not be of any more help…not that she had been much in the first place. Obviously, Jack was here in his office. The only problem was she had no idea where that was and the building was a million stories high with hundreds of offices. She could search all day and never locate him, but she didn't have that time.

She thanked the woman and walked away from the counter looping around towards the elevators. Hopping on the first elevator that dinged open, Lexi stood between several men in high quality suits. As she slowly approached the top floor, she found she was finally left alone with one of the men. Putting on the most girly look she could muster, Lexi cried, "Shoot!" She let the Southern drawl, which she reserved for special occasions, permeate through the word. The man glanced over at her in surprise, but she could see it was also intrigue. He quickly faced the front again not deeming it appropriate to intervene. "Um, excuse me," she cooed drawing his attention back to her.

"Yes, ma'am?" he asked, the perfect gentleman.

"You see," she began huffing a little in embarrassment, "I have an appointment with Mr. Howard today." His eyes widened in surprise. "But I've forgotten where his office is," she told him casting her eyes down and hoping she could find some semblance of innocence in the gesture. "I was wondering if you could maybe point me in the right direction. The woman at the front told me, but Lord, I'd lose my head if it wasn't attached to my body."

He marveled at her unadulterated beauty for a second before answering. "Sure not a problem," he said buying her act. He pressed another button on the elevator and turned to continue to make small talk with her from there.

"What are you seeing Mr. Howard for, if you don't mind me asking?" he asked leaning back against the metal hand railing.

"Uh…" Lexi tucked a loose strand of hair behind her ear. She hadn't thought this far out with her plan and had no alibi for seeing Jack. No doubt she had always been a terrible liar so making something up on the spot wasn't going to work for her. She was amazed she had made it this far with acting.

"It's alright," he said immediately reading her discomfort. "You don't have to tell me. We have a number of people coming in with troubles that need to be solved. You're lucky you got Jack. He's one of our best," the man said admiringly. She had completely forgotten that she was in a place where talking about her problems was confidential business. At least something was working in her favor.

"That's wonderful," she stated dryly, pleased and displeased at the same time that Jack was doing so well for himself. A part of her maliciously wondered how much Bekah had a hand in that.

"Here is his floor," he said when the elevator landed. "All the way down the hallway and on the right. Can't miss it. His secretary should be here. Her name is Gwen. She can take it from here."

"Thank you so much, Mr…" she waited for his name. He had been an invaluable resource.

"Oh, what was I thinking?" he asked smacking himself on the forehead. "Brandon Calloway." He pulled out his wallet and extracted a business card. She took it from him smiling to herself.

"Pleasure to meet you, Mr. Calloway."

"Call me Brandon," he muttered huskily, leaning against the elevator door to hold it open for her while they chatted.

"Brandon," she repeated placing the card delicately into her purse.

"I hope everything works out for you. If Jack doesn't help, just let me know. I'm in office 2404. Stop in anytime," he told her invitingly.

"Well, uh, thanks," she said stepping through the door.

"No problem. What's your name?" he asked smoothly as she passed through the sliding doors.

"Lexi. Lexi Walsh," she said. When she glanced over her shoulder, he was still standing there staring after her. Something had changed in his look and his mouth was hanging slightly open. She wasn't sure what that was about, but she couldn't concentrate on that now. He had played his part and now she needed to bridge the distance between her own troubles.

She followed Brandon's directions and found a blonde, no surprise there, sitting at a desk in front of a large corner office. "May I help you?" the woman asked looking up from her computer screen. She had a British accent, impeccably white teeth, and perfectly fake breasts revealed in her low cut blouse.

"Is Jack in?" Lexi asked smirking at the predictability of the woman's appearance.

"Indeed. However, Mr. Howard is not taking appointments today." She looked down at her screen, scrolled through a program, then glanced back up. "I believe I can squeeze you in Thursday afternoon if that works for you, darling."

Lexi scoffed. "Um, no. I leave this afternoon, and I need to see him now."

"I'm sorry that would simply be impossible. Perhaps when you are next in town then," she stated simply. Lexi rolled her eyes and walked around the desk completely ignoring the girl. "Ma'am, you cannot go in there."

"Sorry. I need to see him," she said rushing to the door. "Jack, can I come in?" Lexi asked knocking swiftly on the large wooden door. "You're…uh…secretary said you were in," she took another glance at the leggy blonde behind her who was just now getting out of her seat to stop her.

"Ma'am, he is unavailable," Gwen said standing with her hands on her hips in frustration. "You can't barge in there."

"Oh, is it not locked?" Lexi asked smiling devilishly as she turned the handle and the door popped open.

"Stop, you're going to get me in trouble," Gwen cried rushing after her.

"Jack," Lexi murmured seeing him sitting behind his desk.

"Gwen, I thought I told you no visitors this afternoon," Jack muttered not even glancing up from his desk.

Lexi's determination wavered at the sight of him. He was wearing a tailored navy blue suit over a crisp white button up. The top button was undone and his navy and silver neck tie was pulled loose. His dark hair fell over his eyes as he scanned through a report bound in a plastic cover with the Bridges Enterprise emblem displayed upon the front. She couldn't even look past him to check out his amazing office as she was so utterly bound by his appearance and commanding presence.

"Sir, I certainly did not let her in. This young lady barged in demanding to see you." Gwen gave Lexi a death glare.

"Well, see her out," Jack said still not looking up. Gwen moved forward and latched onto Lexi's arm. She attempted to veer her out of the room, but Lexi wouldn't budge. When she started yanking on her arm, her long fingernails digging into her skin, Lexi couldn't take it any longer. Jack still hadn't looked up at her.

"Jack, honestly," Lexi cried standing her ground.

"Lex?" he asked surprised to find her standing in his office.

"You know this woman, sir?" Gwen asked dropping her hands and placing them behind her back promptly. She looked between them with poisonous daggers shooting sparks at Lexi's back. She was not too pleased that he knew Lexi. Somehow this didn't surprise Lexi. She wondered if Jack had been sleeping with this woman. The anger at the possibility of him diddling his secretary reminded Lexi why she was there in the first place. She and Jack had a score to settle, and it had to happen today, right now.

"Yes, Gwen. It's fine. You can go," he said dismissing her without breaking his gaze which was still set on Lexi.

"Yes, sir," Gwen said bitterly turning on her designer heels and stalking out the door.

"The door," Jack called out to Gwen.

She stepped back into the room and yanked the handle slamming the door shut. "Well, she's...something, isn't she?" Lexi asked smirking.

Jack rolled his eyes and set his papers down on his desk. Lexi took that opportunity to really take in her surroundings. Like the exterior of the building, the entire perimeter of the office was cased in glass overlooking the city. The view was spectacular and at night time, Lexi could only assume, it would be even better. A large bookshelf was covered with material pertinent to his work as well as the only picture frames Lexi had seen in Jack's presence since her arrival. One picture in a metal frame of him and Bekah vacationing somewhere on the coast stood out to Lexi. Another picture of Jack with the guys in Las Vegas was framed. His diploma was mounted on the wall in a stunning frame with a red, black, and white tassel displayed alongside it.

Lexi's eyes moved to the other side of the room, which opened up to a bathroom. But what caught her eye wasn't the fact that he, in fact, had his own bathroom in his office. Rather was the picture frame that took up the majority of the opposite wall. Her heart clenched as she stared at the picture she had described to Jack less than a week earlier. A picture he had claimed to have gotten rid of, because he couldn't look at it any longer. The frame was different than the original and as she approached wide-eyed, she noticed that indeed there were a few minor tears in the print, but nothing that took away from the shot. The black and white photograph highlighted the beauty of a small creek with an old wooden bridge across the natural barrier. Hundreds of pine trees as tall as the eye could see surrounded the scene as the sun rose across the horizon.

Just as she remembered it. This was her favorite picture. Jack's favorite picture. He hadn't been able to get rid of it, despite everything.

"It's still here," she whispered glancing back at Jack. He was shuffling some papers around on his large mahogany desk, but glanced up at the sound of her voice.

"I had it reframed and brought up here from Savannah earlier this week," he told her attempting to keep the emotion out of his voice.

Lexi shook her head unable to process the many nuances of Jack Howard. Here she was in his office wanting to be so *angry* at him for everything he had ever put her through, and then he did this. One simple gesture that reminded her why she loved him so much.

"Why?" she barely got out choking on her own words.

"What do you mean why?"

"Jack, come on. You made it pretty clear last night."

"Last night I said what we did didn't change things. And, well, it doesn't, Lexi. Sex never changed things with us before."

"Do you really believe that sex doesn't change things?" she asked taken aback by the concept. She wasn't a typical female who believed that sex necessarily meant an emotional commitment on either side. She had had her fair share of one night stands to prove that to herself, but Jack was not one of those men. And she knew that sex did mean something to him whether he was ready to admit it or not.

"I mean that it doesn't change what I have to do or the decision that I have to make. It doesn't make any of this easier."

"A little birdie tells me it does," she said turning her back on the picture.

"Oh yeah, who's that?"

"Who is not the appropriate question," she told him looking into his beautiful blue eyes from across the space of his office.

"Well, you don't have to tell me who would tell you that things have changed between us, because I already know," Jack said triumphantly taking her off guard.

"I suppose you could guess," she said hesitantly not liking the change of subject.

"No guessing needed. I know what you've been trying to do," he told her staring her down.

She gave him a completely flabbergasted look hoping maybe he could explain further what he was talking about. Wasn't she the one who was supposed to storm in here and demand answers? Why was he the one completely confounding her over and over again? Her mouth opened and she tilted her head slightly trying to really assess the situation. The only thing she had been trying to do all week was figure out what the hell Jack was doing with his life. She wanted him…bad, but was only fueled onwards by his obvious desire for her. If he had been aloof and untoward, then she certainly would have done his bidding, hung out with her parents, and then hopped on the first plane out of here.

But that hadn't happened. He had flat out told her that they were meant to be together. That after everything they had been through, he knew what he wanted and all he had to do was tie up some loose ends. Now he was saying that sex didn't change anything along with other unthinkable things, and honestly, she was just lost.

"What am I trying to do besides get answers from you?" she asked unable to keep the confusion out of her voice.

"Don't play all innocent with me. We both know you're not that," Jack said standing and tossing some paperwork into a basket.

"I never said I was innocent," she said a bit confused by the abrupt shift in the conversation.

"Yeah, but you sure try to act like you are."

"Jack, you've lost me," Lexi told him her brow scrunching together.

"I know what you've been up to this week."

"Um…what have I been up to this week? The only thing I've been doing is exactly what you asked me to do. I spoke to Bekah about our relationship. I played the perfect part in your stupid charade. I went to the Country Club, Ramsey's stupid party, your birthday…what more did you want from me? I gave you everything you could want from me. I tried to give you everything, and it seemed like it was going to work out, but now," she drifted off, "I guess it doesn't seem like enough."

He laughed. He actually laughed at the last statement. Lexi's mouth popped open in surprise unable to fathom why he was acting so impertinent. "You actually want me to believe that you gave me everything?"

"Compared to you giving me nothing, yes, I'd say I gave you everything," she spat at him.

"You're ridiculous, Lexi," he said shaking his head. "You think I don't know what you've been up to?"

"Well, I don't know what I've been up to so why don't you tell me," she said completely baffled by this point. She had no idea what he was talking about. She had come here from New York at *his* request to convince his dumb girlfriend that he could commit. She didn't exactly believe it herself, but she had tried. As far as she could tell, she had succeeded as well. Bekah seemed to believe that they were going to be together. And up until last night, when Jack had left her all alone feeling used and violated, she had been certain that Jack was actually going to leave Bekah for her.

"Go ahead, play coy with me. I know what you and Ramsey have been up to."

That really threw her off guard. "What does Ramsey have to do with any of this?" she asked trying to follow his line of reasoning but coming up blank.

He nodded his head a few times. "You don't have to try and play me like this, Lex. I know you, and I know what's been going on."

"Then please fill me in, because I have *no* idea what you're talking about," she said walking to the front of his desk and taking a seat in one of the client chairs. She crossed her arms and legs simultaneously and waited for another outrageous response from him.

"You think I don't know that you guys met before this?"

"Of course we met before this. I told you that as soon as I saw him at the Country Club that we met there when I came up here with Jennifer," she told him still confused as to where this was going.

"Right, that was a pretty good act. When did you become such a good liar, Lexi?"

"If you tell me what I'm lying about, I might know, because as far as I can tell *you* are the only good liar in the room."

"Come on, Lexi," he cried. "Now, I didn't think you would ever play me like this, but I can tell that you are now. How long have you guys been together? Has it been since New York?" he asked placing his hands on the desk and leaning forward towards her.

"We're not together," she stuttered in disbelief.

"Oh, right. You don't do the commitment thing. Have you just been fucking?"

"Excuse me, I'm going to pass right over the very ridiculous accusation that Ramsey and I have been fucking," Lexi said her face clouding over only slightly at the thought that she had almost done just that last night. "And step right up to the plate and take the hypocritical route, jackass."

Jack stumbled a step as he walked around the corner of her desk. He glanced up at her cheeky comment in surprise. "Whatever, Lexi. I know that you know Ramsey from New York. And whether you're fucking or not, I know you guys have been together. I saw you kiss at his party. I saw it again last night. I'm not stupid, alright? I can tell that there is something going on between you two."

Lexi stared at him in awe. So that was why he had been so angry and rough with her the night before. He had somehow deluded himself into believing that she and Ramsey were together. It didn't make sense to her, but she figured if he looked at it from only one side, it might look like that. However, that didn't explain why he thought she had met Ramsey in New York. "What do you mean I know him from New York?"

"You don't deny that you and Ramsey have something going on?" he asked ignoring her question.

"We don't have anything going on, Jesus. We did kiss, but we're not together. I don't even understand how you could think that."

"I don't think that. I know that something is going on between ya'll. You've been fucking with my mind since you got here."

"Excuse me? You're the one who has been flip-flopping the whole goddamned time I've been here. You come home early to see me. Then you're an asshole to me at Ramsey's party. Then you want to be with me again and you're going to break things off with Bekah. After that we have sex, and you're just another asshole all over again. What the fuck, Jack?" she asked demanding his attention.

"It's only because you've been playing me the whole time that I keep changing," he told her his blue eyes stormy.

"I have *not* been playing you!" she yelled at him. "And I don't know Ramsey from anywhere."

Jack laughed again. "You're good. You know that?" Lexi sighed exasperated. "You and Ramsey met in the club the night we got back together in New York."

Lexi glanced at him in surprise. Her heart raced in her chest at the faint memory of a night long ago. She had met someone in that club. In fact, she had almost gone home with that guy. A series of flashbacks took over her mind.

A man in an Armani suit buying her drinks and barely glancing at Chyna as he offered to take Lexi home. A faint memory of Ramsey saying they had met somewhere previously before they kissed on his balcony. The way he programmed her number into his phone as if he already had it in there. Ramsey somehow knowing she didn't drink Jack Daniels or Sex on the Beach. How familiar his lack of personal space felt. The way he had touched her last night, as if he had been waiting to do that for much longer than the week he had known her.

Her stomach plummeted, shock radiating out of every pore. Could Ramsey be the elusive Armani Guy? She had lost all the numbers programmed into her phone, so when Ramsey had given her his number it wouldn't have been in there. He must have known all along, and he hadn't mentioned it to her.

"See you can't even deny it," he said shaking his head as if he hadn't really believed it himself until her confirmation.

"How did you find out that I'd met him?" she asked.

"I remember Chyna talking to you about some guy from Armani calling you when we were together. I knew you were at the club where Ramsey was that night, because I was the one he was supposed to interview." Lexi's heart jumped again. Jack had been there that night. In fact, when she had seen a guy that looked like him, that actually could have been him. She couldn't believe all of this. "I know you've been seeing each other since then. He told me about this woman he met once in New York a couple weeks ago. He didn't even know he was talking about you, and, honestly, until I saw the two of you together last night, I wasn't entirely sure myself."

Lexi's hand rushed to her mouth unable to believe what he was telling her. "I knew Ramsey in New York," she murmured.

"So you admit it?"

"Yeah. I guess I do, but he never told me that he knew me," she said still in a state of shock. Why wouldn't he have told her? It wasn't like she had given him some reason not to trust her. Sure, she hadn't exactly been up front with him about her reasons for being in Atlanta, but she hadn't considered that something like this would happen.

"Right," he said in disbelief resting back against the corner of the desk and turning to face her.

Lexi stood brushing the cobwebs out of her mind. She took a turn around the room trying to process what this new information meant besides the fact that it seemed everyone was lying to her in some way. What more could she find out to make matters worse? She finally settled her mind, and walked back to Jack. "I don't know how we got onto this subject, but Ramsey is not the reason I barged into your office to speak with you."

Jack waited. "What's the reason then?"

Lexi took a deep breath before starting. "I'm leaving tonight for New York, and I need to know what's going on…with us," she said the last part unsure if she really wanted the answer. At the same time, she knew that she would never be able to leave Atlanta happy without answers.

Jack sighed and buried his head in his hands. "Always back to this conversation."

"It's the only one that seems to matter," she said standing her ground in front of him.

"Lexi, I have a whole life here. I have more than a few loose ends to tie up."

"What about everything you said?" Lexi asked her voice quivering.

"What do you want me to say, Lex?"

"What about the goddamn truth?" she cried throwing her hands in the air. "Do you want to be with me? You said that you did. Was that all a lie too?"

"It wasn't a lie. I just…I want to be with you when I'm with you, but when you're gone I doubt everything. We have too much history, Lex. You know that. I don't know what's been going on with us lately, and," he took a deep breath, "I don't know if I can leave my life behind."

"So, this is it then?" she asked, their history the only thing keeping her from collapsing.

"I don't know…"

"No, don't fucking do that. Make up your mind already," she cried rushing forward and pressing herself against his chest.

He instinctively wrapped his arms around her body and held her against him. She breathed into him pushing her hands up his chest and around his neck. "We have to figure this stuff out."

Jack pulled back from her holding her face softly between his strong hands and staring into her confused brown eyes. "I know we do."

"I can't do this anymore," she told him closing her eyes as his thumb trailed down her cheek.

"Can't do *what* anymore?" a voice asked walking into the room behind them.

Lexi jumped back at the sound of the voice. Jack immediately released Lexi's face dropping his hands to his sides. She tried to hide the expression on her face, but there was no point. Bekah had to know something was up by now.

"Hey, babe. When did you get here?" Jack asked hesitantly.

"Just a little while ago. Hey, Lexi," Bekah said cheerfully.

"Bekah," Lexi said nodding her head in greeting.

"Are you here about the news?" Bekah asked smiling as politely as ever as she strolled into the room. Her naturally blonde hair had recently been highlighted and fell down to her chest as pin straight as ever. She wore a crisp white pencil skirt with a baby pink silk blouse that tied up around her neck making a bow. A white suit jacket was folded in half over her left arm. She looked like a vision of perfection, and it made Lexi sick.

"Uh…news?" Lexi asked glancing between Jack and Bekah.

"Didn't Jack tell you?"

"Apparently not," she uttered anxiously.

Bekah held up left hand and squealed with joy. "We're getting married."

Lexi gasped as she looked at the cut of the ring in front of her. It seemed so familiar, but…it couldn't be. He wouldn't.

25

PRESENT

She was seeing spots.
Anger so fierce came over Lexi she couldn't even see properly. Every negative emotion that she had ever conjured up combined seemed insignificant compared to this feeling. She could remember a time when she thought things could be right with her and Jack. Now it seemed like that was such a very long time ago. How could she have ever told herself things were going to be alright? She now knew with every ounce of her being that there was absolutely nothing left of the man she had once loved.

Where had the fun, easy going guy that worked in the coffee shop and brought her muffins after class gone? Where was the guy who had taken her to the carnival and paid the guy to stop them on the top? Where was the guy who got her on the gymnastics team, who marveled in her every achievement, who followed her to New York, who would have followed her to the world's end? Had that man left a long time ago, and she had just missed it?

A part of her, and she wasn't sure how large that part was, realized that this was her fault. Her continual desire for him had only pushed him to compensate for her affections. They had been playing this game for six years now, and it had changed him. He couldn't hold back any longer. He lacked self-control and his selfish and self-righteous behavior only intensified his demeanor. Somewhere in their past, they had mutually agreed that cheating was somehow alright. She didn't know where that began, if it was the first time he had asked her out, the first time she had gone to see him knowing she wasn't available, or that moment on the pier, which changed everything, but it had begun.

And that's how she knew this moment in time was partly her fault. The sex before the proposal was like old times all over again. She had attempted to fight him, but she couldn't fight Jack. When he was persistent, and damn was he persistent, he got what he wanted. That is how it had always been. That is how she had let it become. Cheating was as much a part of them as breathing, no matter how much Lexi tried to fight it.

However, she had made it pretty clear, up until last night, that she had realized her mistake and wasn't going to continue on that path. If Jack hadn't ran in New York, she would have taken some time away from him. She had wanted to show him that what he had done was not right. They had cheated and deluded themselves into thinking it was alright, but it wasn't and it never would be.

But the other part of her knew that this was just as much Jack's fault, if not more. He had been the first to cheat. He had been the first to tell her that it was always going to be okay, that they could just be friends, that it didn't matter what they had done, rather what they felt. He had never given up.

And up until today, she thought he had always kept that one important promise that had saved them through so many battles. He had promised that he would never lie to her. Through everything, he had told her exactly what was going on and exactly what happened. He had even told her when he had cheated on her. Yet, she realized, through her mind clouded with anger, Jack had lied to her all along.

Because he had always said that he wanted to be with Lexi, and it was pretty obvious now that that was simply not the case.

The memory of Jack pulling out an exquisite wedding ring and all but proposing was still fresh in her mind. She could remember every little emotion she had felt that day from his confession, to her depression, to his attempt at making amends.

And now her ring, *her* ring, was on that bony, blonde bitch's finger.

Lexi reared back and with every ounce of force she possessed in her tiny body slapped Jack clear across the face. His head snapped sideways with the momentum of her strike. Her breathing was heavy and uncontrollable fury was ricocheting throughout her entire body. She could hear Jack's ragged breaths in front of her, but she couldn't even stand the sight of him after what he had done. She heard Bekah gasp and rush forward as if to do something about what had happened, but something in Lexi's eyes must have stopped her in her tracks. Lexi wasn't certain what she looked like in that moment, but she was sure it wasn't something that anyone would want to deal with.

"What the…" Jack cried bringing his hand up to his face to rub his jaw line.

"What is wrong with you?" Bekah cried still staying far enough out of Lexi's reach.

"At the moment, everything is wrong with me," she spat back at Bekah.

"How dare you react like this! Now, I knew that you still had feelings for Jack, but honestly this is ridiculous. Coming here, hanging all over him, and then slapping him when you have news of our engagement?" Bekah asked angrily. "That is childish and completely uncalled for. I think you should exit the premises."

"Childish and uncalled for, honestly?" Lexi cried out. She couldn't even form clear words to tell Bekah how absolutely ridiculous her statements were. How could you explain to a woman who was crazy about weddings and had just been proposed to that her ring was never meant for her? Could she break the news to her?

She had never liked Bekah, but she couldn't shatter her dreams just because she was angrier at now Jack than she ever had been in her life. Actually, she might be angrier than she had ever been in her life.

But Lexi agreed with her. Perhaps, she should leave the premises. There was no need for her to stay here and make a fool of herself any longer. Jack had crushed her. That was all there was to it. He didn't want her any longer. He had given her ring to Bekah, which proved that more than anything else ever could.

"Yes, absolutely," Bekah told her, folding her arms one over the other.

"Whatever," Lexi said glaring at Jack who still hadn't spoken up. "There is so much I could tell you that I held back from you to save you heartache."

"Like what?" Bekah challenged steeling herself against Lexi's threat.

Jack glanced between the two girls uneasily. "You really don't even want to know," Lexi announced.

"I do. Please, shock me," Bekah said raising her eyebrows as if challenging her to continue.

"Bekah, ignore her. She's just pissed. I'm getting out of here and you should come too. You don't need this," Jack said snatching up his suit jacket and storming out of the room.

"That's right, just run away like you always do," Lexi called after his retreating back. Bekah stayed put and watched as Jack exited the room in a blaze of fury. "Aren't you going to run after him?" Lexi asked condescendingly. She realized how much of a failure her coming to this place had been. Jack had used her and then threw her out with the trash just like Chyna had said.

"No, I think not," Bekah said a smile creeping onto her face. "I'm actually very happy that we have this moment together."

Lexi looked at her in disbelief. "And why is that?"

"Because I've been waiting for this very moment."

"And again, why is that?"

"For you to finally realize that Jack will never be yours," Bekah stated sweetly, tilting her head slightly to the right as she stared wide-eyed at Lexi.

"What are you even talking about?" Lexi asked staring at Bekah blankly. She wasn't exactly sure about the change of conversation, but was still too angry to process what she was saying.

"Why do you even think that you're here?" Bekah asked placing one hand on her hip and leaning into it.

"What do you mean what am I doing here? I came to talk to Jack."

"No,, I mean, why do you think you're in Atlanta?"

Lexi sighed. "I'm here, because Jack asked me to talk to you and convince you that he was ready to commit to you," she said letting all the words come out in a rush.

Bekah's smile widened. "You thought you were here to convince *me* that Jack was ready for commitment?" Bekah asked sardonically. "What a silly little girl you are after all."

Lexi tilted her head to the side as if evaluating the situation. "What are you even talking about? That's exactly what Jack told me, and fuck you, I'm not a silly little girl."

"Well, yes, of course he told you that. I told him to tell you that, and he believed me," she announced smiling sweetly.

"Then what are you talking about?" Lexi demanded tired of this ridiculous behavior.

"You didn't come here to convince me…you came here to convince him," Bekah stated simply. "I knew all about you. When he gets drunk, he babbles too much, and on occasion you were brought up. He never remembered mentioning you, or if he did, then he pretended as if he hadn't spoken a word. You see, I knew that he wasn't over you. I could tell from the way he looked when he spoke about you."

Lexi stomach began churning. Why was Bekah telling her all this?

"So I made sure you came down to visit. I knew that if you were around, he would finally get over you. And you did just as I suspected, you convinced him that he was ready to marry me. You played right into my hand. I applaud you," she said beginning a slow golfer's clap. "I never thought you would make it so easy for me."

"I…I don't believe you," Lexi croaked her stomach dropping completely out of her body.

"Of course you don't," Bekah said throwing one hand in the air. "You can't see past your stupid little fantasy that Jack is one day going to be yours. You can't see past the history you guys once had. You can't get over the charade you two put on for every other person you have ever been with or ever known. Even your own best friend can't understand that you will *never* get over Jack.

"And I understand because Jack is amazing, but he is not yours. He is all mine. You know if you could have realized that Jack will never be yours earlier, you would have seen what was happening all along." Bekah smirked and fluffed her blonde hair over her shoulder with her left hand letting the giant diamond glitter in the afternoon sun light filtering in through the windows.

"You are completely demented," Lexi cried. "And it is *not* a fantasy, because you know damn well that Jack has been mine for nearly six years now."

"Wow. You really are dumber than I thought," Bekah said chuckling to herself. "Why can't you get it through your head that Jack has never nor will he ever be yours? You are the mistress, the other woman, the second choice. That's all you are or ever will be to him. He could never see you as anything more. That's why he never left anyone else for you. That's why he cheated on you at the first opportunity and then left. That's why he is choosing me…not you."

Lexi's mouth dropped open. She hated the fact that what she was saying actually made sense. She had thought about those facts many times before, but she had never been able to come to that conclusion. She had never been able to believe it was over. How could it ever be over?

Today was the first time she had ever realized that she would lose him. She had thought for a long time that things were not the way they should be between them, but she never lost hope for them to be together. Bekah was right. She was stupid for believing they would work it out after everything they had been through.

"Oh look, I think you might have finally realized it," Bekah cooed as if she were speaking with a toddler.

"What the fuck ever," Lexi said brushing past Bekah and stomping towards the exit. She didn't need this…not from Bekah…not from anyone. She needed to move on with her life and that meant doing just as Bekah ordered: exiting the premises. It was time to leave Atlanta and get back home where things were less drama filled and a bit more reliable.

Bekah chuckled one more time. She turned as Lexi brushed past her and just as Lexi put her hand on the door she said maliciously, "Not to mention my brother played his part perfectly."

Lexi stopped with her hand on the door ready to pull it open. She took a deep breath and willed herself to leave. She knew Bekah was antagonizing her now, and she needed to get out before she got suckered in. She twisted the handle attempting to keep her curiosity at bay. But she couldn't keep it at bay. "What does Ramsey have to do with this?"

Bekah smirked knowing she had caught her interest. "Oh, you know Ramsey," she said shrugging.

Lexi looked at her as if she had no idea what she was talking about. "Bekah," she said warningly, "I'm tired of this bullshit. Just tell me what you obviously want me to know."

"Honestly, I never would have imagined Ramsey to be such a good actor."

"What was he acting about?" Lexi asked afraid to get the answer. There were so many things that could go wrong with this conversation. She wasn't sure what had happened over the past week, but she had begun to trust him. It was a scary feeling for her to allow someone else into her life, but Ramsey was beginning to grow on her. She couldn't imagine what it would mean if Bekah told her something that would shatter yet another relationship. Lexi wasn't sure if she could handle that at this moment in time.

"Really, Lexi, can't you answer that question? The way you were putty in his hands really worked in my favor to be honest."

"Ramsey?" Lexi asked doubtfully.

"Yes, Ramsey. What? Did you think he liked you? He is *my* brother. Who do you think he would choose if it came down to it? Oh, come on, that's a stupid question, he would choose me over you. It was really easy to convince him to fuck around with you."

No, Lexi couldn't believe it. Ramsey wasn't a pawn in his sister's game. He would never play her like a fool. What did he have to gain from Bekah's game?

Bekah continued, "Then planting Jack in the perfect location to witness everything that was going on. Of course I had to leave you and Jack alone some so that he could get pissed off at you. Just enough for you to have a rift and then let the trust issues, which you already have, blossom into true anger."

Lexi didn't know Ramsey all that well. They had only been hanging out this week and if he had been under Bekah's influence the entire time, then it was all a lie. Both of their public kisses had been in front of Jack. Only a day after her date with Ramsey, he had gone straight to Jack and told him that they had been together. No wonder Jack had thought there was something going on. Bekah and Ramsey had set them up.

"It was almost too easy how it worked out."

Lexi's heart was racing as she turned to face Bekah. She knew that something had changed between her and Ramsey in the past week. She hadn't even really been aware of it herself. She had started to like him. Even with everything going on with Jack, she had somehow found her heart could still beat. And it didn't feel manufactured. Was it wishful thinking to believe that he had really had true affections for her?

"Oh, do you care about him?" Bekah asked sounding demented.

"I can't believe you," Lexi finally decided. Her voice lacked the conviction that she wanted to feel. Ramsey, at least, she thought she could count on. She wasn't sure why. Maybe because something about him seemed so sincere. Maybe because they had seemed genuinely interested in each other when they spent time together. Maybe because she had some means of self-control around him and still found that she was attracted to him. But could all of that been from acting?

What did she really know about him? He didn't work for Bridges Enterprise, and she didn't know where he did work. She didn't know where he had gone to school or if he had gone to college at all. She knew he had a trust fund and was around during much of the day. He had a nice ass.

Yeah, that was about it.

Great.

"Again with the not believing me. I have no reason to lie to you. And I can tell you care about him," Bekah said reading her reaction carefully. "You don't even know my brother. You have no idea what he is like. He has shown you one side of him and you fall all over yourself about him. Everyone always does, which is why I was certain if you gave into him even a teensy little bit that you would be lost. And look," she said pointing at Lexi, "you are so very lost."

"You have every reason to lie to me. You're pissed because Jack wanted me. So you had to attempt to sabotage our relationship. I don't think Ramsey is involved. You're just trying to ruin every part of my life so you can have some part of yours," Lexi spat at her. She had been right the first time she met Bekah. She would never ever like this backstabbing bitch.

"Well, I'm not lying to you. Jack didn't want you. He had this crazy idea of you from six years ago. Neither of you are the same people, and you're just stupid to think you could make it through everything that you have been through."

"Just because you are jealous of what Jack and I had doesn't mean you have to be such a bitch."

"It's not being a bitch when you are telling the truth. For instance, Jack has no interest in you. My brother has no interest in you whatsoever. Well, except maybe to fuck you. I told him that was fine," she announced nonchalantly.

Lexi cringed away from Bekah's words. No. This could not be happening to her. She had almost slept with Ramsey. He had been so eager to get with her when he could tell she was broken and in tears. Could this be all that it was? Had he only been seducing her hoping to fuck her and leave? "I may not know your brother very well…"

"At all," Bekah interrupted.

"But I know that the way he was around me was not some kind of act."

"Yes, I'm sure you can delude yourself into believing that, but that is the truth. That is the truth you have been looking for since you got here. Jack is mine," Bekah told her taking a step forward. "He does *not* want you. Ramsey is my brother and he would do anything for me," she said stepping forward until she was standing directly in front of Lexi. "He doesn't want you either. Thanks for your help." Bekah grabbed the door handle and yanked it open. "Please escort yourself off of Bridges property. You are no longer welcome here."

"You're kicking me out?" Lexi asked glancing out the hallway and then back at Bekah. "I believe we have more to discuss here you filthy whore."

"No, I think my work here is done," Bekah said smiling. "Gwen, if she doesn't leave, call security." And with that Bekah stalked right through the door and into her own office.

Gwen hopped off her chair, anxious to rush Lexi out of the office. Lexi's mouth was hanging open still from Bekah's monologue, and she was frozen in place. "Miss," Gwen muttered angrily.

"Oh, right," Lexi said closing her mouth and exiting Jack's office. She took her time walking down the hallway and into the elevators. The steel metal enclosure took her to the bottom floor, and she strode across the marble tiled floor. Her phone dinged just before she reached the sliding doors. She sighed heavily and pulled back from the outside world. She fished her phone out of her purse and clicked on the new text message.

"Delivered your luggage to airport already. Meet me there, chica. Heart you," read Chyna's message.

Lexi smiled to herself, grateful for Chyna's loyalty. It was so nice not to have to worry about at least one part of her life. Chyna had been a true friend throughout it all. She swore as soon as they made it back to New York she was going to treat her best friend to a wonderful dinner and lots of wine.

"You're still here," Lexi heard someone approach her.

She slowly turned to face the man who had dashed all her hopes and dreams of a real relationship into a million pieces. He had walked out on her again leaving her alone with that stupid diamond ring, except this time it was attached to someone else's finger. This was the last person she had wanted to see…the last thing she had wanted to encounter before she left for New York. He had finally made up his mind about her. He had made his decision to be with Bekah, not her. There was no reason for her to ever speak to him, because God knows they could never be friends.

"Yes, I'm still here," Lexi told him not able to keep herself from glaring.

"Can we talk?" he asked looking at least mildly apologetic.

"No," she said turning from him and walking through the double doors. "Taxi please," she told the attendant on duty.

"Come on, Lex," Jack pleaded.

"Just don't," she said holding up her hand.

"Your cab, miss," the attendant said as the yellow car pulled up in front of the colossal set of stairs.

"Thank you," she said sliding into the seat as he opened the door for her.

"Lexi, you have to listen to me," Jack said following her into the taxi.

"I'd rather not," she said emotionless. She would be happier if she never saw Jack again, if she never had to hear his smooth voice or listen to his charming words. She would certainly be happier to go about the rest of her life knowing she had received the necessary closure she had so desperately been seeking while in Atlanta. "Get out of the cab," Lexi demanded pointing her finger towards the door.

"Hartsfield-Jackson," Jack said to the cab driver throwing a few twenties across the seat to keep him from opening his mouth.

Lexi glowered at him as the cabbie followed his instructions. "What the fuck is your problem? What are you even doing here? You have a fiancé inside. There is no need for this conversation. I got the gist of it with the diamond," she growled.

Jack looked apologetically at the cab driver who was glancing backwards through the rearview mirror anxiously. "It's not what you think, Lex."

"First, don't ever call me that again. I hate it," she said crossing her arms over her chest. In fact, she had only ever liked it when Jack said it. The way it came out of his mouth made it sound so sexy. But that was the last thing she wanted now. "And second, waste your time with someone who wants to listen to you like your fiancé, or your secretary, or hell, even your apartment attendant. They all seem very interested in you."

Jack colored slightly at the accusation, but, Lexi noted, he didn't deny anything. "I know you probably never want to speak with me, but I can't end it like this."

"Oh, you can't? Well, I don't give a fuck. If you didn't want it to end like this, then you wouldn't have fucked me in the hallway at Turner Field less than twelve hours before proposing to someone else," she said not caring that the cab driver or anyone else was listening.

"I know," he said nodding his head.

"I don't think you do or you would have taken the slap in the face to mean *stay the fuck away from me* like it was meant."

"I told you I can't leave it like this. I was blinded by my jealousy over you and Ramsey. I couldn't even believe you when you said nothing was going on. We said we'd never lie, but neither of us trusts the other."

Lexi kept that fact that he had been lying to her all along to herself. He would disagree with the statement and there was no need for him to try and convince her otherwise. He was right. She would never believe him. He wouldn't have chosen Bekah over her in the end, if he had really wanted to be with her. He would have cut his loose ends. He would have tried to make it work. He would have loved her the way she deserved to be loved. No, he had lied all along and she could never trust his word again. It had been broken once before, when they had first begun, and she had been stupid to believe in him to this day.

"You don't trust me, right?" he asked mournfully.

"Stupid question," she quipped.

"Right. Well, I guess you have no reason to."

"Yep," she said popping the final sound and staring out across the city.

"I really couldn't help it though."

"Oh, this should be good," she said sarcastically. "You're going to tell me how you couldn't help but propose. Wonderful!"

"No, I was going to propose. Can you just look at me, please, Lex?" he pleaded.

She turned and glared at him. "Do *not* call me that. Why did you string me along if you knew you planned on proposing?" she asked.

"Well, I knew before you got here that's what I was planning to do, but then you showed up and I couldn't think about doing that."

"Then why the hell did you drag me down here? I was supposed to be here to convince Bekah you were ready to commit to her. You told me you wanted her off your back and that you had no intention of doing it. If you really were ready to commit, then why didn't you just fucking tell her that and leave me out of it?"

"Because she found the ring," he cried throwing his hands up in the air in defeat.

"I might hit you again if we continue talking about this," she threatened.

"She found *your* ring," he said more calmly.

"Yes, I fucking realize that moron. The ring that is now currently on her finger. The ring that was meant for my finger," she said waving her left hand around in the air. "Is nothing sacred, Jack? Go ahead. Please try to explain to me how her finding my ring has anything to do with me being down here."

"Because she flipped out and was shrieking, jumping up and down, going insane when she found it," he told her deflecting the glares she was shooting his way, "and then I crushed her when I told her it wasn't for her."

"Guess you changed your mind," she muttered angrily.

"No, I didn't."

"Jack, get out of the fucking cab," she told him. "Sir, can you pull over right here?"

"Ma'am, we're on the highway."

"He can walk," she told him.

"That's illegal. I cannot let you out of the car until we are off the interstate," he said zooming down highway 85 towards the airport.

"I'm not going anywhere anyway," Jack told her.

"Then I'll get out and hail another cab," she told him turning back towards the window.

"Lexi, it's a duplicate," he told her reaching out and turning her head towards him. She yanked her face out of his reach.

"A...wait...what?" she asked staring in the blue pools of his eyes.

"A duplicate. I had another one made, because I couldn't give her your ring," he said reaching into his pocket and pulling out a rather familiar black box. He flipped the top up and Lexi stared down at the wedding ring he had almost given her once. It was as exquisite as she remembered with every detail cut to perfection.

"How do I know this isn't the duplicate?" she asked staring down at the ring and knowing that no one could really duplicate this. The ring itself had an old timey appearance and was completely unlike anything else she had ever seen.

"Why would I go to the trouble of getting you a duplicate?"

"To cover your ass?" she guessed.

"No, to show you that, no matter what happens, you truly will always have a place in my heart," he whispered tucking a loose strand of hair behind her ear. The cab pulled into the line of traffic in front of the airport.

Lexi pulled her gaze up from the dazzling ring and met Jack's look. "I appreciate the fact that you have one redeeming quality, Jack, but that is all it is. Just a hint of redemption with six years of disappointment.

"No matter what you do, it will never make up for what happened between us. I will never trust you. I will never again be comfortable around you. I will never look at you or think of you without considering the destruction you have train wrecked through my life.

"I wish you the very best in your future, because without you in my life I think I might finally have a future. And as angry as I am with what you have put me through, I am so very glad that we are now at this moment. This moment means I can move on to bigger and better things without you constantly weighing on my shoulders.

"I will never again turn a corner in New York terrified that I will run into you and even more terrified that I won't. I can go into any coffee shop I want. I can hope for love again. A love that will be more than anything you ever attempted to give to me. Because the love I am looking for will be reciprocated one hundred and ten percent. There will never be another someone to distract our affections, because *you* will not be in the picture.

"So, as sad as this day is for me, as I am losing a part of myself with the loss of you, it is really just the beginning for me. It is like cutting off the spoiled part to get to the juicy center. So, I would appreciate it this time, if you did not try and contact me. Because, as I'm sure you know, I deserve much better. I want everything this time around, and I deserve it," she said holding her head high as the cab came to a stop in front of the airport terminal. "Take him back to Bridges Enterprise," Lexi commanded stepping out of the cab.

"Lex," Jack called hopping out of the cab.

"Don't call me that," she cried turning around and facing him. As always Hartsfield-Jackson International Airport was crowded with thousands of people destined to travel all around the world. Families were huddled together hugging, kissing, and saying their farewells to their relatives. Lovers were embracing as they came and went through the sliding glass doors. Business men and women carrying similar black luggage took hurried steps around the slower passengers. A few heads had turned at Lexi's exclamation, but she was beyond caring.

"Fine. Lexi," he said taking a more hesitant step closer.

"What do you want? Because all I want is you finally out of my life," she spat at him.

"I know, and I'll get out of your life. I'll let you live yours. Can I make one last request?" he pleaded.

"Take, take, take. That's all you do. What more could you want?" she beseeched him.

"Just a final farewell," he said taking another step towards her.

"No," she said her voice hitching as his hands reached out and lovingly cupped the sides of her face. "Jack, no. You are engaged," she whispered.

"Just a good-bye. That's all," he implored.

His head dipped down slowly. Lexi felt as if she were watching him in slow motion as he descended towards her. She could almost feel the taste of his lips as energy radiated out of every pore. Her skin was on fire and she could feel her body impulsively reacting to his touch. Her eyes stared deeply into the cerulean orbs entrancing her.

Her heart remembered every moment she had given into him like this. She remembered her head feeling dizzy and light headed. Her heart racing along at a sprinter's speed. Her eyes glazing over with desire and fluttering closed in anticipation. Her lips quivering as she wet them waiting for them to be covered with his own. Her cheeks flushing with warmth and desire. A wonderful ringing sound filling her ears.

She could remember every sensation she had ever felt with Jack in that instant as he demanded one last thing from her.

One last kiss good-bye.

As he was about to touch her lips to his own, she took a step backwards and smiled serenely. "Good-bye, Jack," she said turning on her heel, walking through the sliding glass doors, and leaving him behind.

She felt as if she were walking on clouds as she ventured out towards the hanger where the private jet was located. All she had was her purse. No Jack.

No weight on her shoulders. She felt as if she was breathing in new air. Her mind was buzzing with possibilities. Her feet carried her out to the hanger and across the cement tarmac to the waiting plane. As she approached, she noticed someone waiting at the bottom of the stairs.

The closer she got the more she realized that the person wasn't dressed in a uniform of any sort. She knew the person standing there waiting for her. Her heart sped up in anticipation of what was to come. The lightweight feeling she had experienced left her with the prospect that she had one more conversation ahead of her before she left for home, one more conversation that she didn't want to have.

"I'm glad I didn't miss you," Ramsey said walking confidently to her side and enveloping her in a hug. She sighed into his chest and wrapped her arms loosely around his waist. "Chyna told me this is where you'd be."

Bekah and Jack's words rang clear in her mind. At least one thing was certain, she had known Ramsey previously. The more she thought on that the more she realized that he had to be Armani Guy. She knew it was ridiculous to even consider since it was such a strange coincidence. But it would be even stranger if he happened to know things about her like he had since she got here. The thought that he was Bekah's pawn in a game she was playing to hold onto Jack was harder to believe, but it certainly would explain a large majority of his actions.

Ramsey pulled back leaving only a rather small space between them, as usual ignoring any means of personal space. "You look different," he mused out loud.

"Do I?" she questioned.

"I don't know what it is," he admitted.

"Bad?"

"You could never look bad."

"Cut the act," she said turning her head to the side, away from his endearing green eyes.

"I'm not acting. After the way you left my apartment last night, you look like a new woman. It's very becoming," he said eyeing her up and down.

"Well, thank you, but there is no need for your charade any longer," she said taking a step back.

In typical Ramsey fashion, he followed her in a synchronized dance. "Why do you keep saying that?" he asked his eyebrows scrunching together.

"I know what's been going on. They told me everything," she said running her fingers through her hair and sweeping a strand behind her ear.

"They? Bekah and Jack?" he asked and watched her confirmation. "Those bastards."

"So, it's true?" she asked taking a step back in pure shock. She hadn't really believed it until she looked into his face. For some demented purpose, he had played her. But it didn't explain what he was doing here. "If it is true, then what are you even doing here?"

"If you don't want to see me any longer, I would understand, but know that I still want to see you, Lexi. I didn't know when I saw you again at the Country Club that you were *my* Alexa, but I figured it out pretty quick," he told her using her first name rather possessively.

"I wanted to tell you, but there was never a right time, and I thought you might think less of me. I wasn't really in a good place at that time of my life. I thought you would just see me as that guy who had gotten you drunk and tried to take you back to his place. And I knew you were better than that. I wanted to be that other guy for you," he said rambling on like the first time when she had spoken to him outside of the bathroom at the Country Club.

"I don't care about the fact that we knew each other that night. I was just using you to forget," she steered clear of Jack's name, "forget everything anyway." Ramsey's face changed in that moment. It was as if his worries about slipping up had fallen off of his shoulders. He even appeared taller which was really awkward for Lexi who already had to strain her neck to look up at him since he never left more than six inches between them.

"But they did tell you about that? I mean that would be it, right?"

"Sure, Jack told me that. I had the pieces in my mind already but I hadn't knit them together. And I guess your explanation makes sense, but I would have rather you told me the truth."

"You're big on truth, aren't you?"

"Yes," she stated simply thinking about how lying and deceit had ruined her life.

"Now that that is out of the way. When can I see you again?" he asked his full-watt smile reaching all the way up to his eyes.

She shook her head in disbelief. "Never. You're a player, and you played me." She tried to move around him to the stairs of the plane, but he reached out and grabbed her arm. He spun her around until she was facing him again.

"I…what?" he asked his lips parted and eyes stormy. "I've never played you."

"You say that as if you are a player."

He gulped. "Well, I haven't played you."

"Everyone was right when they said I didn't know you and that you weren't everything you seemed."

"Is anyone ever what they seem?" he asked. "You have secrets. Everyone has them."

"But I don't try and ruin someone's life for sport," she spat at him.

"And you think I do?"

"As far as I can tell."

"Who's life am I ruining this time?" he asked staring intently into her eyes. "Please tell me what I've done, and why you are so offended."

"You seduced me. You tried to fuck me. You would have fucked me," she cried disgusted.

"What's the problem with that? It's not like you didn't want me to," he said stepping even closer to her. "You like me, Lexi. I know it. You know it." He reached out to her, pushing his fingers up into her tangled mess of curly hair. "Why is that so wrong?"

"Because you fooled me into liking you," she cried, futilely pushing him away from her.

He shook his head not budging an inch. "I never had to fool you. You just had to open up your eyes."

She clenched her jaw angry that he wouldn't let her back away. "You did it for your sister."

This seemed to take him aback. "Why would I fall for you for my sister?"

"You did her bidding to get rid of me."

"But I want you around," he said smoothly, running his hands gently through her hair. "That doesn't make sense."

"She put you in my path so she could have Jack all to herself," she tried to explain.

That did push him back a step. He released her hair and stared into her wild brown eyes. "This is always about Jack, isn't it?"

"No, nothing is about Jack anymore. And if you come with that territory, then good riddance," she muttered angrily.

"What if I told you that was all a lie?" he asked curious about her answer.

"Could I believe you?"

"Have I given you reason not to?"

"Besides not telling me that you knew me previously?"

"I did tell you," he reminded her.

"Yes, but not about meeting in the club."

"Is that really all that relevant?"

"Absolutely," she told him staring him down. "Half-truths and hiding are still lying."

"Then I apologize, but I had nothing to do with Jack. And I hope to God that I never will," he said inching forward again. His hands came up and secured themselves against her narrow hips. He grabbed her with a tad bit of force and pulled her into him.

"Ramsey," she whispered his name as he locked lips with her. She held still as long as she could before giving into his kiss. His sweet taste of peppermint overpowered her senses and she closed her eyes to breathe him in. His lips moved softly against her own, coaxing out her emotions not demanding them. She couldn't help but give into his adoring affections.

"Yes?" he asked finally breaking away from her, but planting one more feather light kiss upon her plump lips.

"I...I can't do this," she murmured against his lips, the air around them super heated.

"Why? Is it Jack?"

"No," she said quickly. Then sighed and broke away from him. "Yes. It is Jack." He nodded accepting that without questions. "You shouldn't want me. I'm not in a good enough place to be wanted."

"But I do want you. At least, something with you, even if we start slow," he pushed.

"You know how people say you crawl before you walk and walk before you run? Yeah, well, I need to learn to hold my head up before I can even think about crawling," she muttered brushing her hair off her forehead.

"Yeah. I get it, but Lexi…"

"No," she said pressing a finger to his lips. "This is the end of the road."

She turned from him and began to climb the stairs to the jet. Chyna was waiting for her at the top. It was pretty obvious that she had been eavesdropping, but she didn't look displeased. Lexi wasn't sure if that was because Lexi was finally standing up on her own or because they were on their way home. It didn't matter either way.

"Will I hear from you?" Ramsey called as she hit the top step.

She turned around and smiled at him. "When I can hold my head up high."

"You ready to get out of here, chica?" Chyna asked pulling her friend into a hug. When Lexi pulled back, she already had a flute of Champagne stuffed into her hand.

"Very ready," Lexi confirmed.

"A toast," Chyna cheered raising her glass to Lexi, "to being free."

Lexi shook her head. "No. To closure," she announced clinking their glasses together and downing her first glass of freedom.

The End.

ABOUT THE AUTHOR

K.A. Linde is an independent author and publisher enjoys writing novels that keep you guessing to the very end. She wrote Avoiding Commitment in 2009. She studied political science and philosophy at the University of Georgia and received her Masters in 2012. She currently resides in North Carolina. She enjoys dancing in her spare time. She has written a sequel to this novel and plans to have it released in the near future along with her future endeavors.

Avoiding Series:
Avoiding Commitment
Avoiding Responsibility

The Affiliate

You can contact K.A. Linde at:
kalinde45@gmail.com
http://www.facebook.com/authorkalinde

ACKNOWLEDGMENTS

Thank you so much everyone who helped me get to where I am right now. I never thought that I would publish this book, and I am grateful every day to the people who encouraged me to keep writing and to take the next step in the process. Here is just a short list of amazing people who have helped me get where I am today:

S. C. Stephens is one of the most incredible and brilliant people I know. I'm very glad to call you a friend, and I look forward to that Seattle trip we have planned. Who knows, maybe we can get a black Chevelle to drive us around? My editing goddesses: Jenny Aspinall, Rebecca Kimmerling, Lori Francis! You three are a freaking ridiculous bunch, and I can't wait for that drink in Bali. I'll bring the vodka gummies! I am glad to have become friends with a number of book bloggers including Maryse at Maryse.net, Jenny and Gitte at TotallyBooked, Alyssa and Taryn at My Secret Romance, Autumn at Autumn Reviews, Chrystle at The Indie Bookshelf, and Laura at Novel Magic. Thank you for publicizing my work before I'd even thought about putting it out for publication.

Sarah Hansen at Okay Creations did a fantastic job on the cover design for this book. Thanks for putting up with my ever changing thoughts about the cover. I appreciate Mat Kinsey so much for the portrait on the back cover. You have such a talent! Additionally, Colleen Hoover might be one of the coolest people on the planet. Thank you for giving me the push to do this!

Finally, I wouldn't be in this position at all if it weren't for all of my fans at FictionPress. You guys kept me writing throughout it all with your encouragement and reviews. Whether I know you on a first name basis or not…you got me here! Cheers to you!

Made in the USA
San Bernardino, CA
14 December 2012